WITCH

by Ken Warner

Forsaken Hills
River Torsa
River Mayne
MADISON
Orchard Lake
VANCE
STILES
ARTHOS
UNIVERSITY
PERRIN
STROM
ROSES
ULSTER
River Mayne
FOSLAND
OXCART
HIGHGATE
STOUTWALL
Rhun Lake
YORK
SMITHTOWN
STANBRIDGE
MIDDLE
MAEDA

NORTH SEA
BLACKSAND
ROCKPORT
River Arcus
River Ember
SPANBROOK
River Torsa
River Moyne
HIDO
NORTHCOAST
Forsaken
Hills
DORSHIRE
Northern Anihar Mountains
KONG
UNIVERSITY
River Lirth
STOUTWALL
OLDPORT
HIGHGATE
River Hale
MAEDA
Mystic Mountains
KEEPSTONE
Great
Desert
BASTION
WATCHTOWER
Green Mountains
LONELY
SEA
BAYFAST
River Roxa
River Xego
ETERNAL
SEA
River Xago
PYTHA
OSTLAND
OKSET
Southern Anihar Mountains
SHIFAR
N
HORN
ANORIA

CONTENTS

WITCH

CHAPTER ONE
SÉANCE

ezebel crept down the hall as quietly as possible, her cousin right behind her. The house was pitch-black; Jezebel's small candle provided the only light. She opened the back door slowly, cringing when the hinges squeaked. The candle fluttered in the sudden breeze. Jezebel froze, holding her breath as she listened for any noise from her parents' bedroom. All was quiet.

"Go," she whispered. Allison walked past her, out the door. Jezebel followed silently, pulling the door closed behind her. For an instant, Jezebel had second thoughts: maybe this was a bad idea. But she was nearly a woman grown; gone were the days when her parents could punish her for sneaking out in the dead of night.

They walked around the side of the farmhouse, toward the barn. The yard was awash in the light of the twin quarter-moons. Behind the barn, Jezebel squatted down. She picked up the torch and the small bag of salt she'd left there earlier. She handed the sack to Allison and lit the torch with her candle.

They set out across the cornfields, Jezebel leading the way. For this part of the journey, at least, she was confident she knew the way. She'd lived on the farm her whole life; she couldn't count the number of times she'd played hide-and-seek here as a little girl. Her friends could never find her. She led Allison through the maze, up one row of corn stalks, along the path between fields, and down another row.

But when they emerged from the far field, Jezebel wasn't sure where to find the trail. She'd ventured into Devil's Wood only a few times in her life. Her father's land ended here; going into the forest had always been strictly forbidden.

Jezebel hesitated, looking back and forth along the wall of trees before them.

"I thought you knew how to get there," Allison said.

"I do," Jezebel replied. "It's this way."

Allison followed her a quarter-mile along the perimeter of the cornfield. Finally, Jezebel found the path. They set out into the woods. The trail was narrow and not well-trodden. Jezebel had trouble following it at times. More than once, they had to retrace their steps to find it again.

"This is impossible," Allison cried in frustration. Jezebel turned to find her cousin desperately attempting to untangle her hair from a web of low-hanging branches.

"Hold this," she said, handing Allison the torch. "I warned you to tie it back." She went to work liberating Allison's flaxen locks from the twigs. She removed a tie from her own bushy mane and pulled her cousin's hair into a ponytail.

"Thank you," Allison said apologetically, turning to face her. Jezebel couldn't believe how pretty Allison looked, even with her messy hair and work clothes. People often commented that they could pass for sisters. Despite her curly brown hair, Jezebel supposed this was true; they shared the same hazel eyes, high cheekbones, and narrow lips. But there was a halo of beauty about the princess that Jezebel knew she'd never possess. A life of hard work on the farm had endowed Jezebel with a darker complexion and stouter build.

They resumed their course. The path wound its way up a rocky slope. Jezebel slipped and scraped her knee. Soon, they found themselves crossing a bog.

"This is disgusting," Allison muttered. Jezebel could feel the water seeping through her shoes.

Before long, they entered a thicker area of trees. Suddenly there was a noise—it sounded like a branch breaking somewhere behind them. Jezebel turned, holding the torch in front of her.

"What was that?" Allison asked.

Jezebel shook her head. "I don't know. Let's keep moving."

"Is it much farther?"

"I'm not sure."

But a few seconds later, there was a crash. Jezebel thought she heard something growl. Allison screamed; Jezebel turned again, waving the torch around. "Who's there?" Allison cowered behind her.

The forest was silent.

"This is stupid," Jezebel said. "We should go back."

"No. I want to do this."

"There's something out there, Alli—it might be a wolf. This is too dangerous."

"Don't be silly. Wolves haven't lived in this area for ages," Allison replied, but didn't sound so certain. "You promised we'd go."

Jezebel swallowed her objection. She *had* promised. "Fine."

They walked along, listening intently for any more noises. After a few minutes, Jezebel lost the path again. They doubled back, but couldn't find it. But it didn't matter; she knew they had to go north, so she pressed ahead through the trees. Several minutes later, they stumbled upon a new trail, much wider than the path they'd been following before.

"We must be close," Jezebel observed. They headed east.

But before they'd taken three steps, there was a bang in the woods. This time, something definitely growled. Allison screamed again.

"Let's go!" Jezebel yelled, grabbing her cousin by the hand. They ran down the trail. Crashing sounds followed them in the forest, punctuated frequently by snarls.

Suddenly, Jezebel stopped short: someone was on the trail in front of them. It looked like three people, one carrying a torch. The forest fell silent.

"Who's that?" Allison whispered.

Jezebel opened her mouth to reply, but one of them called out: "Who's there?" Jezebel knew that voice. "Will?"

"Jez?" The three figures approached them. Jezebel recognized them immediately. Will, Edward, and Zeke worked for her father— they were farmhands. Will was the biggest; his muscles bulged out of his shirt. Zeke was new; he'd only been on the farm two weeks.

"What are you three doing out here?" Jezebel demanded.

Will regarded her with a smirk. Jezebel noticed the blue bottle in his hands. He was probably drunk. "We might ask the same thing, little lady. Does your daddy know you're sneaking around the forest in the middle of the night?"

"No, and I forbid you to tell him," Jezebel declared. "Now, tell me what you're doing out here."

"I don't work for you, darling."

"We're going to Rockhedge," Edward told her. "What about you?"

"Rockhedge?" Allison asked, stunned.

"Why are you going *there*?" Jezebel asked.

"We're meeting some of our friends from town," Edward said sheepishly. "They're bringing… uh… booze."

"You mean there's a party at Rockhedge?" Allison asked.

"That's where we're headed, too," Jezebel stated. "You know the way?"

"Where do you think this trail leads?" Will asked sardonically, walking away.

Jezebel and Allison followed the boys.

"Did you… hear anything in the forest?" Jezebel asked Edward a minute later.

"No, it was quiet except for you two," he replied. "Why?"

"Something was chasing us," Allison told him. "We heard growling."

"You sure it wasn't just Tess? She follows me around the farm all damn day. She probably would've been curious if she saw you two wandering out in the woods."

Jezebel hadn't thought of her dog. That probably explained it.

"It sounded way bigger than Tess," Allison replied skeptically.

"No, he's probably right. Little noises always sound bigger in the night," Jezebel said.

As if on cue, a large shepherd dog bounded out of the woods onto the path. Allison squealed in surprise. The dog stood on her hind legs and put her front paws on Edward's chest, trying to lick his face.

"Told you," he said to Allison. "Get down, Tess!"

The dog walked to Jezebel and nudged her leg. Jezebel patted her head once, and Tess ran back into the trees.

They continued along the trail for several minutes and finally emerged in a large clearing. The area was well-lit by a bonfire; there were at least twenty people here. A wagon stood by an enormous stone obelisk. Jezebel and Allison followed the boys over to it. A mule grazed nearby.

A small group was huddled around the back of the wagon; it was loaded with green bottles. Jezebel picked one from the top of the pile and uncorked it. She took a swig and handed it to her cousin.

"That's my uncle's mead," she said to nobody in particular. Allison took a long drink.

"Uh… yeah," Edward said shiftily. "One of my friends works at Trey's. He usually supplies the alcohol for our… get-togethers."

"He's stealing from my uncle?" Jezebel asked.

"Uh… I don't… maybe…" Edward stammered.

Just then, a short girl came running over to them. "You made it!" Jezebel pulled her aside. Allison followed.

"Prudence, you didn't tell me this was a *party*!" Jezebel hissed.

"Well, it wasn't at first. But Anabel told a couple of people and… you know how it goes."

"I suppose," Jezebel replied. "Is she here yet?"

"No, I haven't seen her," said Prudence.

The three girls walked across the clearing, away from the crowd, and sat down on a slab of rock. Jezebel pushed the butt end of the torch into the soft ground. She took a drink from the bottle. Her uncle produced the sweetest mead in Spanbrook; none of the other innkeepers could figure out his recipe.

Jezebel didn't recognize many of the people here and assumed most were townies. A small group had gathered around a boy playing the lute. A plump girl was dancing to the music. The top of her dress had fallen around her waist. A boy in the crowd reached out and fondled her breasts; she didn't seem to mind.

Will, Edward, and Zeke were milling around behind the wagon; Jezebel thought they were staring at her. She handed the bottle to Allison. Zeke left his friends and headed across the clearing to the girls.

"You're the princess, aren't you?" he said to Allison as he sat in the grass in front of them.

"Yes," Allison replied nervously.

"I apologize—I didn't recognize you in commoners' clothes. I'm Zeke," he replied, holding out his hand. Allison shook it delicately. "You're a little young for this sort of thing, aren't you?"

"I'm two months older than Jez," Allison replied indignantly. "You don't seem to think *she's* too young."

"True, but she grew up on a farm," Zeke said with a shrug. "The rules are different for highborn."

"Hmph," Allison replied, taking a swig from the bottle.

"I hear your father's been trying to find you a suitable mate," said Zeke.

Allison snorted. "Unfortunately, his idea of 'suitable' differs from mine. I think…"

She didn't get to finish her sentence. Will stumbled over, Edward close behind.

"We told you, Zeke, you're wasting your time," Will scolded him. "The princess *doesn't like boys*."

Jezebel was on her feet in a heartbeat. "That's a lie, you stupid oaf." She stood only inches from him. Despite a height advantage of at least a foot, Will backed away, seemingly intimidated.

"Then explain why Her Highness has rejected nearly a dozen suitors in less than a year," Will replied with a smirk.

"Her standards are higher than yours," Jezebel told him. "She's not going to bed down with the first thing that walks by on two legs. She's waiting for the right man."

Edward and Zeke laughed at her.

"Maybe she's not waiting for a *man*," said Will. "In fact, you should know better than anyone. From what I hear, you two aren't just cousins; you're *kissing cousins*."

"Maybe you should watch your mouth," Jezebel retorted. "Or I'll speak to my father and have you kicked off the farm."

"You've been missing out, darling," Will said, ignoring her. "Come here and let me show you what a man's touch feels like." He grabbed her by one arm and kissed her full on the lips. Jezebel could taste liquor and chewing tobacco in his mouth. He squeezed her breast with one hand.

Jezebel wrenched herself out of his grasp. She grabbed him by the shoulders and drove a knee into his groin. Will doubled over, groaning in pain. "You stupid bitch!"

Edward helped Will walk away. He looked over his shoulder and seemed to apologize with his eyes. Jezebel glared at him.

"Uh… I'm sorry about that," said Zeke. "He's stupider than usual when he's got some drink in him…"

Allison got to her feet and walked farther away from the fire.

"Get out of here," Jezebel said to Zeke.

"I'm sorry," Zeke repeated, backing away.

"I need more mead," Prudence announced, getting to her feet. She'd been sitting there watching the exchange unfold, her eyes wide. She followed Zeke to the wagon.

"Come and get us when Anabel arrives," Jezebel called after her. She approached Allison.

"Is that what the whole princedom says about us?" she asked, turning to face Jezebel. A tear was streaming down her cheek. Jezebel wiped it away with one finger.

"Of course not—Will's only letting his fantasies get the best of him," she said. She thought she knew exactly what had given him that idea, but she didn't want to tell the princess. "He's an idiot; trust me, he doesn't speak for the rest of the populace."

They walked around the edge of the clearing, sharing the rest of the bottle. More people arrived at the party. The girls sat on their rock again, but a moment later, Prudence ran over to them. A taller girl with big teeth ran up behind her, clutching a board to her chest.

"Anabel's here," Prudence told them needlessly. "Where do you want to do this?"

"Not here," Jezebel replied. She plucked her torch out of the ground. "We need some privacy. Follow me." She led Allison, Prudence, and Anabel across the clearing. She stopped at the wagon to grab another bottle of mead. Then she walked past the stone obelisk.

She'd been to Rockhedge only once before. It had been the daytime then. But she thought she remembered the layout well enough to navigate by torchlight.

There were a dozen tall obelisks spread out in a giant circle. Smaller stone beds lay between them, along the perimeter. Within the ring, nothing grew; the ground was packed dirt. A smaller group of stones lay in the center of the circle. It looked like they'd once stood in some sort of pattern, but had long since toppled over. Jezebel walked past these to the opposite side of the circle.

Jezebel had no idea what this place was. But it felt ancient—much older than anything else in Spanbrook. They approached one of the stone beds. The trees grew close on the other side.

"Whoa!" Prudence shouted.

Will was lying on the rock with his trousers down around his ankles. The plump girl who'd been dancing earlier had her head between his legs; she was completely naked now. Will opened his eyes. When he saw them standing there, he scrambled to get to his feet and pull up his trousers. The girl made no attempt to cover her nakedness.

"I… uh… What are you doing here?" Will demanded. He seemed so drunk, Jezebel was surprised he could stand.

"Get out of here, Will," she ordered.

"Hey… I won't tell your dad you were out here if you promise not to say anything about… before."

"Yeah, sure. Whatever—just leave," Jezebel replied impatiently. She knew he'd never remember anything about this night.

Will walked away with his nude friend.

"Let's do it here," Jezebel suggested. "Do you still have the salt?"

"Yes," Allison replied, handing her the sack.

"What's that for?" Anabel asked, looking at her askance.

"Protection," Jezebel said simply. She walked around them, drawing out a circle of salt.

"From what?" Prudence asked.

"What do you think?" Allison asked sharply. "That's a shadow board—we're using it to call upon the dead. We don't want anything… unwelcome coming to visit."

"Oh, right," Prudence replied, looking scared. "Of course."

"So, what is this place?" Anabel asked.

"Nobody knows," Allison replied. "It's much older than the princedom."

"I heard that there's an old necromancer who lives in the Devil's Wood," said Prudence. "He comes to Rockhedge to summon his demons."

"That's bullshit," said Jezebel. "There's only one necromancer in Spanbrook, and he lives in the castle."

The circle complete, Jezebel sat down inside of it. The others took their places around her. Anabel placed the board between them all. She pulled something out of her dress and held it up for everyone to see.

"This is the planchette," she told them. It was a heart-shaped piece of wood with a circular hole cut out near the point. Anabel placed it on the board. "The spirits will use it to spell out messages."

The board itself was rectangular. It had all the letters of the alphabet and the numbers from zero to nine inscribed across it in three rows. At the top corners were the two words "Yes" and "No."

"How do we start?" asked Allison.

Anabel instructed them each to place one finger upon the planchette. She closed her eyes. "Denizens of the spirit world," she chanted in a falsetto voice, "we open our minds and our hearts to you. We mean you no harm. We seek only communion, not control. Speak to us tonight."

Jezebel rolled her eyes. This was ridiculous. She didn't think Anabel had the first clue what she was doing.

"Now what?" Prudence whispered.

"Can anyone hear us?" Anabel asked in the same high-pitched tone. Each girl kept one finger in contact with the planchette.

Nothing happened.

"This is stupid," Jezebel hissed. But just then, the planchette jumped to "Yes."

Anabel's eyes snapped open in surprise.

"Who did that?" Prudence asked.

"Not me," Jezebel whispered, looking at Allison. Allison shook her head.

"What is your name?" Anabel asked, using her normal voice now.

The planchette sat motionless for a moment. But then it jumped very quickly across five letters: L-A-Y-N-E.

"Layne?" Jezebel asked quietly.

The planchette moved to "Yes."

"When did you die?" Anabel asked.

The planchette moved. 7-6-3.

"Over a hundred years ago," Prudence whispered.

"Enough," Allison said impatiently. "I want to talk to my mother."

"Right," Anabel replied. "Layne, we'd like to speak to Leda of Spanbrook. Is she with you?"

"Yes."

"Mom, are you there?" Allison asked, a quaver in her voice. "It's me—it's Allison."

The planchette sped across four letters: A-L-L-I

"Mom!" Allison cried. "I miss you—I love you so much."

"Love you," the board replied.

A tear slipped down Allison's cheek. "Mom… I wanted to ask you… I never had the chance…"

Before she could ask her question, the planchette raced across the board, spelling out one word: danger.

"What?" Allison asked, confused. "What danger?"

The planchette moved again. "Leave now."

"That's enough," Jezebel blurted out. "Which one of you is doing that?"

Prudence shook her head, looking frightened.

"I would never," Anabel said, sounding affronted.

"This is a cruel joke," Jezebel accused. But at that moment, there was a gust of wind. It blew away the salt. A jet of fire engulfed a nearby tree, and a growling voice cried out in the night. Jezebel thought she could hear a word in the cry; her heart froze.

Allison jumped to her feet and screamed, looking around frantically for the source of the noise. The shadow board burst into flame. Anabel and Prudence bolted, screaming in terror.

Allison grabbed Jezebel by the hand, and they ran. Jezebel heard a ripping sound behind them, deafeningly loud. She turned in time to see the flaming tree torn out of the ground as if by some invisible giant. It fell across the spot where they'd been sitting.

Suddenly the entire forest brightened. It lasted only a second, like a lightning strike. But in that instant, an image burned itself into Jezebel's eyes. A figure was standing in the trees, silhouetted against the light. An enormous dark form was bearing down upon it.

Jezebel ran again, pulling Allison along. They arrived back at the party to find the few remaining stragglers dashing away. Edward was helping his friend hitch the mule to the wagon. The animal brayed nervously.

"What the hell happened out there?" Edward demanded.

"No idea!" Jezebel shouted, running for the trail, still clinging to Allison's hand. Jezebel knew she'd never find the path back to her house. They followed the trail west, all the way to the road, running the whole way. The demonic voice cried out in the night, as if in anguish.

But by the time they reached the road, the noise had died down. They headed east toward Jezebel's house, kicking up a cloud of dirt as they walked. The moons provided the only light; Jezebel had left the torch at Rockhedge. It took them a few minutes to catch their breath.

"What the hell was that back there?" asked Allison.

"I don't know, but did you hear that voice?"

"Yes—it sounded like the growling we heard earlier."

"But this time it was saying something," Jezebel replied. "You didn't hear it?"

"No," Allison said fearfully. "What did it say?"

"It was calling your name," Jezebel told her. "It said 'Allison.'"

CHAPTER TWO
KISSING COUSINS

ezebel and Allison returned to the farmhouse. They crept inside through the back door and tiptoed upstairs to Jezebel's room. They changed into their nightgowns and climbed into the large feather bed.

They lay in silence for several minutes, each alone with her thoughts. Jezebel stared at the thick wooden beams that ran across the ceiling. Her room occupied the entire western half of the second story. The roof sloped at an angle to meet the north and south walls, making the large room feel smaller than it was.

"That was scary," Allison whispered finally. Jezebel had wondered if she'd fallen asleep.

"I always suspected the shadow board was a load of bull," Jezebel said. "I guess I was wrong. We shouldn't have messed with it."

"Maybe," said Allison. "But it worked—I talked to my mom. I want to try it again."

"Are you *crazy*?" Jezebel demanded. "After what happened tonight?" Allison didn't reply. "You're going to have to find another shadow board. Anabel's is gone. And maybe we should talk to Myrddin first—this *is* his area of expertise."

"We can't," Allison replied. "He'll tell my father."

They fell into silence again. Jezebel turned to face Allison; she was staring back at her. The princess rolled onto her side and kissed Jezebel on the lips. Allison tasted faintly of honey—much nicer than Will. They kissed tenderly for a few minutes, but then Allison pulled away.

"How did Will find out about us?" she asked.

Jezebel frowned. She'd danced around this question earlier in the hope that it wouldn't come up again. But she didn't think she'd get away with it a second time. "I don't know for sure, but I'm guessing that Edward told him."

"Edward?" Allison asked, incredulous.

"He walked in on us when we were in the barn a few weeks ago," Jezebel explained. "You didn't notice because you were a little… occupied at that moment."

"Why didn't you tell me?"

"I knew it would only upset you," said Jezebel. "He promised me he'd keep it to himself…"

"He broke his word. Now everyone's going to know."

"I doubt it," Jezebel assured her. "Will was extremely drunk; I don't think he's going to remember much. But even if he screams it from the mountaintops, who would believe him?"

Allison paused for a moment, then shrugged. "You're probably right."

"I'll talk to Edward again and make sure he keeps his mouth shut this time," Jezebel promised.

"Are you in love with Will?"

"Definitely *not*," Jezebel replied with a grimace. "He's an ass."

"You said his name in the barn that day," Allison pointed out. "You were thinking about him."

"I was," Jezebel admitted. "He's attractive for an imbecile. But there's a big difference between love and *lust*."

Allison let out a long sigh. "Do you remember the first time we made love?" she asked. Jezebel could tell from her eyes that she was far away.

"Of course I do," she replied. "It was only a couple of years ago."

"How did you feel?"

Jezebel giggled. "After all that wine? Drunk."

"Seriously," Allison chided. "What was it like for you?"

Jezebel lay flat, recalling the encounter. "Well… it was like a game at first. It was fun—you know, we were just fooling around. But it was scary and exciting, too… I'd never kissed anyone before. It was like we were exploring a mysterious new world, full of danger."

"It was different for me," Allison whispered. She was silent for a minute, collecting her thoughts. "When was the first time you ever noticed a boy? I mean, *that way*?"

Jezebel giggled again. "Easy. Four years ago. When Will first came to work for my father. How about you?"

Allison took a deep breath. "Will was right. I don't like boys."

"What are you talking about?"

"I've known it since we were little. My mother always talked about how I'd grow up and marry a prince. It didn't sound right. I imagined myself growing up to marry a *princess*."

Jezebel was stunned.

"The first time I ever thought about anyone *that way* was when your breasts started growing," Allison continued.

Jezebel snorted. "You must be joking."

"I was fascinated—I couldn't stop looking at you. Why do you think I began sleeping here more often?"

"To see me naked?"

Allison giggled. "Exactly! And that night after your party, it was like I'd gone to heaven. I was always afraid you'd never speak to me again if I told you how I felt. When I kissed you, I was so nervous I was shaking."

"I remember," Jezebel said quietly.

"But you kissed me back. And then I knew that you wouldn't hate me."

"But Allison," Jezebel said hesitantly, "I like boys. This is fun, but that's all it is. We're both going to marry *men*."

"It doesn't have to be that way…"

"Yes, it does. That's the way the world works."

"But I'm in love with *you*. I don't want anyone else. And besides, Princess Salerna from Highgate likes women. She didn't marry a man. Why should I?"

"But she didn't marry a woman either," Jezebel retorted. "That's not allowed. And she did take a *male* lover eventually, didn't she?"

"Only to produce an heir," Allison countered. "Her female lover lives with her in the castle. Everyone knows that."

"That's true," Jezebel replied pensively. "You know… I wouldn't mind living in the castle with you." This wasn't an option she'd ever considered before.

"Truly? You're not just teasing?" Allison asked hopefully.

"Truly," Jezebel agreed. "But… you *will* have to produce an heir someday. You're going to have to take a man to bed, just like Salerna."

"Eww," Allison said, crinkling her nose. "Repulsive."

They both giggled.

"What were you going to ask your mother?"

Allison didn't respond for a minute.

"If she loved my father," she whispered finally.

Jezebel tried to imagine her aunt Leda's face. She'd been gone only a year and a half, but already Jezebel had started to forget her features. She remembered only her golden hair and her deep brown eyes. And she recalled too well how she appeared after she fell ill. During her final days, she'd looked like someone three times her age. Her mind had gone, too; she didn't recognize her family anymore. She'd caught a rare disease, and the healers had been utterly stymied. Everything they tried failed.

But Jezebel could no longer remember Leda's face before she was sick. It felt like losing her all over again. She could only imagine the depth of Allison's grief.

The girls fell asleep in each other's arms. But Jezebel woke with a start a few hours later. It was still dark outside. A violent storm was passing through the area.

Jezebel climbed out of bed, careful not to disturb Allison. She looked out the window. There were flashes of lightning every few seconds, the thunder instantaneous: this storm was right on top of them.

For a moment, Jezebel thought she could hear a voice in the thunder. Suddenly a bolt struck the lightning rod on the barn. There was a loud explosion; Allison woke with a scream.

"What's going on?" she asked, jumping out of bed.

"It's just a storm," Jezebel told her, returning to bed. "Go back to sleep."

But at that moment, there was a pounding on the door downstairs. Jezebel and Allison looked at each other, fear in their eyes. Who would come knocking in the middle of the night?

Jezebel heard her parents stirring on the first floor. Whoever was at the door pounded again, louder this time. Allison and Jezebel crept out of the room and partway down the stairs.

Jezebel's little sister cracked open her bedroom door and peered out. Emma was only seven; she looked terrified. Jezebel beckoned her to the stairs, but she shook her head vigorously and stayed put.

Jezebel's father was standing by the door with a club in his hands. "Who's there?" he yelled.

Jezebel heard only a muffled reply. But her father opened the door.

Allison's father, Prince Aldo Barclay, strode into the room, his steward behind him. Aldo was tall and thin, with balding silver hair and a neatly trimmed beard. Oswald, his steward, was short and slender: a mere wisp of a man.

"My prince," said Jezebel's father, dropping to one knee. "To what do we owe this honor?" Jezebel's father was shorter than Aldo. His dark hair looked like a mop on his head. His face was weather-beaten, like old leather.

"I've told you a million times, Robert, don't give me that 'my prince' garbage," Aldo said impatiently. "I'm your brother."

"As you wish," Robert replied, getting to his feet.

"Where are the girls?"

"Here, Father," Allison said, moving down the stairs. Jezebel followed.

"Where did you go tonight?" Aldo demanded.

"They've been asleep in bed," Robert told him. "What's the meaning of this?"

"We weren't here the *whole* time," Jezebel said. "We left... for a while."

"*What?*" Robert asked. "Where exactly did you go?"

"There was a party," Jezebel replied. "Out at Rockhedge. We wanted to go. We didn't stay long…"

"A party," Robert repeated in disbelief.

"And is that where you used the shadow board?" asked Aldo. "At Rockhedge?"

Jezebel was shocked. How did he know about that? "Yes," she admitted.

Aldo shook his head. Robert still looked stunned to learn that the girls had left the house without his knowledge.

"It's called the Devil's Wood for a reason," Aldo told them. "Evil lurks in that forest. It was unwise to attempt contacting spirits there."

"I'm sorry, Father," Allison said, looking at the floor.

"You're both unharmed?" Aldo asked, genuine concern in his voice.

"Yes," Jezebel assured him. "Things got a little weird, but we came straight home. We're fine."

Outside, the sky began to clear. Jezebel hadn't realized the time: it was dawn. Rays of sunlight streamed through the windows.

"It's time for breakfast," Jezebel's mother announced. "Will you join us, Aldo?"

Aldo stared at Allison for a moment longer before replying. "No, thank you, Vivien. I'll speak to my daughter alone for a few minutes, then I must return to the castle.

"Allison, please dress yourself more appropriately, and I shall meet you outside."

With that, he strode out the door. Jezebel saw two of the prince's guards waiting on the porch.

Jezebel accompanied Allison back to her room and she helped the princess into her dress. Neither said a word. Jezebel escorted her downstairs; Allison went outside to join her father.

Jezebel sat at the kitchen table with Robert. Emma came downstairs finally and helped her mother with breakfast.

Vivien was hardly taller than Jezebel. Her skin was every bit as dark as Robert's. She didn't have the figure of a princess, but honest labor kept her stout rather than plump. Jezebel smiled to herself when Vivien muttered something about not being able to find the salt.

"I ask you," said Robert, "what were you thinking? Bringing the princess out to the Devil's Wood in the middle of the night? You know that place is forbidden."

"I'm sorry, Father," said Jezebel. "Allison wanted to talk to her mother. A girl from town had a shadow board. She said Rockhedge was the best place to commune with the dead. We figured we'd give it a try." Jezebel shrugged. She felt stupid telling her father this.

Robert let out a long sigh. "Jez, you must be more careful where Allison is concerned. With Leda gone, and Aldo's refusal to remarry, Allison is the only heir. Aldo fears for her safety. I daresay this incident will not make him rest any easier."

"Why didn't they have more children?" Jezebel asked.

"They tried," Robert said with a shrug. "Aldo always wanted a son. But it wasn't meant to be. In the absence of a male heir, Allison will inherit the throne—she *will* rule the princedom one day."

"So why is Aldo in such a hurry for her to marry?" Jezebel had never grasped the rules of primogeniture; they seemed so arbitrary, utterly devoid of logic.

Robert looked sad. "Because he wants her to produce offspring—as many as possible. That way, if something should happen to Allison, Aldo's line will continue."

"But what would happen if Allison died before she had children?" Jezebel's heart sank just imagining Allison's death. She'd never considered this before.

"In that case, you would become Aldo's heir," Robert replied. "He named you next in his line of succession."

Jezebel froze. "You never told me…"

Robert shrugged. "You never asked. And I didn't want to fill your head with such notions."

"But if that's true, why aren't you rushing *me* into marriage?"

Robert laughed. "You have someone in mind?"

"No!"

Robert took a deep breath. "When we were young, I watched our father pressure Aldo to marry, the same way he's pushing Allison now. Nobles seldom marry for love—necessity dictates their choices. I thanked the stars that *I* wasn't firstborn. And I promised myself I'd never put my children through that."

"But, I thought Aldo and Leda married *older* than usual?"

"Indeed," Robert confirmed. "Aldo refused to bend to our father's will. When your mother and I began courting, your grandfather even threatened to name *me* his heir. Aldo had met Leda by then, and it was love at first sight. But he prolonged the engagement just to make it clear that he was doing things on his own terms.

"No, I'll never do that to you, Jez. When you're ready to marry, you'll let me know."

Jezebel thought back to her conversation with Allison the previous night and grinned.

"What about Princess Salerna?" she asked. "She's never wed, but she was allowed to name Albert her heir."

"Salerna?" Robert asked, surprised by the question. He sat back in his chair with the same look of concentration he always wore when he worked on the accounting for the farm. Nearly a minute went by without a reply. But finally, he grunted to himself.

"Salerna's situation is unique, so far as I know," he began slowly. "Typically, bastards are never allowed to ascend to the throne. Without a proper heir or next of kin, Highgate would have passed to some lesser lord upon Salerna's death. But the people of Highgate love Salerna dearly, and Albert nearly as much. He's grown into a respectable young man with a family of his own. Given the circumstances, the people have accepted him.

"But one thing you—and Allison—must understand is that Salerna's reign nearly ended in disaster. Her actions caused an uproar across the entire continent. The neighboring princes were ready to wage war over Albert's appointment. They would have attacked were it not for Highgate's military prowess—and the fierce loyalty of its commanders." He locked eyes with Jezebel. "You understand?"

Jezebel nodded, considering his words for a moment.

"You're old enough to make your own choices now. I just hope you'll be mindful of the consequences of your actions. One day this farm will be yours; you need to learn to make responsible decisions."

"Yes, Father."

Allison came inside a few minutes later. Aldo had departed. Vivien served them breakfast: steak and eggs and potatoes. Jezebel hadn't realized how hungry she was. After they ate, Jezebel went outside with Allison. They sat on the front porch.

"How'd it go with your father?" Jezebel asked.

"Better than expected," she replied with a weak smile. "He was upset, of course. He threatened to restrict me to the castle from now on. And he was suspicious that going to Rockhedge was your idea. But I swore it wasn't."

"I would have taken the blame," Jezebel told her.

"No, this way is better. If he believed that you'd dragged me out there, he certainly wouldn't let me come here anymore. I told him I wanted to talk to Mother. He melted. I only had to promise not to venture into the Devil's Wood again."

"That's fair," Jezebel observed.

"But he *knew* we were out there," Allison said. "How?"

Jezebel could provide no answer.

CHAPTER THREE
THE NECROMANCER

ater that morning, Allison went off with Vivien to tend to the laundry. Jezebel ventured out to find Edward, under the pretense of helping him break in the new team of oxen. She caught up with him in the southeastern field.

"Hey," she yelled as she approached the plow. Tess, her shepherd dog, ran ahead.

Edward turned and waved. "What's on your mind?"

"You're an ass," Jezebel said, sitting in the dirt.

Edward sat next to her. "Nice to see you, too."

Tess nudged Edward's arm with her nose. He scratched her behind one ear.

"Why'd you tell Will?"

"I was trying to protect my turf," he replied. "Although that didn't quite work according to plan."

"Excuse me?"

"He expressed an interest in you at the party last night. He planned to act on it. I figured I could scare him away."

Jezebel shook her head. "I am not your *turf*. And I can handle myself."

"Yes, as you proved."

"And I told you, I'm not interested in you."

Edward shrugged. "I know. But you'll come around eventually. I have far more to offer than Will."

"Oh yes, your formal education," Jezebel replied, rolling her eyes. "I may not be highborn, but I am educated."

"Perhaps," Edward conceded. "But homeschooling can hardly match…"

"I can do the accounting, Edward. I can manage the employees and figure out the crop rotations. I don't need a man to run this place for me. And I'm not interested in *Will* either."

Edward spat in the dirt. "You can't marry the princess, Jez."

Jezebel got to her feet and started to walk away. But she stopped and turned to face Edward. "I can do whatever I want—it's none of your business. Just promise me you'll keep your mouth shut from now on."

"As you wish," Edward replied.

"Let's go, Tess," Jezebel called to the dog. Tess didn't move.

Edward petted her on the head. "The dog knows," he said with a smile.

Jezebel stormed off and headed back to the house. She had to admit, Edward *would* make a respectable husband. She knew her education was no match for his. And although he was landless, he *was* the fourth-born son of a nobleman. A farmer's daughter couldn't hope for much better than that. But she wasn't attracted to him.

Why couldn't she find a man with Edward's intellect and Will's looks? Of course, what she valued most was the connection she shared with Allison—who also happened to be attractive and intelligent. She was truly the perfect mate. If only one of them had been born male…

That afternoon, Allison expressed a desire to return to the castle. She wanted to talk to Myrddin, her father's necromancer. She hoped he could make some sense out of what had happened to them at Rockhedge the previous night.

"Might as well," Jezebel told her. "No need for secrecy now that your father knows what we did."

Robert offered to drive them in the wagon. But the girls preferred to walk—it was a beautiful summer day. So after dinner, they set out.

They headed west along the road. Robert's farm was several miles away from the castle, so the journey took over two hours. They passed other farms on the way. Fields hugged the road on both sides; gentle hills rolled in the distance. Three separate horse and wagon teams drove by. Each offered them a ride, but the girls refused. They were enjoying the walk too much.

As the sun approached the horizon, the town came into view, Castle Spanbrook towering over it. Jezebel's great-grandfather had built a wall around the entire community. But since her grandfather's time, Spanbrook had known only peace. The eastern edge of the wall had fallen into severe disrepair. Near the road, it had collapsed completely.

To the north and west, the wall still stood. The town had grown beyond it in those directions. In many places, it had been incorporated into the structure of newer buildings.

"What's this?" Allison asked. Dozens of gray tents were set up outside the wall. It looked like a small city.

"No idea," Jezebel replied, yet something about the scene felt vaguely familiar.

As they drew closer, Jezebel realized that the tents were only gray because they were covered in grime. Underneath, each was a different color; some were blue, others green, a few red. She imagined they'd have been rather bright were they not so filthy.

People were moving about between the tents. Nearly all of them had olive complexions and dark hair; they appeared to share a common ancestry. But a few had lighter hair and fairer skin. Most of the men wore trousers and tunics. Some of the women did, too, but most wore plain dresses.

As they passed the tents, Jezebel noticed a young man, perhaps a year or two older than herself. He wore tan trousers and a purple tunic and held a wooden staff. His long hair was pulled back in a ponytail. His almond-shaped eyes were so dark it seemed like he was wearing eyeliner. Jezebel couldn't take her eyes off of him: he was gorgeous.

Allison poked her. "You're staring."

"He's attractive."

"More so than *Will*?" Allison teased.

"Definitely."

"He's too young for a walking stick," Allison observed. "Must be a wizard."

"Doesn't look old enough for that," Jezebel replied.

"What's with his friend?"

Jezebel hadn't noticed the second man, although they were standing right next to each other. He was taller than the attractive one. He wore long black robes, an oversized hood covering his head. Jezebel couldn't see his face.

They appeared to be deep in conversation. The younger one spotted the girls. He waved.

Allison giggled. Jezebel hesitated a moment before waving back.

They walked past the ruined wall, into the town. Jezebel turned to look over her shoulder; the boy was still watching them.

Allison continued along the main road toward the castle. But Jezebel caught her by the elbow. "I want to stop by my uncle's first."

An inn was located on the corner. Jezebel walked inside. The door opened into the tavern; all the guestrooms were upstairs. The bartender was wiping down the bar. There were only three patrons sitting at one of the tables.

"Hello, Trey," Jezebel called out.

The bartender looked up. "Jez!" He scurried out from behind the bar and ran over to meet them. He was short and stocky, with flaming red hair. "How's my sister?" he asked, pulling Jezebel into a hug.

"Mom's doing well," she replied.

"And what brings you—ah, Princess Allison," Trey said, noticing her behind Jezebel. He took her fingers delicately in his own and brushed his lips against the back of her hand.

"Alli, please," she replied. "You're practically *my* uncle, too, Trey. We can dispense with the formalities."

They followed him to the bar. The girls each took a stool.

"What can I get you today? I've brewed a new cinnamon mead—care to try some?"

"Sure," said Jezebel, and Allison nodded. "Uncle, it's your mead I wanted to talk to you about."

"Oh?" he asked, pouring their glasses.

She spent a few minutes telling him about the party and how a wagon-load of his best mead had turned up there.

"Corny," he said with a frown.

"Excuse me?" Jezebel asked.

"Cornwall's his proper name," Trey explained. "Caught him stealing once before. I'll have to have a chat with him. Thanks, Jez."

Suddenly, there was a commotion outside. Jezebel looked out the window to see several of the prince's guards go by on horseback. Behind them rode the steward and the necromancer.

"I wonder what's going on," Allison said, getting off the stool to look out the window.

"Probably going to lay down the law with them wayfarers," Trey suggested. "Saw them set up their tents this afternoon. I could use the business, that's for sure. But I don't know how happy the prince is going to be about this. Seem to encourage drunken revelry and mayhem, wayfarers do."

"Wayfarers," Jezebel muttered. She hadn't seen the wayfarers in ages. "Let's go check it out," she said, already heading out the door. Allison followed her.

"Good night, ladies," Trey called after them.

"Bye, Trey!" Jezebel yelled back.

They ran back the way they'd come, beyond the wall. The prince's men had moved off the road, toward the tents. The girls walked past them, but stuck to the road, careful to keep their distance. Allison expressed worry that Oswald would send them away if he saw her. They stood behind a tree, close enough to hear what was going on.

One of the guards was questioning the boy they'd seen earlier; he was leaning on his staff. Myrddin and Oswald hung back with the rest of the guards.

Myrddin, the prince's necromancer, wore long robes, similar to those of the wayfarer they'd seen earlier, only his were gray instead of black. He'd thrown his hood back, revealing a full head of long gray hair and a thick mustache and beard. His skin was strangely ashen and almost translucent. Jezebel could see the muscles in his neck and face. But his eyes were his oddest feature: the irises were white.

Two men approached from the tents. One was the hooded figure they'd seen earlier. The other was slightly shorter, with the familiar olive complexion and dark hair. His beard and ponytail were long and straight, his smile friendly. A group of people followed in their wake, apparently curious to see what the fuss was about.

"What seems to be the trouble, Khaldun?" the smiling man asked the boy.

Khaldun, Jezebel repeated to herself.

"You're the leader?" the guard asked.

"Yes," the man replied. "Badru's the name."

"Prince Aldo welcomes you to Spanbrook," the guard told him. "He expects your people to abide by our laws during your stay. And he hopes you will perform at the castle."

"Of course," the man agreed. "Please send the prince my greetings. We are at his service."

"The prince has information that you have a wanted outlaw traveling in your troupe. You'll need to surrender this man into our custody."

Badru looked puzzled. "I assure you, I would never allow a criminal to join us."

Myrddin spurred his horse forward. "The man is wanted for rape and murder. Undoubtedly he's taken great care to conceal his identity from you."

Badru looked horrified—Jezebel couldn't tell what scared him more: Myrddin's words or his appearance. "Please, sir, help me find the rogue, and he's yours."

Myrddin closed his eyes. The wind picked up, blowing dirt from the road. Suddenly a man in the back of the crowd screamed and ran toward the town. He was light-haired and fair-skinned—certainly an outsider among the wayfarers, Jezebel noted.

The man hadn't gone twenty feet before he was lifted into the air by some unseen force. His feet moved frantically as if he were still trying to run. He came to rest directly in front of Myrddin—ten feet above the ground.

"You are Seth of Highgate," Myrddin said calmly. It wasn't a question.

"Yes," the man screamed. He was cowering from something only he could see.

"You are wanted for raping and murdering an eight-year-old girl."

He closed his eyes. "Yes!"

"Do you deny these crimes?"

"NO!"

The man stopped screaming. He opened his eyes and looked surprised to find himself hanging ten feet in the air.

Jezebel heard a low buzzing noise. Suddenly serpentine clouds of smoke crawled all over the man's body. He looked terrified. They entered his body through various orifices. He screamed much louder than before. Blood dripped from his eyes and ears.

Allison turned away.

Seconds later, the screaming stopped. The man went rigid, then totally limp. Whatever was holding him up suddenly let go. His corpse landed in the dirt, broken and bleeding.

"Bury that," Myrddin commanded.

Four of the guards dismounted. Two of them picked up the body by its arms and legs and carried it across the road. The other two followed with shovels.

"It's good to see you, Nomad," Myrddin said calmly, nothing in his tone to suggest that he'd just killed a man.

The hooded figure bowed.

"Enjoy your stay in Spanbrook," Myrddin continued. "But remember. We'll be watching."

Myrddin trotted away on his horse; Oswald followed. Badru eyed their backs apprehensively for several seconds before returning to the tents with Nomad and Khaldun. The remaining guards joined their comrades across the road.

Allison looked pale.

"That was unpleasant," Jezebel commented, feeling slightly nauseated.

"I've seen him do that before," Allison said. "But I'll never get used to it."

As they walked away, Jezebel caught a glimpse of Khaldun standing by the corner of one of the tents. He was watching them.

"Your Highness," a voice called out. Jezebel looked up. It was Oswald. He'd spotted them and reined his horse in their direction. Myrddin waited behind.

"Damn," Allison muttered.

"I am sure your father will not want you associating with these wayfarers," he said. His voice was as wispy as his hair. "It would be inappropriate for someone of your high station to be seen cavorting with such rabble."

"Then I promise not to *cavort*, Oswald," Allison replied stiffly.

Oswald nodded and rode back to Myrddin at a trot. The two of them resumed their course into town.

"We could talk to Myrddin now," Jezebel suggested.

"No," Allison replied. "Not in front of Oswald. I can't stand the way he looks at me—as if he were undressing me with his eyes. And anyway, they'll have to report to my father. We can catch him later."

The girls walked into town. Jezebel kept looking back at the wayfarer camp, but Khaldun was gone.

Paved in cobblestones, the road cut straight through the town. The marketplace occupied the last dozen blocks on the approach to the castle. Vendors on both sides of the street sold their wares: fruits and vegetables, meat, fabric, clothing, shoes—the market was the center of commerce in Spanbrook.

As they passed, Allison took her time, chatting with every one of them. It was clear to Jezebel that Allison's people loved her. She didn't know if it was the same outside of Spanbrook Town. But looking at their faces, Jezebel had no doubt these people would accept any heir Allison cared to name, regardless of the circumstances.

By the time they arrived at the castle, full night had fallen. Castle Spanbrook's name described it accurately: the structure itself straddled the River Ember.

The castle rose forty feet high. The eastern towers stood at the corners, this side of the river. The road led directly to the main entrance, right in the middle of the wall. Jezebel had never seen the gates closed. She gazed up at the figure standing sentinel on top of the gatehouse as they passed underneath.

"Which one is that again?" she asked. Two of Aldo's witches were twins; Jezebel could never keep them straight.

"Camilla," Allison replied. "They're not identical. I've told you— Gemma's the one with the longer face."

"If you say so," Jezebel muttered.

After they passed through the tunnel, the great hall was located on the right, the administrative chambers to the left. As the girls neared, a young woman came charging out of the prince's office. Jezebel caught a glimpse of Myrddin closing the door behind her.

The woman stood only a few inches taller than Jezebel. A wild mane of dark hair flowed behind her. Her skin was pale, her eyes green. She gazed at the girls intently as she passed. The woman was beautiful, Jezebel thought. And she carried a staff.

"Is she one of your father's?" Jezebel asked uncertainly once they were out of earshot.

"No," Allison replied. "I've never seen that witch before."

As they continued through the passage, Jezebel knew the Ember flowed beneath them. She'd been down there when she was younger. Three rows of massive steel gates barred the progress of unwelcome vessels. Commercial traffic had no reason to sail south of Spanbrook; the wharves were located at the northern end of town. Only boats or barges supplying the castle itself were allowed to pass the gates. And beyond the castle, the Ember truly amounted to little more than a brook.

The girls emerged into the vast central courtyard. The keep sat directly across from them; the western towers stood at the far corners.

Jezebel followed Allison inside the keep. The guard saluted and opened the door for them. Allison's chambers occupied the northeastern corner of the second floor.

Once inside, Allison strode across her bedroom and sat in the bay window. Jezebel took a seat across from her. From this vantage point, they could look out across the courtyard. Myrddin lived in the northwestern tower; they'd see him when he left Aldo's offices.

"You know," Jezebel said quietly, "maybe with Myrddin's help, we won't need to find another spirit board."

"What do you mean?" Allison asked.

"Communicating with the dead is his specialty. He could help you contact your mother directly…"

"No," Allison replied. "I need to talk to her without the conversation getting back to my father. That's why I didn't go to Myrddin in the first place."

"Good point," Jezebel murmured. "Anabel found the board in her attic. I wonder how common those things are."

Allison only shrugged.

Twenty minutes later, they spotted Myrddin making his way across the courtyard. They intercepted him outside the entrance to his tower.

"Good evening, ladies," he said with a smile. He looked surprised to see them.

"I wanted to talk to you," Allison said. "Do you have a few minutes?"

"Of course," Myrddin replied, opening the door with a great skeleton key. "As a matter of fact, I was planning to schedule some time with Your Highness."

Myrddin led the way inside; the girls followed. They climbed a narrow staircase that wound its way around the inside of the tower wall. Myrddin opened another door at the top, and they emerged inside his office.

The circular room occupied the whole of this level. Thick carpets covered the stone floor. There were four thin windows, each facing one of the cardinal directions, and torches spaced evenly along the wall. With a wave of Myrddin's hand, the torches burst into flame.

Myrddin sat at his desk, motioning the girls into the chairs across from him. They each took a seat. A large crystal ball sat in its wooden stand on one corner of the desk.

"Have you come to a decision regarding Prince Caldwell of Northcoast?" he asked conversationally, a smile twitching the corners of his mouth.

Allison crinkled her nose.

"He was the one who could barely grow a beard, wasn't he?" Jezebel asked.

"Yes," Allison replied, "and with all the pimples and body odor."

"Your father will be sorry to hear that you're rejecting him," Myrddin noted. "The boy is a second son from a very wealthy princedom. Marriage with him would provide a fine alliance…"

"Why shouldn't she marry a firstborn?" Jezebel asked. "Isn't she good enough?"

Myrddin opened his mouth to reply, but Allison answered first. "A mating with a firstborn wouldn't be practical unless it were with someone from an adjoining princedom," she explained. "The thrones would merge, you see. Great difficulties would arise governing a princedom split into nonadjacent regions."

"Not to mention the fact that your father would never approve of such a union," Myrddin added. "Even if there *were* any eligible firstborns in the neighboring princedoms."

"Why not?" Jezebel asked.

"I'm female," Allison replied simply. "Spanbrook would cease to exist as a sovereign entity. The *prince's* throne always dominates in such arrangements."

"Well, you should have a bit of a respite," Myrddin said. "I convinced Oswald that it was high-time for your father to tour the princedom and meet with his vassals. The parade of princes will have to take an intermission, I'm afraid, until he returns."

Allison's face registered only surprise for a moment until she cracked a grin from ear to ear. "Thank you *so much*," she said.

Myrddin bowed his head slightly. "But you didn't come here to discuss your marital prospects…"

"No," Allison agreed. She took a deep breath. "I'm sure you've heard about my foray into the Devil's Wood?"

"Certainly," Myrddin replied. "I'm the one who informed your father of your… activities."

"What?!" Jezebel blurted. "Then… how did *you* know?"

"By the prince's command, I always keep an eye on the princess when she leaves the castle," Myrddin explained. "My skills enable me to watch from afar. And of course, I can intervene should the princess encounter any kind of danger. Until now, no such situation had ever arisen. But I must say, setting foot inside of Rockhedge was extremely dangerous."

"Why?" Allison asked. "What is that place?"

"It's hard to say what purpose it might have served in the beginning. It's older than the princedom, that goes without saying. But it also predates the Pythan Empire or even the first Kingdom of Dorshire. Indeed, my research indicates that when the first men crossed the Lonely Sea and set foot on this continent, Rockhedge was already here.

"At some point, it functioned as a burial site for an ancient civilization. Human sacrifices were made there to appease vengeful gods. From that time forward, Rockhedge has acted as a magnet for demons and malignant spirits.

"By using a spirit board on that hallowed ground, you girls wakened something that was better left asleep. You caught the attention of a powerful demon. I tried to fight it off, but it proved much too strong—I was no match."

"You were there," Jezebel said. "I saw you—there was a flash of light, and an enormous shadow towered over you…"

"I was not there in physical form," Myrddin corrected her. "But using every force available to me, I vied for control of the demon. He nearly broke me. I lost track of Her Highness in the struggle—but you did the right thing by fleeing the forest. The demon failed to find you again.

"I checked in at your home, Jezebel, to make sure you were both safe. Then I spent the rest of the night pursuing the demon. When I was sure it was gone, I alerted the prince. He left for his brother's farm at once."

Jezebel's heart jumped into her throat. What exactly had he seen when he "checked in" at her house? Did he know? No, he couldn't, she told herself. Nothing in his face or voice hinted at any knowledge of the girls' true relationship. And surely he would have informed Aldo if he'd discovered their secret.

"What were you trying to do with the spirit board?" Myrddin asked.

"I wanted to talk to Mother," Allison replied quietly. "A girl in town told us that Rockhedge was the best place to communicate with… the dead."

"Oh, child," Myrddin said, compassion in his eyes. "You should have come to me. I can put you in contact with Leda without exposing you to danger."

"I know," Allison said. "But the things I wanted to talk to her about… were personal. I'm sorry, it's not that I don't trust you—"

Myrddin held up one hand. "There's no need to apologize. I understand. But I am at your service should you change your mind. Your mother was very dear to me. I will confess, I have spoken with her myself."

"You have?" Allison asked.

"Oh yes," he said. "She came to me a few weeks after her passing. She asked me to watch over you—she loved you very much, you know."

Tears welled up in Allison's eyes.

"But you must promise me that you will not attempt to contact her again by spirit board," Myrddin said. "Opening such a channel would make you visible to the demon you disturbed at Rockhedge. I do not wish to confront him again."

"No," Jezebel muttered. "Neither do I."

CHAPTER FOUR
WAYFARER

ezebel lay in bed, curled up in her nightgown, her head on Allison's stomach.

"This is the way I want it to be," Allison said, absentmindedly playing with Jezebel's hair. "Always."

Jezebel gazed up at the canopy of the enormous four-poster bed, and at the oil lamp burning on the nightstand. She looked across the room at the massive fireplace and thought of the plumbing in the adjoining washroom—a luxury that existed nowhere else in Spanbrook. And she turned to look at Allison, breathtakingly beautiful with her wet hair cascading down her bare shoulders.

"I could certainly get used to it," Jezebel observed with a sigh.

"I'm serious," Allison insisted. "I never want anyone else to share my bed."

"I don't see how this is going to work…"

"What do you mean?" Allison asked, sounding distressed. "I thought you said you would live here with me?"

"I would *love* to," Jezebel replied. "But let's be realistic. You're going to tell your father that you refuse to marry, and you're taking me as your lover instead?"

"Well… no," Allison admitted.

"How did Salerna do it?"

"She inherited the throne when she was fifteen," Allison explained. "Her parents and brother died from the plague."

"And her brother was the designated heir, I assume."

"Yes."

"Which means Salerna's parents probably didn't pressure her to marry," Jezebel noted absently. She considered the situation for several seconds. "I don't think you can avoid this. You're going to have to take a husband."

"No! You don't understand. This isn't a choice. *I can't be with a man.* That's not who I am."

"You're not being practical," Jezebel told her. "You are going to inherit the throne one day. You have to ensure your line continues—and for that, you need a man."

"But—"

Jezebel pressed a finger to Allison's lips. "Hear me out. Didn't you tell me that the prince from Northcoast was only interested in the political alliance with Spanbrook? That he didn't care about you at all?"

Allison nodded.

"Then he's perfect," Jezebel told her. "Marry him."

"*What?*"

"*You* will be the ruler—he's not firstborn. So marry him, copulate, produce an heir, and boot him from your bed."

"Dissolve the union?"

"Maybe not formally," Jezebel said. "But you told me once that at least half the ruling princes on the continent don't share a bed with their wives."

"It's true. Most end up taking a mistress. Or three." Allison giggled. "That's why there are so many bastards floating around most of the princedoms."

"What's sauce for the goose is sauce for the gander," Jezebel said. "I'm not going anywhere—my father is in no rush for me to marry. Do what you must to fulfill your duty. The farm will pass to my sister, and I can come live here with you."

"You'll be my mistress," Allison said with a mischievous smile.

Jezebel laughed. "I hadn't thought of it quite that way. But yes, I will."

They lay quietly for a few minutes. Jezebel found herself imagining what her future would be like by Allison's side.

"Have you ever toured the princedom?" she asked. "You know, gone to see the vassals like your father's going to do?"

"Yes," Allison replied. "I accompanied him once when I was a little girl."

"Maybe you should go again."

"I'll have to eventually. The lords will need to know me before I ascend to the throne."

"No, I mean as soon as possible," Jezebel said. "And as often as possible."

"What? Why?"

"I watched the way the vendors in the market reacted when they saw you. Those people adore you. And you charmed them very effectively. It would be smart to charm the vassals the same way, don't you think?"

"I wasn't *charming* them," Allison replied. "But what are you getting at?"

"My father said Salerna could only get away with what she did because her people love her. If you sow the seeds now, perhaps you can achieve the same loyalty here. And with enough support... who knows? Maybe someday I could be your wife instead of your mistress."

"Ah... Yes, I think I'd prefer that role for you." Allison said. "You know, you're quite astute for a farmer's daughter."

"It's only common sense," Jezebel replied.

Allison extinguished the lamp, and they went to sleep. Jezebel had a dream that *she* had inherited the throne. She was standing at the top of Myrddin's tower, looking out across Spanbrook Town. Suddenly someone screamed.

Jezebel woke with a start. Allison was standing by the foot of the bed, screaming her head off, pointing at the canopy. Her hair was a mess, and her nightgown was hanging off her shoulder, exposing one breast. She looked slightly insane.

The doors flew open, and light flooded the room. Two of the prince's guards rushed inside.

"Your Highness!" the older one yelled, scanning the room for the source of her alarm. "What's wrong?"

The other guard simply stood there, staring at the princess's chest. Allison dropped to her knees, sobbing. Jezebel climbed out of bed and sat down next to her. She fixed Allison's nightgown and put her arms around her.

"What is it?" she asked. "What did you see?"

Allison took a deep breath, forcing herself to calm down. "There was someone on the canopy," she said, pointing. "I woke up, and I saw an arm reaching over the edge. I jumped out of bed…"

The guard climbed the bed and peered over the top. "There's nothing here," he informed them.

"It was only a nightmare," Jezebel reassured the princess.

Allison shook her head. "It seemed real… I feel so stupid—I'm sorry I disturbed you," she added to the guards. "Thank you for coming so quickly."

"Of course, Your Highness," the older man replied. "Can we be of further assistance?" His young companion was still staring at the princess.

Allison shook her head, and the guards left the room. Jezebel coaxed Allison back into bed.

"You're shaking," Jezebel whispered, holding her tight.

"I've never had such a vivid dream," Allison told her. "I'm glad you're here."

"Who was the new guard?" Jezebel asked. "He was staring at you."

"Preston," Allison replied, rolling her eyes. "He's smitten with me, I'm afraid."

"The poor child," Jezebel said.

They slept through the rest of the night without incident.

Allison had her training session with Badrick, the prince's master-at-arms, the following morning. Jezebel accompanied her to the courtyard. She sat on a bench in the covered walkway along the south wall to watch the lesson.

Allison fought with a double-edged blade in one hand, a dagger in the other. Badrick wielded a great two-handed broadsword. They both wore chain mail over heavy leather jerkins, as well as helmets and facemasks.

Jezebel knew nothing about sword fighting; she didn't grasp the instructions Badrick gave Allison. But she did understand that her cousin possessed uncanny skill with a variety of blades.

Oswald strolled over from the administrative offices and stood next to Jezebel, acknowledging her only with a nod. He watched the lesson for a few minutes, whistling or clapping each time Allison bested Badrick.

"She's quite good for a girl," Oswald said, sitting next to Jezebel.

"She's quite good. Period," Jezebel replied.

Oswald stared at her for a moment. "You're closer to Her Highness than anyone else. Would you care to offer some insight into her refusal to choose a husband?"

"Isn't this something you should discuss with Her Highness?"

"We have," said Oswald. "The prince has reasoned with her, pleaded with her, bribed her… The princess is willful and stubborn. Her father has made it clear she can pick anyone she wants; he has not placed any conditions upon her choice. Yet the princess chooses nobody."

Jezebel watched Badrick lunge at Allison with his blade. Using her sword to parry, she moved in to stab him in the chest with her dagger.

"But the prince *has* placed conditions on her selection," Jezebel said. "He won't let her marry a minor lord, for example. Or a farmer's son. Nor will he allow her to choose a firstborn prince."

"Interesting," Oswald replied. "Are you implying that the princess has already taken a lover? Someone, perhaps, who would stand no chance of earning the prince's approval?"

Jezebel wished she'd kept her mouth shut. But she was also certain that Oswald was nowhere near guessing the truth.

"I'm not implying anything," she said. "I was simply pointing out that you misspoke."

"It goes without saying that Her Highness must marry a prince," Oswald replied. "She has certain obligations…"

"To produce an heir," Jezebel said impatiently. "I know."

"Yes. With someone of suitable pedigree. But perhaps you can let the princess know… I can help her. Once her obligations are met, arrangements can be made for Her Highness to resume relations with… whomever."

Although Jezebel had suggested this exact scenario herself, it sounded dirty coming from Oswald. The man reminded her of a rat, sneaking around a kitchen, unfit to join the people at table.

"I'll give her the message," she said quietly.

When the lesson was over, Jezebel bade farewell to the princess. She left the castle and began her journey back to the farm. Her head swam with thoughts of Allison's predicament.

As she passed the wayfarer camp, she searched hopefully for any sign of the beautiful wayfarer boy. He was nowhere to be seen.

She trudged up the road. But a moment later, someone called out behind her.

"Hello there!"

Jezebel turned; it was Khaldun. She did her best to stifle a giggle. "Hello," she said, feeling herself blush. Up close, the wayfarer was even more handsome than she'd realized. He was a few inches taller than Jezebel, thin but strapping. His smile touched his eyes, and his teeth sparkled. Jezebel fought an impulse to kiss him.

"I saw you walking yesterday," he said, "with the princess. Do you live in the castle?"

"What? Oh, no—I'm her cousin. Jezebel. I live nearby," she said, pointing down the road. "On my father's farm." As soon as she'd spoken, she wished she'd lied. She should have told him she lived in the castle.

"Khaldun," he said, shaking her hand. *I know*, Jezebel thought. "We probably passed your land on our way in. We came from Newberry."

"Oh, is that where you're from?" Jezebel asked, and immediately felt like an idiot. Wayfarers weren't from *anywhere*.

Khaldun chuckled. "No, we travel a lot, never stay in one place very long. We're doing a show tonight, though, if you'd like to come and watch."

"I'd love to!" Jezebel replied. "I saw a wayfarer troupe perform once when I was a little girl. It was… delightful!" She cringed at her choice of words; only old ladies called anything *delightful*. How could this boy cause her to turn stupid? "How much does it cost?"

"Nothing," Khaldun said with a grin. "If you attend as my guest."

Jezebel smiled at him. "I'd like that."

"The princess is welcome to join you—also as my guest, of course," he added.

"I don't know if she'll be allowed," Jezebel said, recalling Oswald's admonition.

"That's too bad," Khaldun replied with a frown. "Well, the show's at eight. I'll meet you in front of the big tent."

"See you then!" Jezebel said as he walked away.

She continued along the road, a spring in her step. She looked back repeatedly to catch as many glimpses of him as she could before he disappeared.

A man in a wagon drove by and offered her a ride. Jezebel accepted. It was farmer Smithwick, who owned one of the neighboring farms. She made small talk with him the whole way back, but couldn't keep her mind off of Khaldun.

She ran up to her room when she arrived home. Looking through her closet, she wished her invitation had come *before* she'd left the castle. Jezebel's dresses were plain. She could have borrowed something fancier from her cousin if she'd known. She picked one and decided it would have to do.

She went back outside to find her father. He was in the barn with Emma, straightening a plowshare.

"Can you drive me to town tonight?" she asked breathlessly. "Or can I take the team?"

"What for?"

"The wayfarers are here. I'm going to the show."

Robert grunted. "Team's yours, I suppose. You should take your sister. She's never been to the circus before."

"What do they do there, Father?" Emma asked.

"Lots of things," Robert said with a shrug. "Trapeze, high-wire, juggling… and magic."

"Magic! Please take me, Jez! I wanna see magic!"

"Father!" Jezebel protested. "I'm meeting a boy there!"

"Ah," Robert replied. "I'll tell you what, Emma. You and I will go see the show tomorrow."

"But why can't I go with Jez?"

Robert winked at Jezebel. "You owe me one, kiddo."

Jezebel smiled at him.

She spent much of the day working on the farm. After dinner, she decided to take a bath. This was a much bigger project than it would have been at the castle, she reflected. Once she'd set a pot of water to boil on the fire, she went outside and dragged the tub into the barn. It was the same vessel they used for laundry.

She filled a bucket at the well and dumped it into the tub. Impatient, she went upstairs and laid out her clothes. When the water was ready, her mother helped her carry the pot out to the barn.

"Your sister could use a bath, too," Vivien said. "She's a little ripe."

"Yes, Mother," Jezebel said with a sigh.

She went inside and dragged Emma out to the barn. Emma hated bathing; Jezebel had to wrestle her out of her dress. But she finally got her sister into the tub and stripped out of her work clothes. She climbed in next to her sister.

Jezebel tried to soap up, but Emma wanted to play; she kept splashing water at her. But eventually, Jezebel managed to wash herself and her sister.

Fifteen minutes later, she was dressed and ready to go. She went back to the barn and hitched the team to the wagon. Normally she would have ridden one of the horses, but doing so in a dress wasn't ladylike.

Robert walked in as she was about to leave.

"Have fun," he said. "Don't stay out too late."

"I won't," she said, kissing him on the cheek.

Jezebel climbed up and drove out of the barn, thinking about Khaldun the whole way to the show. She couldn't believe how nervous she felt. By the time she arrived, the butterflies in her stomach were so bad she thought she might be sick.

Several horses and wagon teams were tied to posts in the field next to the wayfarer camp. Jezebel left her team there and hurried off to find Khaldun. She could hear music and the noise of a large crowd. She followed the sounds, and sure enough, Khaldun was waiting for her right outside the big tent.

"Here you are," he said, taking her arm. He held his staff in his other hand. "I was beginning to worry you weren't coming. The show's about to start!"

"I'm sorry—I had to give my little sister a bath. She was difficult."

He grinned and led her inside. There was a large ring in the middle, demarked by colorful wooden blocks. Rigging for the trapeze and high-wire acts spanned the open space above it. A band was playing on the other side of the tent. Benches surrounded the ring on all sides; the place was packed. Jezebel followed Khaldun to the far set of benches.

"Jezebel, this is Nomad," he said as they took their seats in the front row. The man next to her nodded. It was the hooded figure from the previous day, only now his hood was thrown back.

Jezebel gasped. Like Khaldun, Nomad wore his long black hair in a ponytail. His skin was golden, not tan or brown as if from the sun, but actually golden and metallic-looking. But his eyes, not his skin had made Jezebel gasp: the irises were blood red. She also felt an aura of energy around the man, as if there were electricity in the air.

Jezebel remembered her manners. "Pleased to meet you," she said, shaking his hand. The man nodded in reply. She forced herself to stop staring.

"Ah, here we go," Khaldun said pleasantly. A man walked into the center of the ring. Jezebel recognized him as Badru, the wayfarer leader. He welcomed the audience and introduced the first act. His baritone voice filled the enormous tent, even without a megaphone. A minute later, the show began.

Jezebel enjoyed herself immensely. She marveled at the trapeze artist but cringed throughout the high-wire act. She wasn't afraid of heights, per se, but did have a fear of *falling* from a great height. At one point, the man ran along the wire with the woman standing on his shoulders. He teetered for a moment halfway across, and Jezebel screamed. Khaldun chuckled at her.

"He does that on purpose," he told her. "It creates suspense."

A group of clowns entertained them next. Some juggled, two performed acrobatics, and the rest acted out a series of gags.

Khaldun watched Jezebel more than the show. She noticed that he seemed to hang on her every reaction, deriving pleasure from her enjoyment. Jezebel knew she was probably Emma's age the last time she'd gone to the circus. She barely remembered it—none of the acts seemed familiar. Until the magic show.

As the magician performed, Jezebel vaguely recalled a similar routine. She hadn't thought of that memory in ages. And when the man placed his scantily-clad wife in a large box and made her disappear, Jezebel was overcome with a flood of recollections. She distinctly remembered running around her house with a "wand" that was really a stick she'd picked up in the yard. She pretended to make things vanish. The fun had ended when Tess, only a puppy at the time, ran off with the stick. She fondly recalled wishing she could become a real magician.

After the show, Khaldun escorted her out through the rear entrance to avoid the crowd. "Some of us are going into town," he said. "There's a tavern just inside the wall. Would you like to accompany me?"

"Sure," Jezebel replied, beaming at him.

They walked with a group of wayfarers. Jezebel recognized the magician and his wife, and the trapeze artist. The others chatted, but Khaldun and Jezebel didn't say a word. She felt awkward—like she should say something, but didn't know what. She didn't want to risk sounding stupid again, the way she had earlier, so she kept quiet.

They entered Trey's tavern to find that business was booming.

"Grab that table in the corner," Jezebel shouted over the din. "I'll be right there."

Khaldun nodded and moved through the crowd. Jezebel scurried behind the bar.

"Jez!" Trey said in surprise. "What are you doing here?" He was dashing around frantically, pouring drinks.

"Hi Trey," she replied. "I went to see the wayfarers perform."

"Ah. Wish I could've gone. Been a bit busy—help yourself!"

Jezebel took two bottles of mead from under the counter and joined Khaldun. He was sitting with his back to the wall, his staff propped against the corner. He raised one eyebrow at her as she set the bottles on the table.

"It's my uncle's place," she said with a grin.

Khaldun uncorked his mead and took a swig. He furrowed his brow for a moment, savoring the flavor. Then he took a longer drink.

"This is excellent," he said.

"Sweetest mead in the princedom," she told him.

"So... how did you like the show?"

"I *loved* it," she said. "Especially the magic—I wanted to be a magician when I was little."

"Ah, well, of course, that's only *stage* magic," Khaldun replied. "It's not real."

"Are you a wizard?" Jezebel asked, nodding toward his staff.

"In training," he said. "Nomad is my mentor—he's a sorcerer. He's been with our troupe for ages."

"So, what is *real* magic like?" Jezebel asked. "You don't practice that scary stuff that Myrddin did with the smoke yesterday... do you?"

"Definitely not," Khaldun replied, a note of fear in his voice. "That's necromancy. Normal magic doesn't use specters."

"Can you show me?"

"Certainly," Khaldun said, looking around the room. "But not here. Why don't you meet me tomorrow and I'll give you a demonstration. Say around noon?"

"Sounds like a plan," Jezebel said. "But I was hoping for more than a demonstration. Do you think you could teach me?"

"To do magic?" he asked, surprised. Jezebel nodded. "I can try. Not everyone can do it—magic runs in families. If you don't have any relatives who can do it, you may be disappointed."

"I'm not sure if I do or not," she said. "One way to find out!"

There was a ruckus at the door. Jezebel turned to see what was going on. To her dismay, Will walked in with Edward, Zeke, and several townies. She rolled her eyes and turned her attention back to Khaldun.

They talked about the show for a while. Jezebel recounted her memories of going to the circus when she was a little girl. Khaldun told her that he used to be in the magic show—she'd probably seen him.

Khaldun described some of the other places they'd traveled recently; Jezebel told him about her life on the farm. She worried she was boring him, but he seemed fascinated.

It turned out that Khaldun was only two years older than Jezebel. Yet he was so much more experienced and worldly. Jezebel had never traveled outside of Spanbrook.

She found herself slipping into an easy rapport with this wayfarer boy as the evening progressed. The conversation flowed naturally. She felt the kind of connection with him that she'd only ever shared with Allison. But eventually, the discussion turned to the princess.

"So why isn't she allowed to come to the show?" Khaldun asked.

For the first time since walking into the tavern, Jezebel felt uncomfortable. "Well... I guess Prince Aldo doesn't hold wayfarers in high regard."

To her surprise, Khaldun smiled at this. "It's a typical reaction. The highborn often find our nomadic lifestyle a little... threatening."

"Threatening? Why?"

"Princedoms rely on law and order to survive. Every citizen fits into the social hierarchy somehow. But we're different. We come and go as we please, and don't assume the traditional roles. So usually, the ruling class look down on us as dangerous rabble."

"I'm sorry they treat you that way," Jezebel said. "But clearly, it bears no reflection on you personally."

"There's no need to apologize," Khaldun replied. "It doesn't bother me. And besides, we're performing at the castle in a few days. I'm sure Allison will be there. Are you two close—do you think you could introduce me?"

"Oh… uh, yes. Sure," Jezebel stammered.

"I find her stunning," Khaldun confided, staring down at his mead, which Trey had replaced several times. "I don't think I've ever encountered anyone so beautiful… with maybe one exception."

"And who was that?" Jezebel asked with a sigh. This certainly wasn't where she thought the conversation was headed.

Khaldun gazed at his bottle for a long moment. "Her name is Mira," he said finally. "We were deeply in love. But it wasn't meant to be."

"Why? What happened?"

"She inherited a small holding when her father and older brother were killed in a hunting accident," he explained. "It had been in their family for generations. So, she left our troupe to return to her ancestral home."

"I'm sorry to hear that," said Jezebel. "But how did she end up with the troupe in the first place?"

"Her mother is a wayfarer," Khaldun explained. "Mira lived with us when she was younger, but her father brought her to his castle when she was twelve. She longed to return to the wayfarers, though, and finally did when she came of age. But then tragedy struck."

"Why didn't you go with her?" Jezebel asked.

"I'm a wayfarer," he replied with a shrug. "Their people had accepted Mira as one of their own, but only because she was family. And once she came into her inheritance, it became her duty to marry another highborn and produce an heir."

"Ah, yes," Jezebel said with a knowing smile. "Allison bears the same responsibility."

"Has she… Well, is she with anyone? The princess—has she chosen a husband?"

Jezebel laughed. "No, she hasn't. And I'm sorry to disappoint you, but I don't think you have any chance with her."

"Oh?"

"She didn't find you attractive," Jezebel said, almost apologetically.

"Yesterday, you mean? When you walked by? Did she actually say so?"

"She didn't have to," Jezebel replied. "Let's just say I know my cousin's mind when it comes to this sort of thing."

Khaldun smiled, looking relieved. "We'll see."

Jezebel opened her mouth to reply, but Trey walked over to their table.

"Jez, do Robert and Vivien know you're out this late?" he asked, looking concerned.

"What time is it?" Jezebel asked, suddenly alarmed.

"Well after midnight," Trey said.

Jezebel was shocked; she'd had no idea so much time had passed. "I'd better go," she said, getting to her feet.

Khaldun stood up as well. "I'll walk you out," he offered.

"No need," Jezebel said. The tavern was still packed. Khaldun's friends had spotted him getting up, and beckoned him to the bar. Jezebel noticed that Will, Edward, and Zeke were sitting with them. "Say goodnight to your friends for me."

Khaldun bent down and kissed her on the cheek. Jezebel's heart skipped a beat.

"We're still on for tomorrow?" he asked.

"Noon," she said, hurrying out of the tavern.

CHAPTER FIVE
MAGIC

ezebel thought of nothing but Khaldun for the entire trip home. She remembered how his laugh had put her at ease, and the way the corners of his eyes crinkled when he smiled. She realized that physically, he wasn't as attractive as Will. He lacked Will's muscles, for one thing. And his facial features were softer. But he possessed a magnetism Jezebel had never sensed in anyone before. Based purely on looks, she would choose Will in a heartbeat. But in Will's presence, she wanted only to strike him. In contrast, she'd spent the entire night resisting a desire to rip Khaldun's clothes off and make love to him right there in the tavern.

But more importantly, she could *talk* to him. Their conversation had lasted hours but seemed like only minutes. She couldn't wait to see him again.

Back at the farm, she unhitched the horses inside the barn and returned the team to their stalls. She found her father on the front porch, sitting on his rocker, smoking his pipe.

"You're home late," he observed.

"I'm sorry," she said, taking the adjacent chair. "I was at Trey's. I lost track of time."

"Good night, then?"

"Great night," she said, smiling ear to ear. "The boy I met was in the magic show when he was little."

"No kidding."

"He's not anymore. He's a real wizard now. I'm seeing him again tomorrow, and he's going to try to teach me… Do you know if we've ever had any mages in the family?"

"Not on my side," he replied. "Can't say for certain about your mother's. I don't think so, but you'd have to ask her. Leda's mother was a witch; I know that. But of course, that doesn't affect you."

"Huh," said Jezebel. "I never knew Allison had mage's blood."

She spent the next twenty minutes telling her father all about her evening. He smoked his pipe and listened.

"Sounds like you really like this… Khaldun, is it?"

"Yes, Khaldun," she repeated, enjoying the sound of his name. "And yes, I do like him."

"Husband material, you reckon?"

"Father! I just met him. Let's not get carried away."

"I'm sorry. This is the first time I've ever seen you react this way to a boy."

He was right, no question. Jezebel had never met a boy like Khaldun before. And the truth was she *had* considered what he'd be like as a husband. But she knew it would never work: he was a wayfarer; she was a farm girl. Her future with Allison still seemed much more compelling.

"I don't know if he's interested in me," she said. "He kept asking about the princess."

"Oh?" He sounded surprised.

"It's no wonder, is it? She's much prettier than I am."

Robert frowned at her for a second. "I don't think I'd agree with you there."

"You're only saying that because I'm your daughter," she said, rolling her eyes. "Father… what do you think about Princess Salerna? I mean, the way she lives."

Robert took a long draw on his pipe and blew the smoke out in rings. "What *I* think doesn't count for much. It's not our place to judge others, Jez. Salerna's an effective leader. So long as her choices don't harm anyone, it seems to me they're nobody's business but her own."

"You don't think there's anything… *wrong* with it?"

"Just so I'm clear, are we talking about Salerna, or you and Allison?"

Jezebel gasped. He knew. She stared at him for a moment, afraid of what might be coming next. But he merely sat there, calmly smoking his pipe.

"Father… I don't… We're…" She was at a loss for words.

"Listen to me, Jezebel. You have to choose your own path in life. Nobody else can decide it for you, not even me. Like I told you before, it's important to consider the consequences of your actions. But as long as you do right by others, there's no issue of right or wrong.

"Before I married your mother, the Lord of Hempstead passed away without an heir. My father planned to assign the holding to me. But I wanted a simple life. I abdicated my noble birthright and became a farmer against his wishes. He was never able to come to terms with my decision.

"You're going to have a rough road ahead if you choose a life with Allison, make no mistake. But I'll support you if that's what's in your heart."

Jezebel sat there for a moment, stunned. Tears came to her eyes. She threw herself at her father, grabbing him in a hug.

"Thank you," she whispered.

Robert went up to bed a few minutes later. Jezebel stayed on the porch a while longer, staring up at the stars. But suddenly something caught her eye. She wasn't sure what it was at first—there was a flash out above the forest. But she saw it again: it was a tongue of fire rising over the trees. She couldn't be certain, but it appeared to be in the direction of Rockhedge.

Jezebel stood up, wondering what could be going on out there. Tongues of flame licked the sky several more times, but it stopped a few minutes later. She stayed on the porch, waiting to see if anything else would happen. But before long, she grew tired and went upstairs to bed.

Jezebel woke at dawn and spent the morning working on the farm. She ran into Will at one point and did her best to ignore him. He wouldn't stop staring at her.

But before lunch, she took Pashta out of the stable and left the farm. She rode bareback as she always did on short trips. She'd been riding since she was a little girl; Pashta had been in the family longer than Jezebel.

The trip took little more than half an hour at an easy trot. Jezebel left her horse in the field behind the wayfarer camp. As she walked between the tents, she unbuttoned her shirt a little lower than was strictly proper. She was still hoping to attract Khaldun's attention despite his apparent lack of interest the previous night.

Unsure where to find him, she walked past the big show tent. She looked around but didn't see him anywhere. Suddenly she heard someone call her name. She turned around to see Khaldun walking toward her, his staff in one hand, a sack hoisted over the other shoulder.

"Hi," Jezebel said, running a hand through her hair. "I wasn't sure where to find you."

"I figured you'd look for me here," he said. "I forgot to mention it last night, but I live in the blue tent in the far corner." He pointed across the camp without taking his eyes off of her. He looked her up and down. "Are you ready to learn some magic?"

"I'm ready to try," she replied.

Khaldun led her through the tents, beyond the edge of the camp. "I found the perfect place."

Trees lined the far edge of the field. Not far beyond that, a stream ran through the woods. Jezebel knew it emptied into the Ember farther west.

They came to a meadow next to the stream. Khaldun dropped his sack in the grass and sat down with his legs crossed, his staff across his knees. Jezebel took a seat next to him.

"I'm not exactly sure where to start," he said. "I realized I have no idea how much you might already know about magical theory."

"Not a thing," Jezebel confessed.

"Ah. Well, in that case, I should first explain that this isn't *officially* the right way to do this. Although most mages do start out learning a few things from a mentor—and usually at a younger age. But anyone who's serious attends the university."

"Is that how you learned?"

"No," Khaldun replied with a frown. "Nomad has been my only teacher. The university doesn't accept wayfarers."

"Oh. Then where did Nomad learn?"

"He didn't grow up with our people," Khaldun explained. "His grandmother was a wayfarer, but she left the troupe and married a lord in Northcoast. And they require sorcerers to train at the university regardless. But he joined us when he graduated."

"Why won't the university accept wayfarers?"

"I'm not sure, to tell you the truth," he said with a shrug. "Just an old prejudice, I think. But let's get started. The first thing to understand about magic is that forces control everything in the world." He pointed at the stream. "The water flows from the mountains toward the sea. Why?"

"Gravity?" Jezebel replied.

"Exactly. The earth exerts a force that pulls the water downhill. But the water itself carries a force, too. It can smooth stone or eat away at a rock wall. And in the case of a flood or a tidal wave, it can cause great destruction.

"Air acts as a force, too. It moves the clouds and gives birds flight. And of course, fire provides another force."

"What's this got to do with magic?" Jezebel asked.

"Everything," Khaldun said. "Hold up your hand."

"What?" she said with a giggle.

"Do it. Hold up your hand."

Jezebel moved her arm over her head, felt stupid, and retracted it immediately.

"How did you do that?" Khaldun asked.

"How did I move my arm?" Jezebel asked incredulously. "Simple. I just did it."

"Everything in the world acts under the influence of forces. So which force caused your arm to rise?"

"None of them. It was *me*."

"Yes, it was you. And you're right, none of the four natural forces lifted your arm. Living creatures can use their thoughts to move their bodies. And they can apply force to objects in their environment."

Khaldun picked up a stone and threw it in the stream. "Which force acted upon the rock?"

"Gravity again," Jezebel said. "The earth pulled the rock down."

"True, but which force set it in motion in the first place?"

"Your thoughts?"

"Precisely. If I hadn't picked it up, that stone would have stayed where it was."

"And… when do we get to magic?"

"We just did! Strictly speaking, magic is the way we use our thoughts to control the world around us. Normally we have to use our limbs. But by extending the force of our thoughts beyond our physical form, we can channel the four natural forces and influence objects in our environment."

"Show me!"

Khaldun got to his feet. He held his staff in front of him and muttered something under his breath. Suddenly a jet of water sprang from the stream and splashed Jezebel.

"Hey!" she yelled, scrambling to her feet. She slapped Khaldun on the arm.

"I'm sorry!" he said, chuckling sheepishly. "I didn't mean for it to hit you—I swear! Water spells aren't my forte."

"What is your forte?" she asked, still standing very close to him. She could feel the warmth of his body. But suddenly she was distracted—something nudged her ankle.

Jezebel looked down to see a black cat staring up at her. She bent down and stroked the back of its head. It purred loudly.

"Where did you come from?" she asked.

Khaldun cleared his throat. Jezebel looked up, and he tipped his staff toward the animal.

"You called him here?" she asked, confused.

"In a manner of speaking."

"I don't understand," she said, petting the cat.

"It's not real."

"What?! Of course it is—I can feel it…"

Khaldun squatted down and reached for the animal's head. But his hand passed right through it as if it weren't there.

"How did you…?"

"I told you. There's no cat here. I conjured the image you're seeing."

"That's impossible! It's—"

"Close your eyes," he said, taking her hand. Jezebel swore she could feel a spark when their skin touched. He moved her hand a few inches, very slowly. "Look."

Jezebel opened her eyes and gasped. Her arm appeared to pass through the cat, her fingers sticking out of its hindquarters.

She stood up and backed away fearfully. "How did you do that?"

Khaldun waved his hand, and the animal vanished. "Illusion. *That* is my specialty."

"Which force is that?"

"Magic itself can act as a force," Khaldun said, sitting down again. He lay his staff beside him. Jezebel sat facing him, her legs crossed. "You can use it to make things appear or disappear—but you can't actually create or destroy anything. It's only an illusion."

"Can you make *yourself* invisible?" Jezebel asked.

"Yes, that's one of the first things Nomad taught me," Khaldun replied. "But the magical force can be used to do many things. Sorcerers can use it to feel other people's spells. Where you saw and felt a cat, Nomad would have sensed magic as well. If he'd paid attention to it, he would have figured out that the cat wasn't real."

"What else can you do with the magical force?" Jezebel asked, fascinated.

"You can imbue objects with mystical properties, for one thing," Khaldun said. "Nomad and I have a set of mirrors we can use to speak to each other across any distance. And I've heard of stones that you can use to see what's happening in faraway places. But only extremely powerful mages can *create* such objects.

"And there are spells that can use the magical force to read people's minds or change their memories. But those are banned by the university."

"Why?"

"According to Nomad, such spells are dangerous. They can damage a person's mind and make them go mad."

"How is a sorcerer different from a witch or wizard?" Jezebel asked.

"They're much more powerful," Khaldun said. "In theory, anyone with magic in their blood can become a witch or wizard—although some people are naturally more talented than others. But sorcerers aren't like the rest of us."

"What do you mean?"

"You saw Nomad's skin, his eyes?" Jezebel nodded. "Most mages—magical folk, that is—need a wand or a staff to do magic. But a sorcerer can cast spells the same way you or I can walk. They don't need any special instrument; they can channel the magical force with their minds and bodies."

"How do you become a sorcerer?"

"Not by choice," Khaldun said. "It's in your blood—either you are one, or you aren't. I guess it's only possible if you inherit magic from *both* of your parents, but even then, you won't necessarily become one. Sorcerers are extremely rare. Nomad told me there are fewer than twenty living today in the whole world, whereas normal mages are fairly common. The university regulates the education of sorcerers very strictly; in fact, most of them spend their whole lives there. Very few are allowed to take assignments anywhere else."

"And what about necromancers?" Jezebel asked. "How common are *they*?"

"As far as I know, Myrddin's the only one."

"What? On the whole continent?"

Khaldun nodded. "Necromancy died out hundreds of years ago. The university banned its practice and destroyed every book on the subject. Most people believe that a necromancer's power meddles with evil. Nobody knows how Myrddin became one."

"How are they different from other mages?"

"I'm not sure exactly," said Khaldun. "I did learn recently that only a sorcerer can become a necromancer. But even normal mages can contact the dead and control them to some extent—using a spirit board, for example." Jezebel thought it would be best not to mention her own experiment with that device. "Sorcerers can achieve much more direct contact with the spirit world. But it comes at a cost— sorcerers can be possessed by demons. Nomad wears a ring to protect him from spectral invasion. All sorcerers do.

"But necromancers achieve a level of power, using spirits, that goes far beyond what any other mage can do. You saw what Myrddin did to that man the other day?"

Jezebel shivered despite the warmth of the day. "Yes."

"That was an example of necromancy."

"Well, I don't ever want to learn *that*. But you did say you'd teach me normal magic."

"I haven't forgotten," Khaldun said, reaching into his sack. He pulled out a long, rectangular box, ornately carved with patterns of flowers and strange runes. He opened the box to show Jezebel. She gasped.

Inside, sitting on a bed of red velvet, was a wand. It looked like a gnarled tree branch, except that it was black and polished. Jezebel could think of no tree that grew wood so dark.

"It's beautiful," she said, reaching for it slowly. "Can I?"

"Go ahead," Khaldun said, smiling encouragingly.

She picked it up gingerly as if it were fragile. It felt oddly warm in her hand; she guessed it was probably because Khaldun's sack had been sitting in the sun.

"What kind of wood is this?" she asked.

"Ebony. It's extremely rare. Hold it by the thick end," he instructed; she'd been grasping it in the middle.

Jezebel pointed it at the stream, half-hoping to repay Khaldun with a water spray of her own. But nothing happened.

"So, how does this thing work?"

"As I said, it's an instrument to project the force of your thoughts into the world around you," Khaldun said. "Wands and staves have powerful charms placed upon them that render them magically conductive. Most of the time, they're made from certain kinds of wood, but bone can be used, too. Sorcerers at the university make them, and I guess only material that used to be alive can work. And only such an instrument can be used to cast spells. Every spell consists of two parts. First, you have to define your objective. Then you speak the word of command to release the spell."

"But you didn't say anything when you made the cat appear."

"Not out loud," Khaldun replied. "But you still have to *think* the words. Some mages can cast their strongest magic nonverbally. It requires more power and proficiency to do it that way—I still have to vocalize most of my spells."

"So, you can cast illusions without speaking because they're your specialty?" Jezebel asked.

"Exactly. But illusions also lend themselves more readily to nonverbal casting than most other spells."

"Teach me something," Jezebel said with a grin.

"Oh, right. Let's do a flame. Fire is usually the easiest force to call."

He spent the next ten minutes teaching Jezebel the incantation and the word of command. Jezebel recited the spell over and over again, but nothing happened.

"This is so frustrating! Can I see you do it?"

Khaldun held his hands in front of him, the staff in his right, his left palm-up. He muttered the spell, and suddenly a tongue of blue fire ignited in his left hand. Jezebel stared in awe. With a flick of Khaldun's fingers, the flame vanished.

Jezebel cast the spell again, concentrating as hard as she could, and imagining the flame. Suddenly it appeared. She cried out in surprise.

But Khaldun's face registered shock. "I… that's remarkable!"

"You didn't think I could do it?"

"Truthfully, no. Certainly not this fast."

Jezebel tried to put out the flame by shaking her hand, but it persisted.

"Terminate the spell," Khaldun told her, still looking impressed.

"What?"

"Recite the spell again," he said. "But imagine it going out."

Jezebel formed the thought, then spoke the same words she'd used to cast the spell. The flame vanished.

"Well, it's clear there must be magic *somewhere* in your family," he observed.

"My mom's side," she replied. "It must be—my father has no mages in his family."

"I guess I shouldn't be too amazed," Khaldun said. "My first time was quite a bit more dramatic."

"How so?"

"I was eight. It was in the middle of the magic show—we were playing for a full house. Chuma was doing a trick that was supposed to make me disappear. But really, the cabinet had a revolving partition. When he said the 'magic words,' I was supposed to release the mechanism that allowed the back wall to turn. But that night, it jammed. I panicked. I knew he was about to open the cabinet, so… I vanished."

"You mean you did real magic," Jezebel said. "But how did you do it without a wand or a staff? I thought only sorcerers could do that?"

"That's usually true. But sometimes young children under great distress can make it happen. It's not something they can control, and it's rarely anything they can repeat.

"I told Chuma what happened after the show. He didn't believe me. The release mechanism in the cabinet worked fine by that point. But Nomad overheard us. He took me under his wing. He said that children who spontaneously cast spells like that usually grow up to be powerful mages. And after that incident, he wasn't surprised when I showed a predisposition for illusion."

"Have you ever done any more magic without your staff?" Jezebel asked.

"Not once. But that brings me to an important point. You should practice as much as you can. Your wand will learn spells as you do. The magic embeds itself in the wood."

"So, if I used your staff, I'd be able to do everything you can do?"

"No," said Khaldun. "It won't work for anyone else. The most powerful wizard in the world could pick up my staff, and it would be as if they were starting over—they would be able to cast only the simplest spells."

Jezebel placed the wand back in its wooden case. She held it out to Khaldun. "Where can I get one?"

Khaldun smiled at her but didn't take it. "It's yours."

"No—I can't," Jezebel said, startled. "It's much too valuable…"

"A wand is *priceless*," he agreed, "but only to the witch who wields it. This wand has displayed an affinity to you. I cannot take it back."

"But I'm no witch," she persisted. "It must belong to someone else."

"It would have been mine," Khaldun told her. "But I preferred the staff. Nomad's kept it ever since. I told him I was going to work with you, and he suggested that we use it. He said you could have it if you wanted—and he'll insist that you keep it once he hears how easily you were able to conjure with it."

Jezebel tried once more to hand it to him, but Khaldun backed away. She imagined herself becoming a powerful mage, casting spells from the top of Myrddin's tower, and finally gave in. It felt strange to take this tangible step toward her childhood dream so many years after the fact.

"What happens if I lose it?"

"Well, try not to," said Khaldun. "If you do, someone like Nomad could transfer your power into a new one, but it would take a few weeks to regain your full strength."

Khaldun picked up his sack and his staff, and they headed back to the camp.

"You must be hungry—you're welcome to join us for lunch," he said.

"I'd like that," she said. "I am rather famished."

Jezebel followed him to a gathering at the center of the camp. Dozens of wayfarers were seated at long tables, partaking in what she could only describe as a feast.

"Looks like you started with dessert, eh, Khal?" a man yelled. Jezebel recognized him as the stage magician from the show. The others laughed heartily; Jezebel turned red. *Don't I wish*, she thought.

"Mind your manners, Chuma," Khaldun said, unabashed.

They sat down to eat, and he introduced Jezebel to everyone. The wine flowed freely and she sampled a number of meat and vegetable dishes she'd never seen before. She enjoyed the food immensely and the company more. The wayfarers were friendly, wholesome people. It felt like they'd already accepted her into their family.

But as they finished the meal, Jezebel spotted someone on horseback galloping east along the road. It was Allison—something was wrong.

"I have to go," she said to Khaldun.

She bade farewell to everyone, and Khaldun walked her to Pashta. Jezebel mounted her horse, and Khaldun handed her the box with her wand.

"Send the princess my greetings," he said, a hint of longing in his voice.

"I will," Jezebel replied before galloping away.

CHAPTER SIX
VIOLATION

ezebel pushed Pashta harder than usual. She knew it must be something dire for Allison to be in such a hurry. She arrived at the farm in half the ordinary time.

Allison was in front of the house, talking to Robert. Jezebel pulled up and jumped down from her horse. Robert nodded to her and walked inside.

"We need to talk," Allison said. She looked terrified.

Jezebel led her into the barn. They climbed up to the loft and sat in the hay. Allison eyed the box in Jezebel's hand but didn't say anything.

"What's wrong?" Jezebel asked.

"It may be nothing," Allison said, a note of hysteria in her voice. "But I'm afraid. You remember the nightmare I had?"

Jezebel nodded. "You thought you saw an arm reaching over the canopy of your bed."

"I saw it again. Only this time, I was wide awake."

"*What*?!"

"I woke up last night because I thought I heard a noise. I lay awake for a while, and I heard it again. There was a clinking sound, like someone dragging metal chains. And something growled, like in the Devil's Wood that night."

"Maybe that wasn't just Tess after all," Jezebel said, recalling the night in the forest.

"I think not," Allison agreed. "I didn't sleep well after that. I've been tired all day. I lay down to take a nap, and that's when I saw the arm. I tried to tell myself that I must have imagined it again—perhaps I'd been dozing off without realizing it.

"I got out of bed and drew a bath. I thought maybe that would soothe my nerves. But matters grew worse. I was brushing my hair in the mirror, and I saw a face. Jezebel, there was someone in my room, standing right behind me. But I turned, and he was gone."

"What did he look like?"

"Not human," Allison said, her voice quavering with fear. "The face was blackened, as by fire, and gnarled, with glowing red eyes. I've never seen anything like it…"

"We should go to Myrddin," Jezebel said. "He'll know what to do."

"No! I can't. If my father hears of this, he'll think I'm crazy."

"But Myrddin said we disturbed a demon at Rockhedge. What if it's haunting you?"

"That's why I came to get you. I want you to stay with me. If you see the same things, we'll go to Myrddin. I have to be sure, though. I need proof that I'm not losing my mind."

Jezebel ran inside and put her wand away in her closet. She let her father know where she was going, then rode back to Spanbrook Town with Allison. They spent much of the afternoon shopping in the market. Allison purchased a fancy dress for Jezebel.

"The wayfarers are coming to perform in a few days. Father said I could invite you, but he wanted to make sure you wore proper attire."

"Fair enough," Jezebel said.

"I'll enjoy dressing you up in this," Allison whispered with a mischievous smile. "You're going to look ravishing."

They returned to the castle and looked in on Prince Aldo at dinner. He was in the Great Hall with Myrddin, Oswald, and his other advisers, planning his tour of the princedom. The girls supped in the private dining room in the keep. Jezebel hardly touched her food; she was still full from her feast with the wayfarers.

Afterward, they retired to Allison's chambers. They sat in the bay window, watching people bustle around in the courtyard below. Once the sun had gone down, they changed into their nightgowns and climbed into bed.

"I don't want anything to happen," Allison said quietly, "yet at the same time, I'm counting on it."

They lay there for a while in silence. Jezebel was on her side, behind her cousin, her arm around Allison's waist. Everything was quiet.

Jezebel grew bored. She started kissing Allison's neck; Allison moaned softly. She turned and kissed Jezebel full on the lips. Jezebel pulled Allison's nightgown off of her and they made love.

Jezebel lay back with a sigh when they were done. Allison pulled her close and draped her arm across her stomach. Within a few minutes, Jezebel started to doze off.

"What did you do with the wayfarer boy today?"

"He taught me magic," Jezebel replied sleepily. "He gave me a wand."

"Is that what you had in the box?"

"Mmm."

They were silent for a moment.

"Did you kiss him?" Allison asked.

"No. Why, are you jealous?"

"Not if you didn't do anything."

"Would you be if I had?"

"Of course," Allison said. "You're *mine*."

"Well, you have nothing to worry about. Khaldun is madly in love with *you*."

"No!"

"Truly. We went to Trey's after the show. You were all he could talk about. I think he's hoping to take you to bed."

Jezebel could feel Allison shiver slightly. "Disgusting," she said. Jezebel giggled at her.

They fell asleep a few minutes later. Jezebel had sweet dreams of floating in the clouds. She woke up a few hours later because she had to urinate. She got out of bed and walked into the adjoining washroom. As she sat on the ceramic bowl, she decided that this alone provided enough reason to move into the castle. The same situation back home would have necessitated a trip outdoors. This proved particularly troublesome during the winter.

Jezebel knew they'd run pipes from a lake in the nearby hills to provide water to the castle. Her grandfather had spent a fortune to have the system built, but she felt it was well worth it.

She climbed back into bed and curled up next to Allison. But as she started to drift off, she heard a noise. Jezebel sat bolt upright, listening intently, her heart hammering in her chest. There was another noise—a muffled snarling. She looked around, trying to determine the source of the sound. Suddenly she heard scratching—something was clawing at the edge of the bed. A scream escaped Jezebel's lips as she pulled her cousin away from it.

"What is it?" Allison asked groggily.

There was a bang, and the bed jolted violently. The girls scrambled off the mattress and dashed across the room. Allison fumbled around on her bureau to light an oil lamp. It flared to life, casting a yellow glow across the floor.

Despite her terror, Jezebel took the lamp from her and crept toward the bed.

"What are you doing?" Allison hissed.

Jezebel dropped to her hands and knees. She pushed the lamp ahead of her and peered under the bed.

There was nothing there. Jezebel let out a sigh of relief.

They went back to bed but lay awake for a long time. Jezebel held Allison close. Eventually, Allison fell asleep. Jezebel remained alert for the rest of the night but didn't see or hear anything else.

Jezebel and Allison went to see Myrddin first thing in the morning. But he wasn't in his tower. They searched the entire castle, but nobody had seen him. The girls were heading back to the keep when they spotted him riding into the courtyard on his horse. They followed him into the stables, accosting him as he dismounted.

He smiled as he greeted them, but a look of grave concern grew over his features as the girls told their story. They recounted each incident in great detail and expressed their suspicion that it was the demon from the Devil's Wood.

Myrddin appeared lost in thought for a moment. "I think you must be correct. The entity you disturbed in the Devil's Wood has followed you here, Your Highness. When you opened yourself to the spirit world at Rockhedge, it must have imprinted upon you. I find it most disturbing that it was able to enter the keep without my knowledge."

"What should we do?" Allison asked. "Can you drive it away?"

"I believe so," Myrddin replied. "I will establish a barrier around the keep—the demon should not be able to penetrate it. But if you experience another encounter, come to me immediately.

"Also… there is one more precaution we should take. The demon may try to possess you. Normally this is quite difficult. But you appear to have a natural affinity for the spirit world—that would help explain the demon's attraction to you."

"What can we do?" Allison asked, panic in her voice.

"Come with me," Myrddin said, striding away.

They followed him to his tower. Inside his chamber, he opened a cabinet that contained dozens of glass bottles. After a minute, he selected two small flasks. He brought them to his desk along with a vial. He poured a few drops of each liquid into the vial. Next, he held his hand over the glass and muttered an incantation. The contents began to smoke.

"Quickly, drink this," he said, handing it to Allison.

She took it in one swig. "What is that?" she asked, crinkling her nose. "I've never tasted anything so bitter."

"Close your eyes," Myrddin instructed. He placed his hands on her temples and spoke several words in a language Jezebel didn't recognize. Allison swooned; Myrddin caught her before she hit the floor. But an instant later, she recovered.

"What happened?" she asked, her eyes slightly unfocused.

"I have closed your mind to the spirit world. It will now be impossible for the demon to possess you. But I cannot stress this enough: do *not* use the spirit board again. Doing so would force your mind open again and make you an easy target."

"I understand," Allison said earnestly.

Jezebel decided to stay with the princess for a few days. Allison sent a messenger to notify Robert and Vivien. But it seemed that whatever measures Myrddin had taken were effective. The demon did not return.

The wayfarers came to the castle two days later. Jezebel and Allison ate a light meal in the private dining room late that afternoon. They returned to the princess's chambers to prepare for the show. After sharing a bath, they helped each other into their corsets.

"I can barely breathe," Jezebel complained. "What is the point of this thing?"

"It accentuates your figure and pushes up your bosom," Allison explained. She adjusted Jezebel's breasts inside the garment. "There. Maximum cleavage."

Jezebel put on her dress next. It was much fancier and more colorful than anything else she owned. Finally, Allison spent nearly an hour applying their makeup.

Jezebel gazed in the mirror. "I hardly recognize myself."

"I told you I'd make you ravishing," Allison said over her shoulder. "The only trouble is now I want to rip your clothes back *off*."

"That'll have to wait, I'm afraid."

They walked into the great hall five minutes later. The room was crowded; every wealthy merchant and craftsman from Spanbrook Town was in attendance, as well as many of the larger landholders from the surrounding area. Jezebel knew her father had probably received an invitation, but he avoided the castle as much as possible. "I spent enough time there growing up," he always said.

There was a stage at the front of the hall. Chairs and benches filled the rest of the room. Jezebel accompanied Allison to the front row. They took the two seats next to Prince Aldo. Jezebel spotted Khaldun sitting with Nomad and Badru, the wayfarer leader, at the end of the row. Khaldun smiled at her.

The show began a few minutes later. It was different than the one Jezebel had watched at the wayfarer camp. The clowns had tamed down their shenanigans, and there were no trapeze or high-wire acts. In the middle of the show, several actors performed a short play. Jezebel had seen it once before—it was a tragedy about a king who unknowingly murders his father and marries his mother.

Jezebel kept sneaking glances at Khaldun throughout the production. But *he* wouldn't stop staring at Allison. The princess didn't seem to notice, but Aldo certainly did. His expression grew more austere by the minute. Before long, he took his daughter's hand, as if to defend his territory.

By the end of the show, Jezebel decided she'd enjoyed the first performance much more. The wayfarers seemed more reserved here. And the absence of the aerial acts detracted from the excitement.

Aldo pulled Allison aside the moment the performers finished taking their bow. Allison looked upset. She walked back to Jezebel a moment later.

"What's going on?" Jezebel asked.

"He's making me leave!" Allison said indignantly.

"What? Why?"

"He doesn't want me *mingling* with the wayfarers!"

"Ah," Jezebel replied knowingly. "I guess I'm not surprised. Khaldun couldn't take his eyes off of you. Your father noticed."

"But that's ridiculous. Is he afraid I'm going to run off and join the troupe?!"

"I doubt it. But Khaldun's stare was rather predatory. I'm sure your father doesn't want you to become his prey." Jezebel noticed that Aldo was glaring at them. He caught her eye and pointed at the doors. "Come on," she said to Allison. "I'll go with you."

"No, stay. There's no reason for you to suffer too."

"You're sure?"

Allison nodded. "I'll go to my chambers like a good little girl. But don't keep me waiting *too* long." She kissed her platonically and strode out of the hall.

Jezebel followed her progress. Several heads turned in her wake. One fat old merchant made the mistake of ogling her in full view of his wife. The woman grabbed his chin and turned his face back to her.

"She is quite alluring, isn't she?" someone said over Jezebel's shoulder. She turned. It was Khaldun.

"Indeed," Jezebel replied.

"It's a shame she's leaving so soon. I was hoping to meet her."

"Yes, well, that's exactly *why* she's departing," Jezebel told him. "The prince caught you staring."

Khaldun did his best to look affronted. "I did not *stare*. His Highness is imagining things."

Jezebel rolled her eyes.

She joined him and socialized with the guests for a time, introducing him to the people she knew from town. Although she knew they shared Aldo's low regard for wayfarers, most greeted him politely.

After a while, Jezebel grew bored. "Do you want to get out of here?"

"I thought you'd never ask," Khaldun replied. "Perhaps you could give me a tour of the castle? Nomad described the way the Ember flows through the building, but I'd love to see it firsthand."

"Certainly," she said, smiling to herself. Jezebel knew the docks would be deserted at this hour. She wouldn't mind spending some time alone with him. For a moment, she thought of Allison waiting for her in her chambers and felt a twinge of guilt. But she didn't expect anything serious to develop with Khaldun. Given his preoccupation with the princess, she'd be lucky to steal a kiss.

"Nomad would love to see this," Khaldun said, scanning the room. "Let me see if I can find him."

Jezebel shook her head in exasperation—so much for being alone. But Nomad was nowhere to be seen. She led Khaldun out a set of doors on the side of the hall. They walked down two flights of stairs and along a narrow hallway. Jezebel hadn't been down here in ages, but she remembered the way perfectly. She and Allison used to go exploring when she was little. For years, their favorite pastime was searching for secret chambers and hidden tunnels. Jezebel knew about two passages that led out of the castle; one ended at the wall in the west end of town, the other behind a smithy. She and Allison had always suspected there were more, but couldn't find them.

A few minutes later they emerged into a dimly lit expanse that spanned the width of the castle. The Ember flowed through a channel in the stone floor. The air was cool and moist. Open space extended to the castle walls on both sides of the river. Great arches straddled the water at regular intervals. Stone steps protruded from their faces, providing passage across the channel. Khaldun walked to the first of these structures.

"Quite the feat of engineering," he said, running his hand across the stone. "Nothing like this exists anywhere else on the continent."

"One of Spanbrook's many treasures," Jezebel said, taking his hand and batting her eyelashes at him. He hardly seemed to notice.

They strolled along the river for a while. Khaldun told her about some of the other castles he'd visited in his travels.

"Spanbrook seems to strike a balance between form and function," he said. "Many of those I've seen are little more than forts, but some would be utterly useless in battle. Stoutwall, for example, has a palace made to *look* like a castle. It's got enormous stained glass windows on the ground floor and lacks a proper gate. An enemy could march right inside—it's totally indefensible."

"Why do they call it Stoutwall?" Jezebel asked.

"Well, the *old* castle's damn-near impregnable. But I guess Augustine grew tired of living in it. He figures they could relocate there pretty quickly if anyone ever attacks."

"I'd love to visit some of these places," Jezebel said.

"Funny," Khaldun replied. "I was thinking I wouldn't mind settling down here."

"Truly?" Jezebel asked, surprised. "After all the places you've been, Spanbrook hardly seems interesting."

"That's only because you've lived here your whole life," he said. "I find it quite attractive. Say, do you think we might pay Princess Allison a visit? Would I be allowed inside the keep if I came as your guest?"

Jezebel sighed. Aldo certainly wouldn't approve. And undoubtedly he'd instructed the guards to be on alert for unwanted visitors tonight. But they knew Jezebel was part of the family. Odds were good they wouldn't prevent *her* from bringing a wayfarer inside. "Why not? I must warn you, though: you're wasting your time."

"We'll see," he said with a smile.

She led him across one of the arches. They entered a maze of corridors on the other side of the river and made their way up a long flight of stairs. Eventually, they emerged in the courtyard. It appeared that the party had broken up. Numerous couples were walking about, arm in arm.

Still holding Khaldun's hand, Jezebel walked up to the main entrance of the keep. The guard gave her a strange look but bowed and opened the door. They walked upstairs and down the corridor.

"You're in for a rude awakening," Jezebel said with a smile as they approached Allison's chambers. But suddenly she froze—someone had screamed. It was Allison.

Jezebel flung the doors open and ran inside. The sight before her nearly stopped her heart. Allison was lying in bed, the bodice of her dress torn open. A man was on top of her, totally naked. He held her wrists pinned to the bed as he thrust his hips between her legs. Allison screamed and thrashed, but couldn't stop him from raping her.

Khaldun ran past Jezebel. He grabbed the man and wrenched him off the princess, throwing him to the floor. The figure stood slowly, and Jezebel realized who it was: Nomad.

Only something was wrong. His golden body looked like it had been carved from stone, every muscle chiseled to perfection. But his face was contorted, and his red eyes seemed to glow.

Nomad threw a fireball, knocking Khaldun across the room.

Allison tried to scramble off the bed. But with a gesture, Nomad pulled her back and turned her over, mounting her again. A scream ripped from Allison's throat.

Jezebel sprang into action. She dashed across the room to the fireplace—Allison's two-handed sword was propped in the corner. She removed it from its scabbard and ran to the bed. With a great overhead stroke, she smashed the blade across Nomad's back.

He screamed in agony. Jezebel tried to pull the sword free, but it had lodged in his flesh. Dismounting the princess, Nomad reached back and yanked the blade free. He climbed out of bed and moved toward Jezebel.

"You're next, my precious," he said, casting the sword aside. But his voice was wrong—it sounded more like a growl.

At that moment, half a dozen of the prince's guards flew into the room. Nomad lunged at Jezebel. He grabbed her dress and ripped it open. The guards descended upon him. It took four of them to wrestle him to the floor.

Jezebel backed away and nearly fell over Khaldun. She dropped to her knees next to him. He sat up, conscious but groggy.

Aldo strode into the chamber, Myrddin, Oswald, and Badru on his heels. He scanned the room. The guards had Nomad back on his feet. He was covered in blood and seemed to wilt between the two men holding him up. Allison was on the bed, holding a sheet around her half-naked form, sobbing uncontrollably.

Jezebel ran to Allison. She jumped into bed and pulled her close.

"What the hell is going on?" Aldo demanded.

The guards explained what they'd seen. But they'd arrived late.

"He raped the princess!" Jezebel shouted, pointing at Nomad.

Aldo's eyes snapped to the sorcerer. Badru looked at the man in horror and disbelief.

"It wasn't me," Nomad said quietly, his voice back to normal. "A specter entered my body. I tried to banish it, but… it was much too powerful. It made me do terrible things." He looked at Allison, tears streaming down his face. "I am so sorry, Your Highness… I tried to stop it…"

"*WHAT IS THIS NONSENSE?!*" Aldo roared. "Did you rape my daughter, or did you not?"

"I did," Nomad said, closing his eyes tight and turning away from the princess, as if the sight of her were too much to bear.

"Your Highness," Myrddin said quietly. "If I could have a word…"

"What is it?" Aldo shouted, rounding on his necromancer.

"Perhaps if we stepped outside…"

"Speak your mind, Myrddin."

"As you wish. You recall the demon Her Highness disturbed in the Devil's Wood? I have reason to believe it has been haunting her. Here."

"*WHAT*?! Why wasn't I informed?"

"My apologies… When Her Highness came to me, I put certain protections into place. The demon could no longer enter the keep on its own. I was attempting to track and bind the monster—I didn't want to bother you with this until…"

"Is the sorcerer telling the truth?" Aldo demanded.

Myrddin looked at Nomad and nodded. "I have no reason to doubt it. Sorcerers do run the risk of demonic possession. The same channels of power that allow them to project the magical force also leave them open to unwanted entry from the spirit world. The demon must have invaded Nomad's body to bypass my barrier and enter the keep."

"It's true," Jezebel said timidly. "His face was wrong… and his voice didn't sound human. I believe him."

Aldo turned to Badru. "If what they say is true, then I will not hold you responsible for bringing a rapist into my castle." Badru looked relieved. "But if I ever find out differently, I will hunt you down to answer for this crime."

Aldo turned to Myrddin. "Kill him."

"Your Highness?" Myrddin said, confused.

"What?!" Badru shouted. "You just said…"

"THIS MAN RAPED MY DAUGHTER!" Aldo yelled, spittle flying from his mouth. "He will be held accountable for his actions. Myrddin—NOW!"

Myrddin let out a long sigh and bowed his head. "I am sorry, Nomad," he muttered. He held his arms out to his sides.

The guards backed away from the sorcerer. Nomad nearly toppled over when they let go of him, but managed to catch his balance. He held both hands in front of him. Out of nowhere, a glowing sheet of red light formed above him and covered him like a blanket.

Serpents of black smoke slithered around the sorcerer but couldn't penetrate the barrier. They disappeared. Tiny balls of fire took their place—dozens of them. They burned through the barrier in seconds. Nomad screamed as the smoke serpents returned, using the openings to eat holes in his flesh. They burrowed deep inside his body.

Jezebel turned away as Nomad fell writhing to the floor. She cowered against Allison. Nomad's screams lasted only seconds more. The room fell silent except for Allison's sobs.

"Allison, are you injured?"

Jezebel looked up. Aldo was standing at the end of the bed, a haunted look in his eyes. It was he who had spoken.

"She was just *raped*, Your Highness," Jezebel said with cold fury. "Of course, she's *injured*."

Aldo turned away. "Guard—fetch the healer!"

One of the men nodded and ran from the room.

Aldo departed next, Badru and Oswald right behind him. Jezebel could hear Badru yelling all the way down the hall.

Myrddin moved to the bed. "Help will be here soon," he said, taking Allison's hand.

"Thank you," she replied with a whimper.

Myrddin knelt next to Nomad's body. Khaldun, on his feet now, stood behind him. Myrddin removed a ring from the man's finger. He handed it to the wayfarer.

"I thought that ring was supposed to protect him from possession," Jezebel said.

"The soul of a sorcerer burns like a beacon in the spirit world," Myrddin said. "This ring only hides that light; it does not close the channels of power. If it did, the sorcerer would be unable to cast spells. The ring only makes the sorcerer difficult to find; apparently the demon found a way around that particular defense."

"Nomad had a mirror," Khaldun said, and Jezebel noticed for the first time that he was crying. "I'd like to keep it, if… if I could."

"Check his robes," Myrddin replied, pointing to the corner of the room.

Khaldun retrieved the mirror. Myrddin ordered the guards to remove the body and escorted Khaldun outside.

"I'll be right back," Jezebel whispered, kissing Allison on the top of the head. She followed them into the hallway, closing the door behind her.

"You need to capture the demon and put a stop to this madness," she implored Myrddin.

Myrddin nodded, sorrow in his eyes. "We are beyond that now. The monster must be *destroyed*, not captured. There's only one way to do it; I will need Aldo's approval."

"Get it soon," Jezebel hissed. "I won't see her go through this again."

Myrddin walked away with Khaldun. Jezebel waited till they'd gone around the corner, then returned to Allison's side. They were alone now. She held the princess tight. Listening to her cousin's sobs, she broke down in tears herself.

CHAPTER SEVEN
QUEST

he healer arrived a few minutes later. Only when he removed Allison's sheet did Jezebel realize the princess's thighs were blood-streaked. She helped Allison take off the remainder of her dress so the healer could examine her.

Jezebel sat beside her and held her hand. The healer noted a bruise forming on Allison's cheek.

"He punched me," she explained.

He proceeded to clean the blood from her legs and groin. Allison flinched when he touched her genitals.

"You're lucky," he proclaimed a few minutes later. "You'll have some bruising on the pubic bone. But there is only minor tearing of the labia—that was the source of the bleeding. The hymen's long gone, otherwise…"

"Yes, thank you," Allison said impatiently.

The healer left, and servants arrived to clean the room. Allison covered herself in her sheet. "I feel dirty," she said, starting to cry again.

"I'll draw a bath," Jezebel said, getting out of bed.

"Don't leave me," Allison pleaded. "I'll come with you."

They walked into the washroom and closed the door. Jezebel stopped the drain in the tub and opened the faucet. Once the tub was full, she removed her clothes and climbed in with Allison. They sat in silence while Jezebel washed the princess from head to toe.

"I've never been so scared," Allison said finally, crying again. "I thought he was going to kill me."

"You're safe now," Jezebel told her.

"I don't understand how he got inside the keep… Why didn't the guards stop him?"

"He was a sorcerer," Jezebel said. "He could make himself invisible. He must have followed someone else inside."

"I thought it was you when I heard my door open," Allison said, staring across the room. "I tried to scream, but he did something… no sound would come out. The next thing I knew…" Allison sobbed, unable to get the words out. "He threw me on the bed and… ripped my dress…"

Jezebel pulled her into a hug and spoke softly to her. "It's over now. He'll never touch you again. Let's dry you off and get you to bed."

She climbed out of the tub and walked to the closet to grab a towel. But when she looked in the mirror, she gasped. She saw Nomad standing behind her, sneering. Jezebel whirled around and slipped on the wet tile. Recovering her balance, she saw that no one was there.

"What's wrong?" Allison asked, suddenly alarmed.

"Nothing," Jezebel lied. "I nearly fell, that's all."

She dried them both off, wrapped Allison in the towel, and walked her into the bedchamber. The servants were gone. The bed was made, and the room held no trace of the night's events.

Jezebel fetched two nightgowns from the bureau. They both got dressed and went to bed. Allison cried for a long time. But eventually, she fell asleep in Jezebel's arms.

Jezebel stayed awake the whole night, fearful that the demon would return. But mercifully, there were no more intrusions.

Sunlight streamed through the bay window at dawn. Allison woke with a start. She sat up abruptly, scanning the room.

"What is it?" Jezebel asked.

Allison shook her head and gathered Jezebel into a hug. She got out of bed and dressed for her training session with Badrick in silence. Jezebel walked her down to the courtyard and watched her lesson for a few minutes. Allison seemed unfocused; she was only going through the motions. Yet Badrick hardly criticized her; Jezebel wondered if someone had told him what happened. It was unlike him to go easy on the princess.

Jezebel went to Myrddin's tower. The door was unlocked. She let herself in and walked up to the necromancer's chamber. She found him sitting at his desk, his head in his hands. Jezebel cleared her throat.

"Ah," Myrddin said, looking surprised to see her standing there. "Good morning."

"Have you spoken to the prince?"

"I have," he replied, shaking his head. "His Highness will not allow me to perform the necessary—"

"*What*?! Why?"

"He has forbidden me to speak of it. But I assure you, I will do everything in my power to keep the demon away."

"No! You said yourself it has to be destroyed!"

"I am sorry, child," he said. "There is no more I can do. But I believe the danger to the princess will be minimal."

"You can't be serious! The demon possessed Nomad and *raped Allison*. You call that *minimal*?!"

"Only sorcerers can be possessed so easily—and there are no sorcerers in Spanbrook. The odds of the demon finding a way to invade and control anyone else…"

"This is unacceptable! You speak of odds? I won't let you *gamble* with her safety. The demon found a way to possess Nomad despite his ring. Do you expect me to believe that it will be incapable of possessing someone else and raping her again? The demon entered her chambers again last night—despite your spells and barriers. Am I supposed to stand aside and watch it terrorize her?"

Myrddin stared at her for a moment. A tear slipped down his cheek. "My hands are tied. I'm sorry."

Jezebel stormed out of the tower. She marched across the courtyard, past Allison and Badrick and barged into Aldo's offices.

Finding the antechamber empty, she walked through the room and flung open the doors to his private chamber.

Aldo looked up in surprise. Oswald, sitting across the desk from him, jumped from his chair as if he'd sat on a bed of nails.

"What do you think you're doing?" he demanded, grabbing her by the arm to escort her out of the room.

"Wait," Aldo called. His face was drawn, and there were dark circles under his eyes. "What is it, Jezebel?"

Suddenly the brazenness of her actions caught up with her. One did not intrude upon the prince's privacy uninvited. Yet the deed was done, and Allison's situation was desperate. Jezebel found her uncle intimidating, but she pressed ahead.

"Your Highness, Myrddin tells me he knows a way to destroy the demon… but he says you won't allow…"

Aldo let out a long sigh and ran his hands over his head. "Oswald, please excuse us for a few minutes," he said, sitting up straight. He motioned Jezebel to a chair.

"I want to thank you," he said once Jezebel had sat down, and Oswald had left the room. "These past many months have been rough on Allison—on both of us. She confided in Leda in a way she's never done with me. They were close. The way you are now. I've allowed Allison to stay with you as often as she wants because you've filled that void for her."

"Yes, sir."

"You must understand, I would do *anything* to protect my daughter. But the method that Myrddin has suggested is madness. The risk to Allison would be far too great—not to mention the danger to Myrddin."

"Forgive me, uncle, but I cannot imagine a danger greater than—"

"I've made my decision. I will not imperil her any further."

"But what could Myrddin's spell possibly entail that…"

Aldo shook his head. "It is *unthinkable*. Do not ask me to describe it. We will have to rely upon Myrddin's skill to keep the monster away."

Jezebel returned to the courtyard. Allison was gone—Badrick must have ended her lesson early. She found the princess in her chambers, sitting in bed, hugging her knees to her chest.

Jezebel sat next to her. "How did your training go?"

Allison didn't reply.

"I'm hungry—will you come have breakfast with me?"

Allison shook her head slightly.

Jezebel could only imagine the torment she was enduring. The princess had to carry on with her life as if nothing had happened. Yet the demon was still out there; it could victimize her again at any time.

Why wouldn't Aldo allow Myrddin to destroy the monster? Jezebel couldn't fathom anything more harmful to her cousin than the ongoing threat the demon represented.

She had to do something. Later that morning, she told Allison that she was going to return home to visit her parents. Allison begged her not to leave; Jezebel assured her she'd come back as quickly as possible. Allison told her to take her horse to make the journey faster.

In reality, Jezebel had no intention of going to the farm. Instead, she rode to the wayfarer camp. But when she arrived, most of the tents were gone. The wayfarers were packing up and getting ready to move on. She found Khaldun inside the blue tent he'd told her was his—it was one of the few still standing.

"What's going on?" Jezebel asked. "Why are you leaving?"

"The prince thought it would be best," he said with a shrug. The gleam in his eyes and his easy smile were gone. "Badru agreed. He's furious about Nomad. I can't say I blame him—Nomad was like a father to me. I never knew my parents; they died from the plague when I was very young."

"I'm so sorry…"

Khaldun looked at the ground, then back at Jezebel. "How's the princess?"

"Not well," Jezebel said. "In fact, that's why I wanted to talk to you…"

She told him everything that had happened with the demon, starting with the night in the Devil's Wood. And she related her conversations with Myrddin and Aldo.

"Things make more sense now, at least," Khaldun said, looking troubled. "I was puzzled last night when the necromancer talked about the demon. I didn't realize the princess was being haunted—that can be extremely dangerous. Nomad knew a witch once who was… well, never mind. It's not important."

"No, tell me—what happened to her?"

Khaldun paused for a moment. "The haunting grew in severity over time. It drove her to madness. In the end, she took her own life."

Jezebel shook her head. "I won't let that happen to Allison. Do you know what Myrddin was talking about—do you know how to destroy a demon?"

"No," Khaldun said. "I don't think Nomad did either—that clearly falls within the purview of necromancy."

"Do you know anyone who might be able to help us?" Jezebel asked, desperation in her voice.

Khaldun looked thoughtful for a few seconds. "As I told you, Myrddin's the only necromancer on the entire continent. And the university banned that field of study ages ago. But Nomad's old mentor sits on the school's board of governors—he's a sorcerer named Enigma. He's no necromancer, but if anyone would know the necessary spells, he would."

"Truly? Do you think he'd talk to me? How do I find him?"

"He lives on the campus," Khaldun said. "I've met him a couple of times. He's very wise, I'm sure he'd be willing to help…"

"That's good news!" Jezebel's desperation finally yielded to this small glimmer of hope. "But I've never traveled outside of Spanbrook—how do I get to the university?"

Khaldun chuckled. "You don't. Not alone, anyway. The journey is extremely perilous—things are different outside of Spanbrook."

"But I must! Don't you understand? Allison is in danger—I have to try. Please, tell me how to get there!"

"I'll do better than that," Khaldun said. "I'll go with you."

"You… No, I can't ask you to do this," Jezebel said, although her heart lifted at the prospect.

"With Nomad gone there's nothing left for me here with the troupe. And even if I drew you a map, you'd never make it alone. As you said, you've never journeyed outside these borders. I'm an experienced traveler—and I know the way."

Jezebel grabbed him in a hug so forcefully that she nearly toppled him over. "Thank you."

"You may not be so grateful once we get underway," he said, hugging her back. "It's going to take weeks to get there."

"*Weeks*?!" Jezebel said, pulling away. She'd anticipated a journey of a few days.

"Maybe as long as three weeks," he confirmed with a nod. "But we could do it in two and a half if we make good time."

"But… Then it will take that long to get back, too…"

"Yes," Khaldun replied with a grin. "That's generally how it works."

"What are we waiting for? Let's go!" She started walking out of the tent.

Khaldun grabbed her by the arm. "Slow down—we can't just run off. We need provisions and gear… and horses."

Jezebel stopped to consider the situation. She realized she was being foolish—he was right, of course. "How soon do you think we can leave?"

"In the morning. I'll collect the gear we need… and I'll have to let Badru know. He isn't going to be happy. With Nomad and me both gone, he won't have anyone left to protect our people. He'll have to find a new mage. And he may not let me take much in the way of food or supplies…"

"I'll take care of that," Jezebel said. "We can stay at my house tonight. I have to tell my parents. They won't be pleased either. We have plenty of provisions, but I don't know what to do about horses. We have two, but Father's going to need them for the farm."

"It'll take longer on foot, but we'll manage," Khaldun said with a shrug.

"That's it then. I'll go tell Allison what we're doing, and I'll meet you back here."

She started to walk away again, but Khaldun called her back.

"Hang on—give this to the princess." He was rummaging through his pack. "Here it is." He handed her a small circular mirror in a frame of black resin.

"Why? Wait—is this the mirror you told me about?"

"Yes," he said, holding up its twin. "This will allow us—*you*—to communicate with her on the journey."

Jezebel hugged him again. "This is perfect. But…" She backed up a step, eyeing him suspiciously. "You're not coming with me to try to win the princess's heart or anything stupid like that, are you?"

"What? No—of course not…"

"Because I am telling you, you are wasting your time if—"

"Jezebel, I am doing this for *you*. As I said, you'd never get there alone. And besides… I was thinking of leaving the troupe anyway. I like it here in Spanbrook." He shrugged.

Jezebel nodded. "I'll be back."

Jezebel left the camp and rode back to the castle. She found Allison sitting in her bay window, staring outside. The princess didn't even turn to see who it was when Jezebel entered her chamber.

"I have to go away for a little while," Jezebel said, sitting next to her and taking her hand.

"Go away?" Allison asked, turning to her, sadness and confusion in her face. "Why?"

Jezebel explained everything that had happened with Myrddin and Aldo. She felt horrible dumping this news on the princess, but she had no choice. It was the only way to make her understand why she had to leave.

"Khaldun knows a sorcerer at the university. He'll help us find a way to destroy the demon."

"But it takes weeks to travel that far," Allison said, panic in her voice. "How will you find the way?"

"Khaldun is going with me—he knows how to get there. And he gave me this." She handed her the mirror. "He's got its twin. We can use them to talk to each other. Look for me every night at sunset."

Allison took the mirror and examined it skeptically.

"He's used it plenty of times," Jezebel assured her. "It will work."

"What are you going to do about horses?" Allison asked. "Surely you're not planning to walk the whole way?"

"I'm going to talk to my father. I might be able to take our team," she said doubtfully.

Allison got to her feet. She walked to her desk, pulled out a sheet of paper, and scrawled a note upon it.

"Give this to the stable master," she said. "You can take my mare and another."

Jezebel took the note and nodded. Allison began to cry. She pulled Jezebel into a hug. "Thank you," she whispered.

"I'm going to save you," Jezebel told her, her own eyes starting to water.

"Hurry back," Allison pleaded.

Jezebel took her head in her hands and kissed her on the lips. "I will, I promise."

"I love you so much," Allison said, smiling for the first time.

Jezebel kissed her once more and left the room. She retrieved the horses and returned to the wayfarer camp. She found them packed up and ready to depart. Khaldun was standing by the road, talking to Badru. They hugged as Jezebel approached, and then Badru walked back to the troupe.

Khaldun greeted Jezebel; his eyes were red and puffy. They packed the gear onto one of the horses and headed east along the road. Back at the farm, Jezebel stabled the horses. She dragged Khaldun into the fields to find her father.

They located Robert with several hands in a pasture on the southern edge of the property. Jezebel introduced him to Khaldun and told him they needed to talk. Will and Edward both cast jealous glances at Khaldun. Seeing the three of them together, Jezebel knew for sure she'd choose the wayfarer.

Robert strolled off with Jezebel, leaving Khaldun with the hands. They moved out of earshot and sat on the fence. Jezebel told her father the whole story.

He sat in silence for a minute, considering everything she'd told him. "Your mother's not going to like this," he said finally. "Traipsing off into the wide world with some wayfarer."

"But I *have* to," Jezebel pleaded. "You didn't see what that thing did to Allison—"

"I'll handle Vivien," he said, holding up one hand to silence her. "You do what you have to do."

Jezebel was overcome with gratitude. She discussed her plans with him for the next ten minutes. She told him about the horses and listed everything Khaldun had packed already.

Robert nodded as she spoke. "Sounds like you've got this under control."

Sure enough, Vivien objected vehemently. But Robert managed to win her over. She busied herself packing food for their trip: dried meats and fruit, a wheel of hard cheese, and flatbread specially prepared to keep on long trips.

They sat around the fireplace that night, plotting the journey on an old map Robert dug up in his desk. Emma was especially curious about the trip; like Jezebel, she'd never traveled outside of Spanbrook.

Jezebel had never contemplated the sheer size of the continent before. The university seemed incomprehensibly far, but the northern half of the mainland spanned more than four times that distance. And it looked half again as large north to south. The southern half of the landmass was much narrower; it looked like the Eternal Sea had taken a giant bite out of it. Jezebel thanked the stars that the university was as close as it was in the grand scheme of things.

"What's that?" Emma asked, pointing to an enormous island off the southwestern coast.

"Ostland," Robert said. "Nobody lives there. My father told me once that some of the princedoms have sent explorers there. But it's a big jungle, full of wild and dangerous animals."

"What's out there?" Emma asked, tracing her finger along the eastern edge of the map.

"They say the world is round," Khaldun told her, "like a big ball. And according to legend, there's another continent on the other side. That's where the elves live. But as far as I know, nobody's ever sailed a ship far enough to find out for sure."

"I heard stories about the elves growing up," Robert said. "Our nursemaid told us that men once lived on their land. But they left and journeyed here across the Lonely Sea."

"Yes, and she was the same woman who believed in dragons," Vivien said, shaking her head. "Nothing but old wives' tales."

"I'm not so sure," Khaldun said. "Nomad told me that he saw a dragon once. Far away in the northern hills, near Kong—that's the only place they inhabit."

"I hope we don't encounter any," Jezebel replied with a shudder. "They're supposed to be able to fly and breathe fire—and eat entire herds of livestock."

Robert chuckled at this. "They're only a myth. I don't know what your sorcerer saw, but I don't think it was a dragon."

"Perhaps," Khaldun said skeptically. "But, we won't need to go anywhere near those hills at any rate."

Soon it was time for bed. Jezebel offered to let Khaldun sleep in her room, but Vivien refused.

"We'll be sharing a tent on the road, Mother," Jezebel protested. "This is no different."

"Not under my roof," Vivien insisted. It was as if she were taking advantage of this last opportunity to exert control over her daughter. But she held her ground, and Khaldun slept downstairs by the fireplace.

Jezebel had tremendous difficulty getting to sleep. Come dawn, she'd be leaving behind everything she'd ever known. She couldn't suppress the feeling that nothing would ever be the same. Who could tell what dangers they would encounter? But she would do whatever was necessary to save Allison. Her love for the princess was the driving force behind this quest.

CHAPTER EIGHT
BORDERS

t was still dark when Jezebel woke. She'd slept only a few hours but felt energized by the prospect of the journey before her. She dressed and went downstairs to find Vivien in the kitchen, already preparing breakfast. She chatted with her mother for a while until she asked Jezebel to wake Khaldun and Robert.

The sun came up as they ate. Jezebel took her time, savoring every bite. She knew this would be her last home-cooked meal for a long time.

She said goodbye to her mother and went outside with Robert and Khaldun to pack their gear on the horses. After a teary-eyed farewell to her father, she climbed her mount, and they departed.

But before they'd even reached the road, Jezebel stopped.

"I forgot my wand!"

Jezebel turned back, jumped off her horse, and ran inside, startling her parents. She dashed upstairs and retrieved the wooden case from her closet. Moments later, she left her room again, pushing the wand into her pocket.

But as she started down the stairs, Emma emerged from her room, rubbing sleep from her eyes. Jezebel hugged her and kissed her on the top of the head.

"I wish I could go with you," Emma said.

"I know," Jezebel replied. "I'll be back as soon as I can. Take care of Mother and Father."

"I will," Emma said solemnly.

Jezebel hugged her parents one last time and dashed out the door. Khaldun watched her in amusement as she mounted her horse.

"Some witch you are," he chided. "How do you expect to do magic without a wand?"

"I know," she said as they set out again. "After everything that happened, I haven't practiced at all."

"We'll have plenty of time to rectify that."

They headed east on the road. Jezebel had to squint to shield her eyes from the dazzling sunlight. Before long, they passed Smithwick's farm. An hour later, they moved beyond the farthest point Jezebel had ever traveled to before.

All day they followed the road. They saw nothing but endless fields and rolling hills in the distance. The horses were eager and energetic; they let them gallop a few times, but kept them to a walk or a trot the rest of the day. They stopped twice to eat. Jezebel enjoyed the fare but suspected she'd tire of it before long.

As the sun set behind them, they made camp by the side of the road near a wood. Khaldun pitched the tent, and Jezebel laid out the bedrolls inside of it. There was barely enough space for the two of them to sleep side by side. The thought of lying so close to the wayfarer aroused her; she couldn't wait.

Khaldun went to collect firewood, and Jezebel pulled the mirror out of her pack. She sat down in the tent, unsure how this was supposed to work. But the instant she looked in the glass, she saw Allison staring back at her. It was odd—she could see her own reflection still, but it was shadowed behind her cousin.

"Jezebel! Thank the stars—I've been waiting for you. I didn't think this would work."

"Did something happen?" Jezebel asked, afraid of the answer.

"No… It's just… I've missed you," Allison admitted, looking slightly abashed. "I grew accustomed to your constant presence."

Jezebel breathed a sigh of relief. They chatted for only a few minutes. But her heart lifted—this was the most Allison had spoken since the incident with Nomad. Jezebel knew it was only due to their separation and the novelty of using the mirrors, but it was encouraging nonetheless.

Khaldun returned with the firewood. He made a small pile of twigs and erected a cone-shaped structure over it with several small sticks and branches. Above that he built a second structure with larger pieces of wood.

"Would you care to ignite it?" he asked.

"What?" Jezebel asked, surprised. "Oh, with magic." She pulled out her wand and pointed it at the kindling. "I don't remember the incantation," she admitted sheepishly.

Khaldun reminded her of the spell. She recited it and spoke the word of command. It took a few tries, but eventually, the fire burst to life. Jezebel stared in awe for a minute, proud of her accomplishment.

"You say you haven't practiced at all?" Khaldun asked. Jezebel shook her head, smiling ear to ear. "It's remarkable that you were able to do it again so quickly. You must have sorcerer blood in your family."

"Not that I know of," she said with a shrug. "What language do these words come from?"

"I guess they originally came from an ancient tongue that died out many hundreds of years ago. But the way you speak them matters more than the actual words. The sound of your voice should reflect the intent of your spell."

"How so?"

"Well, calling a simple flame is fairly gentle," he said. "If I wanted a real conflagration, the sound would be harsher, stronger. Watch."

Khaldun held his staff in front of him and shouted words that did indeed sound much more violent than the spell Jezebel had used. He spoke the word of command, and suddenly the campfire erupted into a wall of flame, ten feet high. Jezebel backed away in surprise.

Khaldun lowered his staff, and the fire returned to normal.

"Can you teach me *that*?" Jezebel asked.

He taught her the incantation, and she recited it several times before attempting it. Finally, she pointed her wand at the fire and cast the spell. As it had for Khaldun, the fire burst into a jet, towering above her. She spoke the words again to cancel the magic, and the fire returned to normal.

They spent the next twenty minutes battling each other over their little campfire. Khaldun would ignite it, and Jezebel tried to extinguish it. After a while, they switched roles. He also taught her how to call fire without producing an open flame.

"The force can act inside an object," he explained. He taught her a spell to heat a stone from within. Jezebel was able to cause a rock to grow so hot that it started to glow.

"Incredible," Khaldun said, shaking his head. "It took me months to master that."

"How hot can *you* make it?" Jezebel asked.

"No more than you," he replied. "But I've seen Nomad use it to melt stone. Let's try something else. You've clearly got a flare for fire…"

Jezebel giggled. "A *flare* for fire? That's tacky."

"I've got a way with words," he said with a grin.

Khaldun tried to teach her to call air. He performed a simple spell that blew her horse's tail straight up. But Jezebel couldn't duplicate it, despite numerous attempts. The animal whinnied at her and walked away.

They tried water next. Khaldun caused dew to form on his pack. "There's water in the air," he explained. "So this spell is as easy as it gets—you're simply wringing the moisture out of the atmosphere, like a wet towel."

He taught her the incantation, but Jezebel couldn't call water, either.

"Hmm," Khaldun said, his brow furrowed. "It's unusual for anyone to favor one force so strongly."

"What about earth?" Jezebel asked, crestfallen by her failures.

"Well, that's generally the hardest force to call. But we might as well try. Who knows—it comes the easiest to me out of the basic four."

He pointed his staff at his pack again and instructed Jezebel to lift it. She grabbed it with one hand, but couldn't move it. Instead, she squatted down and grasped it with both hands. Though she struggled and strained, pushing with her legs against the ground, she could lift it only a few inches.

"It weighs a ton!" she said, exhaling deeply from the effort.

"Not quite," Khaldun replied, sounding impressed. "But I'm surprised you could move it at all. You're strong for a girl."

"Farm life will do that," she said.

He taught her the spell, but Jezebel had no more luck calling earth than she had water or air.

They decided to call it a night. Jezebel put out the fire, and Khaldun walked around their camp, muttering words under his breath.

"What are you doing?" she asked.

"Making us invisible," Khaldun said. "It's only a precaution—I doubt we'll encounter trouble as long as we're in Spanbrook."

Jezebel held her hand in front of her. "I can still see myself."

Khaldun chuckled. "Of course you can. You're inside the spell. But walk over to the road and see what happens."

Jezebel did as he said. When she turned around, she could see only cornfields under the bright moons. She cried out in surprise. The sound of Khaldun's laughter drifted to her through the spell, but she couldn't see him again until she walked back inside the enchantment.

They went inside the tent. Khaldun removed his shirt and lay down on his back. He was snoring softly within minutes. Jezebel lay awake for a long time, admiring his body and savoring his scent. Her dreams that night were quite erotic.

They woke at dawn and shared a light breakfast. Ten minutes later, they broke camp and continued along the road.

"I reckon we covered twenty-five miles yesterday," Khaldun said. "If we keep up this pace, we'll be there in no time."

They spent the next two days exactly as they had the first. All day they rode, stopping only to eat. They made camp at sunset, Jezebel spoke to Allison, and they practiced magic. Farmland extended as far as the eye could see, broken only by low hills or patches of forest.

Early on the fourth day, they came to an old signpost by the side of the road.

"This marks the border with Newberry," Khaldun told her. "The princedoms out here are much larger than those around the university. Some of those can be traversed in a single day."

Jezebel half-expected to feel different somehow once they'd crossed the line. It was the first time she'd ever left her uncle's princedom. But were it not for the wayfarer, she would never have known. Nothing about the road or the land changed in the slightest.

Yet Khaldun seemed different. He was more watchful and alert and less talkative. He didn't tell her anything, but his change in mood made Jezebel nervous as if they were in some kind of danger.

But their journey continued to be uneventful. They met travelers on the road and chatted amicably; Jezebel encountered nothing to explain Khaldun's wariness. They passed to the south of Newberry castle—Jezebel could see the buildings in the distance, like a ragged crown on the hill. By night, the lights of the town flickered and danced. They traveled through a few small villages in the ensuing days, crossing Newberry and entering Cambry. And still, all was well.

Late in the afternoon on the twelfth day of their journey, they came to a mighty river, with a giant wooden bridge providing a way across. The ruins of some old structure stood by the side of the road.

"We've arrived here sooner than I expected," Khaldun observed, dismounting his horse. "This is the River Torsa. It marks the ancient boundary between Maeda and Dorshire."

"I thought we were still in Cambry," Jezebel said, jumping down to stand next to him.

"We are," Khaldun said. "But long ago, Cambry, Newberry, and Spanbrook were all part of the Kingdom of Dorshire. That's Vance," he said, pointing across the river. "But it used to be part of Maeda."

"I remember learning about this when I was little," said Jezebel. "There were five kingdoms, right?"

"Yes. Kong lies beyond Maeda, on the eastern end of the continent. Shifar runs along the western edge, south of Dorshire. And Pytha occupied the land east of the Anthar mountains."

"We don't have kingdoms anymore," Jezebel noted. "What happened to them?"

"Pytha conquered the others. The first Pythan Emperor slew the kings and their families. At its height, the Pythan Empire spanned nearly the entire continent. Only a few lands at the extreme eastern and western edges remained free.

"The empire endured almost three hundred years. But eventually, things started to fall apart. There had always been minor uprisings and rebellions. But at one point, the lords of nearly every house joined forces to overthrow the emperor. It's said they had help from the elves. The lines of every king had been destroyed, so the princedoms were established instead. Generally, the most powerful lord in each territory became the prince."

"And when did that happen?" Jezebel asked.

"Eight hundred and seventy-two years ago," Khaldun said with an air of amusement.

"Oh!" Jezebel said in surprise. "So, that's why it's the year 872."

"Precisely," he said. "Time is counted from the fall of the Pythan Empire. But that's enough history for now. We should make camp."

They set up the tent next to the ruins and built their fire. Jezebel talked to Allison; the princess told her that she was leaving in a few days to accompany her father on the tour of the princedom. Jezebel thought this was an excellent idea. It would allow her to establish a rapport with the vassals, and hopefully, it would also help her move beyond her trauma.

After they ate, Jezebel and Khaldun explored the ruins. Jezebel called a flame to light their way.

"What was this place?" she asked.

"It was probably a watchtower," Khaldun explained. "This road is as old as the Five Kingdoms. The ancient kings would have kept constant watch at every crossing—the tower on the opposite shore still stands. We'll pass by it tomorrow."

They practiced magic that night. Jezebel's proficiency with fire continued to improve. But not once could she call the other forces. On a hunch, Khaldun tried teaching her a simple illusion—he turned her hair green. But Jezebel failed to produce the same effect on him.

After that, it took her thirty minutes to get him to change her hair back. He teased her, telling her she might start a new trend this way. She ended up wrestling him to the ground and sitting on him before he'd cancel the illusion. Jezebel acted angry and exasperated, but she relished the excuse to touch his body.

As usual, Khaldun drifted off to sleep almost instantly when they went to bed. Jezebel resisted a strong temptation to kiss him. She'd been flirting with him almost incessantly since leaving her house. But either he hadn't noticed—which Jezebel found hard to believe—or he was ignoring her. She gave it up as a lost cause.

When Jezebel woke, Khaldun was already outside. She gazed out the flap to see him standing beside the ruins, eating his breakfast and staring across the river. Jezebel picked up her mirror to make sure *all* of her hair was turned back to its normal color, and found Allison staring back at her.

"You startled me!" she declared. But Allison was crying. Jezebel's heart jumped into her throat. "What's wrong?!"

"The demon—it's back! I haven't seen it since… since that night. But I was drawing a bath just now; I took off my nightgown, and it was watching me in the mirror!"

"Did anything else happen?"

"Only growling. I've been sitting in bed for a half hour, waiting for you to look in the mirror. You said you'd check every morning—I thought I'd missed you."

"I overslept a bit," Jezebel said.

"I'm so scared—are you almost there?"

"We're crossing the river into Vance today; we still have a long way to go. Allison, go to Myrddin. He needs to know that the demon's penetrated his barrier."

Allison nodded frantically. "I will—I'm going to, I just wanted to see you first."

"Go now," Jezebel told her. "Right away. I'll talk to you tonight. I love you."

Allison smiled tremulously, and her image disappeared.

Jezebel set about breaking camp. She told Khaldun about her contact with Allison as they mounted their horses.

"We're making good time," he said. "We'll get help soon."

They rode across the bridge on horseback, the animals' hooves clattering noisily on the wooden deck. It took a few minutes to get to the other side.

"Good thing we didn't have to swim across," Jezebel commented.

"We probably wouldn't have made it," Khaldun told her. "The current is too strong—at the very least, it would have carried us a long way north of here."

Several yards beyond the far shore, they spotted the other watchtower. It was surrounded by tall trees, which was why they hadn't been able to see it the previous afternoon. Jezebel wished they could stay and explore, but they pressed on.

There was less farmland and more forest on this side of the river. The road rose and dipped through hilly terrain.

Later in the morning, they approached a covered wagon going the other way. The man driving it reminded Jezebel of her father with his mop of dark hair and weather-beaten face. But he looked rundown and afraid. A slender woman sat next to him; Jezebel assumed she was his wife.

"Good morning," Khaldun called out.

The man reined in his horses. "Hello," he replied. "Where y'all headed?"

"The university, we hope."

The man shook his head. "You won't get there this way. You'd be better served to go north, hook around through Arthos."

"Arthos?" Khaldun replied, surprise in his voice. "That's pretty far out of the way."

"Not these days," the man said. Jezebel could see two faces peering out from the wagon. One was a boy, probably a few years younger than her; the other a little girl, maybe two years older than Emma. "That bastard from Fosland's overrun half of Stiles. One of his men tried to have his way with my little Kara. Killed him, I did. And nearly got his partner, too. But the son of a bitch ran off. I'm getting out—probably have half a regiment on my tail before long."

"Henry's moved his forces this far north?" Khaldun asked, sounding worried.

"Declared himself King of Maeda," the man said with a scowl. "King my ass. No, you'd best turn back, or go around north as I said. Filmore's raising an army, but too little, too late if you ask me. What was he doing when Henry sacked Perrin? That woulda been a good time to prepare, don't ya think?"

"No doubt," Khaldun said, looking troubled. "I've got friends in Stiles Town; I was hoping to meet them on my way."

"Good luck," the man said with a snort. "My farm's a day's march down the road from here. Well, ain't my farm no more—the army's there, and you're gonna have to go right through them to make it to the castle."

"Where will you go now?" Jezebel asked, feeling sorry for this man.

"West," he said with a quick nod. "As far away from *King Henry* as possible."

"I come from Spanbrook," she told him. "It's pleasant there. My father could help you get back on your feet. If you tell him I sent you…"

"*Spanbrook*?" the man asked, suddenly terrified. "I won't bring my family there. That land's cursed! I'd sooner turn around and meet my fate here. No, we're aiming to keep going till we run into the Eternal Sea. And we'd best be off. Good day to y'all."

The man drove off, and Jezebel stared at Khaldun in disbelief.

"Spanbrook's not cursed," she said. "What was he talking about?"

"Welcome to the world," Khaldun said with a grim smile. They resumed their course. "This is what I was afraid of, although I hoped we wouldn't encounter it so soon.

"Jezebel, life is different in Spanbrook. With Myrddin there, nobody will dare attack. Not even the most powerful warlord would stand a chance against him. The people in the other princedoms are deathly afraid of necromancy. Luckily for them, Aldo's not a conqueror.

"But Spanbrook is an oasis. There's almost perpetual warfare on much of the continent—particularly in Maeda. It's usually limited to skirmishes and border disputes. But it's not uncommon for some prince to get restless or greedy and attack a neighbor.

"Henry's the worst. He's the prince of Fosland, well south of here. But he's been annexing neighboring princedoms for many years now. I shudder to think what would happen if *he* had a necromancer. His wraiths are bad enough."

"*Wraiths?*" Jezebel had no idea what they might be, but she didn't like the sound of the word.

"Henry's managed to assemble a whole team of powerful witches and wizards," Khaldun explained. "Dredmort is their leader. He's no necromancer, but he's got a power over the dead. The wraiths used to be men and women. But Dredmort murdered and resurrected them. They're bound to his will. And they're terrible to behold."

"You've seen them?" Jezebel asked.

"I have. But you feel them before you see them—they cast a shadow over your heart when they come near. We fought them a couple of years ago when we were passing through lands south of Fosland. They're tough—magic doesn't work on them. They avoid sunlight, though; that's about their only weakness."

"But why would they attack a wayfarer troupe?"

"Nomad," Khaldun said simply. "Henry would do anything to get his hands on a sorcerer. The wraiths were no match for him, but he had a hard time fending them off and protecting the whole troupe at the same time. We avoided Henry's lands after that."

They rode in silence. Finally, Jezebel understood the increased wariness Khaldun had exhibited since leaving Spanbrook. Now she felt it, too.

CHAPTER NINE
HONOR

hey encountered many people fleeing west that day. Some were running from the enemy forces, others avoiding conscription. But many had simply heard news of Henry's invasion and didn't wish to live under his rule.

Jezebel and Khaldun crossed into Stiles and followed the road into a wood shortly before sunset. Khaldun found a clearing in the trees a little farther from the beaten path than they usually camped. He set up the tent while Jezebel went to collect firewood.

Khaldun started the fire when she returned. Jezebel fetched her mirror and spoke to Allison. Myrddin had been surprised to learn of the demon's latest appearance but assured Allison that he would strengthen the barrier. He also believed that Allison's departure from the castle might provide her a respite from the haunting. Jezebel left the mirror in the tent and joined Khaldun by the fire.

"Wouldn't the demon follow her?" she asked, once she'd told him the news.

"I don't see why not," Khaldun said, puzzled. "Maybe Myrddin knows some way to trick the demon into thinking she's still inside the castle."

"That could be," she conceded.

Jezebel practiced her spells for a while, and Khaldun tried again to teach her how to conjure with the other forces. She didn't make any progress.

"I give up," she said in frustration, getting to her feet. "And I have to pee."

"Don't go too far," Khaldun warned her.

Jezebel walked out of the camp, only a few feet beyond the field of invisibility. She pulled down her trousers and squatted. As she relieved herself, she idly called fire, lighting a small twig on fire.

Suddenly there was a shrill cry, deafeningly loud. In a flash, Jezebel could see the camp again—and Khaldun was gone.

Jezebel pulled up her trousers, careful not to stand too straight. Standing by their fire were two figures clad in black robes and hoods. Jezebel couldn't see their faces. They were swaying slowly, looking back and forth across the camp. One of them ripped open the tent flap.

But in addition to seeing them, Jezebel could *feel* their presence. They cast an overwhelming sense of dread and fear upon her. She knew these were wraiths. As she stood there, stooped low, trying to decide what to do, one of them seemed to spot her. Suddenly they were both moving in her direction. One of them shrieked again.

Jezebel stood tall. Fear froze her heart; her first impulse was to run. But she mastered herself, pointed her wand and called fire. She remembered what Khaldun had told her about the wraiths, so she didn't attempt to burn *them*. Instead, she conjured a wall of flame, twenty feet across, directly in their path.

The wraiths cried louder than ever and backed away from the fire. For a moment, Jezebel worried that she'd overdone it—a nearby tree burst into flame. The last thing she needed was a forest fire.

She held her wand in front of her and moved forward, pushing the wraiths back slowly with her spell. But one of them appeared to throw something, and suddenly the fire disappeared. Before Jezebel could call it again, the other one shrieked, and this time there were words in the cry. Something hit Jezebel in the chest, and she flew back, losing her wand. The wraiths advanced on her again.

But an instant later, someone called out from the road. Jezebel turned—through the trees, she could make out a figure robed in gray, sitting on a horse: Myrddin.

The necromancer held out his hands, and an enormous shadow, wreathed in flame, erupted from the ground before him. The wraiths fled before it. They mounted their horses and withdrew, galloping down the road.

Jezebel recovered her wand and sprang to her feet. What the hell was Myrddin doing here? She went to the road to meet him, but he was gone.

Suddenly Khaldun appeared by her side. Jezebel nearly jumped out of her skin.

"Don't do that!" she yelled, punching him in the arm.

"Sorry," he said with a frown, caressing his triceps.

"And where did you go?! The wraiths attacked, and Myrddin showed up… What?"

Khaldun was chuckling at her. "That wasn't Myrddin," he said, holding up his staff.

"*You* did that?"

"Only when they disarmed you. I was impressed with your spell work until then."

"I'm confused," she said.

"We need to move—they're sure to return. I'll explain everything once we've set up camp again."

Jezebel felt drained from the sudden shock of fighting the wraiths. She broke camp wearily, dragging her feet. They packed up and traveled a few miles farther up the road. Once Khaldun was satisfied that they'd covered a sufficient distance, they moved off the road and set up camp again.

They didn't light a fire. Once Khaldun had circled the area and rendered them invisible, they retreated inside the tent.

"I've masked our sounds this time, too," he told her. "The spell won't follow us when we're traveling, but it works as long as we're stationary. I'm sure that's what gave us away last time. The wraiths must have heard us as they passed by on the road. I'm guessing they're after that family we met this morning. They probably won't trouble us again.

"Because they *knew* we were there, they were able to cancel my spell. You'd gone off by yourself, so I had no choice—I made myself invisible and crept around them. I was about to cast my spell when I saw you call fire. That was quite impressive, I must say. But once they disarmed you, I let Myrddin loose."

"Ah, so that was only an illusion," she said.

Khaldun nodded.

"They weren't as tough as I thought they'd be," Jezebel told him. "If you can scare them off with an illusion like that, how bad can they be?"

"Don't be fooled," Khaldun cautioned her. "They weren't seeking us—they were merely curious to see who we were. You took them by surprise, no doubt. But they would have killed you if I hadn't scared them off. And I'm sure that illusion didn't fool them for long. They'll have gone back to search for us after we left, you can count on it.

"And on top of all that, there were only two of them. Dredmort commands twelve in total. If they'd had reason to look for us specifically, or if they'd arrived in force, we wouldn't have been so lucky."

Jezebel shivered. "I feel bad for that family if they catch them."

"Let's hope they made it across the river by now," Khaldun replied. "I doubt Henry's letting the wraiths venture into Dorshire just yet."

Jezebel lay awake very late that night. She couldn't banish visions of the wraiths from her mind. Once she did drift off, she had nightmares about the confrontation.

Jezebel woke to find Khaldun's arm around her, his face only inches from hers. She smiled, breathing in his scent. She'd finally worked up the nerve to kiss him when he opened his eyes. For a moment, he gazed at her and smiled. But then he sat up, stretched, and yawned.

"I'm starving," he muttered, fumbling his way out of the tent.

Jezebel sighed. This was going nowhere. She couldn't wait to go home to Allison. After lying in her bedroll for a few more minutes, she emerged from the tent herself and joined Khaldun for breakfast.

"I'm torn," he told her. "We're only a day or two from Castle Stiles, where we might enjoy a good meal and a night in real beds. And from there, we can make the university in a day or two."

"I wouldn't mind a reprieve from the road," Jezebel said.

"But I fear the farmer's words. Perhaps he's right—it might be safer to go around."

"How long would that take?"

Khaldun thought about it for a minute. "From here… it could take ten days. Maybe more. We'd have to go around Orchard Lake and we'd be reduced to footpaths in some places. There are no roads that follow the exact route we'd need to take."

"It'll take longer on the way back as well," Jezebel reminded him. "I think we should risk the direct path. If you make us invisible, we can march right past any troops we come across. Allison needs us."

"Yet she's leaving to tour the princedom, and Myrddin thinks she'll be safe while she's gone. That buys us some time—how long did she say the trip would last?"

"It could be as long as thirty days," Jezebel said.

They both considered their choices in silence for a few minutes. Finally, Khaldun got to his feet.

"Let's give it a shot," he said. "Henry's men won't be expecting trouble from the rear. Their attention will be focused on any threat that might come *from* Stiles, not toward it.

"And besides… I'm feeling lucky," he added with a grin. Jezebel smiled back at him.

They broke camp and set out. Khaldun cast his spell, hiding them from all eyes. But he reminded Jezebel that passers-by could still hear them, and see the dust they kicked up from the road. He advised her that they should move off the road and stay silent if they encountered anyone. And he told her to keep her wand at the ready.

Jezebel felt her anxiety rise. But half the day went by, and they hadn't met anyone. The land seemed deserted. But eventually, they came to a village swarming with troops.

Khaldun held his finger to his lips and motioned Jezebel behind him. She followed his lead, moving as quietly as possible. They wound their way through the community, careful not to alert anyone to their presence. Everywhere she looked, Jezebel watched soldiers mistreat local residents. They'd set fire to several houses; the families stood outside watching in despair.

At one point, a column of troops moved past them on the road. Khaldun steered Jezebel into a small pasture, and they waited while they went by. But finally, the two of them made it through the village and continued on their way.

The road was clear for a while. But they came to another town an hour before sunset. There weren't as many soldiers here. But they were much less disciplined. Jezebel saw one group stagger out of a tavern, clearly drunk. She and Khaldun had nearly made it back to open road when Jezebel saw a sight that enraged her.

The last house in the village was in flames, the family outside. The father was lying dead, face down in the yard, a stake through his back. The mother was huddled by the road with her little boy, crying hysterically, a soldier keeping watch.

Two other men were holding down a girl; Jezebel guessed her age at twelve or thirteen. She was naked and screaming. A third man pulled down his trousers and dropped to his knees to mount her.

Jezebel snapped. She pointed her wand and called fire. The man burst into flames, from the inside out. The other two gaped at him in horror. Jezebel repeated the word of command twice more, and they were engulfed in fire as well. The girl scrambled to her feet and ran to her mother.

Khaldun grabbed Jezebel by the arm, fear in his eyes. He pointed frantically down the road. An instant later, he galloped away. Jezebel followed.

They didn't stop at sunset. They rode for another hour, putting as much distance as possible between them and the village. Only when they found a spot to camp for the night did Jezebel think about what she'd done. She burst into tears, sobbing uncontrollably.

Khaldun sat on the ground next to her and put one arm around her.

"I don't blame you for your actions," he told her. "I should have done something myself, but I was thinking only of our safety. I was afraid the wraiths might come—they would have pursued us."

"I'm sorry… I had to stop him…" Jezebel couldn't get the words out.

"It worked out for the best," he said. "And we're safe."

"This is so horrible," she said. "Henry's army is destroying these people's lives."

"That's war, I'm afraid," he replied. "Like I said, Spanbrook is an oasis. Myrddin's protection has sheltered you from this sort of thing. But it's all too common in many other places."

"But why isn't the prince doing anything to protect his people?"

"I don't know," he said with a shrug. "But Fosland's military is formidable, and it doesn't sound like Stiles has a standing army. The prince has probably gathered his available forces to protect his castle."

Khaldun held her for a long time. Once she'd calmed down, they set up camp. They didn't light a fire, going straight to bed instead.

They set out again the next morning. Jezebel heard from Allison that she'd left the castle with her father. She'd arrived at the first manor house and felt safe. Aldo's witches, Camilla and Gemma, were traveling with them. Jezebel reminded her to schmooze as much as possible with all the lords and ladies.

Khaldun and Jezebel didn't encounter any more of Henry's men. They met few people on the road. The land itself seemed to be holding its breath in anticipation of the coming battle.

Late in the afternoon, Castle Stiles came into view. Its surrounding town looked much like Spanbrook Town, only it was bigger, and there was no wall. Khaldun made the two of them visible. Filmore's army was camped in fields outside the community. As Khaldun and Jezebel approached the encampment, two guards halted them.

"Identify yourselves and state your business in Stiles," one of them ordered.

"I am Khaldun. I'm here to visit Princess Fina."

"Her Highness is expecting you?" the guard asked doubtfully.

"No… We're old friends, and I was passing through…"

"You're wayfarer folk, aren't you?"

"That's right."

"What about you, little lady?"

"I'm Jezebel of Spanbrook."

"Wait here," the guard commanded. He jogged off, leaving his partner to watch them.

"What's going on?" Jezebel asked quietly.

"Standard procedure in time of war," Khaldun said. "They have to make sure they're not letting hostile forces into the town. Don't worry."

The guard returned a minute later with an older man, who appeared to be his superior. "Dangerous time to be traveling," he said to them. "You folks come all the way from Spanbrook?"

"Yes," Khaldun replied. "We didn't realize war was looming until we heard the news from others we met on the road."

"And you stuck to the road the whole way?" he asked suspiciously. Khaldun nodded. "How'd you get through Henry's forces?"

"Lucky, I guess," Khaldun said evasively.

The man grunted. "Well, we're under orders to take travelers into custody. Especially wayfarers," he added apologetically. "Times being what they are. Probably be set free once you've been interrogated, as long as your stories add up. Shouldn't be long." He nodded to the two guards and walked away.

Jezebel looked at Khaldun in disbelief as the guards instructed them to dismount. They confiscated Khaldun's staff, but didn't bother patting them down, and Jezebel didn't look like a witch—her wand remained safely in her pocket.

Two more guards ran over. One of them led the horses, and the other marched Khaldun and Jezebel up the road into town.

They arrived at the castle to find it bustling with activity. A moat surrounded it; the drawbridge was up, and the gate closed. After a brief exchange with their captors, the men in the gatehouse lowered the bridge. The gate rose only high enough to admit them, closing again with a clang once they'd passed.

Jezebel could see people rushing about in the courtyard, but they didn't go that far. Their guard led them into a passage while his partner took the horses away to be stabled.

They walked through a corridor and down a narrow flight of stairs. At the end of a hallway was a large room lined with cells, half of them occupied. The guard opened an empty one and motioned them inside. He closed and locked the door.

"His Highness has been a bit sensitive about wayfarers ever since the troupe came through six months ago," he told them through the bars. "The interrogation might be a little rough—it's nothing personal."

"I thought you said you had friends here," Jezebel hissed once he'd left.

"I do," Khaldun whispered. "Don't worry; I'll straighten this out." Jezebel didn't think he sounded terribly confident.

"I've got my wand," she whispered in his ear. "Is there anything I can do to get us out of here?"

"I don't think it will be necessary," he said, sitting on the stone floor. "Have patience."

The last thing Jezebel felt was patient. An enemy army was preparing to attack the castle, they were still at least a couple more days from the university, and now they were locked in a prison cell. She was infuriated. But she didn't have to wait long.

A man strode into the room, backed by six guards. He was short and skinny, with a scraggly beard and severe features. "So it *is* you," he said.

"Prince Filmore," Khaldun said, getting to his feet and bowing slightly. "It's good to see you again."

"The feeling is mutual," the prince replied. "I've been hoping to meet you again ever since I learned of your insolence. Khaldun, is it?"

"Yes, Your Highness. But I'm sorry, I don't know what—"

"The thought of filth like you touching my daughter… It makes me sick."

Surprise and fear washed over Khaldun's face. Filmore nodded to one of his men; the guard opened the cell door and stood aside.

"After you," Filmore said icily.

Jezebel followed Khaldun out of the cell. The guards led them out of the room and down the hall, around a corner, and into another chamber. This one had a barred window high in one corner. Chains and shackles adorned the opposite wall.

"Remove your clothes," Filmore said with a grin. "Heaven knows you hardly kept them on the last time you were here." Khaldun stared at him for a moment, then began unbuttoning his tunic. "Both of you," Filmore added when Jezebel failed to move.

"*What*?!" she yelled.

Filmore nodded to one of the guards. The man produced a dagger and moved toward Jezebel. "Now, or my guard will do it for you."

Jezebel hesitated. The guard grabbed her by one arm. She yanked herself free. "I'll do it myself."

A minute later, they were both standing there, naked. Filmore's man put his knife away and picked up Jezebel's clothes. He found her wand and handed it to the prince.

"Ah," he said, turning it over in his hand. "We have ourselves a witch."

"I'm Jezebel from Spanbrook," she said. "I'm Prince Aldo's niece." She hoped her noble kinship might buy her some leverage.

"I see," Filmore said, raising his eyebrows. "Somehow, I find it comforting to know that my daughter isn't his *only* victim. I hope this experience teaches you a lesson, my lady—to avoid such rabble in the future."

He turned and strode from the room. The guards shackled their wrists and ankles to the wall, their arms out to their sides. A minute later, they were alone.

"This is a fine mess you've landed us in," Jezebel said.

"I know!" Khaldun replied incredulously. "I was expecting a hot meal and a feather bed."

Jezebel was scared. It wasn't like they were being tortured—she suspected that Filmore only wanted to humiliate them. And he was succeeding. But she feared their situation would worsen. At this moment, they were utterly helpless, with an enemy army on its way. What would happen if the castle were overrun and they were still chained in this dungeon? She didn't want to think about it.

Yet despite the circumstances, Jezebel couldn't help admiring Khaldun's body. He was wiry muscle from head to toe. And he was well-endowed, she thought with a nervous giggle.

"*What* could possibly be funny?" Khaldun demanded. He stared at her for a second but turned away immediately.

"You're not *embarrassed*, are you?" Jezebel teased. "I'll confess I've thought about getting naked with you—but this was *not* how I envisioned it!"

"How can you make light of our situation? You have no idea what Filmore might do to us. Princes take their family honor very seriously."

"Don't blame me! *You're* the one who slept with his daughter. But if he were planning to harm us, he'd be doing it already, wouldn't he?" she asked, still trying to convince herself. "You heard him—he just wants to *teach us a lesson*. And besides—he's got a princedom to defend. He's got bigger things to worry about than us."

"I hope you're right," Khaldun muttered.

So do I, Jezebel thought. But she worried more for Khaldun than for herself—she knew only too well the way the highborn tended to look down on the wayfarers.

Hours went by. Jezebel's shoulders felt like they were on fire. She tried to relax and let the shackles hold her arms up. But it was extremely uncomfortable. Before long, her wrists hurt from the pressure of the metal.

Sounds of activity drifted in through the window. All night Jezebel could hear people moving about in the courtyard, shouting orders and moving equipment and horses. She grew drowsy and dozed off a few times. But she found it impossible to sleep very much standing up.

By the time daylight arrived, Jezebel's arms were completely numb. Her breathing was labored, and the muscles around her ribcage burned.

She heard footsteps in the hallway, coming toward them. Khaldun had seemed to be asleep but suddenly became alert. A young guard entered the room.

"Parker—thank the stars!" Khaldun said, relief in his voice.

"It's good to see you, Khal. Hello," he added to Jezebel, looking her up and down. "But don't count your blessings just yet. I don't bring good news. Drink this." He held a flask to Khaldun's lips and tipped it into his mouth. Khaldun sputtered and drank eagerly.

"My lady," Parker said, offering the flask to Jezebel. She hadn't realized the burning in her throat for all her other hurts. The water soothed the pain.

"Henry's on the march. He'll be here by sunset tomorrow," Parker said to Khaldun. "Filmore plans to execute you before they arrive."

"*What*?!" Jezebel and Khaldun said at the same time.

"You'll be released," Parker said to Jezebel. "But he's been fuming over you for months, Khal. He's had us on the lookout for any sign of your troupe anywhere within our borders."

"Can't you release *me* too?" Khaldun asked desperately.

"Not without risking my own neck," Parker replied.

"What about Fina?" Khaldun demanded. "She could get us out of here!"

"She doesn't know you're here," Parker said. "Filmore's keeping it a big secret. I only found out when I came on duty."

"How can he possibly afford to pay so much attention to *us* when he's got an entire army bearing down on his castle?" Jezebel demanded.

Parker shook his head, exhaling in frustration. "Filmore's made his preparations—he believes that his forces will successfully defend the castle."

"You don't sound so convinced of that notion," Jezebel noted.

"I'm not, based on what Fina's told me." Parker agreed. "The prince's advisers have urged him for months to prepare to evacuate should Henry attack in force. But he refuses to listen. He's survived countless skirmishes with neighboring princedoms, and his family has held Castle Stiles for hundreds of years. He believes his forces can repel this attack as they always have. Filmore fails to appreciate that Dredmort and his wraiths make Heny vastly more powerful than anyone he's had to face before. Unfortunately, he's determined to carry out his plans for you."

"Well, get Fina!" Khaldun shouted. "She'll put a stop to this!"

"I plan on it," Parker assured him. "But it will have to wait until I'm relieved. I'm sorry. But if I'm caught abandoning my post…"

Khaldun swore in frustration. He took a deep breath, coughing it out. "I understand. But see if you can get off early—this isn't exactly comfortable."

Parker nodded, gave Jezebel one more look, and left the chamber.

Throughout the day, the noises outside became more urgent and frenzied. Jezebel fell in and out of consciousness. By sunset, she could barely breathe.

Suddenly there was a commotion in the hallway. A young woman charged into the room, followed by two guards. She could only be the princess. The girl was short and a little portly with round, rosy cheeks. Her chest was huge, Jezebel noted, suspecting this to be the source of Khaldun's attraction. Tight blond curls fell to her waist.

"Fina!" Khaldun exclaimed. Before he could say anything else, she'd moved across the room. She locked her lips with his, reaching to his groin and fondling him with one hand. Jezebel rolled her eyes. Khaldun managed to pull his face away from Fina, despite being chained to the wall. "Your father plans to execute me! You have to get us out of here!"

"Yes, of course," the princess said, staring dreamily at Khaldun. She nodded to the guards.

"But Your Highness… The prince made it very clear…" one of them stammered.

"*You idiot!*" Fina bellowed, rounding on the guard and suddenly looking very menacing. "His Highness has abandoned reason—we're on the verge of losing this castle, and he's worried about avenging my *honor.*"

"But if His Highness discovers I've disobeyed his orders…"

"His Highness will be *dead* by morning, and I'll be the ruling princess in exile!" Fina shouted. "*NOW DO AS I SAY!*"

The man cowered and moved around her. He removed Khaldun's shackles first, then Jezebel's. The other guard handed them their clothes. Jezebel's entire body was so stiff she found it extremely difficult to dress herself. Once they were ready, Fina led them from the chamber.

"I'm so sorry," she said to Khaldun. "Father became irate when he learned about us."

"How did he find out?" Khaldun asked.

"Millicent, my servant girl," Fina said with a scowl. "Don't worry; I had her reassigned—now she spends her time emptying chamber pots."

"Yuck," Khaldun said. Jezebel grimaced.

"But we have to hurry," the princess told them. "Henry's forces arrived much sooner than expected. The battle isn't going well. There's no leaving through the main gate—I wish I'd known you were here earlier."

"Then how are we supposed to get out of here?" Khaldun asked, confused.

Fina didn't reply.

They walked upstairs and emerged into the courtyard. Archers lined the castle walls. Dozens of men on horseback crowded the middle of the square. Soldiers ran by, heading toward the walls, their faces full of despair. Sounds of battle drifted over the walls.

Fina led them around the edge of the courtyard to the stables. Yet before they went inside, there was a loud explosion beyond the main gate. A voice cried out in the night, unnaturally loud.

"By the king's command, surrender, and you will be spared. Resist, and you will be destroyed!"

The archers fired a volley of arrows in response. But suddenly, a tower of flame erupted beyond the wall, incinerating the shafts mid-flight.

"Dredmort," Khaldun muttered.

"Let's go!" Fina hissed, pulling them into the stable.

Parker was there with the horses. He handed Khaldun his staff and Jezebel her wand. He and Fina grabbed a section of the stable wall and heaved. To Jezebel's surprise, it moved aside, revealing a passage right through the stone wall.

Fina kissed Khaldun again. "Go," she told him.

"Come with us," Khaldun suggested. "This is clearly a lost cause."

Fina shook her head. "I'll not abandon my people. Unlike my father, I understand the forces arrayed against us—and I have a plan."

"Parker?" Khaldun offered.

"Thank you, my friend," he said. "But, my destiny lies with the princess."

Khaldun nodded. He led his horse into the tunnel; Jezebel followed. The entrance closed behind them, leaving them in darkness. Khaldun called a flame to light their way. The passage sloped downward, barely big enough for the horses to pass. Jezebel guessed it had been built for this exact purpose.

"Does Filmore have mages?" Jezebel asked.

"A few," Khaldun replied. "Enough to prevent Dredmort from incinerating every man, woman, and child inside the castle. But none powerful enough to repel him."

They walked for thirty minutes. The tunnel descended for a while before leveling out. It made several abrupt turns, finally ending at an enormous iron door. Khaldun managed to force it open. They emerged into the end of an alley. The door clanged shut behind them. They walked to the street and turned to see Castle Stiles in flames behind them.

"I hope Fina made it out alive," Khaldun said.

"I'm sure she did," Jezebel assured him. "No doubt this wasn't the only secret passage—Castle Spanbrook has a few."

"I'm sure," Khaldun agreed. "But it's still going to be tough for them to get out of the city with the whole army watching out for them."

"Well, Fina seemed to know what she was doing."

Khaldun nodded, and they hurried down the street. Before long, they found a path that led north into the woods. They set out, the moons lighting their way, trying to get as far from the castle as possible.

CHAPTER TEN
TRANSFORMATION

ezebel's entire body ached. She was so tired she could barely keep her eyes open. But they trudged ahead, leading the horses along the narrow path for hours. Jezebel focused on putting one foot in front of the other. Finally, they came to a broader trail that ran roughly east to west.

"Can we camp here?" Jezebel asked.

Khaldun sighed. He looked as weary as she felt. "We should keep going. If Fina and her people did manage to escape, Dredmort and his wraiths would be hunting them down. They'll capture anyone they find who might be fleeing the castle. We should do our best to avoid them. We must eschew the road at all costs—it will be much more dangerous for us than it was on the way *into* Stiles. I don't know these woods, but this trail heads due east. It should at least get us closer to the university."

Jezebel nodded in agreement despite her fatigue. She had no desire to meet Dredmort.

Khaldun held his staff out toward the path they'd been walking. He muttered an incantation. Suddenly a gust of wind picked up along the trail, carrying sparks through the air.

"What was that?" Jezebel asked.

"It's a spell to prevent anyone from tracking us. Humans leave signs—footprints, broken twigs, and the like—that trackers can follow. Mages can detect even subtler clues. But what I did should erase all record of our passage, magical or mundane."

The two of them kept moving for several more hours. They were able to ride much of the way, but Jezebel found herself becoming drowsy. She would start nodding off only to jerk awake as she began to slip out of the saddle. Khaldun repeated his spell to cover their trail every so often.

An hour or two before dawn, Khaldun decided they'd gone far enough. They found a clearing off the path and set up the tent. Jezebel was asleep before she hit the bedroll.

The sun was high in the sky by the time they awoke. They broke camp and set out immediately, eating as they rode.

"I think we're going too far north," Khaldun observed. "We should try to turn south or southeast if we can."

An hour later, they came to a path that veered to the right. It was rougher and narrower than the trail they'd been following, so they had to lead the horses on foot. And Khaldun still worried about hitting the open road, which they'd do if they moved too far south. They didn't stay on this path for more than a couple of hours, turning east again when the opportunity arose.

It was slow going traipsing through the woods. But they avoided contact with any other people, which would have been impossible on the road. Every muscle in Jezebel's body ached. And she could think of nothing but their danger. Whenever she heard a noise in the trees, no matter how innocuous, she'd stop and turn in panic.

They made camp at sunset. Despite Jezebel's misgivings, Khaldun felt they'd traveled far enough from the castle to risk a fire. He went to collect firewood while Jezebel used her mirror to contact Allison. They hadn't spoken in a few days, and Allison was worried. She grew quite alarmed as Jezebel told her what had happened.

But Allison had been perfectly safe. She continued her journey with her father and his party. There had been no sign of the demon.

Khaldun returned, and Jezebel built a fire. Once Khaldun had hidden them from sight, he rummaged through the gear, pulling out a small pot and a metal grate. He set up the grate over the fire, placed the pot upon it, and filled it with water from his canteen. He produced a handful of unusual leaves from the pocket of his tunic and added them to the water once it was boiling.

"What are you doing?" Jezebel asked.

"It's a potion that may prove useful to us," he said distractedly. "I always try to keep a stock; it's got some medicinal value. I ran out in Spanbrook."

"How much farther to the university?" Jezebel asked. "Will this route delay us much?"

"It's hard to say," he replied. "We're certainly going slower, and our course is less direct. But after another day I think we'll risk the road. We should be far enough from Stiles to avoid trouble by then. And I wouldn't mind spending a night at an inn."

"Neither would I," Jezebel agreed with a smile. "I sorely missed that hot meal and feather bed in Stiles."

They marched from sunrise to sunset the next day. Seemingly out of immediate danger, Jezebel thought about what she'd learned in Stiles. The knowledge of Khaldun's relationship with Fina had been hanging over the edge of her consciousness like a storm cloud. Now that she had time to pay it mind, she realized she was extremely jealous.

She knew it was ridiculous to feel this way. Khaldun had traveled the world; undoubtedly, Fina hadn't been his only lover. And Jezebel's heart belonged to Allison. But during their journey, her attraction to Khaldun had only increased. She knew she was falling in love with him. Meeting one of his former paramours and seeing them embrace had stirred surprisingly deep emotions in her.

They made camp that night, only a few feet from the trail. Jezebel started a fire, and Khaldun made them invisible. He insisted that she try calling the other forces again.

"I don't see the point," she complained. "I'm only good for fire."

"Nonsense," he said. "I've never heard of a mage who could call only one force. Everyone possesses strengths and weaknesses, but you're still new to your talent. It will come with practice."

They tried various spells for the next thirty minutes. Jezebel could do none of them. Finally, Khaldun taught her a simple incantation to call earth.

"It has the effect of throwing an invisible stone," he explained. "Watch."

He pointed his staff at her and cast the spell.

"Ow!" Jezebel exclaimed, rubbing her chest. "Something hit me in the breast."

"Sorry—my aim is never very good."

"I think that's what the wraiths used to disarm me," she said, recalling their encounter. "*Something* hit me, anyway—but it was bigger. It knocked me right over."

"I've seen Nomad use this spell to knock holes through a stone wall," Khaldun said. "That takes a lot of power, though."

He taught her the incantation, and Jezebel tried it. She pointed her wand at Khaldun and cast the spell. It worked. Something invisible crashed into his chest, lifting him off his feet.

Jezebel jumped with glee. "I did it!"

Khaldun got to his feet and coughed several times. "Yes, you did. Knocked the wind out of me. Do it again—but not so hard."

Jezebel practiced for thirty more minutes. She could cast the spell every time but had great difficulty controlling the amount of force.

"That's enough for tonight," Khaldun said eventually. "This is a huge step. Don't worry; earth is subtle. Not everyone can master it. But at least you've moved beyond a single force."

They resumed their course at first light the next day. The path kept turning farther north. Khaldun tried to choose trails that led more southerly. He hoped to find the road the next day, their third full day of travel since leaving Castle Stiles. But by the time they made camp that night, they'd seen no sign of it. Early on the fourth day, they decided to follow a stream that ran due south. But before long, they encountered a dead end.

The stream ran over the edge of a cliff in a narrow waterfall. There was no path here, and they couldn't lead the horses through the dense underbrush. They ended up having to turn back to resume their course along the trail.

On the fifth day, late in the afternoon, the woods began to thin. Before long, they discerned a large clearing in front of them. They emerged from the trees to find themselves in open pastureland.

"This is a farm," Jezebel observed, gazing across the field. "And there's a town—look!" she said, pointing.

"Yes," Khaldun agreed, looking troubled.

"Where are we?"

"I don't know. Let's investigate. But keep your guard up and your wand drawn—we may find trouble."

They mounted their horses and crossed the field. On the other side, they found a small dirt road. They followed this into the town.

"I recognize this place," Khaldun said, looking around. The community wasn't big. Jezebel guessed it at less than half the size of Spanbrook Town, no more than an overgrown village. "This is Raymour."

"Never heard of it," said Jezebel.

"It's a small holding in the princedom of Madison. The keep is on the other end of town. We're about two days south of the prince's castle—and that means we've traveled much too far north."

"Wonderful," Jezebel muttered.

"The worst part is that there's no direct route to the university from here. We'll have to get to Arthos, then take the road south from there."

"At least we're out of that infernal forest," Jezebel said with a sigh. "Is there any risk of running into Henry's men here?"

"I don't think so," he replied. "But I didn't expect them in Stiles either. There's an inn here. We should stay the night—hopefully we can gather some news."

Jezebel beamed at him.

"An inn? That's what I like to hear."

They rode through the town, eyes open for any threat. But all seemed well. They met several passers-by, each of whom greeted them amiably. These people showed none of the fear or distress they'd witnessed in Stiles.

They found the inn. Khaldun went inside while Jezebel stayed to watch the horses. He returned a few minutes later.

"We've got a room," he said with a smile, "and dinner's on the stove."

Khaldun and Jezebel stabled the animals and unpacked their gear. They shouldered the packs and walked into the inn.

The front door opened into a large common room. There was an enormous hearth at one end, the bar along the left. A handful of patrons sat eating their dinner. It was nothing fancy, but the place felt warm and inviting.

Jezebel followed Khaldun across the common room, down a narrow hallway. They climbed the stairs in the rear of the building to the third floor. Khaldun opened the door to their bedchamber.

"Home for the night," he said with a grin.

Jezebel walked inside and dropped her gear in the corner. The room was tiny, with barely enough room for the bed and a chest of drawers.

"There's only one bed," she said, stifling a giggle.

"I thought that would be all right," Khaldun replied, sounding slightly worried, "considering we've been sleeping in such tight quarters this whole trip. It's bigger than both our bedrolls combined. But I can get us a second room if you'd prefer."

"No, this will do," she said quickly. "I was simply making an observation."

They returned to the common room. Jezebel chose a table in the back corner, and Khaldun propped his staff against the wall. She sat down, and Khaldun went to the bar. He returned with two large glasses of some black liquid.

"What's this?" Jezebel asked, sniffing it.

"Beer," he replied, sitting across from her. "Madison is known for its stouts."

"I've never tried beer," Jezebel said. "It's mead and wine in Spanbrook." She took a sip and crinkled her nose. "That's *bitter*!"

Khaldun took a swig and smiled at her. "It's an acquired taste. Most of the princedoms seem to favor pale ales. But I'd take a good Madison stout any day."

Several more people arrived. Jezebel thought they must be farmers, based on their sunburnt faces and manner of dress. Khaldun and Jezebel were finishing their second beer by the time the food arrived. Jezebel ate greedily. There was roast venison, potatoes, mushrooms, and spinach. It was simple fare, but delicious. Jezebel finished much faster than Khaldun.

"Better than jerky and dried fruit?" he asked when she put down her fork.

"Definitely," she said, nodding earnestly. "I wouldn't mind seconds," she added, craning her neck to look at the bar. Khaldun chuckled.

Jezebel had another helping of venison. Khaldun ordered them each another beer. It turned out that the innkeeper was a local authority, and brewed several varieties himself. He recommended a porter next. The common room had grown busier by the time the beer arrived. Jezebel sampled it uncertainly.

"This is quite good," she declared in surprise. "It's almost sweet next to the stout."

They moved to the bar before long to make room for some new arrivals. Jezebel thought Trey would be jealous. The only time she'd ever seen her uncle's tavern this busy was when the wayfarers came to town.

They ordered another porter, and Jezebel felt the alcohol going to her head. She wasn't going to complain. This was the first time they'd been able to relax on their entire journey. She intended to enjoy it. A minute later, she overheard two farmers at the end of the bar discussing the recent events in Stiles.

"You heard wrong, Zed," one of them said. "There's no way Henry's come this far north. Overreaching himself already, he is. Hasn't got the resources to control *another* princedom."

"I'm telling you. My brother was there to buy a horse—you know how they breed them down there. He was on his way back and nearly got run over by a column of soldiers. All wearing the uniforms of Fosland, they were."

"He's right," Jezebel piped in loudly before the other man could retort. "We just came from Stiles. Henry sacked the castle."

"No!" said Zed. "That quickly? What about Filmore's army?"

"Dredmort was there," Khaldun told them. He didn't need to say anything else. Both farmers blanched at the name.

"What about his wraiths?" asked the innkeeper. "Were they there?"

Before long, Khaldun and Jezebel became the center of attention for the whole common room. They ended up recounting their entire journey, from Spanbrook to Stiles—careful to leave out any mention of Allison's ordeal or the motivation for their travels. One of the farmers wanted to know about news out of Spanbrook. It turned out he was related to Jezebel's neighbor, old Smithwick.

They were delighted to meet Khaldun as well. The wayfarers had performed in Madison many times and enjoyed a highly favorable reputation—among the citizenry at least. Khaldun hinted to raucous laughter that much like Filmore, the prince might have reason to imprison him.

The farmers ended up taking turns buying drinks for Jezebel and Khaldun. Jezebel tried several different stouts, porters, and even a hard cider. She liked the cider best—she couldn't get used to the bitterness of the beer.

Before she knew it, Jezebel was drunk. It was only the second time in her life she'd ever experienced more than mild intoxication. She enjoyed herself tremendously, sharing stories with the farmers.

They stayed at the bar late into the night. But finally, the guests began to depart. They all invited Khaldun and Jezebel to stay in Raymour for a few more nights. One of them even volunteered to pay for them to stay at the inn.

Khaldun and Jezebel made their way across the common room, stumbling toward the back hallway when suddenly there was a commotion at the doorway. Four soldiers barged into the inn, pushing aside two farmers who were trying to leave. They sat at a table in the middle of the room and loudly ordered beers. Jezebel's heart jumped into her throat: these were Henry's men.

Khaldun ushered her quickly out of the room. They made their way up the stairs. Jezebel collapsed on the bed, staring at the ceiling. The room seemed to spin slowly around; it was soothing, somehow, rather than unpleasant.

"What are Henry's men doing *here*?" she asked. She probably would have found their presence more alarming if she were sober, but on the other hand, the soldiers didn't have any reason to trouble *them*.

"I don't know," Khaldun said, lying next to her. "They're scouts, probably. Maybe he's planning his next conquest."

Jezebel giggled. "*His next conquest.* How about *your* next conquest?"

She rolled over on top of him and kissed him hungrily. Khaldun tried to push her away at first but gave up after only a few seconds. He started unbuttoning her shirt, but Jezebel pulled it off over her head instead.

Still kissing him, she wriggled her way out of her trousers, too. She moved her lips to his neck and began opening his tunic, one button at a time. Jezebel kissed down his neck and chest as she moved. His shirt off, she rolled to her side and started removing his trousers.

But then she stopped. She kissed him on the lips once more and asked, "How many have there been?"

"What..?" Khaldun asked as if pulled out of a trance.

"How many girls have you been with?"

"Oh. Well, there have been a few..."

"I know about Fina and the princess here in Madison. How many others?"

Khaldun thought about it for a moment. "Um... Six."

"Six!" Jezebel cried. "Including those two?"

"No..."

"Eight!"

"Wait—nine."

Jezebel laughed. "You're quite the harlot, aren't you?"

Khaldun shrugged. "That's the life of a wayfarer. Have you ever been with a man?"

"No," she replied proudly. "I've been waiting for the *right* man. You have the honor of deflowering me," she added with a giggle.

"And is Allison the only girl you've been with?"

Jezebel was stunned that he knew. She turned away, embarrassed.

Khaldun rolled toward her, kissing her neck. "It's nothing to be ashamed of. In fact, same-sex pairings are not uncommon among my people. I was simply curious."

"How did you find out?"

"That Will character told me the first time I met him. The night you and I went to your uncle's place actually. After you left. I didn't believe him at first—I assumed Will had simply invented that as an excuse for failing to get you into bed. But when I saw you with her at the castle, I realized it was true. The look you two shared… I could tell you were lovers."

"She's the only one," Jezebel whispered. "The first time was a couple of years ago—on my birthday. She slept over. I was drunk then, too, come to think of it."

"I'm sensing a pattern," Khaldun said with a sly grin. "Had you been attracted to her before that?"

"In a way. I've always thought she was beautiful. But I'd never thought about girls that way. She kissed me, and I was surprised. But it was… nice. I'd never been kissed before. I liked it. The next thing I knew, we were both naked. She touched me… and I touched her in return. We stayed up all night, exploring each other's bodies. It was like we'd discovered a secret, that was totally forbidden. It was exciting."

"But you like men, obviously," Khaldun said.

"Yes," she said with a mischievous smile, turning to kiss him.

"How is it you've never…"

"Gone to bed with a man?" she asked. Khaldun nodded. "Well, for one thing, there *are* certain pragmatic benefits to my relationship with the princess." Khaldun looked puzzled. "Girls can't make each other pregnant."

"Of course," he said with a nod.

"But more than that, I realized a few things with Allison. I discovered that physical attraction isn't enough for me. Will is *extremely* good-looking, but he's an imbecile." Khaldun chuckled. "Edward is intelligent but arrogant. Allison, on the other hand, is gorgeous, smart, wholly unconceited—"

"And female," Khaldun interrupted. "I think I begin to understand your dilemma. You've been unable to find a man who fits the bill as well as she."

"Yes, exactly… Until now," she said, smiling at him.

"You flatter me," he replied.

"You should know, however, that Allison does *not* like men. So you're barking up the wrong tree if you think you have any chance with her!"

"Ah," Khaldun said. "That explains your certainty."

Jezebel giggled at him. "I guess you'll have to settle for me, won't you?"

She kissed him and started removing his trousers again.

"You do bear a strong resemblance to the princess," he teased. "I guess you'll do."

Jezebel pretended to be offended. But then Khaldun got out of bed. "Where are you going?"

He opened his pack and returned to bed with a vial. He uncorked it and handed it to her. "There are other ways to avoid pregnancy. One mouthful will do."

Jezebel stared at him in disbelief. "Is this the potion you were brewing?"

"I told you it might come in useful."

Jezebel slapped him on the rear end. "You've been planning this all along!"

"Not *all* along," he said. "Only since our night in captivity."

"You ignored my flirting for weeks, but saw me naked and couldn't resist?"

"Precisely!" he said, grinning at her. "Now, drink up."

Jezebel took a swig and recorked the vial. Khaldun placed it on the chest and returned to bed. Jezebel pushed him onto the mattress and climbed on top of him. Kissing him passionately, she made love to him. He whispered Allison's name, so quietly that Jezebel could barely hear it.

Suddenly he froze and groaned deep in his throat. But then the pleasure seemed to turn to pain. His body seized up, and he cried out in agony. Jezebel got off of him, and he curled into a ball.

"What's wrong?!"

Khaldun couldn't answer. He started shaking violently. Jezebel tried to talk to him or soothe him, but to no avail. He began foaming at the mouth, and his eyes rolled up into his head.

Jezebel jumped out of bed—she had to get help. She threw on her clothes, not taking the time to button her shirt all the way. As she ran out the door, she remembered her wand. Jezebel grabbed it off the chest and left the room. She stumbled down the stairs, still inebriated.

CHAPTER ELEVEN
THE FERRY

ezebel emerged into the common room. Her eyes had adjusted to the dark; she thought the light would blind her. She squinted and made her way to the bar. The soldiers were still at their table, ogling her. She tried to ignore them.

"Everything all right?" the innkeeper asked, looking concerned. The three farmers at the bar turned to see what was going on.

"No—the wayfarer I was with—there's something wrong. He's sick."

"You folks had an awful lot to drink," he said with a knowing smile. "He'll sleep it off, don't worry."

"It's not that. He's having a seizure. Is there a healer near here?"

"Seizure, you say? Closest healer's in Madison Town. That's two days' ride…"

"Ugh!" Jezebel cried in exasperation. "That won't do—I'm scared he might be dying!"

"Let me take a look," the man said, walking around the end of the bar. "I've seen just about every kind of illness there is in my time. Maybe I can help."

"Thank you!" Jezebel said, following him across the room. But one of the soldiers got up and followed her.

"Hey there, sweetie! That wayfarer boy not man enough for you?"

Jezebel tried to keep walking, but the man rushed up behind her. He reached around and grabbed her chest. Jezebel turned and backed away violently, his grip ripping her shirt the rest of the way open. She pointed her wand and called fire. A wall of flame erupted between them. The soldier retreated clumsily and fell over a table. Jezebel canceled her spell and followed the innkeeper upstairs, doing her best to cover herself.

They found Khaldun sitting up in bed, the sheets pulled up around him, shivering. He looked horrible—his face was pale, and he was sweating profusely.

The bartender walked to the side of the bed. "She wasn't kidding— you don't look so good…"

Khaldun locked eyes with Jezebel. He pulled the sheet down to expose his chest. Jezebel stared in horror: his skin was turning golden before her eyes.

"Are the soldiers still here?" Khaldun asked quietly.

"Yes, sir," the innkeeper said, scared. "I've been trying to get them to leave…"

"No—make sure they stay!" Khaldun said urgently. "We're going to sneak out the back door. It's imperative that I escape their notice!"

The man nodded. "If you go east out of town, follow the road about a mile. You'll come to the River Mayne," he told them. "You can take the ferry across. I heard them talking—these soldiers are tracking Filmore and his family. Our prince ain't gonna take kindly to Henry's men invading our land. Tell the ferryman what's going on—and tell him I sent ya. He's a regular here. He'll tie up on the other shore for the night, and these goons won't get across."

"Thank you," Jezebel said fervently.

The man scurried out of the room.

"What the hell's going on?" Jezebel hissed. "What's happening to you—"

Khaldun got out of bed and let the sheet fall to the floor. He stood naked in front of her. Most of his body had turned golden in color. And while he'd been muscular before, something had changed. His body now looked like it had been chiseled from stone, every muscle in sharp relief.

Jezebel gasped. "You look like…"

"Nomad," Khaldun said with a nod. "It's the transformation. I'm becoming a sorcerer."

"But you can't—you told me it's in your blood. Either you are one, or you aren't—that's what you said!"

"Yes, but you aren't born that way! The metamorphosis can take place any time after the onset of puberty until early adulthood."

"Will you… survive?"

A harsh laugh escaped Khaldun's lips. "That depends. If we can get out of here without Henry's men seeing me, my odds should be quite good."

"Henry! I'd forgotten—you said he'd do anything to get his hands on a…"

"Sorcerer."

"We need to leave!" Jezebel said, suddenly frantic to collect their belongings. She handed Khaldun his clothes; he dressed quickly. They shouldered their gear, Khaldun grabbed his staff, and they left the room.

They went down the stairs as quietly as possible. No noise came from the common room. Khaldun crept out the rear door, Jezebel close behind.

They had to go around the back of the adjoining building to get to the road. Jezebel followed Khaldun to the stable, quiet as shadow. But inside, they heard voices. Jezebel peered through the entrance—it was the innkeeper and two of the soldiers.

"I can't let ya take their horses," the innkeeper said.

The men chuckled. "Who are you to tell us what we can't do?" one of them asked.

"These are fine animals," the other soldier said. "Well-bred. They don't look to be from Stiles, though. Where'd you say those two come from?"

"The boy's a wayfarer—he don't come from anywhere, you idiot," the first soldier replied.

"The girl does. And she's a witch—you saw her throw fire at me. Cordy's right. We have to report."

"*You* report—them wraiths give me the chills. They ain't gonna care about some stupid farm girl."

Khaldun grasped Jezebel's elbow and pulled her away.

"Our horses!" she hissed. "We can't go without them."

"Forget it—we need to get out of here. Now!" he whispered, walking away.

Jezebel grabbed him by the arm. "There are only two of them. We can handle this. We need the horses."

"No! We can't risk them seeing me!"

Khaldun looked panic-stricken. Jezebel couldn't understand it. But she followed him back the way they'd come, behind the buildings.

But suddenly the door of the inn burst open, and the other two soldiers walked out. One of them bumped into Khaldun. He backed away a step, hurling insults at him, then caught a glimpse of his face. The man froze.

Khaldun's skin had turned completely golden. The muscles in his face and neck stood out prominently.

"Sor-sorcerer," the man stammered, pointing at Khaldun. He grabbed his comrade and ran to the stable.

"Let's go!" Khaldun yelled, running to the road. Jezebel sprinted behind him, struggling to keep up.

They ran into a thick fog rolling up from the river. After a mile, they found the ferry lane. They might have missed it, but for the lamppost glowing in the dark. They stopped for a few seconds to catch their breath. Jezebel had a cramp in her side; she tried to relax and breathe deeply.

"I don't hear any pursuit," Khaldun observed. "Let's go."

They walked down the lane, gravel crunching under their feet. The fog was so thick they could barely see their hands in front of their faces. It grew pitch dark as they moved away from the lamppost. After about a hundred yards, they could discern another light ahead of them. They drew closer and saw the ferry tied to a small dock.

But suddenly they heard a noise. There were horses approaching fast. Khaldun and Jezebel scampered into the trees along the side of the lane. They ducked down and waited, watching apprehensively.

Jezebel's heart hammered in her chest. If the wraiths had caught up to them, they were doomed. They had no hope of outrunning them. And she clearly recalled Khaldun's warning after their last encounter. Unlike that night, now the wraiths *would* be seeking them specifically.

Seconds later, three horses appeared out of the fog. Jezebel held her breath as they trotted by. But they slowed down right in front of her; Jezebel could make out only one rider. He seemed to be scanning the lane, searching for something. He drew closer. Jezebel pointed her wand, ready to call fire. But the rider moved past them.

Khaldun and Jezebel didn't dare to move. They couldn't see anything, but they knew the rider would return any second.

Suddenly Jezebel heard a voice through the fog. "Hello there!" it called. That was no wraith—it was the innkeeper. Overcome with relief, Jezebel bolted out of the trees, Khaldun on her heels. They ran to the dock.

"There you are," the innkeeper said. The ferryman had just emerged from a small boathouse to greet him. He spotted Khaldun and stopped in his tracks. "Me and a couple of the farmers managed to waylay them soldiers. But one of them got away. Sounds like three of Henry's wraiths are camped a mile up the road. Reckon you'd better hurry."

"I couldn't agree more," said Jezebel.

"I brought you your horses," he said, handing them the reins.

"Thank you so much," Jezebel cried with gratitude.

"How can we repay you?" Khaldun asked.

"No need," the innkeeper said, "they were yours to begin with. Couldn't just stand by and watch them rob you like that."

"Thank you again," Jezebel said earnestly.

She and Khaldun packed the horses while the innkeeper helped the ferryman untie the boat. It was actually a small barge, big enough to transport a dozen horses or up to three wagon teams.

The innkeeper explained the situation to the ferryman. He sounded perfectly happy to tie up on the opposite shore for the night.

The innkeeper mounted his horse and disappeared into the fog. They shoved off from the dock. The ferryman lowered a pole into the water and began the task of pushing them to the opposite shore.

But suddenly, Jezebel heard a ghastly noise. A shrill cry emanated from the dock behind them; two more answered it. Dread and fear filled Jezebel's very soul. She strained her eyes to peer through the fog. Silhouetted against the lamplight, she could faintly perceive a horse and rider.

"Wraiths," Khaldun muttered.

There was another shriek. Suddenly a fire sprouted on the back of the boat. Jezebel pointed her wand and canceled the spell.

The ferryman looked back with terror in his eyes. He redoubled his effort, heaving his pole. Khaldun grabbed a pole and helped hasten their progress. Jezebel had her hands full blocking spells from the wraiths. But they gave up before long. Ten minutes later, they reached the other side. Khaldun helped them dock.

"How far to the next crossing?" he asked the ferryman.

"There's a bridge about ten miles upstream," he replied.

"We have to fly," Khaldun said to Jezebel. "We need to get to Arthos as quickly as possible."

"Arthos?!" the ferryman said. "That's two days' ride from here. You'll kill your horses before you get there."

"You have a better idea?" Jezebel asked impatiently.

"I'd hide if it were me. There's caves up in them hills," he said, pointing vaguely south. "'Bout ten or twelve miles down the road."

Jezebel opened her mouth to argue, but Khaldun spoke over her. "It may be our only hope. That will put some distance behind us, at least. And if we can evade them till dawn, we can travel all day in relative safety. Thank you," he added to the ferryman. He paid him, and they mounted their horses.

They had to keep the animals to a trot for the first mile—the fog made it impossible to go any faster. But after that, they let them gallop for almost two miles. They stopped to rest for a few minutes, then proceeded at a trot.

It was only about ninety minutes before they'd traveled into the hills. Soon after, they found a hunting path that veered to the east. They dismounted and led the horses into the woods.

They walked for nearly an hour. The path wound its way up and down increasingly rough terrain. Trees grew in the valley, but the peaks quickly turned into barren wastelands.

Finally, they found the perfect spot. It wasn't exactly a cave. Instead, it was a deep crevice in the rockface, wide enough for the horses, but narrow enough to be easily defended.

They led the animals inside and sat on the ground. Jezebel closed her eyes, rubbing her temples. The effects of the alcohol had worn off, but she had a terrible headache.

"You should do that spell to hide our trail," she suggested.

"I can't."

"What? Why not?"

"I can't do magic."

"What the hell are you talking about?"

"When you left the room to get help, I realized what was happening to me. I tried to call fire. Nothing happened."

"I don't understand."

"Neither do I," Khaldun said with a sigh. "I tried it with my staff, too. But that didn't work."

"Sorcerers are supposed to be able to do magic without wand or staff, right?"

Khaldun nodded.

"Your eyes are still normal," Jezebel observed. "Nomad's were red. Does that have anything to do with it?"

"I don't know. Sorcerers' eyes always look like Nomad's. I don't understand why mine haven't changed. Maybe it takes a while for the metamorphosis to complete.

"But that's why I didn't want to risk confronting the soldiers. If I hadn't lost my magic, it would have been easy. I could have made myself invisible. But like this?" He raised his arms in exasperation.

They sat in silence for a minute.

"So if the wraiths do come… I'm our only defense," Jezebel said quietly.

"Yes," Khaldun confirmed. "You can do it, Jez. Your command of fire is formidable—I still don't understand it, but it's perfect. With any luck you can use that to hold them off until dawn."

"They were able to disarm me last time," she pointed out.

"True. But if it happens here, it'll be easy to find your wand again," Khaldun replied, looking around them. "Where's it going to go? It's not like you can lose it in the underbrush."

"Should we light a fire?" she asked. "If I lose my wand in the dark, I'll never find it. Even here."

"Good idea," he said. "Darkness will provide no protection if they find our trail. We might as well."

They left the horses in the crevice and went to collect a night's supply of kindling. Jezebel started the fire when they returned.

"You should try calling earth again," Khaldun said. "It could be useful."

Jezebel hadn't tried it since their flight from Stiles. Khaldun had to remind her of the incantation. She pointed her wand at the wall and cast the spell.

Something enormous smashed into the rock. Dust and debris flew everywhere. Jezebel had to turn away to shield her eyes. When she looked back, she saw that she'd blown a hole through the corner of the wall, effectively widening the entrance to their hiding place.

Khaldun stared at her for a moment, his mouth open. "Don't do that again," he said. "We don't want the hill crashing down upon us."

"No," she agreed, thrilled, and scared at the same time. How could she possibly possess so much power?

"Try it on one of the trees," Khaldun suggested.

Jezebel moved out of the crevice. The land was awash in moonlight. She aimed straight across the valley, at one of the larger trees. She cast the spell, and the trunk splintered with a sharp crack as if someone had thrown an enormous boulder at it. The top third of the tree toppled over and crashed, hanging by a few strands.

"Perhaps that's enough practice," Khaldun said mildly.

"You're impressed, aren't you?" Jezebel said, smiling broadly.

"Certainly. The scope of your power remains fairly limited, but your command of earth now seems to rival your skill with fire. I've never seen anything like it."

Khaldun sat before the fire, his back against the wall. Jezebel settled down as well, leaning against him. "We're not going to make it, are we?" she asked quietly. "Even if we survive tonight, we're still a couple of days from Arthos. I'm not strong enough to defend us from three wraiths by myself. And if Henry wants a sorcerer as badly as you say he does, we'll be facing more than three of them before long."

Khaldun didn't reply at first. "It's true," he said finally, his voice grim. "When they attacked the wayfarers, they were relentless. Nomad could have handled them if he didn't have to protect the troupe. They only wanted him, so he could have fled to draw them off, but they would have butchered our people in the process. We had another mage at the time, too, but even so, we suffered several casualties."

"How did you defeat them?" Jezebel asked.

"We were in Stoutwall at the time. I rode ahead to the castle with a messenger from the local holding. The prince rode out with his sorcerer and some of their troops, and together, we drove the wraiths away."

They sat quietly for a long time. Jezebel strained her ears listening for the wraiths' ghastly cries. But the land was quiet. The crackling flames and the crickets in the woods provided the only noise.

"You're in love with Allison, aren't you?" Khaldun asked eventually.

"Yes," she replied without hesitation. "And I fear what she'll say when I tell her about tonight."

Khaldun chuckled softly. "It's not like you're *married*."

"No," she said. "But we started making plans to spend our lives together. Flirting with you was one thing. But sleeping with you was clearly out of bounds."

"So why did you do it? You spurned plenty of other suitors."

Jezebel sighed. "I was drunk. I gave in to my feelings. I'll admit, I've fallen in love with you, too."

"Would you choose me over Allison?"

"No. But I wish I didn't have to choose. My heart is big enough for both of you."

"You'd make a good wayfarer," Khaldun told her.

"Oh? How so?"

Khaldun collected his thoughts for a moment. "Our lives are less structured and rigid than what I've seen in the princedoms. When we're hungry, we eat; when we're tired, we sleep."

"And when you're horny, you fornicate?" Jezebel asked with a grin.

"Yes," Khaldun said with a shrug.

"Don't wayfarers get married?"

"Some do. But it's not too common. Most people have multiple partners."

"What about children?"

"What about them?"

Jezebel giggled. "How do you keep track of who's whose? If everyone's sleeping around all the time, there must be bastards everywhere."

"We don't have *bastards*," he said. "The concept is foreign to us. I grew up with Nomad because my parents died. But truthfully, I have no way to know for sure if my father was my *biological* father. It wouldn't have mattered. My parents would have raised me along with any other children my mother birthed. And besides, in large part, wayfarers raise their children communally."

"Interesting," Jezebel said. "And practical, given your nomadic lifestyle. But what about you? Are *you* in love with Allison?"

Khaldun let out a long sigh. "I don't know. There's something about her. I suppose I can't *love* her—I've never even spoken to her. But she's… enchanting."

"You just want to get her into bed," Jezebel teased.

"Of course," Khaldun admitted. "But it's much more than that. There's an attraction that I can't explain. When you two walked by our camp that day, I *felt* her before I saw either of you. It was the same sensation I always had when Nomad cast a powerful spell. A tingling, almost.

"I felt it again when we performed at the castle. Sitting so close to her was nearly unbearable. I was drawn to her like a magnet. You tell me, is that love?"

"Maybe," Jezebel said. "I've felt something similar—around both of you, to be honest. But tell me, why did you sleep with me if you think you're in love with *her*?"

Khaldun grinned. "There's a big difference between love and *lust*."

Jezebel laughed. "For certain."

"You're not upset?" Khaldun asked sarcastically. "I haven't broken your heart?"

"Not at all," Jezebel replied. "You've made my decision simple. I could never be with someone who didn't love me. So I choose Allison—if she'll still have me."

They didn't talk for a while. Jezebel grew drowsy.

"Sleep," Khaldun told her. "You're going to need your strength. I'll wake you if they find us. I should be able to sense them from far away now. We'll have sufficient warning."

Jezebel wasn't going to argue. She curled up with her head in his lap and drifted off to sleep immediately.

CHAPTER TWELVE
THE BLACK DRAGON

haldun shook Jezebel awake. She jumped to her feet.

"They're coming," he said, his face grim.

Jezebel moved to the edge of the crevice, looking out over the valley. The sky in the east was growing brighter above the opposite hill.

"Dawn in an hour, I think," Khaldun told her. "Maybe sooner. But they're almost upon us."

"I don't hear anything," Jezebel said.

"Neither do I. But I can feel them."

The next few minutes were tense. Jezebel had her wand drawn, ready to call fire or earth. Suddenly she heard a noise. There were voices echoing across the valley.

Jezebel retreated into the crevice. She picked out a branch from the unused firewood. Lighting thc cnd on fire, she handed it to Khaldun.

"Those voices belong to men," she told him. "That'll be better than nothing if they make it in here."

He nodded and moved a little deeper into the gap. Jezebel stood at the opening, scanning the path below. A few seconds later, she saw them.

There were four soldiers on horseback. She thought she recognized them as the men from the inn the previous night. Jezebel didn't wait to confirm her suspicion. She pointed her wand and called fire.

Jezebel showed no mercy. She ignited all four from within. They fell screaming from their horses. They rolled down the stony hill, into the valley, like so many torches. The horses whinnied in panic, turning to gallop back the way they'd come.

Suddenly there was a shrill cry in the forest below. Two others answered the call. Something massive struck the wall to Jezebel's left. She ducked inside the crevice as dust and debris exploded around her. One of the wraiths had blown a hole in the side of the hill, more substantial than Jezebel's earlier that night.

"How the hell do I defend against that?!" she shouted. "If they hit me, I'm dead!"

"Don't let them hit you!" Khaldun yelled back.

Jezebel dropped to her belly. She crawled to the path, careful not to present them too much of a target.

Far below, she could see two riders moving through the trees: these were the wraiths. But the innkeeper had said there were three—where was the third? She didn't wait to find out.

She called fire again, igniting two enormous trees directly in front of the riders. A second later, she called earth. Something huge smashed into the first rider's horse; it reared, throwing him from its back. Jezebel hit the second horse and its rider jumped off. Both animals bolted in terror.

Suddenly a tower of flame erupted directly in front of Jezebel. The heat was overwhelming; Jezebel scurried deeper into the opening. The horses whinnied nervously.

"Cancel it!" Khaldun yelled.

Jezebel shouted the incantation and spoke the word of command. The flames went out, leaving scorched earth.

Jezebel crept to the edge again. The two wraiths were clambering up the hill. She pointed her wand and called a wall of fire directly in their path. One of them extinguished it an instant later.

The other stood tall, holding his hands out to his sides. He shrieked, and there were words in his cry. Suddenly a coiled serpent appeared next to Jezebel. It reared its flat head, hissing at her. Its giant teeth were only inches from her face.

"It's not real!" Khaldun told her. "It's an illusion."

Jezebel didn't know what would happen if she were bitten by an imaginary cobra. She didn't wait to find out. Backing away carefully, she pointed her wand and incinerated the snake.

Another shrill cry rose from the valley. It felt like an earthquake had struck. Dirt and stones dribbled down on them from overhead.

Jezebel had an idea. Creeping closer to the edge again, she chose two of the nearest trees. She called earth twice in rapid succession, hitting each of them near the base of their trunks. The trees exploded as if struck by lightning. An instant later, she summoned fire, igniting them.

It worked: both trees fell toward the hill. The wraiths turned in surprise. One of them shrieked, casting some kind of spell. But it failed. One tree landed right on top of him. Jezebel could hear him wailing as his black robes caught fire. He was pinned.

Please, let him be roasted alive, Jezebel thought.

The second wraith had managed to avoid the danger. He resumed his climb up the hill.

But suddenly, there was a scream much closer. Jezebel turned: the third wraith was storming up the path on his horse, bearing down on her. She scampered out of the way, only just in time. The wraith had called earth. The spell slammed into the ground, forming a crater across the opening to the crevice. Dirt and rocks showered Jezebel as she rolled away.

She got to her feet and spat dirt out of her mouth. The wraith had reined in his horse and now stood across the crater from her. Jezebel hated to do it, but she called fire and ignited his animal from the inside. It burst into flames, engulfing the wraith.

The dead animal fell over, taking its rider with it as it toppled down the hill. Jezebel climbed into the crater and peered over the far edge. There was nothing to see. But she crawled out the other side just as the last wraith crested the hill, directly in front of her.

Jezebel backpedaled and lost her balance. She fell into the crater, dropping her wand. The wraith called fire, and a wall of flame sprung up around the edge of the hole. The circle tightened, closing in around her. Jezebel saw the wraith jump over her as she scuttled to retrieve her wand.

She put out the flames and scrambled out of the crater. The wraith was bearing down on Khaldun. He brandished the flaming branch in front of him, trying to light the wraith's robes. But the wraith extinguished the flame.

Jezebel pointed her wand, reciting the spell to call earth. But the spell had no effect. The wraith rounded on her and hit her with a spell of his own. It walloped her in the midsection, launching her clear across the crater.

Jezebel hit the ground hard and lost her wand. She tried to regain her balance but failed, rolling uncontrollably down the hill, past one of the flaming trees.

She came to rest in the valley and scrambled to her feet. It took a few seconds to get her wind back. Jezebel's heart sank—Khaldun was still up there.

And then she saw the fallen wraith only feet away, moving toward her. Panic-stricken, Jezebel started her climb back up the hill, desperate to find her wand. But suddenly there was a horrible scream from above. It was much louder than anything before. And in that instant, Jezebel's heart lifted. The sun peeked over the opposite hill, its light filling their crevice.

A black shape flew from the opening and streaked down the hill like the wind. It disappeared into the forest, shrieking the entire way. The other wraith looked up, saw the sunlight, and bolted after its partner.

Jezebel clambered up the hill. It was difficult, with stones slipping beneath her hands and feet. She saw the wraith pinned under the burning tree as she went by. Somehow, the thing was still alive. It was silent but struggling to free itself.

Khaldun called out to her from the path. Her heart soared: he was still alive. She made it to the top, and he helped her to her feet. Jezebel told him about the trapped wraith.

"We should kill it before we leave," he said. "There will be one less for our pursuit."

"How do you kill a wraith?" Jezebel asked.

"You'll see," he said with a grim smile.

They packed everything first and searched for Jezebel's wand. It had rolled down the hill, landing close to where she'd fallen earlier.

Khaldun found a large stone, and they climbed back toward the wraith. He instructed Jezebel to put out the burning tree. She did so, and they approached their enemy.

The wraith seemed to be unconscious. It moved jerkily as if having a nightmare. Its robes were charred to dust, revealing its blackened body. In some places, its bones showed through the skin.

Khaldun crawled within inches of the monster. He smashed its skull repeatedly with the rock. Then he pulled a knife from his belt and began cutting off its head. It was grisly work. It took more than thirty minutes to saw through the tendons and sinews and sever it completely.

Once he was done, he left the head next to the body. They clambered away.

"Dredmort might still be able to bring it back," he told Jezebel once they'd reached the path. "You need to call the hottest fire you can. It will burn now, but you need to reduce it to ash to make sure it can't come back."

Jezebel nodded. She turned to face the wraith. Focusing for a minute, she pointed her wand and cast the spell. A blaze erupted that consumed the entire hillside, burning white-hot around the wraith. They had to move into the crevice to escape the heat.

Jezebel looked at Khaldun. His eyes were still normal. But his face was golden. There was no mistaking what he was.

"Has your magic returned?" she asked.

"No," he said with a sigh. "I don't understand it."

Jezebel removed her shirt. Khaldun stared at her. "What are you doing? This is hardly the time…"

"Don't worry, I'm not in the mood," she said with a grin. "But we need to make some attempt to disguise you. Until your power comes back, we don't want people knowing what you are."

"Good point," he muttered.

"This is already ripped to shreds," she said, tossing him her shirt. "See if you can fashion a hood out of it. We've got to cover your face."

Jezebel dug through her pack and removed another shirt. She threw it on while Khaldun tore her old one apart.

Twenty minutes later, Jezebel put out the conflagration. They couldn't approach the remains of the wraith because of the heat still emanating from the ground. But Khaldun was pretty sure she'd done the job. They mounted their horses and set out down the path.

When they emerged from the woods, they stopped for a minute by the side of the road. Khaldun donned his makeshift hood.

"You look ridiculous," Jezebel told him.

"Thank you," he said. "We'll probably be safe as long as the daylight lasts. We don't want to injure the horses; we'll have to keep it to a trot if we want them to last the entire journey. But we need to put as many miles behind us today as possible."

"What makes you so sure Dredmort won't come here himself?" Jezebel asked.

"He probably will," Khaldun replied. "But it will take time for the wraiths to get a message to him. And it will take days for Dredmort to get here. We've got enough of a head start that we should be able to make Arthos well before he does."

"And what then?" Jezebel asked. "What's to stop them from attacking us there?"

"Arthos is a free democratic city. It's independent of any princedom. And it's got a strong military—it has to, to survive. They won't allow Dredmort to enter the city in force."

"They have witches and wizards?"

"Yes," Khaldun replied. "A dozen or more. Arthos is something of a haven for mages. Probably due to its proximity to the university."

"Let's hope we make it that far," Jezebel said. "I'm worried about surviving another night."

They headed southeast on the road.

"You know, you should consider attending the university," Khaldun told her.

"I don't think so," Jezebel said. "My life is in Spanbrook."

"Suit yourself," he said. "But you'd thrive in that environment. With your power…"

"What power? I can only do a few spells!"

"True," Khaldun said. "But you're more powerful than I am—well, than I *was*. I couldn't have produced that inferno you summoned back there."

"Truly?"

"Not even close, and I've been doing magic for years. But I'm only a novice. There are people at the university who could teach you things I couldn't even begin to describe."

"I guess I'll think about it," she said.

They rode all day, stopping a few times to eat and let the animals rest. As sunset approached, they tried to find somewhere sheltered to make camp. But the country was flatter here. In between the random town or village, it was mostly farmland.

Eventually, they found a stand of trees and made camp in the hollow between them. But as they set up the tent, they noticed flashes of light in the western sky.

"Is that lightning?" asked Jezebel.

"I don't think so," Khaldun replied, gazing intently back the way they'd come. "There's not a cloud in the sky."

"What is it then?"

Khaldun didn't reply for a few moments.

"It's magic," he replied finally. "I can feel it."

"Magic? Is it the wraiths? What are they doing?"

"I don't know. Perhaps we should keep going," Khaldun suggested.

"What, overnight?" asked Jezebel.

"The wraiths' mounts are normal horses," he said. "If they force them to gallop too far, they'll die. We've probably gone over twenty miles today. It would take them most of the night to catch us—but they *would* catch us. If we keep going…"

"Wait a minute—you haven't slept in days. You stayed awake last night watching for the wraiths. And before that, you didn't sleep since before the inn."

Khaldun shrugged. "I'm not sleepy. We should go as far as we can."

They broke camp and continued on their course. But by midnight, Jezebel was struggling to keep her eyes open. She followed Khaldun off the road. They didn't bother making camp; Jezebel curled up on the soft ground. Khaldun stood watch, and within minutes, Jezebel fell asleep.

Khaldun woke her before dawn. She sat up, instantly alert. "What is it?"

"Nothing," he said. "It's been quiet. I'm a little surprised we haven't at least encountered any soldiers. The wraiths may hide from daylight, but the rest of Henry's men do not."

"Maybe our lead is too great," she said. Jezebel was famished. She pulled some meat and fruit out of her pack and ate.

"Perhaps," Khaldun said skeptically. "But we should get moving as soon as you're ready."

They rode all day. Jezebel failed to understand how Khaldun was able to go so long without sleep.

They stopped at sunset to eat. Jezebel fetched the mirror from her pack. She spoke to Allison for a long time. She told her everything that had happened since the last time they talked, omitting only her sexual encounter with Khaldun. She decided that conversation would work better in person.

Allison seemed to be enjoying herself. Not once had the demon made an appearance. She socialized as much as possible with everyone she met. And she'd even had two marriage proposals. Aldo wasn't amused.

Khaldun and Jezebel traveled late into the night again. By the time they stopped, Jezebel was exhausted. Khaldun kept watch again while she went to sleep.

Jezebel woke to find the sun well above the horizon. Khaldun was eating. She stretched and groaned.

"I can't wait to sleep in a bed again," she said.

Khaldun smiled at her. "Tonight, hopefully. We should make Arthos before sunset."

Sure enough, they arrived at the city with almost an hour of daylight to spare. Jezebel's first glimpse of the area had taken place as they rounded a low hill. She couldn't believe its sheer size. The city seemed to sprawl to the horizon. It was bigger than anything she'd ever imagined.

They skirted the outlying houses and found a barn. It was far enough from the farmhouse for them to enter unseen. Khaldun hid there with his horse and sent Jezebel into the city to find his favorite inn.

"It's called the Black Dragon," he said. "Stick to the road into the city. It's two or three blocks past the guard station, on the right. You can't miss it."

"Is there a sign?" Jezebel asked skeptically.

Khaldun laughed. "Yes, an enormous one. Take this." He handed her their money pouch. "Pay for three nights."

"Three?"

"We have to figure out a way to leave the city unnoticed by Henry's men," Khaldun said. "I know some people here who might be willing to help us."

Jezebel raised her eyebrows at him.

Khaldun laughed again. "Don't worry—I've never slept with anyone in Arthos. This won't be a repeat of Stiles, I promise. Anyway, it might take some time to find my friends. If we need more than three nights, we can extend our stay. Come right back once you've secured us a room. It should be dark by then; I'll be able to sneak into the city unseen."

"What if Henry's men show up here?" she asked. "What will you do?"

"They won't. Our lead is certainly too great by now."

Jezebel nodded. She kissed him on the cheek and mounted her horse. She approached the guard station five minutes later. To avoid attracting undue attention, she stuffed her wand inside her shirt. The guards waved her through without questioning her.

Arthos was bustling with activity. There were people everywhere. Jezebel rode up the street and, sure enough, found the Black Dragon without a problem. A black signboard ran across the entire front of the building, with a dragon carved into it in gold. A separate sign hung over the door with the words "Black Dragon."

The building was enormous. It was four stories tall and appeared to take up an entire city block. Jezebel tied her horse and went inside.

The front room served as a reception area. Jezebel walked up to the counter. The man there was friendly and helpful. She paid for three nights and requested something on the ground floor. He gave her a set of keys and told her where to find her room.

Jezebel thanked him and walked through the double doors at the end of the counter. She emerged into a huge common room, not too crowded, with a separate tavern behind it. Across the common room, she went through another set of doors and down a long hallway. At the end of the passage, there was an exit to her right. Their room was across from that.

"Perfect," Jezebel muttered with a smile.

She let herself into the room. It was much more spacious than the accommodations in the last inn. And it had a back door.

Curious, Jezebel walked to the window. She moved the drapes aside to reveal a courtyard in the center of the quad.

She left the room by the front door, locked it, and went out of the adjacent exit. Jezebel found the stables next to the inn. She returned to the front of the building and mounted her horse. The sun had set by the time she made it back to Khaldun's hiding place in the barn.

She told Khaldun how to find their room, suggesting that he use the side entrance to the inn. He handed her the reins to his horse, and they left the barn. Khaldun disappeared into the night. Jezebel rode back into town, leading the second animal.

The guards on duty gave her a strange look. She guessed it must have looked rather odd for someone to be leading a packed, saddled, riderless horse. But luckily, the shift had changed; these weren't the same people she'd seen earlier. She figured those men probably would have questioned her if they'd seen her pass through a second time after so short an interval.

Jezebel stabled the horses and carried her gear into the room. She had to make a second trip for Khaldun's packs. After that, she waited by the door. Five minutes later, there was a soft knock. It was Khaldun.

They settled into the room, and Khaldun collapsed on the bed.

"I'm getting tired now," he said with a sigh.

"No wonder," Jezebel replied. "How long has it been since you slept? I'm not sleepy, but I *am* starving. I'll go get us some food."

"Yes, a hot meal sounds good right now," he agreed.

Jezebel wandered down the hall to the common room and went into the tavern. The place was reasonably busy now. She sat at the bar and ordered dinner. The fare was fancier here than in Raymour. Jezebel selected the house specialty: a chicken dish with noodles and fresh vegetables. She also chose a bottle of wine from a local vineyard.

Jezebel scanned the room while she waited. There were many farmers here. But there were also merchants and businessmen. She spotted two women who could only be prostitutes. And in the far corner sat a very strange-looking man.

His robes were a patchwork of brown and green. He had wild, scraggly hair and a long beard. He was smoking a pipe. And Jezebel realized with a start that he was staring back at her from under his bushy eyebrows. He lifted his mug to her.

Jezebel turned away. She had no idea who he might be, but she didn't like the look of him. He was probably some local lunatic. She knew the type; there was one in Spanbrook who frequented her uncle's place. He was always predicting people's futures based on the movements of the stars and foretelling the end of the world.

Her food was ready a short while later. The bartender brought it out on a large tray. She stuffed the wine bottle under one arm and carried the tray out of the room. The old man in the corner was gone.

Jezebel walked through the common room and down the hall. But as she approached her door, the crazy-looking old man walked in from the outside.

"Good evening," he said, his voice low and resonant. "Jezebel of Spanbrook, I presume?"

"Never heard of her," she said, suddenly very frightened. Who the hell was this man? And how did he know her name? She banged on her door with one foot; it opened to admit her. Jezebel slid inside, and Khaldun closed the door behind her, careful not to reveal himself.

"Who was that?" he whispered.

Jezebel told him the whole story.

"Apparently, Henry has men stationed in Arthos," Khaldun said, looking scared. "They must have been watching for us. This makes matters more difficult."

"How would they know about us? No messenger could have arrived here any faster than we did."

"They might have mirrors or seeing stones," Khaldun said.

"Damn. I forgot about that. What are we going to do?"

Khaldun thought for a minute. "We need to leave. We can sneak out the back and disappear into the city. I know Arthos well."

"What about the horses? And our gear?"

"It'll only slow us down. Once I locate my friends, and we find a way to leave the city unnoticed, we can buy what we need."

"Not horses—we don't have enough for that."

"No matter. We're close to the university now. We can walk the rest of the way."

Jezebel took a deep breath. She looked longingly at the food and the feather bed. "So be it. Let's go."

She moved to the window and pulled the drapes aside an inch or two, peering outside. "It's clear."

Khaldun opened the door. But as Jezebel crossed the threshold, the crazy old man appeared out of nowhere, holding a wand to her throat. He pushed her back into the room.

CHAPTER THIRTEEN
RAPHAEL

ezebel backed away, stumbling into Khaldun. The old man moved into the room. The door slammed shut behind him, seemingly of its own accord.

"You're… You're a wizard," Jezebel stammered, staring at his wand.

"Well spotted," the man replied, a twinkle in his eye. "I'm called Raphael. I would have introduced myself earlier if you'd given me the opportunity."

"What do you want?" Jezebel asked. She knew very well what—or whom—he wanted. But she was trying to buy some time to think of a way out of this. Her wand was in her pocket. If she could distract him somehow, get his eyes off of them for just a moment, she might be able to draw it.

"My primary goal is to get the two of you out of this city," Raphael replied.

Jezebel started inching away from Khaldun. If she could put enough distance between them, and get the man to look in Khaldun's direction, she could slide her hand into her pocket without attracting his notice.

"What's the point?" Khaldun asked spitefully. "Wouldn't it be easier to keep us here until the wraiths arrive? They'll probably be here by morning."

"Sooner than that, I'm afraid," Raphael said. "And that is why we must leave immediately. We won't make it out of the city tonight— we'll have to hide you for now. I've secured a room across the quad.

If we can move you there unseen, you should be safe for a day or two. With a little luck, the enemy might even assume you've departed when they find your room empty."

"You want to *keep* us from the wraiths?!" Khaldun asked, befuddled. Jezebel took a few more steps away from him. "What—are you trying to upstage Dredmort or something? Earn points with Henry for bringing him a sorcerer yourself?"

"*Why* would I want to bring you to Henry?" Raphael demanded. "That's exactly what we must avoid!"

Khaldun and Jezebel both stared at him incredulously.

A look of sudden comprehension washed over Raphael's face. "You don't remember me, do you?" he asked Khaldun. "I guess that shouldn't surprise me. We met only once, many years ago. Right after Nomad started teaching you."

Jezebel turned her body slowly, hiding her right side from Raphael. She slipped her hand into her pocket.

"I don't know any *Nomad*," Khaldun said.

Raphael shook his head disapprovingly. "You're not a good liar, Khaldun. You're obviously a wayfarer, and every mage on the continent knows that Nomad travels with the troupe."

Jezebel drew her wand, pointing it at Raphael. "That's enough. Drop your wand. *NOW!*"

Raphael stared at her in surprise for a moment. Then he shook his head. "I assure you, Lady Jezebel, I mean you no harm. But if you wish to escape those who do, we must remove Khaldun from this room as quickly as possible."

"Why should we trust you?" Jezebel demanded. "We've never seen you before. How do we know the wraiths aren't waiting for us across the quad?"

"You are wise to be suspicious. But if I intended to bring you to Henry, we wouldn't be standing here enjoying this pleasant conversation. You'd both be unconscious by now, probably bound and gagged. And I certainly wouldn't have let you keep your wand."

"*Let* me keep my wand?" Jezebel demanded.

Something smashed into her right arm. Her wand flew out of her hand and vanished.

Raphael raised his eyebrows at her. "Now. Come with me. When we get to my room, I promise I will explain everything."

Jezebel didn't see that they had a choice. She moved to the door, Khaldun right behind her.

"Henry's spies are sure to be watching," Raphael told them. "I'm going to make us invisible. But stay quiet. The spell doesn't block sound."

"What about our gear?" Jezebel asked.

"I'll return for it once we've secured Khaldun," Raphael told her.

He led them into the night. Only a few other people were in the courtyard. One was sitting on the edge of a fountain in the middle of the quad. A young couple strolled along the walkway behind the tavern. Jezebel scanned the windows lining the walls all around them, searching for prying eyes. She saw no one.

They walked through an opening in the far corner and went back inside the building. Raphael opened a door halfway down the hall and ushered them inside.

Jezebel still half-expected to find wraiths waiting for them. But the room was empty. Raphael lit a small lamp on the chest of drawers.

"Wait here, and I'll retrieve your belongings," the wizard said. "I've put a spell on the windows to prevent anyone from seeing inside. Nobody will know you're here, even if they press their nose to the glass."

"Could you bring the food, too?" Jezebel asked. "I'm famished. And the wine. It'll go a long way toward earning our trust."

Raphael grinned at her and left the room.

"I think I believe him," Khaldun said. "I do vaguely recall meeting an old wizard once when I was very young. It could have been him."

"Yes," Jezebel agreed. "It's clear he would be acting differently if he were working for Henry."

Jezebel sat at the table by the window. She peered outside but could see no sign of Raphael's passage. She kept her eye on the door to their old room but never saw it move. Five minutes later, Raphael returned. He seemed to be empty-handed. But with a flick of his wand, their gear appeared in the corner, the tray of food in his left hand. He walked across the room and set it down on the table. He produced the bottle of wine from inside his robes and handed Jezebel her wand.

"How did you carry so much in one trip?" she asked.

Raphael raised one eyebrow at her.

"He called air, Jez," Khaldun explained. "You can make things weightless."

"Oh," she replied, mystified.

"Eat while it's still warm," Raphael suggested. "We have much to discuss once you've finished."

Khaldun and Jezebel scarfed down their food. Raphael sat on the edge of the bed and lit his pipe. Jezebel took a swig of wine and offered it to the wizard. He turned it down with a wave of his hand. She passed it to Khaldun instead. And in the dim lamplight flickering across the room, they talked.

"So. Trust can wait until later," Raphael said. "For now, do you believe that I do not work for Henry?"

Jezebel nodded.

"Who *do* you work for?" asked Khaldun.

"No one," the wizard replied. "At least, officially. I operate behind the scenes, opposing Henry and others like him. I endeavor to undermine his power. I haven't been too successful, you may think—I can see it in your eyes. But I assure you, without my efforts, Henry would be even stronger than he is already. I have, at least, been able to help confine him to Maeda for the time being, and west of the River Mayne. It is a lonely business, for the most part. Although there are a few others like me. The university, shall we say, tacitly approves of our activities, although they cannot openly condone them."

"Why not?" asked Jezebel.

"They must maintain the pretense of neutrality, of course," Raphael said. "As the guardians of occult knowledge on the continent, they cannot be perceived as favoring any one princedom over any other."

"So you're helping us to make sure Henry doesn't acquire me?" Khaldun asked.

"Yes. We must get you to the university. However, given your current condition, that task may prove impossible."

"Why? What condition?" Jezebel asked.

"As I'm sure Khaldun is aware, Henry would stop at nothing to obtain a sorcerer. I shudder to think what he might achieve if he were to enlist such a mage. But finding an *unbound* sorcerer parading across the countryside… That would make his job far too easy for my liking. You can be certain that he will pursue you with particular zeal.

"This begs the question, what was Nomad *thinking*, allowing you to journey alone in your state?"

Khaldun slumped in his chair. "Aldo's necromancer killed Nomad. We set out for the university on separate business. I didn't transform until a few nights ago."

Raphael started in surprise. "*Myrddin* killed Nomad? Why?"

"My cousin—Princess Allison—is being haunted by a demon," Jezebel explained. "It possessed Nomad and… raped her. Aldo ordered him killed. Myrddin told me he knows a way to destroy the demon. But Aldo refuses to allow it. He says it's too dangerous. So Khaldun and I are going to the university to see Enigma. We're hoping he might be able to help us."

Raphael smoked his pipe for a moment, looking troubled. "This is grievous news. Nomad was an old, dear friend. You are right to seek Enigma—he may be the only one who can help you. The university upholds the ban on necromancy with something akin to religious fervor. Enigma is more open-minded and wiser than most.

"But unfortunately, he has left the university."

"What?!" Khaldun blurted. "But he was a governor! He can't leave."

"Normally, that's true," Raphael said, taking a deep breath. "A governorship is a lifetime appointment. But Syllith was censured and forced to resign—I've not been able to find out why. She left the university; Enigma retired soon after. That was almost six months ago."

"Who's Syllith?" Khaldun asked.

"She's a witch, and Enigma's conjurnor," Raphael told them. "He's bound to her," he added in response to their blank stares.

"I'm sorry," said Khaldun. "You used that term before, too—but I don't know what it means for someone to be *bound*."

"Ah," Raphael replied, heaving a great sigh. "This is going to take some explaining. But you must understand.

"The metamorphosis you underwent opens your channels of power. That's why a sorcerer can conjure without wand or staff. Your very body becomes the physical conduit for the magical force.

"For millennia, it has been common practice for a sorcerer to be *bound*. The mage's soul is tethered to another, sometimes a ruling prince or princess—or a king in the old days. The rite is ancient; it predates the Pythan Empire by hundreds of years, at least.

"A sorcerer serves the person to whom he or she is bound—the conjurnor—and cannot cause them harm, magically or physically. Thus it is impossible for such a mage to overthrow the ruler and seize power. And of course, sorcerers are never allowed to rule."

"Why not?" asked Jezebel.

"Too much power," said Raphael. "Only once has a necromancer or sorcerer ever sat upon a throne. The results were disastrous.

"In any event, a sorcerer's binding cannot be undone, unless the conjurnor dies. Furthermore, the rite makes the mage's true name known to the conjurnor."

"*True name*?" Khaldun asked.

"Every mage has one," Raphael said, nodding. "Most never learn it themselves. Knowing your true name would give you power over your own soul. You could stop yourself from dying. But if anyone else were to learn it, they would have the power to banish you from existence."

"What does that mean?" Khaldun asked fearfully.

"It means you would die, and your soul would be destroyed. You would not live on as a spirit or demon."

"So… That means a conjurnor could kill his sorcerer simply by naming him?" Jezebel asked. "Aldo could murder Myrddin with a *word*?"

"Essentially correct," Raphael said. "Every sorcerer—or necromancer, in Myrddin's case—is bound to *someone*. Nomad was bound to Badru. Myrddin to Aldo. There are six sorcerers on the council of governors at the university. Each is bound to a different witch or wizard, who also sits on the board. No one council member is ever allowed to act as conjurnor for more than one sorcerer. This ensures that none of them can ever grow too powerful.

"The same holds for the princedoms. The university rarely allows a sorcerer to take an assignment in the outside world. But it *never* allows any ruler to control more than one sorcerer. The consequences were devastating the last time that happened."

"When was that?" asked Khaldun.

"Don't you know your history?" Raphael demanded. "That's how the Pythan Empire started! King Saliman of Pytha was assigned a sorcerer. Her name was Nyro; she was bound to the king. Soon after her appointment, Nyro became a necromancer—an extremely powerful one. Together, over a period of many years, Nyro and Saliman managed to abduct a handful of unbound sorcerers. The operation was totally clandestine; the sorcerers disappeared on their way to the university, and nobody knew what had happened to them.

"But eventually, the king revealed his true power and began the conquest of the continent. By that time, every one of his sorcerers had become a necromancer. They controlled powerful demons that terrorized the land. Nobody could resist them. Within a few years, Saliman annexed the entire kingdom of Shifar. He murdered the king and his family, leaving no possible heir.

"Maeda fell next. And as Saliman brought more sorcerers into the fold, it wasn't long before they subverted Kong and Dorshire as well.

"But in the end, Saliman was betrayed. Not even Nyro could *undo* her bond. But she discovered a way to *reverse* it—nobody else has ever found the spell. She became the conjurnor, taking back her true name. Saliman no longer had the power to destroy her, and instead was bound to *her*. Of course, the other twelve necromancers—known as the Sacred Circle—were still bound to Saliman, so Nyro kept him alive. She commanded the others through him. When Saliman died, the bond of every necromancer in the Circle transferred to his heir. But the heir also inherited Saliman's bond to Nyro.

"Under Nyro, the continent endured three hundred years of darkness. Her power was unimaginable, and she was like a god. Mortal men were mere chattel to her. Only when the surviving lines of princes united and sought the help of the elves from across the Lonely Sea was Nyro finally overthrown. The elves killed the necromancers and destroyed their demons."

"How did you know Khaldun was unbound?" Jezebel asked.

"His eyes," Raphael replied. "The rite of binding turns the irises red."

"That explains it," Khaldun said with a nod. "But wait—Henry and Dredmort tried to take Nomad once. How would that have worked if he was bound to Badru?"

"They would have murdered Badru and his heirs," Raphael said simply. "That would have left Nomad unbound. Dredmort knows the spell of binding. He would have established Henry, or possibly himself as Nomad's conjurnor."

"Why murder Badru's heir?" Jezebel asked.

"Because Nomad's bond would have passed to that person in the event of Badru's death," Raphael explained. "Typically, naming an heir is a simple legal matter. But in the case of a conjurnor, there is a magical rite that must be invoked as well. It is typical for a conjurnor to name a line of succession at least three deep. That way, even if someone murders the heir, the sorcerer's bond still passes to someone in that person's line.

"That's how Enigma came to be bound to Syllith. Ferdinand, his former conjurnor, was very old. Syllith was something of a prodigy at the university. She was designated heir, and Enigma's bond passed to her when Ferdinand died. To the best of my knowledge, she was the youngest mage ever appointed to the council."

"But I'm unbound," Khaldun said, suddenly seeming to comprehend the magnitude of his danger. "If Henry catches me…"

"You finally understand," Raphael said with a grim smile.

"Can you bind me?"

"I? No. Only the governors possess the spell of binding."

"Then how does Dredmort know it?" Jezebel asked. "Surely, he's not a governor?"

"No. In fact, Dredmort was expelled from the university for experimenting with necromancy," Raphael told them.

"I've heard about that," said Khaldun. "But then I learned that only sorcerers could become necromancers."

"Strictly speaking, that is true," Raphael replied. "But Dredmort has gone farther along the path than any other non-sorcerer. The spell of binding comes from necromancy originally, believe it or not. Dredmort managed to discover the enchantments that make up the rite and performed it on another wizard. But only a sorcerer can be bound to a non-sorcerer—or vice-versa."

"So, what happened?" Jezebel asked quietly.

"That's how he created the wraiths," Khaldun said with a look of dawning comprehension.

"Indeed," said Raphael. "Horrible creatures who no longer possess a soul of their own. They provide Dredmort with terrible power, but he is no necromancer."

"I saw him convert one of them," said Khaldun, "but I didn't know that was the rite of binding—I didn't know anything about that at the time."

"Wait—you *saw* him do it?" asked Jezebel.

"Yes," Khaldun replied, taking a deep breath. "Remember when I told you about fighting the wraiths on the way to Stoutwall?" Jezebel nodded. "That started when Henry sent an army to retrieve an ancient artifact from Stanbridge, and the wayfarers got caught up in the conflict. I ended up breaking into Henry's castle with another mage to retake the artifact, and that's when I saw Dredmort create one of the wraiths. But my understanding was that he wasn't powerful enough to do that without the artifact."

"Yes, but that's only because he was using the rite on normal mages," Raphael explained. "It was designed for sorcerers. Dredmort had to alter the incantations to get them to work on witches and wizards, but didn't possess sufficient power to complete the rite that way—he could only do it with the artifact. But I do not believe he would have any trouble binding a sorcerer."

"Can a sorcerer be bound to another sorcerer?" asked Khaldun.

"No," Raphael replied.

"What happens if you try?" Jezebel asked, imagining something worse than a wraith.

"Nothing," Raphael said with a shrug. "The rite has no effect."

They sat in silence for a few minutes, Jezebel and Khaldun absorbing everything Raphael had told them. Raphael took several long draws on his pipe, blowing out the smoke in rings.

"What am I going to do now?" Jezebel asked finally. "Allison's still in danger. I have to find a way to destroy the demon. But with Enigma gone…"

"Our more immediate concern must be Khaldun," Raphael said. "We should still try to get to the university. Only there will he be safe. And I'm sure Enigma will have left word of his destination."

"They'll bind me?" Khaldun asked.

"Yes," Raphael replied. "Either to a mage at the university, or possibly to a prince or princess somewhere."

"Do I have any say in the matter?"

"Likely not," Raphael said. "The council will decide if they want to assign you to a princedom. If so, you will complete your education first, then relocate to your assignment. But as I said, that happens infrequently."

"I don't want to spend my entire life at the university," Khaldun said. "Is there any way I can convince them to assign me to Badru—to take Nomad's place?"

"Don't count on it," Raphael replied, shaking his head. "Enigma performed the rite for Nomad—countermanding the council's decision. He was always partial to the wayfarers."

"Then I'll wait until we find Enigma," Khaldun said stubbornly. "He can bind me to Badru."

"Perhaps," said Raphael. "For now, we will make for the university to escape the current danger. You must not fall into Henry's hands. Once there, we can decide how to proceed."

"What about my magic?" Khaldun asked. "When will that return?"

"Ah, yes," Raphael said, getting to his feet. "With that, I can help. I realized your dilemma when I saw that you were still carrying your staff. You'll need to remove your clothes."

"What?!" Khaldun demanded, getting up from the table.

Raphael picked up Khaldun's staff.

"We have to transfer your power from your staff back into your body. So… strip."

Jezebel giggled. Khaldun removed his clothing, and Raphael handed him the staff.

"This isn't going to be pleasant," he warned him. "Hold the wood tight to your torso. You must not let go, no matter how painful it becomes."

"I understand," Khaldun replied apprehensively.

Raphael rose to his full height, holding his arms out to his sides and pointing his wand at Khaldun. He spoke a long series of enchantments, finally uttering the word of command. There was a brilliant flash of light, and the staff began to glow. Khaldun winced. But the staff continued to increase in brightness. Jezebel watched his features contort in pain, but soon had to look away to avoid being blinded.

Eventually, there was a quick tearing noise, and the room grew dark again. Jezebel looked up to see Khaldun swoon. Raphael managed to catch him—he moved quickly for an old man, Jezebel noted. He eased him onto the floor. Khaldun's staff was gone.

Khaldun regained consciousness a few moments later. Jezebel helped him back to his feet. He held out his hand and called fire. A small flame formed in his palm; his sense of relief was palpable.

"You see, Lady Jezebel?" Raphael said with an amused grin. "No agent of the enemy would give Khaldun back his magic."

"I'm sorry for doubting you," she said. "And I do trust you now. But if I might ask, how did you know we were here?"

Raphael sat at the table and relit his pipe.

"I was in Stiles when Henry sacked the castle. Unfortunately, Filmore perished… stubborn old goat. But I helped Fina and her people escape. We moved east to the university, while an associate of mine laid a false trail to the north. Fina told me of your ordeal—that was the first I'd heard of your adventure.

"After I left the university, my associate contacted me," he said, producing a mirror slightly larger than Jezebel's. He placed it on the table. "An innkeeper in Madison came to her with an interesting tale. Wraiths were pursuing a young sorcerer and his lady friend. They were fleeing to Arthos—where I was already headed on business of my own. So my cohort did her best to keep the wraiths at bay while I made for the city."

"That's why we didn't see any pursuit after the first night," Khaldun observed.

"And that must explain those flashes of light we saw," added Jezebel. "We owe you our gratitude."

"Save it for now," Raphael said grimly. "You're not out of the woods yet."

"I feel more confident now, though," Khaldun replied. "I was helpless without my magic."

Raphael nodded. "We'll be safe here for tonight, at least. Six wraiths are riding in our direction totally unhindered. Dredmort can't be far behind. For now, I do not think they will attack the city openly. But Henry's spies are everywhere. He'll know which room you were in. Unless I'm much mistaken, the wraiths will sneak into Arthos before sunrise. And as I said earlier, our best hope is that they will find your previous dwelling empty and assume you've departed from the city. That should buy us some time. I will go south tomorrow and find what news I can.

"You should both try to rest now. I'll wake you if anything happens."

Jezebel and Khaldun climbed into bed. Jezebel couldn't help becoming aroused with his body pressed so close to hers. She hadn't noticed it on the run from Madison, but Khaldun's strange magnetism had nearly disappeared with the loss of his magic. Now it had returned in full force. Only Raphael's presence and Jezebel's sense of modesty kept her from making love to him.

The last thing she saw before drifting off to sleep was Raphael sitting at the table. He was smoking his pipe, gazing out the window.

CHAPTER FOURTEEN
DEPARTURE

ezebel woke with a start. Khaldun was standing by the bed; he looked frightened.

"They're coming," he whispered.

Jezebel crept to the table. She and Khaldun huddled behind Raphael, gazing out the window. It was still dark outside; only the moons lit the quad, which was deserted.

"I don't see anything," Jezebel hissed.

"They're not here yet," Khaldun told her. "But they're close. I can feel it."

"So can I, now," Raphael said quietly.

Minutes went by. Motion in the far corner of the courtyard caught Jezebel's eye. She stared intently, trying to make out shapes in the darkness. An inky patch of black slipped across the façade of the building, a shadow moving through the shadows. It stopped outside the door to their old room. Jezebel couldn't see what it was, but a sense of dread and despair overcame her. It had to be a wraith.

Another minute went by in silence. Suddenly a shrill cry pierced the night. The window of their former quarters lit up, as if by fire. Next to it, the wraith held out his hand. The door exploded off its hinges, and the creature moved inside. Jezebel could see other shadows moving among the flames.

Something flew out the window, smashing the glass. It looked like the chest of drawers. A minute later, there was another cry. The light in the room disappeared, plunging the scene into darkness once again.

Jezebel watched for a while longer, hardly daring to breathe. Lamps illuminated several other windows, but nothing else happened.

"Are they gone?" she asked.

"The wraiths have undoubtedly retreated outside the city," Raphael said. "But I suspect Henry's men will search the inn to make sure you're gone. You must hide. And I should assume the visage of the old farmer who paid for this room."

"Will a spell of invisibility suffice?" asked Khaldun.

"Only sorcerers can detect magic," Raphael said with a nod. "Your spell should do the trick—but make sure to hide your gear, too."

Khaldun nodded. He didn't appear to say or do anything. But a few seconds later, Raphael muttered, "Well done." Jezebel knew he must have made them invisible.

"Now stay quiet," Raphael warned, not looking directly at them.

Raphael held out his wand and muttered an incantation. Slowly he transformed. His beard disappeared, and his scraggly hair turned white. Old work clothes replaced his robes, and his complexion became much darker. He stuffed his wand into his pocket.

A minute later, they heard a commotion in the hallway. Someone banged on the door. Raphael opened it.

"I'm so sorry for the intrusion," said the man standing there. Jezebel recognized him from the front counter the previous day. "These men—"

He didn't get to finish his sentence. A soldier in Fosland's uniform yanked him out of the way. He entered the room, another man right behind him. Raphael backed away, appearing to be a frightened old man.

"We're looking for a young man. Golden skin, dark hair pulled into a tail. There's a girl with him. You seen them?"

"No, I haven't," Raphael said, shaking his head vigorously. Even his voice was different—higher-pitched and cracking slightly. "Ain't seen no one."

The soldier scanned the room. He looked under the bed, coming within feet of Jezebel and Khaldun in the corner. But then he nodded to Raphael and left with his partner.

They could hear the soldiers enter the next room. Once they'd moved on, Raphael changed back to his normal appearance. Khaldun removed his spell.

"We should be out of immediate danger," Raphael told them. "It won't be light for two more hours. You should both try to get some more sleep."

Jezebel climbed back into bed with Khaldun but lay awake. She was too anxious to relax. Khaldun was asleep within minutes.

When the sky began to lighten, Jezebel heard horns blaring in the distance. She sat up in alarm.

"What's that?"

"The city guard," Raphael answered, still sitting at the table. "Word must have reached them that Henry's men invaded the city." He got to his feet. "I should investigate. They're probably long gone by now, but I'd like to be sure. I'll return soon." Raphael strode from the room, closing the door behind him.

Jezebel got out of bed. She sat at the table and stared out the window. The quad was alive with activity now as people started their days. A crowd had gathered outside their old room. A group of soldiers surveyed the damage. Jezebel assumed they were from the city guard.

Raphael returned a short while later. Khaldun started awake when he entered the room.

"The wraiths are nowhere near. I rode far down the road, but felt no presence. And Henry's soldiers are gone. The city guard sent a contingent to pursue them along the south road.

"They seem to believe that you've left the city, as I hoped. This should make our departure easier. I have no doubt, however, that Henry's men are still watching the inn. We'll have to leave unseen. And we cannot take your horses—they're certain to be under surveillance. But I'll leave word with friends to look after them."

"How soon are we leaving?" Khaldun asked.

"It would be best to travel under the cover of darkness," Raphael replied. "I will mask our trail, and make us invisible. But our passage would still produce certain signs."

"Like dirt kicked up from the road," Jezebel muttered.

"Yes, precisely," Raphael said. "Such things are harder to detect after nightfall. And there will be fewer people about to spot them in the first place. This will also give me time to go south and gather news. It would be helpful to know what the enemy is doing before we set out."

They shared a light breakfast of dried fruit and meat. Raphael prepared to depart soon after. He warned them not to leave the room under any circumstances.

"I'll return by sunset," he told them.

Khaldun lay in bed and heaved a long sigh. Jezebel sat beside him.

"This journey hasn't exactly gone according to plan," Khaldun observed.

"Truly," Jezebel agreed. "I was thinking, though… Why don't you bind yourself to Aldo? You said you were thinking about settling down in Spanbrook."

"I'd love to," he said. "But you heard Raphael. Nobody's allowed to be conjurnor for more than one sorcerer. Aldo's already got Myrddin."

"Maybe Enigma will allow it," she suggested. "He broke the rules when he let Nomad choose Badru."

Khaldun shook his head. "Enigma has always been partial to the wayfarers. I'm betting he did it because he knew they could use the protection. But Enigma was a governor. He understands the danger of consolidating too much power in one place."

"But Aldo's peaceful. He's not like Henry. What could happen?"

"You have a point," Khaldun conceded. "With Myrddin's power, most princes would probably annex a few neighbors. We can ask Enigma when we find him. The worst he can do is refuse."

"You don't wish to stay at the university?" Jezebel asked.

"For life?" Khaldun said. "No. I do not. They wouldn't have me when I was a normal mage because I was born a wayfarer. Now that I've transformed, they would seek to keep me as a prisoner forever?" He shook his head and sighed. "Being bound at all is bad enough. But if it must be, I would vastly prefer Aldo or Badru to anyone at the university."

The morning wore on. Jezebel watched out the window as people came to repair the damage to their old room. But for the most part, she was utterly bored. And her attraction to Khaldun intensified. He was sitting across the table from her but she could feel the warmth of his body as if she were right next to him. Confinement with him in this small room was overbearing. It was all she could do to stop herself from ripping his clothes off and making love to him.

But suddenly, there was a banging on the door. Jezebel froze, her heart jumping into her throat. Moving as quietly as possible, she grabbed her wand from the table.

Khaldun got to his feet, holding his finger to his lips. Jezebel knew the routine. She went to the corner with him, pressing her body between him and the wall. She knew he was making them invisible.

A second later, the door flew open. Jezebel held her breath. But it was only the cleaning lady. Jezebel exhaled a sigh of relief, which was drowned out by the noise the woman was making. She was singing to herself, but Jezebel thought it sounded more like a dying animal.

The woman changed the sheets on the bed, quickly dusted the furniture, and departed. Jezebel collapsed on the bed and fell into a fit of giggles.

"I'm starving," she said, once she'd calmed down. "It's too bad we have to hide. I'd *love* a hot meal again—and the food here is excellent."

"Agreed," Khaldun said. "But Raphael is right. Henry's spies are everywhere. We can't afford someone spotting us here when we're supposed to be long gone."

Jezebel knew he was right. She dug into their provisions but ate only sparingly. Hungry or not, she could hardly bear to consume the same fare yet again.

By sunset, there was still no sign of Raphael. Jezebel retrieved her mirror to talk to Allison. Her cousin's image formed in the glass immediately. Allison's hair was wet from a bath, and she was already in her nightgown.

"Early night?" Jezebel asked. She was taken aback by Allison's beauty; she found the sight of her arousing.

"Yes, we're leaving before first light tomorrow. If we ride hard, we might arrive at the next holding before nightfall. I'm hoping to get a good night's sleep."

Jezebel brought Allison up to speed with everything they'd learned in the past two days.

"Enigma left the university?!" Allison said, looking crestfallen.

"Don't worry—Raphael believes he will have left word of his destination," Jezebel reassured her. "We'll find him."

"This is becoming far more dangerous than I imagined," Allison said. "The demon has not returned. Maybe you should come back. If you stick to the north roads, you can avoid Henry's forces. "

"No," Jezebel said simply. "We've come this far. We don't have much farther to go before we reach the university."

"But now you've got wraiths pursuing you! I'm so worried something is going to happen. It's not worth the risk; I'll manage."

"I'm not giving up," Jezebel insisted. "The demon may well return when you get back to Spanbrook. I won't see you endure that again."

When she was done with Allison, Jezebel sat for a long time, gazing out the window. She suddenly felt incredibly guilty for sleeping with Khaldun. True, she'd been drunk, but that was a poor excuse. And after talking to Allison, her feelings for the princess flooded her consciousness. She had no doubt she'd choose her over Khaldun. Their separation had only strengthened Jezebel's love for her; she wanted more than ever to spend her life with the princess. But now she worried that she'd ruined that future. Why was her desire for this wayfarer so overwhelming?

She didn't know how she was going to explain it to the princess. And she had no idea if her cousin would find it in her heart to forgive her. But if she were going to have any chance at all, one thing was clear: she couldn't make love to Khaldun again.

Dusk settled into full night. Still, Raphael did not return. Jezebel began to worry.

"Maybe we should leave," she suggested.

"What? Why? How would Raphael know where to find us?" Khaldun said.

"What if the wraiths captured him? If they force him to admit that we're still here… *He* might not be the one coming to find us."

Khaldun took a deep breath. "I hadn't considered that. He did say he'd return by sunset."

They debated for a few minutes, trying to decide what to do. But Raphael finally returned.

"I'm sorry I'm so late," he said, sounding worried. "I journeyed far, and good thing I did. The wraiths did indeed ride south, like a gale, if the reports are true. Six of them flew down the road.

"I made myself unseen and infiltrated a company of Henry's men. The news is troubling. Dredmort himself is coming for you. He brings the rest of the wraiths."

"We've got to get through *all of them*—and Dredmort?!" Khaldun said.

"That's not the worst of it, I'm afraid," Raphael replied. "They believe we are somewhere in the wild, making our way to the university and avoiding the road—which we will be very soon. But they know that at some point we have to cross the River Mayne. There are only two ferries and two bridges where the water may be safely traversed between here and there. The wraiths now protect them all."

"We crossed it by ferry on the way here," said Jezebel. "Why don't we go back that way?"

Raphael shook his head. "My associate informs me that Henry has moved forces into Madison. We would have to pass through lands that he controls to make it to the university that way.

"We must choose between deadly perils. But the southernmost bridge is only a few miles from the university. We *will* encounter the enemy, but I would prefer to delay that meeting as long as possible. I feel that avoiding it until we are in sight of our goal gives us our greatest chance of success. I may even be able to find a way to call for help once we are close enough to the university."

They considered the situation for a few minutes.

"Couldn't we swim across the river somewhere?" Jezebel asked. "That way, we could cross without them knowing."

"I don't recommend it," Raphael said. "The Mayne runs hard and swift. Even a strong swimmer would have trouble with it."

"I'm not a strong swimmer," Jezebel admitted apologetically.

"The southernmost bridge would be my choice," said Raphael. "But the two of you must decide. I will go fetch us some dinner—talk it over."

He left the room. Khaldun looked at Jezebel; she shrugged.

"He's right about swimming the Mayne," he said. "I tried it on a dare once when I was younger—the current nearly overpowered me before I turned back. That was one of the few times Nomad ever chewed me out as a kid. Apparently people have died trying to swim across that river."

"But if we go back toward Madison and cross the river at the ferry, we could avoid the wraiths," Jezebel pointed out. "We could stay invisible the whole way and escape notice."

"True," Khaldun said. "But Henry's men could be everywhere for all we know. We walked right through his army on the way to Stiles, but they weren't looking for us then."

"You agree with Raphael," Jezebel observed.

"I do," he said, nodding. "I know the bridge he's talking about. You can almost *see* the university from there. And Henry hasn't taken any territory this side of the river yet. I think it's our best shot."

"You'd both know better than I," Jezebel said with a shrug.

Raphael returned twenty minutes later with a whole turkey. He set it on the table along with corn, cranberries, and a bottle of wine. They told him of their decision as they ate.

Less than an hour later, they gathered their gear. Khaldun made the three of them invisible—inside the same spell, they could still see each other. They departed, walked across the quad, and left the building by the side exit.

They headed west, avoiding the guardhouse. They crossed a field and came to the same barn where Khaldun had hidden on the way into Arthos. Now sufficiently far from the city to avoid being seen, they turned south.

Raphael planned to lead them in a great arc around the perimeter of Arthos. That way, they would come to the road. They could walk beside it in the grass and make decent time while still avoiding unwelcome attention. If they met anyone, they could take cover in the woods.

"We're already invisible," Jezebel said. "Would it really be necessary to hide in the woods?"

"Better safe than sorry," Khaldun told her.

"We'll leave the road completely once we're closer to the bridge," Raphael said. "So enjoy our easy passage while it lasts."

They kept up their march for the duration of the night, the moons lighting their way. Despite the hour, they encountered people traveling the other way several times and moved off the road to take cover until they'd passed. This made the going quite slow, and moving around the city like this had added many miles to their journey. Raphael explained that typically it took only a day to travel from Arthos to the university. But they weren't making that kind of time on this trip. Finally, when the sun crested the horizon, they moved into the woods and made camp. Khaldun took the first watch while Raphael and Jezebel slept.

He woke Jezebel later in the morning and lay down. Jezebel sat with her back against a tree, her wand drawn. She grew anxious every time somebody passed on the road.

The south road was busier than the one they'd taken into Arthos. Jezebel saw all manner of travelers: farmers bringing produce to market, wagons transporting goods farther inland, a family relocating, even a trio of young wizards. She guessed the last group was headed to the city on holiday from the university.

But her shift was uneventful. She woke Raphael a few hours after noon and went back to sleep. After sunset, they resumed their course. They forged ahead for a little while without meeting any resistance. But then Jezebel heard a bloodcurdling shriek. It was followed several seconds later by another farther away.

She looked at Khaldun in horror.

"Wraiths," he said.

CHAPTER FIFTEEN
DREDMORT

 uickly, off the road," Raphael said, ushering them into the woods. "We're invisible, but the wraiths might be able to detect our presence." They moved several yards away and hid among the trees. Less than a minute later, a horse and dark rider came into view, trotting up the road. Jezebel could feel the creature: this was a wraith.

As if it could sense them, the wraith reined in its horse at almost the exact point they'd left the road. It seemed to sniff the air as it swayed back and forth on its mount. The horse edged closer to the trees.

But suddenly there was another cry from afar. The wraith sat bolt upright on its horse and answered the call. A second later, it galloped away, resuming its course.

"We're near the ferry," Raphael told them. "They'll probably be patrolling the road from here to the bridge. We should stick to the forest to avoid risking contact. But fear not—I know these woods well."

Jezebel and Khaldun followed him farther into the trees. Before long, they came to a path, narrow and lightly-trodden. Raphael led them to the south.

They traveled for hours, following the trail across dell and knoll. They heard the wraiths' cries every so often. Jezebel knew they were never far because she could feel them. The constant sense of dread wore her down.

Jezebel dropped into a daze. Her body ached, and she was exhausted. She was conscious only of one foot falling in front of the other.

But suddenly Raphael threw his arm out to stop them. He was staring out into the trees to their left. Jezebel followed his gaze. In the distance, she could make out a flickering light, as if from a fire.

"Enemy camp," Raphael said quietly. "This path leads right by it. We must proceed with extreme caution."

They forged ahead, careful not to make the slightest noise. As they drew closer, Jezebel could see several soldiers sitting around a campfire. A lone wraith was sitting astride its horse outside their circle.

Only yards from the camp, they came to a fork in the path. Raphael led them to the right. But before they'd taken more than ten steps, Khaldun stepped on a fallen tree branch that snapped in half with a loud crack.

They froze. Jezebel turned her gaze to the wraith—he'd heard them. He edged his horse away from the fire and seemed to be sniffing the air.

Raphael picked up a stone and hurled it through the trees, toward the other branch of the path. The wraith's head snapped the other way when the stone landed. He spurred his horse forward to investigate.

Raphael held out his wand and whispered an incantation. Suddenly an illusion appeared on the other path, several yards ahead of the wraith: perfect duplicates of Raphael, Jezebel, and Khaldun.

"Hurry—this way!" the false Raphael yelled. He ran, and the doppelgangers of Khaldun and Jezebel followed.

The wraith cried and urged his horse to the chase. The men at the campsite got to their feet and hastened in his wake.

Raphael motioned them forward. "The other path leads directly to the bridge," he told them. "With any luck, my deception will keep them searching for us in the wrong direction."

Several minutes later, their path emerged from the trees at the top of a steep embankment, the Mayne rushing along below. To their south, less than a half-mile away, Jezebel could make out the silhouette of an enormous bridge. It arced over the river, high enough to allow boats to pass underneath. Three points of light moved about the near end of the structure. Jezebel guessed they were torches and tried to make out the men carrying them.

"The bridge is held against us, as expected," Raphael said.

"How do we get across?" Khaldun asked, desperation in his voice.

"It won't be easy," Raphael said. "And it won't happen without a fight. The university itself is still a few miles away, but the boundary lies less than a quarter of a mile beyond the bridge."

"A few *miles*?" Jezebel asked incredulously. "How are we supposed to make it that far with the wraiths pursuing us?"

"We won't have to," Raphael replied. "The wraiths cannot pass the boundary—powerful enchantments lie upon it. We'll be safe once we cross the border."

They proceeded along the riverbank, Raphael leading the way, Jezebel taking up the rear. But several seconds later, something went horribly wrong.

A wall of blue flame sprung up between Jezebel and Khaldun. Jezebel stopped short. She fell over as she tried to avoid the fire, dropping her pack.

"We're visible!" Khaldun cried. "Someone canceled the spell!"

Jezebel could see him through the flames. But suddenly he disappeared—she knew that he was now invisible again, but she was not.

She got to her feet, wand drawn, frantically searching her surroundings for the caster of the spell. But suddenly, the wall of flame moved toward her, circling her.

Jezebel pointed her wand and put out the fire. But standing before her on the path was a woman with long, red hair. She was holding a staff. Jezebel uttered the spell to call earth, but the witch was ready. She pointed her rod, and suddenly a sheet of glowing blue energy descended over Jezebel, covering her like a blanket. It constricted, pinning her arms to her sides and binding her legs together.

Jezebel teetered and fell—she couldn't move her legs to catch her balance. But suddenly she found herself lifted off her feet, hovering several inches off the ground.

The witch spoke a word of command, and Jezebel flew through the trees. She let out a scream, but the sheet of energy muffled it. Branches whipped past her, and she was sure she would crash into a tree.

But an instant later, she came to rest, still floating above the ground. It took her a few seconds to take in her new surroundings. There were two tents and a fire—it looked like the enemy camp they'd passed earlier. The witch appeared in front of her. She pointed her staff, and Jezebel moved to a nearby tree.

"Tie her up," the witch commanded.

Two men moved into Jezebel's field of vision. They tied her to the tree, pulling the ropes so tight that she could barely breathe. Once she was secure, the witch removed the spell, and the sheet of energy disappeared. Jezebel tried to point her wand and call fire, but the witch snatched it from her hand.

"Keep this on your person," she said, handing it to one of the soldiers. He nodded, pocketing Jezebel's wand. Jezebel now saw that there were three of them.

"Your friends managed to get away," the witch told her, moving directly in front of Jezebel, her face only inches away. The witch's eyes were green; her face was drawn and pale. She wore black clothes that clung to her wiry frame. "But something tells me they'll be back."

"What do you want with me?" Jezebel asked.

"It's not *you* we want," the witch said with a smile. She turned toward the soldiers, and her hair whipped Jezebel in the face.

"Find Dredmort," the witch said. "Tell him we've got the girl."

One of the men nodded and jogged away. The witch returned her attention to Jezebel.

"Raphael will come for you. His bleeding heart won't allow him to abandon you as he should. And when he does, the boy will be ours.

"I have to be honest; I'm shocked that anyone would allow an unbound sorcerer to travel across the land unprotected. Tell me, where did you find him? And who are you, anyway?"

It surprised Jezebel that this woman didn't know more about them.

"I'm not telling you anything."

The witch smiled at her. She raised her staff. A tongue of fire sprung up on the ground, a foot away from Jezebel. It edged toward her.

"Who are you?"

The flame moved within inches of her. Jezebel could feel the heat on her ankles. She didn't say anything. But the fire suddenly erupted before her, six feet in the air. It singed her hair, and she had to turn her face away from the searing heat.

"I'm Jezebel of Spanbrook!" she cried out.

"That's better," the witch said; the flames decreased in intensity. "What about the boy?"

"He's a wayfarer."

"A wayfarer?" the woman repeated, clearly surprised. "Ah, yes—I thought he looked familiar. Why didn't Nomad escort him to the university?"

"Nomad's dead. Khaldun and I were traveling to the university on our own business when he transformed."

"How interesting," the witch said, giving her a knowing look. "So you must be his lover. This improves our situation—you'll make better bait than I thought."

How could this woman possibly know? Jezebel opened her mouth to retort, but the witch spoke first.

"Don't let her out of your sight," she said to the soldiers. The fire in front of Jezebel disappeared. "Either Dredmort or I will return soon."

The witch strode away, vanishing before she'd left the light of the fire. One of the soldiers walked toward Jezebel, smirking at her.

"So you're the baby sorcerer's *lover*, are you? Are you some tavern wench he picked up somewhere?"

He moved within inches of her. His breath stank.

"I'm Prince Aldo's niece," she said defiantly.

"Almost a princess," the soldier said, sounding impressed. "I should have guessed. You've got that arrogant highborn tone in your voice." He caressed her face with the back of his hand for a moment, then fondled her breasts. "I've always wanted to fuck a princess."

Jezebel spat in his face. The man backhanded her, snapping her head to the side. Jezebel could taste blood in the corner of her mouth.

"What the hell are you doing?" the other man demanded. "You heard Nineve—Dredmort's coming! You want him to catch you abusing his prisoner?"

The soldier wiped the spittle from his face. He grabbed Jezebel by the chin, slamming her head into the tree. With his other hand, he reached between her legs, rubbing her genitals through her trousers.

"You're going to pay for that, you little bitch. As soon as Dredmort is done with you, you're mine."

"We'll leave the torture to Nineve, I think," a voice said.

The soldier wheeled around. A tall man was standing by the fire. "Dredmort…" the soldier breathed. "I'm sorry, sir… I didn't mean… I won't…" Dredmort waved him aside, and the man scampered over to his comrade.

Dredmort was tall and thin. He was bald but wore a long black beard. His robes were blood red. He carried a white staff that was as tall as he was. As he approached, Jezebel realized that it was carved with the features of a naked woman, unnaturally elongated.

"I apologize if you've been mistreated, my lady," Dredmort said with a small bow. "Honorable men are so difficult to come by."

Jezebel glared at him. Dredmort turned toward the trees. When he spoke, his voice rang through the forest like a trumpet.

"You know the terms, Raphael. Give us the sorcerer, and the girl goes free. Otherwise, she dies." He faced Jezebel again. "You'll soon be free. I'm sure Raphael is still nearby—and I expect he will deliver the boy any minute now. Although you might consider joining us. You're a witch, I understand? Henry treats his mages very well."

"Yet he allows his soldiers to rape and kill his subjects," Jezebel said. "No, thank you. I'd never serve that bastard."

Dredmort closed his eyes and shook his head. "You're referring to the unfortunate incident in Stiles. I assure you, Henry does not condone those men's actions. Conquering soldiers will take certain liberties, but such atrocities occur only on the front."

"Yes, I'm sure Fosland is a veritable paradise," Jezebel said sarcastically.

"It is free of lawlessness and violence—much like Spanbrook. You've experienced firsthand the prosperity that comes with peace. Henry seeks only to bring similar circumstances to others. Restoring the ancient kingdom will put a stop to the endless bloodshed the princedoms inflict upon each other. But again, having grown up in Spanbrook, you're probably unfamiliar with conditions on the rest of the continent."

"Your army has caused the only bloodshed I've witnessed since leaving my home," Jezebel told him.

Dredmort started to respond but was interrupted by a commotion behind him. Two soldiers walked into camp, holding Khaldun between them. Two more men showed up behind them.

"No!" Jezebel cried.

Dredmort moved toward the wayfarer. He walked around him in a slow circle. Jezebel couldn't believe her eyes. Had Raphael abandoned them? Or had he been captured, too?

"We found him on the path, walking this way," one of the soldiers reported. "He surrendered."

"Fools," Dredmort bellowed. "This is an illusion!" He waved his arm, and Khaldun disappeared. The soldiers backed away in surprise. "They're somewhere close. Fan out in the trees—find them! They're sure to be invisible, but you'll still be able to hear them and feel them."

Dredmort departed with the four new arrivals, leaving the two original soldiers behind to guard Jezebel. The abusive one sat by the fire, glaring at her.

A few seconds later, Jezebel felt something brush against her shoulder. It startled her—she turned but saw nothing.

"Don't make a sound," someone whispered in her ear—it sounded like Raphael. She could feel his hot breath against the side of her head. An instant later, she saw him. The ropes binding Jezebel to the tree went up in flames, the ashes falling to the ground. Jezebel gasped. The soldiers turned to face her and shouted in surprise.

"Where the hell did she go?!"

Raphael had extended his invisibility spell to include her. The men panicked, running around the camp with their arms extended, trying to find her by touch. Raphael cast a spell that knocked them both unconscious; they fell to the ground. Jezebel retrieved her wand from the abusive soldier's pocket and Raphael led her into the trees.

The next few minutes were tense. Raphael and Jezebel made their way toward the river in fits and starts, dodging and weaving around Dredmort and his men. They avoided the path, walking instead through the trees and underbrush. The noise of the soldiers mostly masked the sounds of their passage.

After several close calls, they made it to the path by the river. They broke into a run, heading toward the bridge. But suddenly Raphael pulled up short. He whistled between his teeth, sounding like a bird. Someone landed on the path in front of them, apparently having jumped from a tree. It was Khaldun. He smiled, handing Jezebel her pack.

The three of them continued along the path. As they approached the bridge, they hid behind an outcropping of rock. Jezebel cursed under her breath: a dozen soldiers patrolled the structure.

"How the hell did you get into the camp like that?" Jezebel hissed.

"Sleight of hand," Raphael said with a grin. "That doppelganger who surrendered to the soldiers wasn't *only* an illusion. It was me! When Dredmort canceled the magic, I cast a spell of invisibility. Luckily, my timing was perfect, and he did not detect the ruse. I may have outsmarted him, but I am no match for his power."

Jezebel had more questions, but at that moment, they heard the cry of a wraith. She peered around the edge of the rock. Two wraiths had joined the soldiers, positioning themselves at the entrance to the bridge.

"They know we're coming," Khaldun observed.

"Yes, by now, Dredmort realizes we escaped his perimeter at the camp," Raphael agreed.

"How are we going to get across the bridge?" Jezebel asked.

"With some help from Nineve," Raphael said elusively. "But first, I should give you both the spell to enter the university—in case we get separated before we reach the boundary."

Jezebel doubted she'd be able to cast the spell, but he spent a couple of minutes teaching them the incantation. Once he was sure they had it, Raphael said, "That will open a portal in the barrier. Cast it again once you're through to close it. Now, follow me—and stay quiet!"

They crept along the rest of the way. The path continued beside the river, under the bridge. Raphael, Jezebel, and Khaldun huddled against one of the iron support beams.

Raphael pointed his wand toward the path that led to the bridge. Suddenly Nineve appeared out of nowhere, escorting a copy of Khaldun. The same blue energy the witch had used against Jezebel now encased the wayfarer.

"Where's Dredmort?" Nineve called out to the wraiths. The monsters moved off the bridge to approach the witch.

"I'll deal with the wraiths," Raphael whispered. "You two take care of any ambitious soldiers who get in our way. Ready?" Jezebel and Khaldun nodded. "Now," Raphael hissed.

They sneaked out of their hiding place and rounded the corner onto the bridge. Jezebel ran as fast as her legs would carry her, Khaldun by her side. Over her shoulder, she caught a glimpse of a huge fire at the entrance to the bridge. She heard the wraiths screaming beyond it.

Three soldiers tried to bar their way, swords drawn. Jezebel pointed her wand and called earth. Something slammed into one of the men, knocking him over the railings and into the water far below; Khaldun took care of the other two the same way. Jezebel thought they were free and clear. But as they reached the center of the structure, a tall man with billowing red robes appeared.

It was Dredmort.

Jezebel skidded to a stop, Khaldun right behind her. She turned to look for Raphael, but he was gone. The wraiths were now approaching.

Jezebel faced Dredmort again and called fire—she tried to ignite him from within. Nothing happened. She summoned a wall of flame instead, directly in front of the wizard. But he canceled it with a wave of his hand the moment it appeared.

"It's over," Dredmort told them, almost apologetically. "Don't waste your time trying to escape—you may be a sorcerer, Khaldun, but you are still new to your power and untrained. I don't wish to harm you, but it may become necessary if you try to flee."

Khaldun looked around frantically, trying to find a way out. But they were trapped. Dredmort stood between them and freedom, and the wraiths drew ever closer.

Without warning, Khaldun lunged toward the railing. Jezebel realized that he was going to dive into the Mayne. But a sheet of blue energy formed in his path, encasing and binding him. He fell to the deck, his body rigid.

Dredmort moved toward him but stopped suddenly, frantically looking around. Jezebel didn't know what was happening at first, but an instant later saw the source of his alarm. The iron beams of the bridge were beginning to glow. Someone was heating them from within.

"NO!" cried Dredmort.

In the next instant, several things happened at once. The energy binding Khaldun disappeared. Something unseen knocked Dredmort into an iron beam and bound him there. And a voice yelled "RUN!"

It was Raphael.

Jezebel didn't need to be told twice. She helped Khaldun to his feet and bolted toward the opposite shore. A tower of flame erupted directly behind them. The bridge shuddered and groaned as the iron beams began to glow white-hot.

They pounded onto the dirt road and didn't stop until they'd crested a hill. There they turned around. Jezebel saw Dredmort and Raphael battling in the middle of the bridge. Raphael was on his knees. Dredmort held out his staff, shooting barbs of lightning at the wizard. Raphael was holding his wand in front of him, casting some sort of shield to block the spell. The wraiths had moved past them, riding hard.

A moment later, Raphael managed to cancel Dredmort's magic. He rose to his feet and pointed his wand. His voice carried to Jezebel and Khaldun as he cast a powerful incantation. There was an explosion, and a huge fireball rose to the sky. The whole bridge swayed and buckled under the force of the spell. In seconds it broke, the entire structure collapsing. Raphael and Dredmort disappeared from view. Jezebel watched in horror as the bridge crashed into the river. She couldn't imagine Raphael surviving that.

"Let's go!" Khaldun yelled, pulling Jezebel along. "We have to get across that boundary."

At that moment, Jezebel heard the wraiths cry—they'd made it to the shore. She wiped the tears from her eyes and ran.

Within seconds she could hear hoofbeats behind them, closing fast. Jezebel willed herself to go faster, not daring to look behind her for fear of stumbling. She was breathing hard and had a cramp in her side. As they descended the hill, she noticed two short towers ahead of them, one on either side of the road.

"That's it!" Khaldun yelled. "That's the border!"

One of the wraiths shrieked—it sounded like they were on their heels. A wall of flame shot up across their path, blocking the boundary. Khaldun held out his hand and extinguished it. Then he bellowed the incantation he'd learned from Raphael.

A shimmering plane appeared in the air before them, an archway forming where it intersected the road. Moments later, they pelted through the opening and stopped short. Khaldun cast the spell again to close the archway. The wraiths' horses skidded to a stop. One of them reared; its rider threw a spell. But the incantation hit the boundary, its power bleeding across the invisible plane. There was a sound like a deep gong as the energy reverberated against the protective enchantments.

The wraiths cried in anger before galloping away. Jezebel fell to the ground, clutching her side.

CHAPTER SIXTEEN
UNIVERSITY

hat's wrong?!" Khaldun asked, moving toward Jezebel with fear in his eyes. "Are you hurt?"

Jezebel shook her head, wincing slightly. "Just a cramp."

Khaldun sat beside her, catching his breath.

"Raphael," she said, still breathing heavily. "He's gone." Her throat burned as she said it; she fought back the tears.

"Let's hope he took Dredmort with him," Khaldun muttered.

They sat there for several minutes. Jezebel's cramp subsided. But the pain of losing Raphael caught up with her. She couldn't stop herself from crying. They would never have made it out of Arthos alive without his help. But now Raphael had sacrificed himself for them.

Eventually, Khaldun and Jezebel got to their feet and headed toward the university.

"What now?" Jezebel asked.

"I don't know," Khaldun replied. "We've got to find out where Enigma is now. I should hide somewhere. Hopefully, they'll give you the information. As long as Enigma went somewhere we can reach without crossing Henry's lands, then we should be in business."

"But if not," Jezebel said, thinking through the situation, "I have to go alone. We can't risk Henry capturing you unbound."

Khaldun let out a long sigh. "If it comes to that, you'd be far safer without me. You've certainly proven that you can take care of yourself. And Henry's men have no reason to go after you if you're alone—it's *me* they want."

"Maybe I can find Enigma and bring him to you," Jezebel suggested. "That way, he can bind you, and you won't have to stay here."

"Perhaps," Khaldun agreed. "Let's not get ahead of ourselves, though. We don't know where he is yet."

They walked in silence. A few minutes later, they came to a crossroads and heard footsteps approaching fast from the right. Jezebel looked fearfully at Khaldun. Could someone have found a way around the boundary? Khaldun grabbed her by the arm and pulled her into the bushes.

A few seconds later, a man came trotting up the road.

"Raphael!" Jezebel cried out, jumping from their hiding place. She gathered him in a huge hug, tears of joy streaming down her cheeks.

"We thought you were dead," Khaldun told him, grinning in astonishment.

Raphael patted Jezebel on the back. "I'm alive and well," he assured them.

"How did you survive?" Jezebel asked, releasing him. "We saw the bridge collapse!" Only then did she realize that Raphael was soaked from head to toe—and now she was wet, too.

"I assume you noticed that I heated all the iron in the bridge?" he asked. They both nodded. "I waited until you were safely off the span, then I called fire. I created an explosion within the structure—beyond the center to make sure Dredmort couldn't cross. With the beams already weakened, it was enough to destroy the bridge.

"I jumped off the span at the same time. Although I tried calling air to blow myself to this side of the river, it wasn't enough. The wind worked against me, and I landed in the river. I swam to shore, but the current had dragged me far to the north. I had to move very quickly to catch you here."

"What about Dredmort?" asked Khaldun. "Was he destroyed?"

"No, it would take far more than that to end him," Raphael replied. "When he realized what I was doing, he fled. I'm sure he made it back to shore in one piece.

"But we should keep moving. We need to get you into hiding before anyone sees you. I'll make us invisible, but there are some here who may detect the spell. Follow me!"

The eastern sky started to lighten as they walked. They passed a few houses, and Jezebel could see larger buildings in the distance. But they turned down a narrow lane. At the end, they came to a small stone house on the edge of the woods.

"Home sweet home," Raphael said with a smile as he opened the front door for them.

"You live here?" Jezebel asked, walking inside.

"I used to teach history at the university until… well, until I changed my vocation. I don't often return here these days, but the house is still mine. Make yourselves comfortable. It will be a few hours before anyone arrives at the administrative offices. Sleep for a while, if you'd like."

Raphael settled himself into a large leather chair in the corner. He put his feet up on the footrest and lit his pipe.

The house was small, only one story. This room seemed to serve as a study. Bookshelves lined two walls, and there was a desk in one corner. Dark wooden beams ran across the high cathedral ceiling. Jezebel could see a kitchen through an adjacent doorway, and a passage led farther into the house. There were at least two more rooms in the back.

Khaldun and Jezebel dropped their packs in the corner. Jezebel sat at the desk, turning her chair to face the others. Khaldun sat on the floor by her feet.

"I'm too anxious to sleep right now," Jezebel said. Khaldun nodded in agreement.

"Suit yourselves," Raphael replied, blowing out smoke in rings. "Khaldun should remain here for the time being. But Lady Jezebel, you are welcome to accompany me on our quest for information when the time comes. I think you may enjoy a short tour of the campus."

"Yes, I'd like that," she said. "I have a few questions, though."

"Go ahead."

"When you rescued me from the enemy camp, you cast a spell to knock out the soldiers. Could you teach us that?"

Raphael cleared his throat. "I would prefer not to. Spells that interfere with the mind are forbidden."

"Why?" asked Jezebel.

"They can cause madness. I don't use that one often, and only when the circumstances are dire. Next question?"

Jezebel collected her thoughts for a moment. "When we encountered Dredmort on the bridge, I called fire. Nothing happened. Why?"

"You tried to ignite him internally?" Raphael asked. Jezebel nodded. "Try it on me."

"*What*?! Why would I do that?"

"Unless I'm much mistaken, it won't work," he said, a twinkle in his eye.

Jezebel raised her wand nervously and cast the spell. Sure enough, nothing happened.

"You build a tolerance to magic as you practice it," Raphael explained. "That tolerance grows with your power. Only someone with extraordinary talent would be able to affect Dredmort that way."

Jezebel nodded. "And how did Nineve know…" She looked at Khaldun and felt herself blush. "She knew we were lovers. She asked where Khaldun had come from, and who had let an unbound sorcerer journey unprotected. I told her only that we were traveling on other business, and Khaldun transformed on the journey. But somehow, she knew."

"That's not too hard to figure out," Raphael said with a grin. "I surmised as much myself."

"Why?" Khaldun asked, looking somewhat embarrassed himself. His face grew a deeper shade of gold rather than red.

"The metamorphosis is almost always triggered by sexual intercourse," Raphael explained. "As I'm sure you know, human thought provides the basis for the magical force. Erotic desire is a very primitive emotion and exists on a more fundamental level than conscious thought. As such, sexual energy can produce potent magic—intercourse in particular. You know, male joining together with female, the coupling of positive and negative forces."

"That's why the transformation never happens until the onset of puberty?" Khaldun asked.

"Indeed," Raphael said. "Powerful experiences usually trigger it—like someone's first sexual encounter."

Jezebel laughed. Khaldun looked at the floor, the color in his face deepening again.

"I missed the joke," Raphael muttered, drawing on his pipe.

"It was *my* first time," Jezebel said, unable to stifle a giggle. "But it certainly wasn't *his*."

"Curious," Raphael replied, sounding more and more amused. "Perhaps this encounter was particularly special or meaningful, in some way. Lust without love isn't nearly as powerful. It's nothing to worry about. The metamorphosis isn't the same for everyone."

Jezebel remembered that Khaldun had whispered Allison's name, and thought she understood perfectly.

"You've talked about *hiding* me," Khaldun said. "Does that mean you're willing to let me go to Enigma to be bound?"

"For now, I am withholding my decision," Raphael replied. "Let's find out where Enigma went before we make up our minds."

They sat in silence for a while. Khaldun drifted off to sleep sitting against Jezebel's legs. Jezebel grew drowsy but remained awake. When the time came, they woke Khaldun. He moved to Raphael's chair, and Jezebel left the house with the wizard.

They strolled down the lane and turned onto the main road. The campus was alive with activity this morning. A few minutes later, they came to the central quad. Several large, brownstone buildings were laid out in a rectangle, with an open courtyard in the middle. Each was a separate structure, but only narrow alleyways led between them, archways spanning those in many places.

Raphael strode along the cobblestone walkway to the building at the far corner. Jezebel followed him up the steps to the entry. The enormous central doorways led into a long hallway. Halfway down the passage, Raphael opened a door on the right. Jezebel walked in, the wizard right behind her. The room was cluttered with bookshelves and cabinets. An older woman sat at a desk in the opposite corner.

"Good morning, Meredith," Raphael called out. The woman turned with a start—apparently she hadn't heard them come in. She stared at them for a moment, until recognition washed over her face.

"Raphael," she said, rising slowly to her feet. She hobbled over to them. "It's been ages—how are you? What brings you back to the nest?"

Raphael stooped low, kissing her lightly on both cheeks. "This young lady is Jezebel of Spanbrook."

"Hello," Jezebel said with a smile, shaking the woman's hand.

"We need to find Enigma," Raphael told her. "I know he hasn't been here in some time, but I'm hoping he left word of his destination."

Meredith frowned, shaking her head slightly. "Dark business, that," she said. "The governors were in an uproar for months. Syllith's removal was bad enough. Seldom in the entire history of this school has anyone from the council been forced to resign. But of course, you know that—professor of history and all."

"Yes," Raphael said with a little smile, "but do you have any idea *why* they removed her?"

"They refuse to discuss it, but I'd tell you if I knew," Meredith replied conspiratorially. "As for Enigma, that was a great dishonor. He left without bothering to seek the approval of the other governors."

"I wasn't aware," said Raphael. "Yet with Syllith gone, and no easy method available to reassign his bond, what else could he do?"

"True, but he should have done the thing properly," Meredith said. "The council would have approved his retirement. But he didn't give them a chance. And he told no one where he was going. His departure was unannounced—he simply disappeared!"

"I didn't know that," Raphael muttered, stroking his beard. "This could be ill news. How do we know he left of his own volition?"

Meredith regarded Raphael askance. "It's Enigma, dear. How else would he have gone?"

"Oh, yes. Of course," said Raphael, shaking his head. "I've been in the wild, fighting Henry too long. Forgive me."

"What?" asked Jezebel. "I don't understand."

"Enigma is a *sorcerer*," Raphael said with a shrug. "An extremely powerful one. It's highly unlikely that anyone could have removed him against his will. And especially here, with the enchantments around the perimeter."

"But what if it was one of the other governors?" asked Jezebel. "Aren't half of them sorcerers?"

"Enigma is powerful even among them, darling," Meredith told her. "I'm sorry, I can't help you. I'm sure he'll check in eventually, and if he does, I'll know about it immediately. I'll get word to you right away."

They left the building. Jezebel despaired of ever finding a way to save Allison from the demon. Without Enigma, her quest was hopeless.

At first, they headed back toward Raphael's house. But the wizard stopped after a few yards, gazing the other way.

"What is it?" asked Jezebel.

"Only a hunch," said Raphael, retracing their steps. Jezebel followed.

They moved beyond the central quad. Raphael chose a path that led past the rear corner, into the trees. Before long, they passed by an odd structure, set back from the walkway. It was some sort of tower, perhaps five stories tall. But it was twice as wide as the towers of Castle Spanbrook and seven-sided. And it had no doors or windows, as far as Jezebel could see.

"What is that?" Jezebel asked.

"I don't know," Raphael said. "It's been there for centuries. But I've never learned what function it serves."

A few minutes later, they came to a row of elegant mansions. They strolled to the very end of the lane, and Raphael walked up to the last house. He peered inside a window before moving to the door. It was unlocked.

"After you," he said, holding the door open for Jezebel. He followed her inside.

"What is this place?" Jezebel asked, looking around in awe. Before her, an enormous stone staircase led to the second floor. A huge chandelier hung from the ceiling high above.

"Enigma's house," Raphael said simply. "The university provides fine homes for each of the governors."

"And what are we doing here?"

"Looking and listening," Raphael said. "I'm wondering if perhaps Enigma left a message when he departed."

Jezebel followed Raphael around the mansion. They walked through a fancy dining room and an enormous kitchen. They searched for clues in a large study and a luxurious living room with a giant fireplace. Upstairs they found a library and several bedrooms. There were no clues or messages.

"It looks incredibly clean for a place that hasn't been occupied for six months," Jezebel observed.

"Yes, it does," Raphael agreed with a frown. "And that in itself is odd."

They were about to return to the first floor when they heard the sound of the front door opening. Raphael held out his wand and made them invisible. He motioned Jezebel behind him, and they crept to the top of the stairs.

An old man walked inside, closing the door behind him. Raphael seemed to relax.

"Hello, Archibald," he called out.

The old man whirled around, clearly startled. "Raphael," he said, holding his hand to his chest. The wizard had removed the spell of invisibility, Jezebel noted. She followed him down the stairs. "You gave me a fright."

"I apologize for that," Raphael said, shaking his hand. "We were trying to ascertain where Enigma might have gone."

"I'm afraid I don't know," Archibald said. "The governors reassigned me, but I stop in now and then to tidy up a bit. Not much to do, as nobody has been here since Master Enigma's departure. But I assume he will return eventually, and we wouldn't want him to find a dusty house."

"Certainly," Raphael said with a frown. "We'll be on our way then," he added, leading Jezebel out of the mansion.

"Farewell," Archibald said, closing the door behind them.

"Who is that, exactly?" Jezebel asked as they strolled down the lane.

"He *was* Enigma's manservant," Raphael explained. "I would have sought him next if we hadn't met him here. But I'm afraid now we have only one chance of finding the sorcerer."

They returned to Raphael's house. Khaldun was asleep in the chair still, snoring away. Jezebel didn't have the heart to wake him.

"We should sleep now, too," Raphael told her through a big yawn. "There is no more we can do today."

He led her down the hallway to a guest bedroom before going off to retire to bed himself. Jezebel lay down in the bed and fell asleep within minutes.

But suddenly something disrupted her sleep. She sat up, confused for a moment about where she was. Unsure what had wakened her, or how much time had passed, she tried to go back to sleep. But then she heard a whisper: someone said her name.

Jezebel sat bolt upright, frantically looking around the room for the source of the speaker. But nobody was there.

She got out of bed and tiptoed down the hall. It was still light out—how long had she been asleep? She heard someone whisper her name again, but couldn't find the source of the noise. For a moment she panicked—could this be the demon? But she didn't think it would shift its focus across so many miles from Allison to her.

Jezebel felt something beckoning to her from outside. Slowly she opened the front door and slipped outside. Walking around behind the house, she ventured into the woods, unsure what was drawing her forward. But she found she couldn't resist this call.

Dead leaves and twigs crunched beneath her bare feet as she walked farther into the trees. But suddenly, she saw a golden glow before her, like a firefly with its light greatly amplified. The glow moved toward her, and Jezebel froze. In the next moment, the light surrounded her.

"*What are you doing here, farm-girl?*" a voice whispered in her ear. Jezebel jumped. She tried to answer, but no words would come out. Instead, she said Enigma's name in her mind.

"*I'm afraid you're too late,*" the voice said. It struck her as feminine, although there was no actual sound. "*Enigma has departed. What do you want with him?*"

Jezebel felt like the questioner withdrew the answer from her mind, but she couldn't say for sure. She found herself fading from consciousness.

Jezebel woke up very disoriented. She was lying in bed. It was dark outside, and she wasn't sure where she was. Delicious aromas were drifting into the room. Memories flooded in, and she remembered that she was in Raphael's house. The last strands of a dream flickered through her mind, something about a golden glow. But as she tried to remember, the memory faded away, like sand slipping through her fingers.

Jezebel sat up. She got out of bed and shuffled down the hall. She found Khaldun and Raphael sitting at the kitchen table.

"I was afraid you were dead," Khaldun said with a grin.

"How long was I asleep?" Jezebel asked, sitting at the table. Platters of bacon, eggs, pancakes, and fried potatoes sat in front of her.

"Approximately thirteen hours," Raphael said with a grin. "Eat—you must be famished." He passed her a dish.

"I am," she said, her stomach growling in anticipation. She filled her plate.

"I told Khaldun what we discovered earlier," Raphael told her. "But, I'd like him to return with us once we've eaten."

"Why?" Jezebel asked, stuffing her face.

"He's a sorcerer," the wizard said simply. "If anything's hiding behind a spell of concealment, he'll be able to detect it. It's a long shot, but it's the last chance we have of finding Enigma."

Jezebel's heart sank. If they couldn't locate the sorcerer, she'd have to return to Spanbrook, unsuccessful in her quest. And there'd be no way to banish the demon.

They finished eating and set out into the night. Rather than making him invisible, Raphael altered Khaldun's appearance. He looked now exactly the way he had before his transformation. Raphael explained that hiding someone entirely would look quite suspicious if they encountered any sorcerers. But many mages used magic to enhance their appearance. Such a spell would be unlikely to attract attention.

They walked along the lane in front of the mansions. The soft light of oil lamps lit most of their interiors. They arrived at Enigma's house, and Raphael let them inside.

"What should I be looking for?" Khaldun asked.

"You aren't *looking* for anything," Raphael said. "If something's being concealed, you won't see it—you'll feel it. Most sorcerers describe the presence of magic as a tingling sensation or like the feeling of energy in the air during a storm. It will be subtle—don't expect to be hit over the head."

"Right," Khaldun muttered as they walked across the dining room. They passed through the entire house, but Khaldun sensed nothing.

"This is it, then," Jezebel said sadly, sitting on the bottom of the stairs. "We failed. There's nothing I can do for Allison."

"Let me try again," Khaldun said. "I am new at this, after all."

Jezebel knew he was only trying to make her feel better. She sat there, twirling her wand while Raphael walked through the house again with Khaldun. But several minutes later, Khaldun called down to her from the second floor.

"Come here," he said. "I've found something."

Jezebel ran up the stairs, into the library.

"I didn't notice it the first time," Khaldun explained, "because it's not in any one place."

"I don't follow," Jezebel said.

"Spells can conceal objects," said Raphael. "But they can also hide energy. Imagine using one spell to hide another."

"And the underlying spell is floating in the air," Khaldun added. "It's not localized."

"Go ahead," Raphael urged him.

Khaldun waved his hand. There was a whispering sound, and suddenly a man appeared in the middle of the room. He was only slightly taller than Jezebel. He wasn't wearing a shirt; his golden skin looked like it had been painted over his thick, rippling muscles. There was no hair on his head, and the irises of his eyes were blood red. Tattoos covered his entire body, including his head and face. Most were runes and symbols of some kind, and they glowed faintly red and black against his golden skin. One ear was pierced, and a silver dragon dangled from it on a short chain.

"Enigma," Raphael said in awe.

The image of Enigma began speaking. "I have to leave quickly, and there's no time to discuss my departure. I apologize for not following protocol, but my need is great.

"As you're aware, Syllith made some startling discoveries. I know you don't approve of her research. But it turns out her most dire predictions were true.

"I am heading immediately to the northwestern watchtower in the Anthar Mountains. I only hope I'm not too late. If you need me, you can find me there."

The image disappeared.

Raphael sat in a chair, seeming deeply troubled.

"What is it?" Khaldun asked.

Raphael looked at him sharply. "Not here."

Jezebel had no idea what was going on. Raphael hurried out of the house, Khaldun and Jezebel on his heels. They walked across campus and returned to Raphael's home. He started a fire in the hearth and sat heavily in his chair. Khaldun and Jezebel sat on the floor in front of him.

"So… What's wrong?" asked Jezebel.

"You remember the story of the Pythan Empire that I told you in Arthos?" Raphael asked.

"Yes," said Jezebel. "The King of Pytha abducted sorcerers, who became necromancers, and took over the entire continent."

"And Nyro betrayed the emperor," Khaldun added. "She reversed her bond and became like a god. She plunged the empire into three hundred years of darkness until the elves came and destroyed the necromancers and their demons."

"Yes," Raphael confirmed, nodding vigorously. "They also laid waste to Pytha. They feared that Nyro might rise again someday. They cast immensely powerful enchantments upon the land and erected watchtowers at several points in the Anthar Mountains. But hundreds of years passed and nothing happened. Eventually, the watchtowers were abandoned."

"But if Enigma went there, something must be happening now," Jezebel suggested.

Raphael stared at her for a moment. "Activity in Pytha can mean only one thing," he said. "Nyro is rising."

CHAPTER SEVENTEEN
ESCORT

ezebel sat in stunned silence. The story of Nyro had seemed like something out of a dark, twisted fairy tale—not real history. Myrddin was the only necromancer she'd ever met—the same was true for anyone alive today, she reminded herself. And he was perfectly benign. But Jezebel recalled the way he'd killed Nomad and shuddered to think what Nyro might be like were she to return.

"But that can't be," Khaldun said, sounding alarmed. "The elves *killed* her…"

"The truth is that we don't know for certain what the elves did," Raphael said. "For years after the fall of the Pythan Empire, the university purged the library of every work concerning necromancy. The governors at the time grew overzealous—the merest mention of the topic was enough for a book to be destroyed. Many purely historical writings were lost in the process. Everything we know about the final battle—which isn't much—comes to us by oral tradition. Legend says that the elves killed Nyro and destroyed her demons. Yet rumors have always persisted that Nyro's soul lived on. And it's entirely possible— she did learn her own name. Such knowledge provides immense power.

"Enigma's message makes me wonder many things; it casts a shadow upon my heart. I would guess now that Syllith was researching the final days of the empire. She must have found something that prompted her to visit Pytha—and it sounds like whatever she discovered was dire indeed. No trivial concern would have driven Enigma to leave so abruptly."

"But you just told us that the university destroyed historical records of those days," said Khaldun. "How could Syllith have been doing that kind of research?"

"Many of the princedoms have libraries of their own," Raphael said with a shrug. "Syllith did travel extensively. Perhaps the purge wasn't as comprehensive elsewhere as it was here. I can't say for sure—but it's clear she found *something*. And the reason for her expulsion seems more apparent now. If she was digging up information about Nyro and the end of her reign, it's no wonder the other governors forced her out."

They sat quietly for a few minutes, considering Raphael's words.

"I still have to try to find Enigma," Jezebel said quietly. "How far is it to the watchtower?"

Raphael rose to his feet. He pulled out an enormous scroll from the top of one of the bookshelves. As he unrolled it on his desk, Jezebel realized that it was a map.

"As the crow flies, we are over five hundred miles from Spanbrook," he said, tracing the route with his finger. He continued to a point in the Anthar Mountains. "The northwestern watchtower is here—more than eight hundred miles from where you now stand."

Jezebel's heart sank. "That's a journey of thirty days, at least. And then I still have to return all that way to Spanbrook..."

"I'm afraid an overland journey will take considerably longer than that," Raphael told her. "The Great Desert occupies much of the distance between here and there. And the Forsaken Hills lie across your path as well. Crossing such terrain is much slower than what you've experienced so far.

"But I think I will accompany you, at least part of the way," the wizard added. "And we may be able to find a swifter course."

"What about me?" Khaldun asked. "Will you force me to remain here to be bound?"

"No," Raphael replied. "Lady Jezebel will need your assistance if she is to make it to the watchtower—I cannot journey that entire distance myself. My business will take me elsewhere, I am sure. But you must give me your word that you will allow Enigma to perform the rite of binding when you find him. I will escort you beyond Henry's reach. But you must not attempt the return trip in your present condition."

Khaldun nodded gravely. "Agreed."

"Very well. Tomorrow I will learn what I can about the best route to take. We will need to stock up our provisions as well. And I suspect I will have some explaining to do to the governors."

"About what?" Jezebel asked.

"They will undoubtedly be curious about my reasons for destroying the bridge," Raphael said with a twinkle in his eye.

Jezebel hadn't been awake long but had no trouble going back to sleep for a few more hours. She left the house with Raphael in the morning. Khaldun stayed behind to avoid contact with other sorcerers.

Raphael led Jezebel into one of the main university buildings. They entered an elegant conference room. There was an enormous stone fireplace, and cherry wood paneling covered the walls. A long bench, like in a courtroom, spanned the front of the room. Raphael and Jezebel took their seats at one of the tables facing the bench.

A minute later, an impossibly large man entered from a door behind the bench. He was as big as a house, with long unkempt hair and a beard that reached his stomach; the golden skin of his face was barely visible behind all the hair. He wore tattered brown robes.

"Who's that?" Jezebel asked in a whisper as the sorcerer sat behind the bench.

"Semblant," Raphael replied. "He's a shapeshifter, and one of the governors."

Jezebel wondered why he wouldn't change his shape to something more attractive.

Moments later, another sorcerer entered from a door behind the other end of the bench. She was as different from Semblant as it was possible to be. Standing no more than five feet tall, she wore a scant, one-piece garment that barely covered her breasts and groin, the black material contrasting against her golden skin. Her muscular body seemed to flow rather than walk across the floor as she moved to take her seat. Black hair fell to her waist, and her skin was a darker gold than any of the sorcerers' Jezebel had seen so far. Sitting down, she stared directly at Jezebel, a smile teasing her lips. She felt overwhelmed by the sexual aura emanating from this woman; she couldn't help but feel aroused by her presence.

"Who is *she*?" Jezebel whispered, wrenching her gaze away from the woman.

"Allure," Raphael replied, clearing his throat. "Don't let her diminutive form fool you: she is one of the most powerful among the governors."

"I can't imagine why," Jezebel muttered.

"Indeed," Raphael said quietly. "But in addition to her powers of seduction, she possesses another rare gift. She can sense the magical potential in a person, and often predict whether a mage will transform into a sorcerer."

The sorcerers looked entirely out of place in this room, elements of the wild within otherwise civilized surroundings. But two others entered and took seats behind the bench: an elderly man, and a middle-aged woman. These were not sorcerers; Jezebel assumed they must be conjurnors. Unlike the sorcerers, they looked like they belonged here.

"I thought there were *twelve* governors?" Jezebel asked.

"Yes, but this is only a subcommittee," Raphael explained.

Jezebel noticed a golden glow coming from the corridor beyond the door the conjurnors had used. She gasped, suddenly recalling the entirety of the dream she'd had at Raphael's house. But the light vanished. She was about to ask Raphael about it when the woman cleared her throat to speak.

"Shall we begin?" she asked. The others nodded.

The woman did most of the talking; the two sorcerers sat in silence the entire time. Semblant appeared utterly uninterested in the proceedings; at some points, Jezebel thought he might have fallen asleep. Meanwhile, Allure couldn't keep her eyes off of Jezebel. She gazed at her invitingly the entire time.

The other woman questioned Raphael about the bridge; he told them most of the truth: Dredmort and his wraiths were chasing him. He left out any mention of Khaldun's transformation. By the woman's follow-up questions, it sounded like she assumed Raphael's activities against Henry had prompted Dredmort's pursuit.

She inquired about Jezebel's presence next, catching her flat-footed. Raphael told the woman that she and Khaldun were interested in enrolling in the university. "Jezebel comes from Spanbrook, where one of the witches has instructed her in the rudiments of magic. Khaldun has lived among the wayfarers until very recently."

The strength of her adverse reaction to Khaldun surprised Jezebel. Khaldun had told her that they didn't allow wayfarers, but he hadn't prepared her for such hostility.

The woman and the old man did express approval of Jezebel's matriculation, however. She thought they seemed eager to enroll someone who could supply them with information about Myrddin's activities. Jezebel was surprised to learn that Spanbrook had long ago severed ties with the university. Myrddin himself had fallen out of their good graces when he became a necromancer. But Aldo's other mages had renounced the governors in a show of solidarity with their chief.

Raphael made no mention of their intent to travel to the watchtower, nor their discovery of Enigma's message. He only inquired about Henry's recent activities to the south of the university. The governors told them that they were expecting scouts to return from the region within days.

"Well, that should conclude our inquiry, Raphael," the woman said. "We appreciate your efforts, as always, but might ask that you try to avoid such property damage in the future. Bridges are expensive, after all."

"I will do my best," Raphael replied with a twinkle in his eye.

They got to their feet, and Raphael led Jezebel out of the chamber. Feeling the weight of someone's stare, she turned to glance at the bench. Semblant and the two conjurnors had risen from their seats, and were heading out the doors. But Allure remained in her chair, smiling seductively at her.

Jezebel followed Raphael out of the building and into the sunshine.

"So you're not in trouble?" she asked.

"Not this time," he said with a grin. "Although I *should* try not to destroy any more bridges."

"Did you notice the golden glow behind that door?" she asked.

"Golden glow, you say?"

She told him about her dream. "I think it was the same thing. But the dream seemed so real; I wonder if it actually happened."

"Hmm," said Raphael, stroking his beard. "Shadow, perhaps..." he muttered.

"What?"

Raphael shook his head. "Old stories and rumors," he said. "Nothing more. I cannot rightfully say what it was that you saw."

Jezebel tried to get him to elaborate, but Raphael would say nothing more.

Back at the wizard's house, they discussed their inquiry with Khaldun. The three of them decided to wait until the scouts' reports came in before leaving the university. Jezebel was happy that she'd have a respite from her journey.

"It would be easiest to travel south through Roses for a time before we cross the Mayne," Raphael explained. "With the bridge gone, we'd lose a few days by traveling north to the ferry. And there is rough country between Strom and Highgate. But the next crossing lies deep within Henry's lands—Roses was one of the first princedoms he sacked. And he's always maintained a presence along the border with the university in the hope of capturing a sorcerer."

"Then we *can't* go that way," Jezebel said. "Won't they be watching for Khaldun?"

"I don't think so," the wizard replied pensively. "New sorcerers always undergo the rite of binding as soon as they arrive. And they stay here for years to complete their education. Henry's people have no reason to expect Khaldun's situation to differ from the norm.

"Moving through the north of Roses will still be dangerous. But depending on the disposition of Henry's troops farther south, it may be worth the risk. It would cut many leagues from the journey."

Raphael cooked breakfast for them again. Jezebel much enjoyed being able to sit down for a home-cooked meal. After that, the wizard left to visit some old friends. Jezebel walked around the study, perusing all the books on the shelves. Many contained histories of various princedoms. Some were about magic, and a few were written in different languages. One documented the founding of the university. Jezebel pulled that one from the shelf and sat down to start reading.

"Look at this," Khaldun murmured from across the room a minute later.

Jezebel moved to his side. "What is it?"

He was holding a portrait of a beautiful young woman; it had been sitting at the end of one of the shelves.

"To my husband, the love of my life," Khaldun read from the back, "on our fifth anniversary."

"Raphael's *married*?" Jezebel asked, taking the portrait from him. "This is dated 835. That was… thirty-seven years ago."

"Oh no," Khaldun whispered. "Read this—it was behind the portrait." He handed her a card. It contained words written in a long, flowing script.

"Raphael, I'm so sorry for your loss," she read out loud. "Helen was a dear friend and one of the most gifted mages I've ever taught. Her death comes as a heavy blow to me personally and to everyone who resists Telbana. I promise you that bastard will pay. I am here if there's anything I can do for you. Your friend, Enigma."

"That's so sad," Khaldun said.

"Who's Telbana?"

"Telbana is a princedom far north of here," Khaldun explained. "It sits in a great bend of the River Mayne. A long time ago, a man named Daphnis ascended to the throne. He was a powerful mage—but he was a lot like Henry. He conquered half of northern Maeda before they stopped him."

"This makes it sound like he killed Raphael's wife," Jezebel said.

"It does," Khaldun agreed. "Nomad once told me that the university became much more directly involved in *that* conflict. Daphnis tried to take over the school, so they didn't have any choice."

"I thought mages weren't allowed to rule," Jezebel said.

"Only sorcerers and necromancers," Khaldun corrected her. "It's frowned upon for normal mages, but it happens now and then."

"This must explain why Raphael gave up teaching," she observed.

"So it would seem," said Khaldun. "I guess Henry's not the first despot he's fought."

This information provided Jezebel new insight into their guide. He'd seemed invulnerable before, especially after surviving the battle on the bridge. She'd come to regard him as something more than a man. But this knowledge showed her that he was human, after all, possessing the same emotions and motives as anyone else. She appreciated him more than ever.

Khaldun and Jezebel agreed not to tell Raphael what they'd discovered. She felt like they'd invaded his privacy. If he wanted them to know about his wife, he'd bring her up himself.

Jezebel spent the rest of the day reading about the early days of the university. She sat in Raphael's chair, legs folded beneath her. And for the first time since leaving Dorshire and encountering Henry's men, she felt safe and secure.

Jezebel spoke to Allison before she went to bed that night. She told her about Enigma's message, and their plan to travel to the watchtower. Allison begged her not to go.

"The demon has not returned," she said. "I'm safe. If you journey that far, you may not return for *months*. I can't bear to be without you so long."

"There's no guarantee the demon won't strike again when you return to the castle," Jezebel insisted. "I've gone this far; I'm not giving up. We know where to find Enigma now. He can teach us how to end this nightmare forever."

Jezebel fell into a deep and dreamless sleep that night. But again, she was wakened by a sense of someone beckoning to her. This time there was no doubt the source was outside, somewhere in the woods.

She ventured out of bed, left the wizard's house, and set out into the trees. Before long, she spotted a golden glow in the distance.

The glow disappeared, but Jezebel pressed her way through the woods, still feeling the mysterious call. Within a few minutes, though, she felt lost and was sure she'd never find her way back to Raphael's.

Suddenly someone stepped out from behind a large tree. Jezebel gasped, startled for a moment until she realized who it was. "Allure," she said.

The sorceress was dressed the same as before. She moaned low in her throat, reminding Jezebel of a cat's purr as she drew closer and caressed Jezebel's face with the back of her hand. A few inches shorter than Jezebel, she stared longingly into her eyes.

"There was a golden glow," Jezebel said nervously.

"What golden glow?" Allure asked with a mocking smile, bringing her face within inches of Jezebel's, and breathing softly on her ear.

"Was that you?"

"What truly brings you here, farm-girl?" Allure asked, ignoring her question.

"It's like I said at the inquiry, I want to learn magic."

"Then you should stay," Allure told her. "There is so very much we could teach you."

"But I can't yet," said Jezebel. "I have to…" Allure ran her tongue along the side of Jezebel's neck, moaning softly again. Jezebel felt frozen with fear, or anticipation, she couldn't decide which. "I need to return to Spanbrook. But one day, I wish to study here…"

Suddenly the forest around her disappeared. Jezebel found herself in a dimly lit room, with a fire burning on the hearth, and a massive four-poster bed with silken hangings around the edges.

Allure pushed her onto the mattress, climbing on top of her and plunging her tongue into Jezebel's mouth. Jezebel kissed her back for a moment, but then pulled away.

"There are many reasons to stay," Allure whispered in her ear. "I wish to entice you."

"I can't stay, I have to…"

Jezebel's clothes disappeared, and Allure turned into Khaldun, also naked, rubbing his manhood against Jezebel's leg. Jezebel moaned, scratching her nails down Allure's muscular back. But again, after a moment of temptation, she pulled away, trying to distance herself from this enchantress. "This is all an illusion," she muttered.

Allure moaned again, but this time the sound spoke of disappointment. She changed again.

"Perhaps you'll find this form more tempting," she said, and Jezebel realized she'd turned into Allison.

"No," Jezebel whispered. But she couldn't resist and kissed the woman hungrily. But then she said "No!" more insistently, pulling away yet again.

Allure sat up, still maintaining Allison's appearance, but Jezebel realized that her skin was golden, glistening in the glow of the hearth. Suddenly the surroundings changed again. The fire remained, but the bed disappeared. Now Jezebel found herself chained and shackled to a stone wall. Allure stood naked before her, still in the form of the princess.

"I could teach you much of the ways of the flesh," the sorceress told her with Allison's voice. "If only you'll stay."

"I can't," Jezebel said weakly.

"This girl is the reason you are here," she declared.

"How do you know about her?" Jezebel demanded. "How can you look like her when you've never seen her?"

"You are trying to save her," Allure said, returning to her own body, and now wearing clothes again. "You are on a quest to find Enigma."

"Yes," Jezebel replied as her clothing reappeared, their surroundings dissolved, and they returned to the woods. "There's a demon haunting my cousin, and I'm trying to save her before it drives her mad."

Allure moved toward her, still holding her gaze. Jezebel felt frozen as the sorceress placed her hands on the sides of her head.

"You *will* find Enigma," Allure told her. "Beyond that is hard to say. But you *would* learn much if you were to stay. There is magic in your blood, doubly strong."

"What does that mean?"

"You've inherited the talent from both of your parents."

"That's impossible," Jezebel said, shaking her head. "My father has no mages in his family."

Allure withdrew her hands and stepped away. "There can be no doubt," she told her. "You would become powerful if you enrolled here."

"Will I become a sorcerer?"

Allure closed her eyes and stood silent for a moment. "No. The metamorphosis is not within you. And for now, you must continue your quest. But perhaps one day, I will entice you to return."

Allure smiled seductively, moving toward her and kissing her passionately once more. But in the next moment, she was gone, and Jezebel started awake, back in her bed at Raphael's house, unsure if it had all been a dream.

Jezebel stayed at the house with Khaldun for the next two days. Her attraction to the wayfarer had not abated, but she resisted the temptation. The encounter with Allure had strengthened her resolve: she was determined to restore her faith to Allison.

Jezebel said nothing to Raphael or Khaldun about her experience with Allure. She felt like she was being toyed with, a pawn in some sort of larger game she didn't understand. But she was determined to figure it out on her own.

She spent much of her time immersed in books. As she read various texts on magical theory, she found herself thinking she might enjoy enrolling at the university. She wasn't a sorcerer, so she'd still be able to go back to Spanbrook. It would mean leaving Allison's side for a time, but it wouldn't be permanent. She decided to bring it up with her father when she returned home.

At the end of the second day, Raphael reported that the scouts had returned. Henry had recalled the majority of his troops to Fosland. He'd left occupying forces in the more outlying areas, but only a token presence in Roses and Ulster. This worked to their advantage; they would be able to take the faster route along the western side of the Mayne.

"Why the withdrawal?" Khaldun asked. "What is he up to?"

They were standing around the desk, looking at the map.

"Isn't it obvious?" Raphael said. "Look!"

Jezebel had no idea what he was driving at. But suddenly, Khaldun said, "Oh no…"

"What is it?" asked Jezebel.

"He's preparing to attack Highgate," Khaldun said.

Jezebel looked back and forth from the wayfarer to the wizard. They both appeared grimmer than the situation warranted. "Why is Highgate so important?"

"Thus far, Henry has confined himself west of the Mayne—Ulster, Roses, Perrin, Stiles," said Raphael, pointing to each. "But Highgate is the linchpin to everything on the eastern shore. None of the other princedoms can match Salerna's might. If Highgate falls, there's nothing to stop him from taking everything from here to Northcoast."

"Only Stoutwall would remain independent in all of northern Maeda," Khaldun observed.

"And once he truly commands the resources of a kingdom, he's bound to take Stoutwall as well. And then no princedom would remain to stop him from conquering southern Maeda," Raphael added.

"Forget Stoutwall," Jezebel said, jabbing her finger at the map. "If he does march to Northcoast, he'll have the university surrounded!"

"Yes, precisely," Raphael agreed. "And in all likelihood, he will capture at least one sorcerer before he bothers with southern Maeda. At this point, I would be heading to Highgate with or without the both of you. But now we must make haste."

"How long before Henry's ready to bring his troops across the Mayne?" Khaldun asked.

"At least a fortnight," Raphael replied. "We can beat him to Highgate, but we must leave right away. Are the provisions and gear ready?"

"Yes," Jezebel said, going through everything in her head.

"Then we should leave at first light," the wizard told them.

As much as she wanted to find Enigma, Jezebel was sad to be moving on so soon. She'd been enjoying her stay at the university and wouldn't have minded spending a little more time there.

She slept poorly that night. She'd been sharing a bed with Khaldun. But she felt like lying next to the wayfarer was making her crazy. Jezebel failed to understand why her desire for him was so insatiable.

Worse, she had nightmares that she'd turned into a sorcerer, and the wraiths were chasing her through a forest. The dream ended the same way every time: Dredmort binding her to Henry.

When Raphael woke them, Jezebel felt like she'd slept only a couple of hours. She dragged herself to the kitchen, where the wizard had prepared them one last home-cooked meal. After that, they set out.

Khaldun made himself appear like a non-sorcerer. Once they were past the main campus, Raphael made the three of them invisible. They approached the southern boundary to find the road was being watched. A group of Henry's men was camped only a dozen yards away. Raphael led them farther east instead.

"The spells required to penetrate the boundary produce a shimmering effect that even non-mages can see," he explained once they were well out of earshot. "There's a path up ahead—we should be safe there."

A minute later, Raphael held out his wand and spoke the incantation. The barrier appeared, energy crackling along its surface, and an archway opened. Jezebel worried that someone might be hiding in the trees, but their passage went unmarked. The wizard closed the portal again once they were through.

They walked all day. Raphael avoided the road, leading them instead along a path that followed the river. The going was slow, but they didn't stop until well after sunset.

They didn't bother pitching a tent, instead laying out their bedrolls and sleeping under the stars. They woke at dawn, ate a light breakfast, and continued their march.

By midday, the river looped to the west, bringing them right next to the road. Raphael cast a spell to disguise them as farmers. They traveled along the main thoroughfare for the rest of the day.

Despite Dredmort's words about Henry's peace, Roses was nothing like Spanbrook. They didn't encounter any soldiers, but they did meet plenty of farmers and townsfolk. Jezebel thought they all seemed downtrodden. None of them offered any sort of greeting, instead casting their eyes to the ground when they passed. These were not happy people.

Although they hadn't seen any sign of troop movement, Raphael worried about camping too close to the road. So as the sun approached the horizon, they took to the trees. They ventured far into the woods before they laid down their bedrolls for the night.

Jezebel collected some kindling and started a small fire. Khaldun rendered them unseen. For a couple of hours before they went to sleep, Raphael attempted to teach Jezebel more magic. But he had no more success than Khaldun. Jezebel started to feel like she would be limited to a handful of spells for the rest of her life.

"Isn't it unusual for someone to have so much power in such a limited way?" Khaldun asked, making Jezebel feel worse.

"It is," Raphael replied, furrowing his brow. "But she is still new to her magic. Give her time."

They returned to the road in the morning, continuing southward. The banks of the Mayne rose higher until the river was flowing through a gorge far below. Before long, they spotted a bridge in the distance.

"This is where we must cross the Mayne," Raphael told them. "But I fear we may encounter troops. We'll go invisible, but we'll have to take great care to make sure they don't note our passage."

"But the lands across the river don't belong to Henry," said Jezebel. "So as long as we get to the bridge, we shouldn't have to worry about them pursuing us across it, right?"

"We'll see," Raphael replied.

As they drew closer, they spotted a shack by the bridge, and two soldiers sitting outside of it. There were six horses tied to a post nearby, though, making them think there were more men inside the building.

"I've crossed here before," Khaldun whispered. "We came this way on the way to Henry's castle. This should be easy—they won't hear us over the noise of the river."

Raphael nodded.

"Let's do it."

The guardhouse sat to the north of the bridge. They moved a little past it, then approached from the south to avoid coming too close to the men. But as they drew closer, one of the men spotted the dirt they were kicking up from the road.

"Who goes there?!" he shouted, getting to his feet and drawing his sword.

His partner joined him, and two more men rushed out of the shack to see what was going on.

"Shit," Khaldun muttered.

"To hell with it," said Jezebel. Raising her wand, she called fire, engulfing the men and the building in a towering inferno. Two of the men ran screaming, falling over the edge into the gorge.

"That'll do it," Raphael said with a grin.

The three of them hurried over the bridge.

"They'll have other troops close enough to see the smoke from that blaze," said Khaldun. "And I'm sure they'll come to investigate. Will they pursue us if they figure out that we went this way?"

"I doubt it," Raphael said. "Their soldiers won't cross the river without authority. But we should move fast. If there are wraiths nearby, I'm sure they *will* pursue us."

They kept up their march for three more hours. Jezebel expected to hear the wraiths' cry at any moment. But it never came. They made camp but didn't risk a fire. Jezebel fell asleep within minutes.

They resumed their course at dawn. They reached another road a mile from the river. Raphael told them that it led to Highgate City. They traveled with lighter hearts now, not bothering to disguise themselves or become invisible.

Jezebel noticed a remarkable difference in the travelers they met. These people greeted them cheerfully. Many expressed concern about the looming war, but their spirits were unfettered.

For three more days, they journeyed along the road; the terrain grew steadily rockier. High hills rose to their east, coming closer as they traveled. They lit a fire every night, and Jezebel practiced her magic. This phase of her expedition was the most carefree she'd experienced since leaving Spanbrook.

From conversations they had with people on the road, Jezebel formed an image of Princess Salerna. It was clear that she was a strong leader who inspired the love and confidence of her people. Jezebel found herself nurturing a great fondness for the woman, even though she'd yet to meet her.

As they walked on the fourth day, Jezebel realized that the hills—which had grown larger—now lay directly in front of them. The road had veered away from the river. And she noticed something on the nearest hill gleaming in the sunlight.

"What's that?" she asked, pointing it out to Raphael.

"That, my lady, is Highgate," he said.

As they drew closer, Jezebel could indeed make out a city on the hill. But she soon realized it was unlike any town she'd ever seen. Even Arthos had been similar to Spanbrook, only much larger.

Highgate was different. Although still some miles distant, Jezebel could tell that the entire city was built from stone. It almost looked like it had been carved out of the hill itself. Tall towers and spires reached to the sky.

"That's incredible," she muttered. At that moment, the westering sun had caught the top of the tallest spire. It glowed like a star.

"The crystal tower," Raphael said. "It's the tallest structure in Maeda. The view from the top is breathtaking."

"I've never seen anything like this place," Jezebel said.

"Highgate is ancient," Raphael told her. "It was the capital of the old kingdom. They don't build cities like this anymore. We'll be there in a couple of hours—wait till you see it up close!"

"I can't wait," Jezebel said, picking up her pace.

CHAPTER EIGHTEEN
HIGHGATE

hey stopped briefly at sunset. Jezebel contacted Allison; they talked only briefly. Allison informed her that they'd finished the tour of the princedom, and she'd return to the castle the following day. Jezebel reiterated her fear that the demon would resume haunting the princess. But Allison remained convinced it was gone. She again urged Jezebel to abort her journey and return home.

"But tell me all about Highgate," she said. "And Salerna in particular."

Only a few minutes after they'd started walking again, a group of soldiers on horseback intercepted them. The leader recognized Raphael.

"Greetings, master," he called, eyeing Khaldun suspiciously. "Her Highness told me you'd be arriving today!"

"Did she indeed?" Raphael said, looking puzzled. "I wonder how she knew. I sent no messenger."

"They say little transpires inside our borders without her knowledge," the man replied with a grin. "We've brought extra horses. The princess is eager to meet with you."

Raphael jumped onto one of the animals, and Jezebel rode behind Khaldun on the other. They followed the soldiers at a canter.

They passed a vast troop encampment a few minutes later. It was clear to Jezebel that Salerna was ready for Henry. As they drew closer to the city, her amazement at its architecture continued to grow. It looked like it had been built from the very bones of the earth. The hill itself acted like a castle wall; the city grew out of the summit. It was surrounded by a great wall of iron and stone that seemed but an extension of the earth and rock below.

Only the western slope of the hill was gentle enough to climb. A single, wide path made its way through several switchbacks up to the main gate. There they stopped as their escort spoke to the gatekeeper.

Jezebel gazed up at the top of the wall, dizzyingly far above, and the crystal tower even higher, and marveled at its construction. How had anyone managed to build something so tall? The gate alone stood higher than the walls of Castle Spanbrook—the city had certainly earned its name.

Once inside the wall, Jezebel was taken aback by the size of the city. It had been hard to judge its dimensions from below. It appeared from this vantage point to be at least twice as big as Spanbrook, yet entirely enclosed within the wall. Stone edifices stood everywhere. Jezebel could now see that the crystal tower rose from the middle of the central keep.

They followed the main road for several minutes until they came to another wall. This one wasn't nearly as high as the first, but still too tall for any enemy to climb. They rode to the southern end of the city before they came to the gate. Once inside, they continued toward the keep. But they came to yet another wall. This time they had to proceed to the eastern side of the city to find the entrance. It became apparent to Jezebel that any invading army would have an extremely difficult time sacking Highgate.

They went through one more wall before finally entering the castle itself from the west. The courtyard was enormous. An entire garrison was camped here—the soldier leading them explained that troops were embedded at every level of the city. They dismounted the horses and walked around the perimeter of the courtyard. The soldier led them inside the keep. They went past the great hall to the throne room at the rear of the building. The soldier opened the door for them but didn't go inside. Jezebel and Khaldun followed Raphael into the chamber. The door closed ominously behind them.

Marble walls surrounded them. Ornate crystal chandeliers hung from the vaulted ceiling high above. Two rows of thick stone columns formed an alleyway right up the middle of the room. There was a dais at the end with a golden throne.

Salerna rose from the chair, beckoning them. Raphael bowed low; Jezebel and Khaldun copied the gesture. As they made their way toward the princess, Jezebel realized she was older than she'd imagined. Her features were severe—as if her face had been carved out of stone—but not unkind. She wore long green robes, and her white hair was pulled back into a bun. A thin diadem encrusted with diamonds sat upon her head. She possessed an air of power and grace; Jezebel could easily imagine this woman as a queen instead of a princess.

When they stopped, only a few feet before the dais, Jezebel noticed a figure standing in the shadows beyond the throne to one side. His black, skin-tight, leather costume, facemask, and black morion caused him to fade into the shadows. When the golden skin and red eyes caught the flickering light from behind his mask, Jezebel realized he must be Salerna's sorcerer. The leather accentuated his lithe, muscular form; he was a little shorter than Jezebel. And although it was subtle, she could feel the magical force radiating from his body.

"Welcome, Raphael," Salerna said, walking toward him. She extended her hand. The wizard bowed, taking her fingers in his own and brushing his lips against the back of her hand.

"Greetings, Your Highness," he replied. "May I introduce you to Lady Jezebel Barclay of Spanbrook, and Khaldun."

They each bowed and kissed her hand in turn.

"An unbound sorcerer," Salerna noted, raising her eyebrows. "And a wayfarer, unless I'm mistaken. There must be an interesting tale here, Raphael."

"Indeed there is," Raphael said. "And I will tell it in time. But I have more pressing matters to report."

"If you're referring to the army Henry's raised across the Mayne, we already know," she told him, retaking her seat.

"Of course," the wizard replied, eyeing the sorcerer. "But more troops are coming, Your Highness. Henry's emptied much of his homeland. He's mounting an invasion that will likely start within days."

"You are correct," Salerna said gravely. "Your information is not news to us, although we appreciate the corroboration you provide. We will hold council tomorrow, and we'd like you to join us. But it is late. My people will escort you to your rooms—you must be weary from your travels. Take some time to bathe and dress yourselves. When you're ready, we'd be honored if you would join us for dinner."

"Of course," Raphael said, bowing low. They left the throne room to find a young woman waiting for them. She led them down a long hallway and up two flights of stairs. Then she showed Raphael to his room and escorted Jezebel and Khaldun farther down the passage.

"Her Highness wasn't sure of your relationship," the woman said, "so we assigned you a suite. Your chambers connect through a common washroom."

"Thank you," Jezebel said awkwardly. The woman nodded and walked away.

Jezebel's eyes nearly popped out of her head when she walked into her room. Wood paneling covered the walls—a dark cherry or mahogany. Lush carpeting blanketed the floor. The canopy bed was even bigger than Allison's.

Jezebel walked across the room to a narrow window. It faced east, looking out on the hills behind the keep.

"Spanbrook looks austere by comparison," Khaldun commented, clearly impressed.

"What, haven't you been here before?"

"Not inside the city," he said. "We performed in some smaller towns when I was little."

Jezebel dropped her pack and followed Khaldun into the washroom. It was almost as big as her bedchamber. The tub was large enough for four people. "They must pipe the water in from a source somewhere high in the hills," she said.

"We could wash together," he suggested with a grin.

"I think not," Jezebel said with a sigh. "I'd be too sorely tempted. I'm determined to avoid further damaging my chances with Allison."

"As you wish," Khaldun replied, sounding only mildly disappointed. "Let me know when you're done." He went into his bedchamber, closing the door behind him.

Jezebel turned on the tap. She peeled off her clothes, realizing only now how dirty they were. Dry mud was caked on in places. It occurred to her that she hadn't had a bath since Spanbrook.

Steam filled the room as hot water gushed into the tub. Jezebel found a rack on the adjacent wall loaded with glass bottles. She opened one and sniffed: scented oil. Another one emitted an aroma that reminded her of Allison. She poured some into the bath and shut off the water.

Jezebel spent the next ten minutes soaping herself up and scrubbing off the dirt. She washed her hair, then just lay in the tub. She felt more relaxed than she had in weeks, and started dozing off.

"Almost done?" a voice said.

Jezebel turned quickly to see who was there, covering her breasts with one arm and sloshing water all over the floor. It was Khaldun. He was leaning against the opposite wall, grinning at her.

"How long have you been standing there?" she demanded.

"Long enough," he said. "You're sure Allison wouldn't be willing to share?"

Jezebel growled at him. Getting out of the tub, she pulled the stopper from the drain. Khaldun handed her a towel. She dried herself off; the wayfarer stood there and watched.

"Don't you have any respect for my privacy?"

"No," he said with a shrug.

She wrapped herself in the towel, picked up her clothes, and stormed from the room, slamming the door behind her. Once in her bedchamber, she dropped the towel again. She realized she had nothing else to wear. But a moment later, she noticed several dresses lying out on a chair in the corner. Most were much too fancy for her taste. She put on the simplest and waited for Khaldun.

She had to confess that she couldn't entirely blame him for intruding upon her. They *had* become intimate. And were it not for her love for Allison, Jezebel would have been amenable to continuing that relationship.

Ten minutes later, they walked downstairs to the great hall. Raphael was already there; they took two seats next to him.

Salerna sat at the head of the table. She was richly dressed in a burgundy gown. A tall woman sat to her right. She looked to be the same age as the princess. Long bronze hair flowed down her back.

"Is that Salerna's lover?" Jezebel whispered to Raphael.

He nodded. "Her name is Jennifer. That's Prince Albert on the other side, the heir to the throne, with his wife, Elsa, and their twins, Dustin and Diana."

"I'm never going to remember everyone's names," Jezebel said. Albert was a big man, not fat, but tall and solid. His brown hair hung to his shoulders, and he wore a beard. His smile touched his eyes. Elsa was young and slender, with blond hair. She hardly appeared old enough to have birthed the twins, who looked a year or two older than Jezebel's little sister, Emma.

"Don't worry, I'll remind you as it becomes necessary," said Raphael.

"What's the sorcerer's name?" Jezebel asked. He was sitting next to Jennifer, still in his tight-fitting leather outfit, though he'd removed his facemask and helmet, revealing a shock of black hair.

"Azure," Raphael told her.

The feast started a minute later, and the servants poured wine. Salerna raised her glass in a toast to Raphael, Khaldun, and Jezebel. Everyone welcomed them.

Jezebel ate more than she'd thought possible. They started with a sampling of shellfish—she couldn't imagine how much it must have cost to import so far inland. After that, they served a succulent veal dish in wine sauce, wild rice with vegetables, and spicy potatoes.

Salerna asked about news from Spanbrook. Jezebel didn't know what to tell her—not much ever happened there. She found herself babbling about the arrival of the wayfarers and her uncle's tavern.

Albert talked to Khaldun at length about the travels of the wayfarers. The prince seemed fascinated by their lifestyle, not at all threatened by it. Jezebel realized that she should have been surprised by Khaldun's inclusion in the dinner invitation. She doubted very much this would have happened in most of the other princedoms.

But the conversation never turned to war. Jezebel had the feeling everyone was saving such grave matters for the council the following morning.

They had pie for dessert. Not long after, the twins dragged Jezebel off to play with them. They reminded her of Emma; she discovered that she missed her little sister very much.

Jezebel returned to her bedchamber late that night. She stripped out of the dress and collapsed in bed. She was exhausted, but content. She found Highgate very much to her liking so far.

Khaldun woke her late the following morning. She dressed in her travel clothes, which someone had laundered the previous evening. They went to Raphael's room and ate breakfast with the wizard. The windows in his chamber looked west over the city and the plain beyond.

"Today's council will be more serious," he informed them. "There is much planning to be done in advance of Henry's arrival."

"Why does Salerna want us there?" Jezebel asked.

"Mostly as a courtesy," Raphael said. "Although given your recent travels, you'll both be able to provide some news from the north."

"What about the watchtower?" Khaldun asked. "As much as I'm enjoying Salerna's hospitality, Jezebel and I should probably get underway before Henry arrives."

"I agree," said Raphael. "I have discussed the matter with Her Highness in private. I don't think we should bring it up in council. But if you can be patient for a couple more days, I believe the princess will help you get to your destination much more quickly than you imagine."

"What? How?" asked Jezebel.

Raphael would say no more. Ten minutes later, they made their way downstairs. There was a large conference room across from the great hall. Salerna, Albert, Jennifer, Azure, and several advisers and soldiers were already there, talking in groups of two or three. Raphael went directly to the princess. Jezebel stood by the door with Khaldun, uncertain where she should go. But when Raphael greeted Salerna, Jennifer excused herself.

"Lady Jezebel," she said with a smile, taking her hand. "The princess has asked me to invite you to sup with us this evening. It's nothing formal—we'll eat in the small dining room off the kitchen. She has some business she'd like to discuss with you privately."

"Oh—certainly," said Jezebel. "You're not staying for the council?"

"I leave politics and war to Her Highness," Jennifer replied. "But I'll see you tonight."

She left the room. Salerna called everyone to order a few seconds later, and they took seats around the table. Jezebel sat next to Khaldun, not feeling like she belonged here. Salerna started by introducing Raphael, Khaldun, and Jezebel to everyone else. Salerna's steward was here, as well as her master-at-arms, her top generals, and two witches who worked with Azure.

"Raphael, I am curious to know your plans," said Azure. "Will you be staying in Highgate for the battle?" The sorcerer's voice was surprisingly deep.

"I will," the wizard replied. "Resisting Henry is my calling."

"Excellent," said Azure. "And what about the boy?"

"He has business elsewhere," Salerna told him.

"It's too bad the university won't be sending more help," said one of the generals.

"Officially speaking, the university did not send *me*," Raphael reminded him.

"Of course," said the general; the others chuckled.

"What are the most recent numbers?" Salerna asked one of her generals.

"Troops are still arriving from some of the outlying holdings," the man said. "But so far we have sixteen thousand men camped north of the city. Eleven thousand are stationed on the southern plain, including the Elite Guard. Fifteen hundred are garrisoned within the city."

"And Henry?" she asked.

One of the other generals spoke up. "Current estimates put his main force at forty thousand."

"Raphael, tell me about his mages," said Salerna. "Will he bring them all?"

"No," Raphael replied. "Some he'll have left behind to guard his homeland. He left sizable forces in the northern princedoms but emptied Fosland and Roses. He has relied heavily on Nineve recently—she will probably turn up here. And Dredmort, of course."

"And the twelve wraiths," Azure added.

"Eleven, actually," Raphael corrected him.

"Did you manage to eliminate one of them?" the sorcerer asked.

"Not I," said the wizard. "The Lady Jezebel."

Jezebel felt herself blush as all eyes turned to her.

"I didn't realize you were a witch," Albert said, nodding appreciatively. "Tell me, how did you come to face Dredmort's devils?"

"Yes," said Salerna. "After speaking with Raphael, I think we would be well-served to hear your tale. Perhaps you should start with your experience in Stiles. I understand you first encountered Henry's men there?"

"That's correct, Your Highness," said Jezebel. She told them about everything they'd seen in Stiles and the way the troops had treated the people. She and Khaldun took turns recounting their escape from the castle, their encounter with the wraiths on the way to Arthos, and the battle with Dredmort before reaching the university.

"Thank you, both of you," Salerna said when they'd finished. "I think your story will reinforce for everyone here why it's so critical that we defeat Henry."

Jezebel knew she was in over her head as talk turned to battle plans. They spent a great deal of time discussing how Henry might cross the river. Salerna was prepared to destroy all the bridges. But the princess informed the others that Henry might be bringing boats from somewhere farther south.

They debated troop deployments, contingency plans, siege preparations, and a host of other concerns that Jezebel barely understood. Raphael, Azure, and the two witches put their heads together to discuss thaumaturgic responses to Dredmort and his wraiths.

The council lasted three hours. But finally, Salerna was satisfied.

"Thank you, everyone," she said, getting to her feet. "Highgate has never fallen to an enemy since the end of the old kingdom. And I don't believe it will succumb to Henry."

The meeting broke up. Raphael went to converse with Salerna. Jezebel turned to Khaldun. "Can we leave?"

"I think so," he said with a shrug.

They slipped out of the room.

"I'd like to explore the city a little today," Khaldun said in the hallway. "Care to join me?"

"Definitely," Jezebel replied with a smile. "The first thing we have to do is find lunch. I'm famished after all that talk!"

They left the keep. Despite Jezebel's hunger, they ended up walking down to the first level of the city before stopping to eat. People stared at them as they passed, some dashing off in fright. It was clear they were unaccustomed to seeing a sorcerer in their midst. Jezebel guessed that Azure probably didn't walk around the city very often.

Khaldun chose a tavern near the gate. They discussed the council meeting over ale as they waited for their food.

"Salerna seems to know what she's doing," Jezebel noted.

"She does, but the math works against her," Khaldun said with a frown. "She's outnumbered pretty badly."

"True, but look at this place," Jezebel countered. "It looks impregnable."

"That only matters if it comes to a siege. In a pitched battle, Henry wins. Although he has to get his men across the Mayne. Salerna's got an advantage there."

"And she's got Azure," said Jezebel. "I know Dredmort's powerful, but surely he's no match for a sorcerer."

"That's true," Khaldun agreed. "Azure should be able to neutralize Dredmort. I hope Salerna wins—I like Highgate. And I'd hate to see Henry take the entire kingdom."

"Agreed," said Jezebel. "I wonder what she wants to talk to me about tonight."

Khaldun shrugged.

They walked around the city after they ate. First, they visited a giant coliseum on the first level. Playbills announced upcoming concerts and theatrical productions. Next, they visited the botanical gardens and war museum on the second level. They tried to go inside the catacombs, which housed the tombs of the ancient kings, but the guard there refused them entry. Finally, they strolled through the central market and stopped to watch a group of street performers. Jezebel thought they looked strangely like the wayfarers. They did juggling and acrobatics primarily.

Khaldun talked to them once they'd finished. Sure enough, they'd been with the troupe many years before. They'd decided to leave and settle down in Highgate. They remembered Nomad and were sad to hear of his death.

After that, they made their way back to the castle. Raphael accosted them in the courtyard.

"There you are!" he said. "I've been looking all over for you."

"What's wrong?" Jezebel asked.

"Wrong? Nothing—I thought I'd give the two of you a tour of the city."

Khaldun laughed. "That's where we've been! We decided to take a walk around Highgate after the council."

"Oh," the wizard said, looking crestfallen. "Well, did you see the coliseum?"

"Yes," replied Jezebel. "It was marvelous—there's a concert there tomorrow night. Perhaps we can attend."

"I see," said Raphael. "But what about the gardens—you've never seen anything like it…"

"We went there, too," Khaldun informed him apologetically.

"The market?"

Jezebel nodded.

"The war museum?"

"That too," Khaldun confirmed.

"How about the catacombs?"

"We stopped there, but the guard wouldn't let us inside," Jezebel explained.

"Aha!" Raphael said, as excited as a child with a new toy. "I can get you in—let's go!"

He strode away. Khaldun and Jezebel followed in his wake, shooting each other amused glances.

The wizard led them back into the city, down one level. And indeed, the guard admitted them into the catacombs with a nod to Raphael.

They followed him through a long tunnel. In the end, it opened into a cavernous hall with a low ceiling. Torchlight flickered on the walls, exposing thousands of human skulls.

"This is the antechamber, where they buried common soldiers in ancient times," Raphael explained quietly. "They believed that they'd rise again in a final battle to protect the city from evil."

Jezebel scanned her surroundings in awe as Raphael led them across the room. She couldn't fathom how many wars it must have taken to fill this place.

Their footsteps echoed eerily as they passed. Jezebel feared they might be disturbing old ghosts. But a few minutes later they reached the opposite wall. Raphael led them through a grand stone archway.

After traversing a short tunnel, they emerged into a vast chamber with vaulted ceilings. Enormous niches lined the walls, each displaying a different scene carved into the stone. Below each vista sat a massive sarcophagus. Raphael led them to the first of these.

"Here lies Gregory the First," he told them. "He was the first king of Maeda."

"I've heard of him," said Khaldun. "He's the one who united all the separate fiefdoms."

"Indeed," replied Raphael. "Although under his reign, the kingdom included only northern Maeda."

"Was he like Henry?" Jezebel asked. "Did he conquer his neighbors and slaughter innocent civilians?"

"History remembers him as a hero," said Raphael. "I suppose the rulers he vanquished might tell a different tale if they could. But Gregory resorted to diplomacy more often than military might. Although he did defeat more than one warlord in his day—men cut from the same cloth as Henry."

They wandered slowly past the graves of dozens of kings. Above each, the sculpture on the wall portrayed a critical scene from the ruler's life. Raphael told them stories of the old kingdom as they walked. Near the end of the hall, they reached a sarcophagus much newer than the others.

"Who's this?" asked Jezebel. The sculpture depicted a man with a two-handed sword facing a naked woman. Rays of light cast in stone emanated from the woman's head.

"This is Verus," Raphael said solemnly. "He was the last king; Nyro killed him herself. The people of Highgate weren't allowed to give him a proper burial. He was relegated to a pauper's grave outside the city. After the downfall of the Pythan Empire, the first prince of Highgate exhumed Verus's remains and brought him here to rest with his fathers. He was a mighty ruler. But none could withstand Nyro at the height of her power."

Jezebel stared at the ancient necromancer's sculpture on the wall. The woman's body appeared lithe and powerful, her face beautiful. She wondered if this was an accurate portrayal, or merely the fantasy of the sculptor—it certainly didn't fit her vision of Nyro as an all-powerful mage. This representation looked entirely human.

"I think I've seen enough," Khaldun said with a shiver. "This place is creepy."

"Yes," Raphael agreed. "I think it's time to return to the land of the living."

CHAPTER NINETEEN
LOOKING GLASS

ezebel accompanied Khaldun and Raphael back to the castle. At sunset, she pulled out her mirror.

"There you are!" Allison said, staring back at her. Her hair was wet, and she was in her nightgown. Jezebel recognized her room at Castle Spanbrook in the background.

"You're back," she said.

"We arrived an hour ago," Allison told her. "I'm exhausted. I decided to take a quick bath and wash the road off of me. How's Highgate?"

Jezebel told her about the council and her exploration of the city. "I'm going down to dinner shortly with Salerna and Jennifer. But tell me—has the demon returned?"

"It's been quiet," said Allison. "I think it's gone."

Jezebel wasn't convinced, but she let the matter rest. Allison made her promise to contact her again when she returned from dinner.

An hour later, Jezebel changed into the dress she'd worn the night before. She ventured downstairs and found the small dining room without any difficulty. Salerna and Jennifer were already there. The princess greeted her with a smile, ushering her to an empty seat.

"I hear you had a chance to see the city today," Salerna said. "What did you think?"

"I love it," Jezebel said, as Jennifer poured her a glass of wine. "It's so different from everywhere else I've been. And it feels so old."

"I know what you mean," said Jennifer. "I've lived in Highgate my whole adult life, but I'm still not used to it. There's so much history here—I feel as though I'm moving back in time to the days of the kings whenever I walk through the city."

"I'd like to bring you to the crystal tower after we eat," said Salerna. "You haven't truly seen Highgate until you've viewed it from there."

"I hope you're not afraid of heights," Jennifer added, shivering slightly. "I've been up there once—never again!"

"They don't bother me," Jezebel replied, "as long as there's no chance of *falling*."

"The chamber is enclosed… mostly," Salerna told her. She took a sip of wine. "I must compliment you on your performance today. My advisers were impressed."

"They were?" Jezebel asked.

"That group can be intimidating," said the princess. "Yet you acted as if you belonged there. You also behaved with great courage against Henry's men when you found them abusing that poor girl. And destroying a wraith is no small feat, either. My mages accosted me this afternoon; they insist that I hire you."

Jezebel could hardly believe her ears. "But I'm a novice! I only know a handful of spells…"

"You're powerful, and you're brave," said Salerna. "That's what matters most. They would train you. But don't worry. As much as I'd love to have you, I know you don't belong here."

Dinner was served before Jezebel had a chance to question Salerna's cryptic remark. The conversation turned to other topics. Salerna told many tales of the kings of old. She also shared some of her family history, telling Jezebel about her father and grandfather, and the battles they'd fought in defense of the city. But still, Jezebel wondered why the princess had requested her presence.

Jezebel enjoyed the meal; Salerna and Jennifer put her at ease. She almost forgot that she was dining with one of the most powerful rulers on the continent.

After dinner, Jennifer kissed Salerna goodnight and left the room.

"Your Highness, what was it you wanted to talk to me about?" Jezebel asked.

"Follow me," Salerna said, striding from the room.

The princess escorted Jezebel to the top floor of the keep. There, they climbed a flight of stairs to the roof. A breeze buffeted Jezebel's dress as they made their way to the crystal tower. Salerna opened a great iron door and led Jezebel inside. The interior of the structure contained only a wide spiral staircase.

"It's a long way up," the princess said, starting the climb. "I hope you're in good shape."

"I'd better be after walking halfway across the continent!"

Jezebel discovered very quickly that climbing steep stairs didn't use the same muscles as walking. Her thighs started to ache, and she became winded after a few minutes. It took more than fifteen minutes to climb to the top. Despite her age, Salerna hardly broke a sweat. Jezebel couldn't understand it.

At the top of the stairs, the princess opened another heavy iron door. Jezebel walked through and was amazed.

The octagonal chamber was built entirely of crystal. A short, circular table stood in the middle. Large openings along the bottom of each wall let the air pass through; it was quite windy here and cold. Jezebel shivered, wishing she'd worn something warmer than her dress.

But the view was astonishing. The twin moons were nearly full, and the sky was clear. Jezebel could see for miles around. The Mayne snaked away to the north, back the way she'd come. Across it, she could see the fires of thousands of troops camped out under the stars. To the north and south lay Salerna's army; it seemed woefully small by comparison.

Minutes went by in silence as Jezebel stared out at the landscape. She'd never imagined it would be possible to stand so far above the ground. The towers of Castle Spanbrook didn't reach nearly so high.

"Tell me, Lady Jezebel," said Salerna. "What truly brings a farmer's daughter halfway across the world?"

"How much did Raphael tell you?" she asked.

"Only that you are seeking Enigma at the watchtower. He didn't say why."

Jezebel didn't know why the princess was so interested in her journey. But she found she trusted this woman. She took a deep breath and told her the full story, starting with the encounter with the demon in the Devil's Wood. She explained what happened with Nomad, and about Aldo's refusal to allow Myrddin to destroy the monster.

"You must love Allison very much," Salerna observed with a knowing smile. "Come here. I'm curious about what you'll see."

Jezebel didn't know what she was talking about. Salerna led her to the center of the chamber. She realized that the structure in the middle wasn't a table. It was a wide, shallow bowl sitting atop a thick base. The bowl was filled with a shimmering liquid, only two or three inches deep.

"What is it?" Jezebel asked.

"It's called the looking glass," said Salerna. "The ancient kings used it to observe their lands." She held her hands over the liquid. Instantly an image formed on its surface. Jezebel recognized it as the same aerial view of Henry's troops she'd just seen. But Salerna waved her hand, and the scene changed. There were troops again, but the surrounding country was desolate, and the men were on the move.

"What are you showing me?" Jezebel asked.

"These are the forces marching toward us right now from the southern princedoms," said the princess. "Henry has allied with a powerful warlord. With his help, he plans to destroy my city."

Jezebel gasped. "I had no idea! What will you do?"

"Don't worry. I have a surprise of my own in store," Salerna told her. "But come. I want to see what the looking glass shows *you*."

"Me?" Jezebel said in surprise. "But how do I… control it?"

"Empty your mind," said the princess. "Hold your hands above the liquid and see what you can see."

Jezebel followed her instructions uncertainly. Immediately an image of Allison formed in the liquid. She was sitting in the bay window in her chambers, looking out across the courtyard.

It was Salerna's turn to gasp. "What is it?" asked Jezebel.

"Nothing—it's just… she's stunning," the princess stammered.

The image changed. Jezebel saw herself and Allison facing each other, smiling joyfully. They were both wearing elegant gowns. Jezebel was squinting, as if from bright light; Allison seemed to glow. As more of the picture resolved, Jezebel realized they were in the courtyard of Castle Spanbrook, surrounded by hundreds of people.

"Are we… No…" she whispered.

"It looks like a wedding to me," said Salerna. "Sometimes the looking glass shows you the future. It showed me an image of you coming to Highgate at a time of great need. That's how I know we'll defeat Henry."

"But I don't understand," said Jezebel. "You said that I don't belong here… I'm going to the watchtower."

"No, the woman I saw in the vision was older than you are now," Salerna replied. "You will come here again one day—and Allison will be with you. We will fight together to defend this city."

"So… You know you're going to win now because in your vision, you still ruled Highgate?"

"Precisely," said Salerna. "You must find Enigma and return to your princess to fulfill your vision as well as mine."

Jezebel stared at the looking glass again, but it had gone dark. "What's it like?" she asked. "For you and Jennifer, I mean."

"It was difficult in the beginning," the princess said, with the same faraway look Allison often had when remembering something long passed. "Not everyone approved. But I knew we'd prevail."

"How?"

Salerna looked her in the eye. "I saw it in the looking glass. Knowing the future can be a great gift, Jezebel. But sometimes it can be a curse. I saw my entire family die. I tried to warn them—I wanted so desperately to stop it. But nothing I did made any difference. Yet the looking glass also showed me my son, and the existence I now enjoy with Jennifer.

"Always in life, you must do what you know is right. You embarked on this quest to save your cousin without a looking glass to show you the outcome. I have no doubt you will be successful. And I think the vision you've seen here proves you will achieve other goals as well."

Jezebel felt like she was walking through a dream as she made her way back to her room. *She and Allison were going to get married.* It seemed too good to be true.

She dug her mirror out of her pack and jumped into bed. Gazing into the glass, she found Allison staring back at her. She was lying in bed, too.

"How did everything go?!" Allison demanded.

Jezebel told her about her conversation with Salerna and what she'd seen in the looking glass. Allison was stunned.

"You're certain? We were truly getting married?"

"You wouldn't doubt me if you saw the gowns," said Jezebel.

"But… When was it? How old were we?"

"Older…"

"*Older*?" Allison asked, looking crestfallen. "By how much, precisely?"

Jezebel laughed. "We were still young—we looked almost the same as we do now. Except… I don't know. I can't put my finger on it. We seemed more mature somehow, careworn perhaps."

"Tell me everything—what were our gowns like? Who was there? Where in the courtyard were we, exactly?"

Jezebel laughed again. "It was hard to see much—the sunlight was glaring. You looked ravishing, I can tell you that much. And the gowns were beautiful. They were white and sleeveless with this sort of lace covering the bodice. We were on a raised platform directly in front of the keep…"

Suddenly Allison gasped, looking around anxiously.

"What's wrong?" asked Jezebel.

"I don't know—I thought I felt the bed move."

"Oh no," said Jezebel. "You don't think…"

Jezebel heard a snarling noise. Allison's bed started shaking violently; the princess screamed.

"Go to Myrddin!" Jezebel yelled. It seemed like Allison had put the mirror down because Jezebel could see the underside of the canopy now. Allison dashed out of her field of view. The princess screamed again, and Jezebel could see only a blur of motion in the mirror. But then there was a crashing sound, and the glass broke into several pieces. Jezebel dropped the mirror in surprise. Picking it up, she realized it no longer functioned. She could see only herself in the cracked face.

"Allison," she whispered. Had she made it out of her room? Jezebel had to know. She ran out the door and back down the corridor, and dashed up to the roof of the keep. The wind was stronger than it had been earlier—she felt like it might blow her away as she raced to the crystal tower. She had difficulty opening the great iron door, heaving it against the wind. Finally inside, she pelted up the stairs.

Jezebel's heart was beating so hard by the time she made it to the crystal chamber, that she thought it might explode. Pulling the door open, she stumbled to the looking glass. She grasped the edges of the bowl with both hands, bracing herself against the wind. Her hair whipped around her face as she stared straight down into the liquid.

"Show me Allison," she murmured, trying to clear her mind. An image of her cousin formed immediately. She was standing in the center of Myrddin's chamber, wearing only her nightgown. As Jezebel watched, the necromancer got to his feet. He walked across to her, clearly attempting to comfort her.

Still trying to catch her breath, Jezebel felt relieved. Allison was safe. Myrddin would find a way to protect her. He had to hold off the demon until Jezebel could find her way back.

Suddenly the image before her changed. It was Highgate—the city was ablaze. The crystal tower in the vision swayed dangerously back and forth. Suddenly it toppled over, the octagonal chamber shattering against the buildings below.

The image morphed again. Jezebel saw Aldo. He was dead; his empty eyes stared up at her. His body was broken, and blood was oozing from his head.

After that, the looking glass went blank. Jezebel panicked. Clearly, the image of Highgate was from the future—but what about Aldo? She tried to see him again, to see anything at Spanbrook but failed. The liquid remained stubbornly clear, showing her only the bottom of the bowl.

Jezebel tried to calm herself. If something had happened to Aldo, Myrddin would have known about it. He wouldn't have been sitting quietly in his chambers. This must have been a vision of the future.

What could transpire to cause Aldo to die such a violent death? And how far in the future would it happen?

Salerna was right, Jezebel reflected as she again returned to her room, and thought of the image of Aldo she'd seen. Such knowledge could indeed be a curse. Should she do something? Salerna had tried to stop her family's death to no avail. Jezebel wondered if taking action to avert such disasters would only help bring them about. Thinking about it made her head ache. She didn't know what to believe.

Jezebel knew one thing for sure, though: this journey had changed her. She'd had the sense, when she left her father's farm, that things would never be the same. And now she knew this was true because *she* wasn't the same. She could never look at the farm or even Spanbrook and not see them as part of a bigger world. And after everything she'd been through, and the visions she and Salerna had in the looking glass, she felt like she was destined to be caught up in events far more significant than she'd ever imagined. She could only wonder what they would be.

Jezebel kept herself up very late that night, fretting about Aldo's fate—and Highgate's. She wanted to warn Salerna about her vision at the earliest opportunity. But at least she knew Allison was safe.

Several hours later, Jezebel woke with a start. Trumpets were blaring. Heavy footsteps walked by in the passage outside her door.

Jezebel didn't know what was going on. She could see the sky through her window—it was dawn.

Jezebel slid out of bed and dressed quickly. She walked through the washroom to Khaldun's chamber and found him still asleep. Once she'd roused him, the two of them rushed to Raphael's quarters.

"What's happening?" Jezebel asked.

The wizard was sitting by the window, smoking his pipe. "Have a look for yourself," he said, beckoning them.

Jezebel walked across the room. On the plain far below, a detachment of troops was headed toward Highgate, directly from the river. The man on the lead horse carried an enormous white flag. A woman rode behind him, her flaming red hair trailing behind her.

"Nineve?" asked Jezebel.

"Mmm," said Raphael, drawing on his pipe. "I wonder where they crossed the river."

"They want to parley?" Khaldun asked in disbelief.

"Doubtful," said Raphael. "More likely, they will demand Highgate's surrender."

At that moment, Jezebel spotted a column of soldiers moving from Highgate's northern encampment to meet the enemy detachment. And she also noticed something strange. An odd-looking bird soared into view from overhead. It looked like a single, enormous wing. It raced through the air and began to circle over Nineve and her cohorts.

The opposing forces met in the middle of the plain. Nineve appeared to be conversing with the leader of Highgate's detachment. Jezebel wished she could hear what they were saying.

A few minutes later, Highgate's commander returned to his men. Nineve raised her staff. Jezebel cried out as a jet of fire shot toward Highgate's soldiers. But something blocked it.

"Look!" Khaldun yelled, pointing to the sky. The strange bird was diving toward the melee. But Jezebel realized it wasn't a bird. Now it looked more like a man standing on a plank. He held out his hands, and barbs of lightning arced toward Nineve. They hit her, blasting the witch from her horse.

Raphael chuckled.

"What the hell was that?" Jezebel demanded.

"You'll see," said the wizard, getting to his feet. "Come with me."

Jezebel and Khaldun followed him from the room. He led them down the passage to the same stairway Jezebel had used twice the night before. A minute later, they emerged on the roof of the keep. Salerna was there with her advisers, surveying the plain below. Raphael moved toward her, Jezebel and Khaldun close behind. Salerna turned and flashed them a smile, nothing in her face to indicate that anything was wrong.

Jezebel looked out to see Nineve and her men beating a hasty retreat across the plain. Highgate's troops hadn't moved. Jezebel could now see a boat tied up on the shore—it hadn't been visible before, but explained how they'd managed to get across the river. Jezebel searched the sky, but couldn't see the strange flying object anywhere.

But a few seconds later, she saw something take to the air as Highgate's soldiers headed back to their encampment. It now appeared to be shaped like a rectangle with a small mound in the center. It was headed directly for them. As it drew nearer, Jezebel realized it was a flying carpet; it landed a few yards away. The mound rose—it was Azure; he approached Salerna.

"What news?" the princess asked.

"Henry demands our surrender," Azure reported. "There was nothing more than his usual drivel: he intends to destroy the city if we don't capitulate."

"I wish you'd fried Nineve," said a man standing next to the princess. Jezebel recognized him from the council as one of her generals. "Calling fire against our men under a flag of truce…" He spat on the ground.

"The flame you saw masked another spell," Azure explained. "She attempted to ignite them from within at the same time. No doubt, her true intent was to ascertain my power. I blocked her magic, but my spell was no more than a slap on the wrist. Better not to reveal my full strength until we join them in battle."

"You acted wisely," said Salerna. "Now, if you'll excuse me, everyone, I need to speak to our guests."

Once the others had moved inside the building, the princess addressed Khaldun and Jezebel. "Henry is moving more quickly than I anticipated. I apologize—I'd hoped you could enjoy Highgate's hospitality a little longer. But you'll need to depart right away. Azure will transport you to the watchtower."

"No—you need him here," said Jezebel. "We can find our way. We'll trouble you for no more than a map and some provisions."

Salerna smiled at her. "The journey is more treacherous than you realize. And it would take you many weeks if you were to survive. No—I insist. Azure can get you there and return before nightfall."

Jezebel gaped at her.

"*Before nightfall*?!" said Khaldun. "But that's impossible…"

"Only if you delay," she said, walking away. "You have an hour to break your fast and gather your belongings. Then you must meet Azure back here."

"An hour…" Jezebel muttered. She hastened after the princess. "Can I speak with you, Your Highness? Alone?"

"Of course," said Salerna. "Join me for my morning meal."

Khaldun looked at Jezebel inquiringly, but she waved him off. He went with Raphael back to their chambers as she continued down the stairs with the princess. They walked to the same small dining room where they'd eaten the previous evening. Salerna sat at the head of the table, motioning Jezebel to sit next to her.

"What's on your mind, Lady Jezebel?" she asked as the servants laid out their food.

Jezebel told her that she'd gone back to the looking glass, and described what she'd seen.

"Interesting," said Salerna. "I cannot speak to your vision of Aldo. But you have foreseen the same future for Highgate that I have witnessed myself."

"But… Will Aldo live long enough to see me and Allison marry?"

"That's impossible to tell," Salerna replied. "I have spent countless hours gazing into the looking glass. It doesn't show the future often. And when it does, it reveals only brief glimpses. Often I see the same scenes over and over again. Only rarely have I been able to infer the order in which events will take place."

"But you're sure the destruction of Highgate isn't going to happen now, in the battle with Henry?"

"Yes, my dear. The crystal tower will not fall any time soon—that's one thing I *have* been able to piece together. You will return here with Allison before that happens."

"What enemy could possess the power to inflict such devastation upon this city?" Jezebel asked.

"I do not know," said Salerna. "I have seen many visions of that battle, but none revealed the identity of the attackers."

"Will Highgate prevail?"

"I cannot say," Salerna replied with a shrug. "I've never been able to see beyond the fall of the crystal tower. That fact alone bodes ill, I know. But the veils of time are closed beyond that moment. Who knows?"

"How can you stand it?" Jezebel asked. "Knowing, but not knowing?"

Salerna smiled. "It's never easy. But as I told you last night, you must always do what you believe is right. Do so, and the universe will pull you toward your destiny. If Highgate does fall, its demise will serve some greater good in the long run. Of that, I have total faith."

Jezebel failed to comprehend how she could remain so serene in the face of such a disaster. She ate her breakfast in silence. When they were done, she returned to her chambers.

She'd never unpacked, so gathering her things took almost no time. Her mirror was useless now, but she stowed it in her pack anyway. She met Khaldun in his room, and they made their way up to the roof.

"I feel bad leaving like this," Khaldun told her. "We're both mages—we could help in the battle."

"No. The risk is too great—you're still unbound. Think of what could happen if Henry's forces were to capture you!"

"I know, I know," he said with a sigh. "But I still feel bad."

Raphael was waiting for them on the roof, talking with Azure. "So this is goodbye," he said as they approached him.

"It is," Jezebel replied, realizing it only now. "Thank you so much for everything you've done for us. We wouldn't have made it without you." She grabbed him in a big hug.

"I owe you," Khaldun said simply, shaking his hand.

"We'll meet again, I'm sure," the wizard told them. "Best of luck in your travels."

Azure led them to the carpet. It looked much bigger up close.

"How does this work?" Jezebel asked uncertainly. She grew fearful imagining herself falling off of it.

"Powerful enchantments reside in the carpet itself, but flying it is still rather complex," the sorcerer explained. "You have to call air to lift and steer it, but summon earth at the same time to avoid falling off."

"Have you ever lost a passenger?" asked Khaldun.

Azure stared at him for a moment from behind his morion. "Not yet."

Jezebel smiled weakly at him.

Azure positioned Khaldun and Jezebel rear of center, near the left and right edges, instructing them to sit with their legs crossed. He deposited their gear in the middle. Once he was satisfied, he sat on the front edge, right in the middle.

Suddenly, Jezebel's legs snapped to the carpet. It was as if they weighed a thousand pounds. She tried to lift them, even an inch, but they wouldn't budge. An instant later, the carpet rocketed off the roof, straight up. Jezebel felt like she'd left her stomach below. They rose higher and higher, and several seconds later, she was looking *down* at the crystal tower.

For a moment, Jezebel was overwhelmed by the beauty of the landscape around her. It was even more striking from this height than it had been from the tower. Here, the troops stationed across the river seemed insignificant, like ants. The entire earth looked like a giant map, the road and the river, fields and hills drawn out in exquisite detail.

But a second later, she was overcome with fear. The carpet shot to the east like an arrow. They were traveling unthinkably fast, and Jezebel couldn't comprehend what was stopping her from toppling right over the edge. She knew that Azure had called earth to lock her in place. But she expected their high velocity to overpower the spell at any moment.

Yet she also noticed that there was no wind. Their acceleration had pushed her back when they first started moving, but Azure must have been doing something to block the rush of air.

She turned to look at Khaldun. He was grinning ear to ear, clearly feeling all of her exhilaration without any of her fear.

Jezebel peered back at Highgate. Already it was fading in the distance, the crystal tower glinting in the sun. She looked down for a second, and her fear of falling was renewed. After that, she tried to stare straight ahead.

Time moved on. Minutes turned into hours, and the sun climbed higher in the sky. Jezebel's back ached, and her stomach muscles burned. She tried to shift to a more comfortable position, but her legs were utterly immobile.

The land grew steadily more barren. Before long, a sea of pale gold extended below them: Jezebel knew they were passing over the desert. The mountains loomed in the distance ahead, a deep shade of purple.

Jezebel wondered if they would make any stops. Her whole body hurt. She was hungry and had to urinate. But they flew on.

As they drew closer, the mountains became clearer. Jezebel could make out individual peaks; most were snow-capped. Rock formations began to grow out of the desert, and rough hills rose before them. Azure climbed higher.

When the sun reached its zenith, Jezebel thought she could see their destination. There was a tall tower nestled between two peaks, still quite some distance into the mountains. They were headed directly for it. Jezebel pointed, and Khaldun nodded: that was the watchtower.

As she stared, Jezebel noticed something strange. There was a disturbance in the air; it seemed to emanate from the tower. It was like a wave on the water, except it had no substance. The air itself was rippling. It was moving toward them very quickly.

Suddenly Azure banked hard to the right and climbed still higher as if to evade whatever was coming at them. But the disturbance followed them. The sorcerer turned the other way, back toward the desert, and nose-dived. The anomaly was gaining on them.

For the next minute, Azure took them on a wild ride. Jezebel thought for sure she was going to fall off the carpet as the sorcerer desperately tried to avoid the disturbance. They weaved and bobbed through the air, climbing and diving wildly.

But it was a wasted effort. The anomaly slammed into them. Jezebel didn't need to be a sorcerer to feel its power. The magic was so strong it nearly knocked her unconscious. It also canceled every one of Azure's spells.

The carpet folded in the middle, suddenly a useless piece of fabric. Jezebel's legs came unstuck to it as she plummeted toward the ground.

CHAPTER TWENTY
MOUNTAIN

ezebel tumbled out of the sky, falling head over heels. At first, she flailed violently against the wind but soon managed to calm herself. Straightening herself out and holding one hand before her face to block the gale, she looked down. The ground was far away; for a time, it didn't feel like she was falling.

She knew she was going to die. Remembering her wand in her pocket, she tried to think of any spell she might cast that could save her. Fire would do no good. Could she use earth to soften the impact somehow? She couldn't imagine how it would help.

Before long, Jezebel perceived the ground rushing toward her alarmingly fast. She couldn't believe she was going to meet her end after coming so far. Jezebel started to panic; she struggled against the wind again, willing herself to fly.

Suddenly it happened. She sensed herself slowing. A strong gust of warm air rose from below; she felt as if an invisible cushion were supporting her. The ground was still approaching swiftly, but not as fast as before. Jezebel thought she might survive.

The terrain directly below her was rocky. Her most significant danger now was hitting her head on one of the large boulders. She squirmed, trying to steer herself to an empty patch of ground. It was too late; there was nothing more she could do.

Jezebel attempted to land on her feet but smashed into the ground too hard to keep her balance. She fell, tumbling painfully across rock and gravel. But she was alive.

Someone shouted her name as she regained her feet. She took a couple of cautious steps, trying to decide if she'd broken anything. Her arms and legs were bruised and scraped, but she felt like she'd avoided severe injury.

"Jezebel!" It was Khaldun. He was running toward her, Azure close behind. "Are you hurt?" He grabbed her by the shoulders, looking her up and down.

"No—I don't think so. I can't believe that fall didn't kill us!"

"It was Azure," Khaldun explained, glancing at the sorcerer. "He dove to make sure he reached the ground first. Then he called air for us to soften the impact."

"Your packs landed close to here," said Azure. "Follow me."

"What the hell happened up there?" Jezebel asked as they set out.

"I'm not certain," said Azure. "Powerful wards enclose the entire land of Pytha. But the approach to the watchtower is supposed to be open, a kind of passage through the enchantments. It turns out they limited the opening to the area near the ground. I tried to counter the magic, but it was much too powerful. It canceled every spell I cast."

"Now what do we do?" she asked.

"You'll have to continue on foot," the sorcerer said apologetically. "I can get no closer. And I must return to Highgate. Make for the pass between those two peaks," he said, pointing to the mountains. Jezebel recognized them—from the air, she'd seen the tower in the saddle point between the two. But from this vantage point, the structure was hidden.

"How long will it take us?" asked Khaldun.

"It's hard to say for sure," Azure replied, gazing off toward the mountains. "I've never been there. But I'd guess that you can make the entrance to the pass by nightfall—I saw it before the attack. It's probably a full day's march from there to the tower.

"The path is treacherous, but you should be safe if the weather holds. It frequently snows at the higher elevations. If you find the route impassable, there is a tunnel that leads through the mountain. I don't know where the entrance lies, but it's supposed to go directly to the tower."

"Would it be safer to make straight for the tunnel?" asked Khaldun.

"Perhaps. I wonder though—before Enigma, it had been centuries since anyone traveled to the watchtower. The tunnel hasn't been maintained. This region is prone to earthquakes; the passage may have caved in."

"We should stick to the pass if we can," said Jezebel. "I'd hate to make it most of the way through the tunnel only to find it blocked."

They reached their packs a few seconds later. Azure's carpet was there as well.

"I must leave you now," the sorcerer said. "I wish you luck." He pointed to the carpet, and it stretched taut, solid as a rock. He sat in the middle and shot into the air.

Jezebel watched him for a few moments until he disappeared in the sky. She wandered off to relieve her bladder behind a large boulder. Returning to Khaldun, she hoisted her pack over her shoulder. "Flying was good while it lasted. But I should've known we'd never go long without walking."

Khaldun sighed, lifting his pack. "I don't mind walking. But the lack of food is going to be a problem."

"Oh no," said Jezebel. "You're right—I didn't pack any provisions. And I don't imagine we're going to find anything edible in this land. What about water?"

"I filled my canteen before we left," he replied. "If we drink sparingly, we'll probably have enough to last a couple of days. We should get moving."

Jezebel wasn't about to argue. She was eager to put this leg of the journey behind them. They set out across the rocky landscape.

The next several hours were filled with misery. The land became steadily more adverse, the hills steeper. Jezebel stumbled and fell repeatedly. One time she lost traction in the gravel, one foot sliding out from underneath her. She stayed on her feet, but with her legs spread far apart, splitting her trousers. Khaldun laughed at her.

The day grew unbearably hot with the sun beating down on them. Jezebel pulled an extra shirt out of her pack and wore it over her head to provide some shade. They drank little water, only enough to avoid heat exhaustion.

The Anthar mountains loomed ever higher as the sun sank below the hills behind them. At sunset, they came to a rock wall and could proceed no farther east.

"We're close to the southern peak," said Khaldun. "If the pass lies between them, we should find it farther to the north."

"Ugh," Jezebel replied, sitting on the rocky ground. "I was hoping we could camp here."

"Let's try to find the entrance," said Khaldun. "It can't be far. I don't like this place—it feels like we're being watched. At least if we find the pass, we can use it as an escape should it become necessary." He held out his hand, helping her to her feet.

It grew dark. They marched for another hour, the moons lighting their way. Finally, they found the path. It was an opening between two enormous pillars of stone. Worn runes were carved in the rock.

"What does this say?" Jezebel asked, running her hand over the bottom of the inscription. It rose much higher than she could reach.

"I don't know," said Khaldun, setting down his pack. "That's no language I recognize. I wonder if it's ancient Pythan."

Jezebel sat down with her back against the rock. She closed her eyes, and uninterrupted would have drifted off to sleep within moments.

"You didn't talk to Allison," Khaldun observed, sitting next to her.

"I can't," she replied. "I never had a chance to tell you—the mirror is destroyed." She recounted her last conversation with the princess.

"So the demon did return," he said. "I hope she's safe."

"She went to Myrddin," Jezebel told him. "Hopefully, he can find another way to keep the monster away until we get back."

"Wait—I thought you said the mirror didn't work anymore? How could you possibly know that?"

"Oh…" Jezebel wasn't sure if she was supposed to tell anyone about the looking glass. But she had to provide some explanation. So she told Khaldun about her two trips to the top of the crystal tower.

"A looking glass?! I've heard of those—but I didn't realize any still existed. Did you see anything else in it, other than Allison talking to Myrddin?"

"I did," she said hesitantly. "Salerna showed me troops marching from southern Maeda to join Henry. Thousands and thousands of them."

"*What*?!"

Jezebel shrugged. "Salerna didn't seem worried. She said she's got a surprise of her own waiting for them."

"I wonder what that could be…"

"It also showed me my wedding day with Allison. And I saw Aldo dead, and I watched Highgate burn and the crystal tower fall."

Khaldun stared at her in shock.

"Salerna said I'm going to return to Highgate with Allison someday. And she saw Highgate burning, too. But she can't see anything beyond that. Do you think it will happen? Does everything the looking glass shows come true?"

"I don't know," he said. "Nomad always told me that divining the future is an uncertain business. He'd never used a looking glass, but he said that predictions like that could only show you possible outcomes. Our actions have the potential to alter the flow of time."

"Well, I hope Allison and I do wed. But I don't want to see Highgate fall."

"Nor do I," muttered Khaldun.

Jezebel curled up on the ground, using her pack as a pillow. She was asleep within minutes. But she awoke a short time later, shivering with cold. Khaldun lay snoring next to her.

She pulled out her wand and called fire. A fountain of flame sprung up before her. It provided warmth, but it wouldn't last. She had no kindling, and the spell would fade out as she fell back to sleep.

Jezebel stared out into the night, wondering if any trees grew in this land.

That's when she saw it. A pair of eyes were looking back at her, glowing in the firelight only a few yards away. Jezebel screamed; Khaldun sat bolt upright.

"What is it?!" he asked, groggy.

Jezebel pointed.

Khaldun held out his hand. A tower of flame erupted next to the eyes. The sight before them terrified Jezebel: wolves. Dozens of the beasts surrounded them. The one Jezebel had seen yelped at the fire, prancing away. A few of the others howled.

"What do we do?" Jezebel asked fearfully, holding out her wand.

Khaldun got to his feet. He held out both hands, expanding his spell to a vast wall of flame. A crescendo of howls and snarls burst from the pack as they backed away from the fire.

But at that moment, a lone wolf darted toward them around the edge of the flames. Jezebel pointed her wand and called fire, igniting the animal from within as it jumped at them. Its charred corpse landed at her feet.

Several other wolves moved in from different directions. Khaldun and Jezebel killed four more before the rest of the pack withdrew.

"We should take turns sleeping and keeping watch," Khaldun suggested.

"Agreed. Why don't I take the first watch? I'm too anxious to sleep now."

Khaldun nodded. "Keep a fire going. That should remind them to stay away. Wake me if they return."

He lay down again. Jezebel sat with her back against the rock, maintaining a large fire between them and the darkness beyond. Once or twice, she saw a pair of eyes approach. But calling fire near the beast was enough to scare it off again.

Khaldun woke a few hours later, and Jezebel went to sleep. When she woke again, she realized that she was starving.

"Is wolf meat edible?" she asked grumpily.

"I don't know," Khaldun replied. "I've never had it. We can try one if you'd like."

"Forget it," she said. "Let's just go. Azure said we could get to the tower in a day."

They started up the pass. At first, it was a pleasant stroll. The path was smooth and wide enough to allow two wagons to travel abreast. They covered ground very quickly. But as the day wore on, their progress slowed. The trail narrowed, in many places hugging the sheer face of the northern peak. To their right was a drop of hundreds of feet; Jezebel tried to stay away from the edge. They stopped at midday to take water.

"I don't like the look of those clouds," Khaldun said, pointing to the south.

Jezebel turned. A tremendous black thunderhead was moving directly toward them. "Lovely," she muttered. "Let's keep going. I don't fancy getting caught in a snowstorm."

They set out again. Soon, the way was barred. The path ended a few feet short of a cave in the wall. Jezebel could see it resume again a few yards ahead, but a chasm lay between.

"What now?" she asked.

Khaldun considered the situation for a minute, eyeing the cave. "We jump," he stated.

"No! That's ten feet across—I'll never make it."

"You misunderstand," he said, pointing to the cave. "We can leap into the opening from here—that's only a few feet. From there, we can get to the far ledge."

"I don't know about this," Jezebel said, remembering her fall from the carpet the previous day. "Azure's not here to save us this time if we get in trouble."

"It's either that or turn back and give up this quest," Khaldun said.

Jezebel let out a long sigh. "You're going to have to help me," she said.

"I will."

Khaldun jumped into the cave first. He made it look easy.

"Throw me your pack," he suggested. "It'll be easier without it."

Jezebel agreed. She tossed it to him, and he set it aside.

"Now swing your arms and push off with both legs," he told her. "Jump as hard as you can—I'll catch you."

Jezebel started shaking, willing herself not to look down. She stood as close to the edge as she dared. Bending her knees, she reached back, swung her arms and leaped.

She jumped so hard that she nearly knocked Khaldun over when she landed. He caught her, holding her in his arms for a moment. Jezebel felt the old attraction to him quite strongly; she was annoyed that his magnetism could arouse her even in a situation like this.

"Now comes the hard part," he said, releasing her. He walked across the mouth of the cave. The wind was strong here, swirling around the opening. Jezebel stayed behind him, keeping close to the wall.

"If I jump that hard again, we're going to fall over the edge," she observed.

"Yes," Khaldun agreed. "It's not as far, though. I could step across if my legs were a little longer. Wait here—I'll go first again."

"Where else would I go?" she muttered.

Khaldun leaped across the abyss like a cat.

"Easy," he yelled over the wind. "Throw me your pack again."

Jezebel tossed it to him, then worked up her nerve to make the jump. She felt stupid—it wasn't very far across. She knew she could do it with ease, were it not for the potential of falling. So she pretended that she was merely jumping across a stream back at her father's farm.

Khaldun was waiting for her, his hand wedged into a crevice to brace himself. Jezebel took a deep breath and launched herself toward him. The moment her feet hit the ground, he pressed her to the cliff face.

"Ow!" she yelled, bashing her head against the stone.

"Sorry about that—I thought you were going to jump too hard again," he said, grinning at her.

Jezebel's heart was hammering in her chest as they resumed their course. She hoped they wouldn't have to do *that* again.

As they walked, the air grew colder. Freezing drizzle pelted them as the thunderhead neared. It started falling more heavily but soon changed to snow. The path widened somewhat but became very slippery. Jezebel found herself practically hugging the rock to their left.

It grew dark. Jezebel was reasonably sure it wasn't sunset yet, but the storm clouds blocked the daylight. The snow fell ever more heavily. Jezebel was freezing; her feet grew numb. The wind was blowing snow in drifts before them and soon, it was up to her knees. Walking became much more difficult, and it grew nearly impossible to see the path.

"This is insane," she yelled over the storm. "Either I'm going to take one wrong step and plummet to my death, or the wind will blow me over the edge!"

Khaldun stopped. "We should turn back. If we can get to that cave, we can camp there for the night. Hopefully, the weather will break by tomorrow."

"You go first," Jezebel shouted. "I can't see where I'm going."

"Thanks!" he said, moving cautiously past her.

They made their way back down the path. Khaldun plowed his way through the snow. It was up to his waist in places; he batted it away with both hands. He tried calling fire to melt it, but the wind was too fierce: it blew any flame he created *away* from the snow.

Eventually, they found the cave. The snow wasn't as deep here; the swirling wind swept it away from the edge.

Khaldun jumped into the opening; Jezebel threw him her pack. Making the jump wasn't nearly as intimidating this time; she knew she could jump as hard as she wanted. So she swung her arms and leaped.

But her foot slipped as she pushed off. She crashed against the ledge, her legs hanging off. She scrambled to gain purchase, clawing at the hard ground, and trying to find a foothold. But it was no good: she was sliding backward.

"Jezebel!" Khaldun shouted. He dropped to his knees, grabbing her arm with both hands. Jezebel held on to him as hard as she could. But her hand slipped out of his grip.

Khaldun grabbed her other arm; Jezebel was dangling off the edge by one hand. Looking down, she saw only snow spiraling into endless darkness. She screamed, squeezing his arm so tight, her nails dug into his flesh. Slowly, Khaldun pulled her back. Jezebel managed to reach over the edge with her other hand. With Khaldun's help, she swung one leg onto the ledge. Finally, he tugged hard, and she tumbled over on top of him. Jezebel hugged him, crying hysterically.

"You're safe now," he whispered.

He held her for a minute while she tried to calm down. Jezebel couldn't stop imagining herself falling into the abyss. But finally, she mastered her fear, forcing herself to breathe deeply.

"I thought I was going to die," she said haltingly between sobs. "Thank you."

"It's over now," said Khaldun. "You're out of danger."

"I've had enough of this place," she said, getting to her feet.

"So have I," he replied. "With any luck, the weather will clear by sunrise. We must be close to the watchtower."

Jezebel looked around the cave. It was dark. Their packs were lying a few feet away, but she could see no farther. Pulling her wand out of her pocket, she summoned a small flame. She walked farther into the cave, surprised at how deep it delved. Looking behind a large boulder, she gasped.

"What is it?" Khaldun asked, moving to her side.

"Look!" she said. Stacked on the floor of the cave was an entire cord of wood.

He looked back and forth disbelievingly between her and the logs.

"What is this doing here?" she asked.

"I'm afraid I have no explanation," he said. "Perhaps people live in these mountains. If they travel through the pass regularly, they might leave wood here for future use."

"Lucky for us," Jezebel replied. She brought a few logs closer to the opening, sat down, and lit a fire.

"Come here," Khaldun called from deeper inside the cave. "You're not going to believe this."

Jezebel joined him. Khaldun had found a large wooden crate. He lifted off the lid. Inside there were jars of dried fruit and meat, and canteens of water.

"A feast," Jezebel said with a smile, opening one of the jars. She scarfed down several pieces of meat.

"Slow down," Khaldun cautioned, laughing at her. "You'll make yourself sick."

Jezebel paid him no heed—she ate until she was full. Khaldun consumed his food more slowly.

"I wonder how far this cave goes," he said. He moved farther inside; Jezebel followed.

They walked carefully, as the floor was strewn with rocks. Beyond the provisions, the opening narrowed considerably. Jezebel had to duck to avoid hitting her head. But after several yards, the walls smoothed. The debris on the floor disappeared.

"This is no cave," Jezebel said excitedly. "It's a tunnel!"

CHAPTER TWENTY-ONE
DARVÛD

ezebel took a step into the passage. Khaldun grabbed her by the elbow.

"What are you doing?" she demanded. "Let's go!"

"This isn't wise," he said. "You heard Azure—the tunnel might have caved in."

"I'll take the chance! It's better than trying to travel any farther along that cursed path. I almost died out there."

Khaldun held his ground. "I have a bad feeling about this route. We have no idea who left the wood and provisions—they may be in there. And they could be unfriendly."

"You don't know that! We're almost there. Azure said the tunnel leads to the watchtower. Enigma's there—I can finally find out how to save Allison. Why delay?"

Khaldun turned back to the cave. "I'm not going in there. If you do, it'll be without me." He walked away.

Jezebel stood there for a moment in disbelief. But she had no desire to journey alone. She walked back into the cave herself and sat next to Khaldun by the fire. They stayed motionless for a long while, staring out at the falling snow.

"You know," said Jezebel quietly, "this whole quest may be for nothing."

"What do you mean?"

"We don't know for a fact that Enigma can help us banish a demon."

"That's true. But you were aware of that from the beginning. If anyone possesses the knowledge, it'll be him. Have faith, Jez."

Jezebel took a deep breath. "I know. But if he doesn't have the answer, maybe I'll take Allison and move far away. The thing didn't follow her on the tour of the princedom. I can't bear to stand by and watch her endure this."

"You truly love her, don't you?"

"I do. I don't think I realized it until this ordeal began. But when I saw the vision of our wedding, I knew beyond any doubt that was what I wanted."

"We're going to have a long journey back, whatever happens with Enigma."

Jezebel sighed. "Indeed. I wish *we* had a flying carpet. I wonder what's happening in Highgate."

Khaldun could only shrug.

They chatted a little longer before Khaldun drifted off to sleep. As Jezebel sat there alone, staring out from the top of the world, she wondered how her journey would end.

In the morning, she woke to find Khaldun standing over her. He was gazing out of the cave, shading his eyes. Jezebel stretched and yawned. She sat up to look outside and was nearly blinded. The world had turned white. Everything was buried under the snow; the morning sun glared off of it.

"It seems our decision has been made for us," Khaldun observed. "There's no way we can continue through the pass."

"Good," Jezebel muttered, lying down again.

They ate a light breakfast and stowed some of the food and water in their packs. Khaldun went back to the mouth of the cave for one last look outside.

"Nomad knew spells to help navigate on cloudy, moonless nights," he said. "I wish I'd learned them—they could be helpful where we're going."

"Azure said the tunnel leads to the watchtower," said Jezebel. "Why do we need to *navigate*?"

Khaldun didn't answer. They set out down the tunnel. Jezebel took the lead this time, conjuring a small flame in front of her. The shaft was straight and narrow; it was also warm and stuffy. Jezebel's body soon ached from walking partially crouched. But eventually, the tunnel ended, intersecting with another that was wider and higher.

"Maybe you were right," said Jezebel. "Which way?"

"Definitely to the right," Khaldun replied. "We still have to go farther east."

Jezebel moved into the darkness. It felt good to straighten up. And there was a cool breeze here—it was faint, but she found it refreshing.

The two of them walked for what seemed like hours. They crossed intersecting tunnels several times, but their passage made no turns. At one point, the rock wall to their right disappeared, revealing an open chasm. Recalling her brush with disaster the day before, Jezebel stayed as far from the edge as possible. But Khaldun peered over the brink. He called fire, then staggered back a second later.

"What is it?" Jezebel asked.

"A bottomless pit, it would seem," he said. "It made me dizzy to look into such deep darkness."

After that, they both avoided the edge. Before long, much to Jezebel's relief, the wall reappeared. The tunnel grew wider and started twisting and turning through the mountain.

Suddenly Jezebel stopped; Khaldun walked right into her.

"What's wrong?" he asked.

She shushed him, listening intently. She'd heard something up ahead but wasn't sure what. Everything was silent now.

"Let's go a little slower," Jezebel suggested. "I don't want to walk into anything unpleasant."

They moved ahead, but within seconds she stopped again. This time the noise persisted.

"Voices," Khaldun whispered.

Jezebel nodded; the sound ceased.

They proceeded very cautiously. Jezebel held a tiny flame in front of her, barely enough to see anything. They heard the voices again, directly ahead. A minute later, they emerged into a large chamber. Some sort of stone structure stood in the center. The voices were louder here, echoing off the walls. They crept across the room, ready for anything.

Suddenly a figure appeared in front of them. Another moved into view beside it. They were somewhat shorter than Jezebel and quite stout. If they didn't have eyes and beards and weren't walking, she might have mistaken them for rocks. Their faces and bare chests were craggy and gray, as if they'd grown out of the mountain.

"Hello," Khaldun called out.

The two figures froze, regarding them apprehensively. They looked as surprised as Jezebel felt. The two of them yammered in some foreign tongue, approaching slowly.

"We don't understand you," Khaldun said, holding his hands in front of him in a gesture of peace.

The two creatures shouted at them, gesticulating wildly.

"This isn't going so well," Jezebel observed, holding her wand tight. She had unintentionally grown her flame quite large.

"We're looking for the watchtower," Khaldun said slowly. "We mean you no harm."

One of the figures drew a sword. Jezebel called fire and ignited his trousers. The other creature batted at his comrade's legs, putting out the flames. Then he drew a long dagger, and the two of them advanced on Khaldun and Jezebel.

This time, Khaldun summoned earth, knocking the creatures back. They charged again, and Jezebel called a wall of flames. The pair turned and ran. Jezebel canceled her spell.

"What were they?" she asked.

"Dwarves, I think," said Khaldun.

"*Dwarves*?! I had a hard enough time believing that elves were real. I'm still not sure about dragons—and now you're telling me that dwarves truly exist? I feel like I've woken up in some strange fairy tale!"

Khaldun shrugged. "They weren't human—I don't know what else they could've been. But that might explain who left the provisions in the cave. And in any case, they've decided our course for us."

"What do you mean?" asked Jezebel.

Khaldun pointed across the chamber. For the first time, Jezebel realized that two separate tunnels led out of it, both in the same general direction.

"The dwarves went to the left. Therefore I think it would be best if we stayed to the right."

"Good idea," Jezebel agreed.

They walked into the tunnel. In a few yards, it opened up, much broader and taller. And it sloped gently downward.

"Azure was wrong," said Jezebel.

"How so?"

"He said that the tunnel led directly to the tower as if there were only *one*. Who do you think built all of this?"

"I don't know," said Khaldun. "It feels ancient, though. The watchtowers were built after the fall of the Pythan Empire—I wouldn't be surprised if these tunnels were just as old."

"Could it have been the dwarves?"

"Perhaps. I don't know much about them."

They walked for at least another hour. The passage grew larger twice more; it was now as wide as the Castle Spanbrook's Great Hall. But suddenly Jezebel stopped—she heard noises again, far ahead.

"What is that?" she whispered.

"I think we're in trouble," said Khaldun. "I hear voices—lots of them. It sounds as if a whole host is marching toward us."

A moment later, Jezebel noticed a flickering light far down the passage. "Should we go back?"

"No—but we might be able to hide," Khaldun said, pointing to the far edge of the tunnel. There was an opening there. Jezebel ran, Khaldun right behind her.

Several yards inside the passage, they found a chamber to the left. There was another opening across the room and a circular stone structure in the middle. Jezebel realized it was a well. They ran behind it, hiding from view.

The noise in the central passage grew steadily louder. Jezebel heard angry voices shouting commands. Soon it sounded like they were passing by. The din started to die down again. But then Jezebel heard two distinct voices much closer. Someone was coming down the side passage. Jezebel held her breath, her heart hammering madly.

A light shone into the chamber, casting a shadow of the well on the wall. The voice shouted something and moved on. The light disappeared.

"They're searching for us," Khaldun whispered. "We need to get out of here."

He crept through the far doorway, Jezebel behind him. There was a narrow staircase leading down. Khaldun walked only a few steps before he stopped. He turned to face Jezebel, fear in his eyes. Jezebel heard voices from below, approaching fast.

"Quick," said Khaldun, "back into the main tunnel. I'll make us invisible."

But the moment they stepped into the chamber, two dwarves walked in from the other side. They were wearing strangely iridescent armor and helmets and brandishing swords.

"Damn!" shouted Jezebel, pointing her wand. She called earth, trying to knock them back. But nothing happened. She summoned a wall of fire instead, but the flames vanished when the dwarves walked through them.

Khaldun flung out one arm, calling fire himself—Jezebel knew he'd tried to ignite them from within. The spell failed.

At that moment, dwarves emerged from the stairway. They grabbed Khaldun and Jezebel, snatched Jezebel's wand, and shoved them into the wall. They confiscated their packs. One of them yanked Jezebel's arms behind her back. She felt her wrists being tied together with coarse rope.

The dwarves forced them roughly from the chamber, shouting at them in their guttural language. Out in the central passage, Jezebel saw hundreds of the creatures waiting for them. She'd thought that Khaldun might be able to free them using magic, but that hope disappeared.

Their captors directed them to the very center of the group. They started marching in one enormous column deeper into the mountain.

"I'm scared," said Jezebel. "What are they going to do with us?"

One of the dwarves struck her in the back of the head before Khaldun could respond. He looked at her apologetically.

They walked for only a short time, passing into a massive hall. An enormous bonfire was burning in the middle. Hundreds of dwarves were gathered here, sitting on benches at long, low tables. It appeared they'd walked into the middle of a great feast. An uproar arose when their captors pushed Khaldun and Jezebel to the front of the room.

There, sitting on a rock throne upon a dais, sat a fat old dwarf. He was wearing a golden crown. As they approached, he addressed them in the common tongue.

"How dare you enter my kingdom uninvited! Who are you?"

"Please, sir, I'm Jezebel of Spanbrook, and this is Khaldun. We're trying to get to the watchtower. We meant no disrespect—we weren't aware… Well, we didn't know you existed."

The dwarf stared at her for a moment. Then he laughed, deep and slow. "We have existed here since before men invaded this land from over the sea. Who do you think constructed this magnificent realm? *Men* have never possessed such skill."

"We apologize again, Your Highness, but we must get to the watchtower," said Khaldun. "We have urgent business with the sorcerer who resides there. What do you plan to do with us?"

The dwarf laughed again, more softly this time. "I plan nothing. I will bring you to Nargûn. He can do with you as he pleases."

"Nargûn?" Jezebel asked apprehensively. "Who is that?"

The king waved them off. The other dwarves pulled them away, toward the bonfire. There, they tied Jezebel to an iron stake, Khaldun to another nearby. Jezebel could feel the heat emanating from behind her; she started to sweat. A group of dwarves was seated at one of the tables immediately before her, ogling her as they ate. She couldn't tell what kind of food was on their plates, but it looked slimy and disgusting.

Time dragged on, and Jezebel grew steadily less comfortable. The heat from the bonfire was overwhelming. The dwarves seemed to drink more than they ate. Soon they broke out in song. A few of those close to Jezebel fell off their benches, apparently intoxicated.

Finally, the king rose to his feet. He addressed the gathering, shouting harshly. The others cheered, raising their mugs to him. It appeared that the feast was over because all across the room, the dwarves started getting to their feet and wandering off. A few minutes later, Jezebel and Khaldun were left alone, except for guards standing sentinel at each of the exits.

"This feels oddly familiar," Khaldun observed wryly.

"Yes, but at least we're clothed this time."

"I think I'd prefer to be naked," said Khaldun. "It's hotter than hell in here."

"So who's this Nargûn they're bringing us to?"

"I don't know," he replied. "But I don't like the sound of him. With our luck, he'll be the torture master."

"Why didn't our spells work against them? They were perfectly effective against the two we met earlier."

"It was their armor," said Khaldun. "It repels magic somehow. I've never heard of such a thing—I didn't know it was possible."

They stood there for a long time. Jezebel thought that hours must have passed. She was sweating so badly that her clothes were drenched. Her eyes burned from the sweat dripping into them.

The king returned with several other dwarves. Jezebel counted eight. One of them had their packs; another was playing with Jezebel's wand.

"Thieves!" the king yelled.

"What?" asked Jezebel. "We've stolen nothing…"

One of the dwarves opened her pack, reached inside, and threw dried meat and fruit at her.

"You had no right to take those provisions. We left them for our scouts, not for filth like you. Nargûn will hear about this. You will go to him now."

"Who is Nargûn?" Jezebel demanded.

"We bring him intruders. He questions them. The last few who entered here were thrown from the mountain."

The king turned and strode from the room. The dwarves untied them from the stakes but left their arms bound behind their backs. Jezebel struggled, but one of the dwarves pressed a knife to her throat, shouting at her. She held still. They escorted them out of the chamber; the dwarf with Jezebel's wand led the way.

They walked along a low, narrow passage. Jezebel had to crouch, which was awkward with her hands tied behind her. The tunnel took many turns, sometimes angling sharply upwards.

Suddenly, Khaldun shouted a spell—he had called fire. Jezebel turned to see that he'd burned off his ropes. He held out his hand, calling earth against the nearest dwarf. It had no effect. Instead, he grabbed the creature and threw him to the ground.

"Free me!" Jezebel yelled.

Khaldun summoned fire again; Jezebel felt the ropes ignite on her wrists and disappear. She shoved one of the dwarves into his companion, knocking them both over. Khaldun and Jezebel ran up the tunnel.

But they hadn't gone more than thirty feet before two dwarves stepped out of a chamber in front of them. Jezebel stopped short. Khaldun called air, creating a gale in the tunnel before them. It didn't help. The dwarves moved directly toward them.

Jezebel turned around to flee, but the others were approaching from the rear. They were trapped. One of the dwarves grabbed her, wrenching her arms behind her back. Another did the same to Khaldun. They marched them up the passage.

"Nice try," Jezebel murmured. Her dwarf kicked her.

They walked for five more minutes. The tunnel widened significantly. They reached two massive iron doors, towering over Jezebel's head. The lead dwarf banged on the metal. Nothing happened. He tried again. This time, there was a clanging noise within. The doors opened slowly outward, seemingly of their own accord.

The dwarves pushed Khaldun and Jezebel through the entrance. Inside was a chamber that looked nothing like the tunnels. The walls and floor were constructed of glossy blocks of black stone with white mortar. The room was big and square and totally empty.

"Nargûn!" the dwarf called out. He sounded nervous, his eyes darting around the chamber.

Suddenly a figure walked through the opposite wall. He was slimmer than their captors but no taller. He wore black robes, a hood hanging low over his head. The lead dwarf spoke to him, an apologetic note in his voice.

Nargûn cast back his hood, revealing a craggy face and short beard. He spoke to the others. Jezebel didn't understand a word he said, but it sounded like he was questioning them.

The dwarf with Jezebel's wand babbled at him. He sounded afraid. When he'd finished, everyone stood in silence, awaiting Nargûn's response.

Finally, Nargûn spoke, and his words sounded like commands. The dwarves dropped their packs and Jezebel's wand and scurried from the room. The giant iron doors closed behind them.

"What are you doing here?" Nargûn demanded in the common tongue.

"I am Jezebel of Spanbrook," she said nervously. "And this is Khaldun of the wayfarers. We're trying to get to the watchtower. We need to see the sorcerer, Enigma…"

Suddenly Nargûn transformed. He grew somewhat taller; his hair and beard disappeared along with his robes, and his skin turned golden.

"You have found him."

CHAPTER TWENTY-TWO
OLD ONES

nigma!" Khaldun said in astonishment.

Jezebel felt waves of power emanating from this man as if his very body exuded the magical force. It was similar to what she'd felt around Nomad and Azure, only much more powerful. He was wearing only loose-fitting black trousers, tied about his waist; the red and black rune tattoos that covered his entire body glowed faintly. They seemed to move about on his skin unless she focused on one—then it didn't appear to move at all.

"It's good to see you again," Enigma said. "And Lady Jezebel. I've been expecting you—I wondered when you would turn up."

"You have? Why?"

"Tell me, how is Nomad?" Enigma asked, ignoring Jezebel's question. "And why has he allowed you to travel here, unbound?"

"I'm sorry, sir," Khaldun replied, bowing his head. "Nomad is dead."

Enigma stared at him in shock for a moment. "I'm so sorry for your loss. Clearly, there is a story here. Come upstairs, and we can talk." He turned and strode from the chamber, disappearing into the wall.

Jezebel looked at Khaldun in confusion, but he merely followed Enigma. He passed right through the wall. She walked up to the place where he'd vanished and ran her hand along the strange bricks. They felt quite solid. She thought back to the very first day Khaldun had shown her magic, making a cat appear out of nowhere. Jezebel knew this, too, was an illusion. Closing her eyes, she stepped forward.

She found herself in a long passage constructed of the same material as the chamber. Enigma and Khaldun were up ahead; she ran to catch up.

"What is this place?" she asked.

"The elves built it," Enigma said, "to connect the watchtower to the tunnels. I traveled this way when I first came here."

"Azure told us there was a tunnel," said Khaldun. "We discovered it by accident—there was a storm, and the pass was too treacherous."

"Yes, come winter, the tunnels provide the only access," Enigma said.

"The dwarves seemed afraid of you," Jezebel observed. "Who do they think you are?"

Enigma chuckled. "Nargûn was an ancient wizard among their people. Mages are rare in their race, but he was one of the strongest. I came here by stealth, avoiding contact with them at first. But I needed their help. I met with their king, disguised as one of them. I convinced him that I was Nargûn returned to life. They agreed to bring intruders to me."

"The king mentioned that you threw the last invaders from the mountain," said Khaldun. "Is that true?"

Enigma grunted. "Henry's men."

"What were *they* doing here?" asked Jezebel.

"We'll get to that," Enigma muttered.

"The dwarves' armor seemed to repel magic," said Khaldun. "How is that possible?"

"The spells are ancient and powerful," Enigma replied. "But you'll be able to cancel them when you come into your full power. Nyro gave the dwarves that armor in the early days of the empire. It helped them defeat enemy mages."

"The dwarves worked with Nyro?!" Khaldun asked.

"Indeed," said Enigma. "They're little more than a drunken rabble now. But their civilization reached its greatest height in Nyro's time.

She enticed them to join the cause—they helped defeat Kong. Sadly that conflict nearly wiped them out, reducing their kingdom to a mere shadow of its former self."

"Forgive me," said Jezebel, "but Raphael told us that records of those days were destroyed. How do you know all of this?"

"We'll get to that, too," he replied. "I promise."

They reached the end of the passage. Enigma held his hand to the wall and the bricks dissolved into nothingness. They entered a small chamber with a spiral staircase. The wall reconstituted behind them.

Enigma led the way up several flights of stairs. They emerged into a large circular room, built from the same glossy black bricks as the passage below. A fire was burning on an enormous hearth. There was a giant iron door directly across from that, and narrow window slits at intervals along the wall. A strange light flickered outside, casting purple shadows on the walls. The center of the room was sunken slightly, containing deep sofas and chairs. A low table sat in the middle.

"Welcome to the watchtower," Enigma said. "Come, sit with me and tell me your tale."

They stepped into the sunken area. They sat down, and Enigma poured them coffee in heavy mugs. Jezebel and Khaldun took turns telling their story, starting with Jezebel's foray into the Devil's Wood.

Once they'd finished, Enigma sat quietly for a few minutes, taking everything in. Suddenly he cracked a smile. "So you two must be lovers," he observed.

Jezebel felt herself blush. "*Former* lovers," she said. "It was our first time when Khaldun transformed."

"I see," Enigma replied with a nod. "I can still recall my metamorphosis—I was with a young wayfarer girl, as a matter of fact. Oh, she was beautiful. I'd never been with a woman before, but she was quite experienced. Yet I have to say that I don't think she was prepared for what happened that night! She ran from the tent, screaming her head off."

Jezebel giggled; Khaldun looked embarrassed.

"But tell me," Enigma continued, "your cousin, Princess Allison—she'd never experienced a haunting before you used the spirit board at… Rockhedge, was it?"

"No, sir," said Jezebel.

"And why did you two attempt to contact the spirit world?"

"Allison wanted to talk to her mother," Jezebel said.

"Ah," Enigma replied with a knowing smile. "I remember Leda well. She was a kind woman. Her death was tragic—it was a heavy blow to Aldo. I understand that her mind went in the end; she no longer recognized her family. Is that true?"

Jezebel nodded. "It was horrible. Allison was devastated—she and her mother were always very close."

"You said that Myrddin believed the demon from Rockhedge followed Allison back to the castle?"

"That's correct," she said. "The first incident took place very soon after we went into Devil's Wood; it made sense that it would be the same spirit."

"I agree," Enigma said, nodding. "Nomad possessed a ring—it would have looked identical to this." He held up his hand. "Was he wearing it when the demon possessed him?"

"Yes," said Khaldun. "He always wore it—but it didn't protect him from the demon."

"What became of the ring?" Enigma asked.

"I took it," said Khaldun.

"Why aren't you wearing it?"

"I didn't see the point," Khaldun said. "It failed Nomad…"

"It doesn't *guarantee* protection," said Enigma. "But it works in most cases. You should put it on—especially here. You've still got it, haven't you?"

"I do," Khaldun muttered. He rose from his seat and fetched his pack. Rummaging around inside of it for a minute, he retrieved the ring. He put it on his finger and retook his seat.

"Now… You say Myrddin explained to Aldo that sorcerers are particularly susceptible to possession, but Aldo ordered Nomad's murder anyway?"

"He was distraught," Jezebel said. "The idea of his daughter being raped… It was too much for him."

Enigma shook his head. "Tragedy begets tragedy, it seems. I can understand Aldo's turmoil, but that's a shame. Nomad was a great man."

"He was," Khaldun agreed. "I miss him terribly."

"After Aldo forbade Myrddin from attempting the banishment, was the necromancer at least able to keep the demon away?" Enigma asked.

"Not completely," said Jezebel. "Whatever he did worked for a time, but the demon returned. Allison joined her father on a tour of the princedom, and that seemed to do the trick—the demon didn't follow. But it came back as soon as she returned to the castle."

"That's not surprising," Enigma said. "It would have been difficult for the demon to track your cousin."

"I've thought that maybe she and I could move far away to escape it," Jezebel told him.

"He'd find her eventually," said Enigma. "When a specter imprints upon a human this way, it learns to sense her life force—like a hound tracking a scent. If Allison stayed in any one place for very long, the demon would eventually feel her presence there."

"Perhaps traveling with the wayfarers would allow her to elude it," Khaldun suggested. "They're always on the move."

"Possibly," Enigma said. They sat quietly for a moment. "Well… It seems that our tales converge."

"They do?" Jezebel asked. "How?"

"Come with me," Enigma said, rising to his feet. "I'll show you."

The sorcerer walked toward the great iron door. Jezebel got up, looking questioningly at Khaldun; he merely shrugged.

Enigma opened the door, and a gust of cold wind blew through it. Jezebel shivered; she hadn't appropriately dressed for this climate.

They followed the sorcerer outside, and he closed the door behind them.

They were high in the mountains now, between the two peaks Jezebel had seen from afar. The sun was setting in the west. The tower sat in the middle of a flat basin. Enigma led them to the eastern edge. Jezebel's teeth chattered with cold. The bitter wind whipped her hair in all directions.

As they approached the end of the basin, Jezebel gasped. A sea of roiling black clouds extended below them, almost as far as the eye could see; the sky above was clear. Lightning occasionally flashed, illuminating small regions of the clouds from within. Far beyond, near the horizon but above the black clouds, Jezebel perceived the sun glinting off a lighter-colored band.

"It looks different, way out there," she said, pointing. "Is that the ocean?"

"It's just a band of clouds, higher in the atmosphere," said Enigma. "Pytha occupies the eastern edge of the continent, between the Anthar mountains and the Lonely Sea. But the water lies many hundreds of miles away, much too far to see from here."

At that moment, the ground shook. It felt like some unseen giant had struck the mountains with a massive hammer. The tremor lasted several seconds; Jezebel stumbled from its force.

"Azure told us this area was prone to quakes," Khaldun said. "I'd never felt one before."

"That was no earthquake," Enigma replied. "It was Xythor."

"What are you talking about?" Jezebel asked.

Enigma didn't answer at first. He stared out at Pytha, looking far away for a moment. "Let's go back inside," he said finally.

Jezebel wasn't going to complain. The black clouds filled her with dread, and she was freezing. Back in the tower, she made straight for the hearth, holding her hands in front of the flames. Enigma poured them more coffee, and they sat down on the couches again.

"I suppose I'd better start at the beginning," said Enigma, taking a deep breath. "You've both heard of Syllith, I assume?"

"Raphael told us about her," said Jezebel. "She's your conjurnor, right? She was one of the governors?"

"That's correct," Enigma replied. "When the governors first appointed her to the council, she became very interested in Dredmort's wraiths. The spirit world is her specialty, you see. She couldn't understand how Dredmort had discovered the rite to create the monsters. Henry had only recently unleashed the wraiths in his campaign against the neighboring princedoms. So when Syllith requested permission to infiltrate Fosland and investigate the matter, the council approved."

"My understanding was that Dredmort found the rite contained in texts in Fosland's library," said Khaldun.

"Yes, exactly," Enigma confirmed. "But such information should not have existed there. Syllith managed to embed herself in Henry's castle, disguised as a servant. Sure enough, she discovered a series of ancient tomes on magic in the library. The books were buried deep in the stacks. Among other things, they contained the spells for the rite of binding. And it turns out that their author was one of the ancient governors from before the rise of the Pythan Empire. He'd been the court mage in Fosland prior to his tenure at the university, and returned there after his retirement. That's when he wrote those books, and left them in the library."

"That explains it," said Khaldun.

"But one of the volumes was missing," Enigma continued. "Syllith broke into Dredmort's private chambers and found it. The book contained information about necromancy—it even outlined the spells required for a sorcerer to become a necromancer."

"Isn't a necromancer simply a sorcerer with a strong affinity to the spirit world?" Khaldun asked.

"That's what I always assumed," Enigma replied, furrowing his brow. "But it turns out that necromancers undergo a transformation similar to the one you and I endured. They do so by choice, so it's not completely analogous. But the spells do change them." He pointed to his eyes. "You've noticed, for example, that Myrddin's irises are white?"

"I wondered about that," Jezebel said with a nod.

"Syllith didn't have time to examine the spells in too much detail—Dredmort caught her in his chambers, and she had to flee—but she was able to glean that much. And along with the book, she found a page of Dredmort's notes. There, he'd written down his ideas for applying the rite of binding to two non-sorcerers."

"And that's how he created the wraiths," said Jezebel.

"Yes," Enigma replied. "But she found something even more disturbing in Dredmort's chambers.

"We long knew that Henry wanted a sorcerer—he'd made requests to the university since the day he ascended to the throne. But with the arcane knowledge Dredmort possessed, Henry undoubtedly intended to force any sorcerer he acquired to become a necromancer. Imagine Myrddin's power in Henry's hands—there would be no stopping him. And in Dredmort's notes, Syllith found references to the ancient demons of Pytha."

"What ancient demons?" asked Khaldun.

"Those controlled by Nyro and the Sacred Circle."

"But the elves destroyed them—didn't they?" Jezebel asked fearfully.

"That's what we always believed," said Enigma. "Tradition tells us that the elves killed Nyro and her necromancers and destroyed their demons. But Dredmort's notes raised suspicions. We knew that powerful enchantments had been placed upon Pytha. Syllith began to suspect that perhaps instead of destroying them, the elves incarcerated the demons, locking them inside the old kingdom. She returned to the university and reported everything she'd learned—and suspected. She asked permission to travel here to research the matter further, but the council refused. Syllith went anyway—that's why they expelled her.

"Syllith came here and saw what I showed you. It didn't take much for her to determine that her suspicions were correct: the old ones survived. The entire land of Pytha was transformed into a magical penitentiary. Immeasurably powerful enchantments lock the demons inside, and keep everything else out."

"So that earthquake before…" said Jezebel.

"That was Xythor. He was one of the necromancers in the Sacred Circle. He possessed an uncanny gift with earth spells," Enigma explained.

"Wait," said Jezebel. "I'm confused. I thought the Circle's *demons* were in there. The necromancers themselves were killed, weren't they?"

"Their bodies were killed, yes," said Enigma. "But what do you think demons are? They are nothing more than the spirits of powerful sorcerers and necromancers. The elves killed the necromancers, but their spirits live on inside of Pytha along with the demons they controlled. Speaking a mage's true name is the only way to destroy her spirit and prevent her from living on as a demon."

"So that's why they created the watchtowers," said Khaldun.

"Precisely," Enigma confirmed. "The elves knew that the demons would spend eternity trying to escape their prison—Syllith learned about this more recently from the many historical texts she found in Highgate. The university should have maintained a perpetual watch upon this land. But over the centuries, complacency set in. The governors who were alive during Nyro's reign died off, and people forgot *why* the watch mattered. The university's purge of information didn't help matters. Eventually, Nyro became the stuff of myth, no longer a real threat.

"And now we have a serious problem. The spells are weakening. Knowledge of how to restore the original wards has been lost. And the demons are doing everything they can from within to accelerate the process. It's only a matter of time before Nyro and the Sacred Circle escape their ancient prison and rise again.

"What's more, not *all* of Nyro's mages are here. She possessed many lesser necromancers and sorcerers beyond the Sacred Circle. Some of their spirits are trapped here, but others still roam free."

Jezebel gasped. "Do you think one of them could be the demon haunting Allison?"

"That's exactly what I fear," said Enigma. "When I first came here, Syllith and I opened a portal. We released one of the lesser demons, and I allowed it to possess me. Syllith destroyed the monster. We managed to eliminate three more of them but dared not lure any of the more powerful ones.

"I stayed here to keep watch, but Syllith went to search for those specters who were never imprisoned. Your cousin's demon is most likely one of those—the ancient power at Rockhedge would have attracted it.

"Syllith went to Highgate first. Buried deep in the library there, she discovered a list of all of Nyro's mages and the demons they controlled. Since then, she has endeavored to find and destroy them while I seek a solution to the crisis here."

"But how can you know what Syllith's been doing if you've been here?" asked Jezebel.

"Mirrors," Enigma said simply. "Until recently, anyway. Hers broke when she fled Roses. Henry has learned of her activities. He knows that she's been to Pytha, and he pursues her relentlessly. He hopes to find out how to unlock the enchantments trapping the demons."

They sat quietly for a minute. Jezebel held her mug in both hands, reflecting on everything Enigma had told them. Her sense of dread was overwhelming. The idea of Nyro returning was like something out of a hideous nightmare.

"But why—*why* didn't the elves truly destroy Nyro and her necromancers the way everyone believed they did?" asked Jezebel.

"It may not have been possible," said Enigma. "To destroy Nyro would have required knowledge of her true name—and she'd taken that back from the emperor. Eternal incarceration was probably the best they could do."

"But you and Syllith destroyed some of them—why didn't the elves do it?" Jezebel persisted.

"No, we didn't capture any of the Sacred Circle," said Enigma. "They are much too powerful—the ones we lured were lesser demons that the Circle once controlled. I imagine that not even the elves were strong enough to implement that spell against Nyro herself. The method requires allowing the demon to possess a living being— attempting that with Nyro would have been catastrophic."

"What happened to the people of Pytha?" Khaldun asked.

Enigma shook his head sadly. "Of all the secrets Syllith unearthed, that is the most tragic."

"What is?" Khaldun asked.

"They were slaughtered," Enigma said. "The spells that the elves cast upon the land killed everyone who lived there. Small bands of refugees had fled during the war, traveling the continent in search of a new home. But your troupe is all that remains of the wandering people of Pytha. And that's why the university has never allowed wayfarers to enroll there. It's an ancient prejudice."

Khaldun was stunned.

"But that's ridiculous!" said Jezebel.

Enigma shrugged. "I would have to agree. In the beginning, the prohibition was based on genuine fear. You see, the magic ran strong in Pythan families. The majority of the Sacred Circle came from Pytha. The governors at the time of the fall worried that the secrets of necromancy might have been passed on within some of the old families. But the tradition of banning Pythans persists today without any basis in reason. Myrddin is the only necromancer who has arisen since Nyro's fall, and his family does not come from Pytha. If the wayfarers were harboring such secrets, surely they would have produced a necromancer by now."

Finally, Jezebel asked the most pressing question on her mind. "Can you help us? Will you teach us the spells to destroy the demon?"

Enigma let out a long sigh. "I cannot. Only Syllith knows them. It was imperative to keep them from me. I had to allow the demons to possess me—they would've shared the knowledge if I knew the spells, and that might have enabled them to cancel the magic. We couldn't afford to take that risk."

Jezebel felt herself come undone; it was as if something had snapped inside her gut. They'd come all this way for *nothing*. She had invested every ounce of her faith in this meeting, and now it was for naught. She'd failed: they couldn't help Allison. Jezebel started to cry.

"Then tell us where we can find Syllith," said Khaldun, looking back and forth between Jezebel and Enigma. "We've traveled halfway across the continent to find a way to save Allison. We can't give up now!"

"I agree," said Enigma. "In fact, I was going to suggest it. This is what I meant when I said that our stories had converged. Syllith will want to destroy your demon as much as you do. The last I knew, she was headed to Northcoast. They have an extensive library, and she was hoping to track down more information about the demons there."

"Well, let's go," said Khaldun, getting to his feet and taking Jezebel by the hand.

"Not so fast!" Enigma replied. "I cannot allow you to leave here until you've been bound!"

CHAPTER TWENTY-THREE
BINDING

h, of course," said Khaldun. "Can we do that now?"

"That depends," said Enigma. "When was the last time you ate?"

"This morning, why?" he asked. "What's that got to do with anything?"

"Internal cleansing is necessary to prepare for the rite of binding," Enigma explained. "You must fast for seven days. Only air and water may enter your body."

"But that sort of thing is just ceremonial, isn't it?" Khaldun asked. "The magic works regardless…"

"The rite is powerful and dangerous. It can prove fatal if not followed exactly."

"Fatal… I thought this was fairly routine," Khaldun remarked anxiously.

"I've performed the rite a few times, but there is nothing *routine* about it," Enigma told him. "I must kill you, tether your soul, and resurrect you. One misstep, and I could lose you permanently. No, we must not tinker with the 'ceremony,' as you put it. Fasting is critical for success. Any impurities in your body could hinder your soul from reconnecting to your flesh."

Khaldun and Jezebel sat in stunned silence.

"I should have realized," Khaldun muttered. "I knew that Dredmort murdered and resurrected those mages to create the wraiths. And Raphael told us that he used the rite of binding… But I never put it together."

"What Dredmort did was an aberration of the true rite," said Enigma. "And as you know, he lost as many wizards as he transformed. In any event, we should put our time to good use. You'll need retraining now that you're a sorcerer."

"What do you mean by *retraining*?" asked Khaldun. "I know I'll grow more powerful now, but magic doesn't work any differently for us, does it? Other than not needing my staff anymore?"

"Strictly speaking, no," said Enigma. "But you'll probably find that you need to *think* about it differently. I'll show you to your rooms for now—you must be exhausted from your journey. But we should begin your lessons first thing tomorrow."

"Do you think you could train me, too?" asked Jezebel. "I'm not that good at magic yet—I only know a few spells."

"She's incredibly powerful," Khaldun added. "But only in particular ways. I've never seen anything like it."

Enigma nodded. "I may be able to help."

Jezebel and Khaldun gathered their gear. Enigma showed them upstairs to the second floor. He led Khaldun to one room, Jezebel to another. The quarters were tight; each chamber was barely large enough for a small bed. There was no other furniture. Jezebel's room didn't even have a window.

"I have to warn you," Enigma said, "you must not engage in sexual activity of any kind while you're here. Our *neighbors* feed off that type of energy. It makes them particularly strong."

Jezebel giggled nervously.

"No, we don't want that," Khaldun agreed.

They went to bed a few minutes later. Enigma was right: Jezebel was exhausted. Yet she found it impossible to sleep. The mattress was too hard; it was little more than a blanket stretched over a wooden frame. And she couldn't stop thinking about the powerful spirits filling the land right outside. She heard the wind howl through the tower walls and wondered if one of them was causing it.

Jezebel lay awake for over an hour, tossing and turning. Finally she got out of bed. Wandering into the hallway, she found stairs leading up. She followed them to the top floor of the tower. There, she spotted a trapdoor in the low ceiling. She yanked a small rope, and it opened; a folded wooden ladder extended halfway down to the floor. Jezebel could see the stars and hear the wind through the opening. She unfolded the ladder and climbed up, emerging on the roof.

Jezebel walked to the edge and leaned against a merlon. Staring over the battlements, she could see the black clouds of Pytha shining eerily in the light of the twin moons. The roiling seemed calmer than before. But lightning still flashed beneath, casting a purple glow.

Jezebel almost thought she could sense the ancient ones enshrined before her. It was terrifying to think that Nyro was still alive in some form. As if in response to her thoughts, a slight tremor shook the ground. Jezebel found it impossible to comprehend the power these necromancers must have possessed. She knew Myrddin was strong but didn't think he could cause earthquakes. She hoped Enigma would find a way to fortify the spells confining the old ones—or better still, figure out how to destroy them.

Jezebel stood there for a long time, staring out across Pytha. Her fear subsided eventually. She began to feel that her destiny was tied up with this place in some way, although she didn't understand how. Jezebel wondered if Salerna had seen something about Pytha that she hadn't shared with Jezebel. But finally, she grew drowsy. She returned to her room and fell asleep minutes later.

Enigma woke her in the morning. As they descended the stairs, Jezebel realized it was still dark out; she couldn't have slept more than a few hours.

Khaldun was sitting in the common area, looking grumpy.

"You, at least, should have some breakfast before we depart," Enigma told her with a wink. There was a crate of provisions sitting by the wall. Jezebel ate some dried fruit and meat, trying her best not to seem as if she were enjoying it too much. Khaldun watched her jealously.

"Let's head out," Enigma said once she'd finished.

"We're not going to practice here?" Jezebel asked.

"That wouldn't be wise," the sorcerer said, hoisting a rolled-up carpet over his shoulder. "With the current state of the protective enchantments, I prefer to keep spell casting near the wards to a minimum. Take that, please," he added, pointing to a pile of metal on the floor. Jezebel realized it was armor—a chainmail shirt, a breastplate, and a helmet. As she picked it up, she discovered it was the same type the dwarves had worn but lacked the strange iridescence.

Khaldun and Jezebel followed Enigma out of the tower. He rolled out his carpet on the ground.

"I didn't know anyone besides Azure used these," Khaldun said.

"He was the first," Enigma replied. "He's got a gift with air spells. He shared his work with me—the magic is clever but complex. I gave my first carpet to Syllith. It proved extremely useful for her journeys."

"She couldn't create one herself?" Jezebel asked.

"Only sorcerers can endow physical objects with magical properties," Enigma reminded her. "And I'm the only one who's been able to duplicate Azure's work. Syllith's a skilled flier, however."

Enigma took the armor from Jezebel and placed it in the center of the carpet. He instructed her and Khaldun to sit by the edges rear of center as he took a seat in front.

But a few seconds later, Jezebel was still standing there. She couldn't bring herself to trust the carpet after her last experience.

"Something wrong?" Enigma asked, turning to look at her.

"Some sort of spell knocked us out of the sky when Azure was bringing us here," Khaldun explained, sounding apprehensive himself.

"Yes, I discovered the wards the hard way," Enigma said with a grin. "Nasty surprise there. But I've had time on my hands, as you can imagine. Don't worry—I found a solution. I won't let you fall, my lady."

Jezebel stared at him a moment longer before taking a seat. She was skeptical but knew Enigma could rescue them the same way Azure had should it become necessary. Enigma nodded to her before turning away.

A second later, Jezebel's legs snapped to the carpet, unmovable. The carpet rose several feet in the air, then shot around the tower. They flew over the edge of the basin, fast as an arrow. Enigma didn't climb any higher. His course hugged the landscape; the rocky terrain went by in a blur.

Jezebel realized he was following the pass they would have used were it not for the storm. And before long, everything around them was covered in snow; their passage kicked up clouds of white. They raced down the pass, the mountain to their right, a sheer drop to the left. At one point, Jezebel thought she saw the tunnel entrance in the cliff wall. But they were moving so fast that she couldn't be sure.

A few minutes later, Jezebel saw two towers of stone rising before them: this was the entrance to the pass. Enigma banked hard to the right; Jezebel wished she'd skipped breakfast.

They went faster now. Enigma moved due north, skirting the mountains. A few minutes later, he turned to the east and climbed steeply. Jezebel was again impressed that she didn't topple right off the carpet.

They rose higher and higher, finally cresting a tall peak. As they flew over the edge, Jezebel realized there was another basin here, extending beneath them. It seemed like an enormous stadium. As they descended, the other mountains disappeared from view. Beyond the ring of peaks surrounding them, Jezebel could see only blue sky. Enigma set them down near the edge. He removed the spells anchoring them to the carpet.

Jezebel got to her feet unsteadily. Her muscles felt rubbery, and her stomach was still unsettled.

"The trick is to stay low," Enigma told them happily. "I tried every method I could think of to cancel the wards, but nothing worked. The spells are far too powerful. I fell out of the sky more times than I care to admit. But the airspace directly over the pass is protected, as long as you don't go too high."

"Good to know," Khaldun muttered.

Enigma picked up the armor. When he touched it, the metal glowed white. The glow faded, but it was replaced by the same iridescence Jezebel had seen before.

"You know the spells Nyro used?" Khaldun asked in awe.

"Indeed," Enigma said, handing the armor to Jezebel. "Put that on, please. The magic is similar to the wards that protect Pytha and the watchtowers, but not nearly as powerful."

Jezebel donned the mail shirt and breastplate, realizing they were intended for someone wider, but flat-chested. It squeezed her breasts together uncomfortably, reminding her of the corset Allison made her wear. Enigma helped her put on the helmet.

"Wand at the ready," he told her.

"What are we doing?" Khaldun asked.

"You're dueling," Enigma said. "To win, you're going to have to cancel the protective spells on the armor."

"And how do I do that?"

"Simple," Enigma said, snapping his fingers. "Will it to happen."

"But I don't know the spell," Khaldun objected.

"You don't need to. Lady Jezebel, feel free to use whatever magic you know. Blow him away, light him on fire—but do it like you mean it! Our young sorcerer will only learn if the threat is real."

Jezebel didn't feel entirely comfortable with this idea. But recalling the time she tried to ignite Raphael from within, she wondered if she indeed possessed the ability to harm Khaldun. He was a sorcerer now. The way Raphael had explained it, she guessed that would afford him a certain degree of protection.

They began a moment later. Jezebel pointed her wand and called fire—she started simple, merely trying to ignite Khaldun's clothes. He blocked her spell.

Khaldun called earth, throwing his hand toward Jezebel. She felt the spell, but it seemed to bounce off the armor. An instant later, a wall of flame erupted directly before her. Jezebel walked through it, and the fire disappeared.

Jezebel called earth, throwing a huge invisible boulder. As Khaldun canceled her spell, she summoned fire. He barely managed to block it; the spell singed his ponytail.

"You're wasting your time!" Enigma yelled. "Deal with the armor!"

"I don't know how!" Khaldun grumbled, hurling another spell at Jezebel. She didn't even know what it might have been, but it did not affect her.

They went back and forth for several minutes. Jezebel was enjoying herself, but Khaldun's frustration only grew. When Jezebel lit his shirt on fire, he reached his limit.

"I don't understand!" he yelled. "You're offering me no explanation…"

"You're a sorcerer now," Enigma replied. "Feel the magic and take it away."

"*I don't know the spell*!" Khaldun roared. "I can't cancel it!"

"You're still thinking like a wizard," Enigma said. "You don't *need* to know the spell anymore. For normal mages, performing magic is like describing a landscape with words. But now you're a painter, and the force of your will is your brush. You don't need words."

Khaldun shook his head. "That makes no sense."

"You could also think of it like language," Enigma said. "When you learn a new tongue, you are limited by grammar and vocabulary. But a native speaker doesn't need to do that—they grow up fluent and don't have to *think* about constructing sentences. Sorcerers are the native speakers of *magic*."

"But how…"

"There is no *how*," Enigma told him. "How do you move your arms and legs—do you need spells for that? No, you just *do* it. This is no different. The magic is there," he said, pointing at Jezebel. "Remove it."

They continued for a while longer, but Khaldun made no progress. Enigma taught Jezebel a simple spell to create a gust of wind. She was unable to do it. But Enigma seemed neither surprised nor disappointed.

"Practice it day and night," he told her. "Don't expect results—but don't stop practicing. Just say the incantation over and over again."

Jezebel didn't see how this would help, but she wasn't going to argue.

They returned to the basin the next day. Neither Jezebel nor Khaldun achieved the slightest measure of success. They dueled for hours, but Jezebel's armor rendered Khaldun's magic useless.

They took a break from the routine on the third day. When they arrived at the basin, Enigma taught Khaldun the spells to control the carpet. Khaldun spent hours trying to make it work. Riding it alone, he was able to rise high into the air and creep forward. However, he failed to land without crashing, couldn't move more than a few inches per second, and lost control entirely if he tried to carry a passenger. Jezebel was not willing to let him experiment with her on board. Enigma rode with him instead but inevitably had to call air for himself and Khaldun to cushion their fall.

Jezebel finally called air on the fifth day. Again, Enigma didn't seem surprised. He helped her vary the spell to create anything from a light breeze to a gale.

They sat down to eat when they returned to the watchtower on the seventh day. Khaldun's mood had darkened steadily, and he was barely talking anymore.

"Don't worry," Enigma said. "You'll figure it out eventually. Many sorcerers awake from their binding much more attuned to the magical force."

Khaldun grunted. "You said that sorcerers don't need spells, but I can distinctly remember Nomad using them. And even when he didn't, he often referred to his magic as 'spell work.' So, I'm not sure I understand…"

"Sorcerers don't *need* to use spells, but that doesn't mean that they *can't*," Enigma explained. "We can learn new magic by sensing its use or presence, without knowing the spell. But learning the words can sometimes make the process easier at first. And for some of us, it's just the force of habit. I still use spoken magic now and then. But the word 'spell' can also be used to describe the magic being performed, not only the words used to cast it."

"That makes sense," Khaldun replied.

"We can proceed with the rite tomorrow if you're ready," Enigma told him.

Khaldun nodded. "The sooner, the better."

"Excellent. We'll have to do it at the basin—we certainly wouldn't be safe trying it here. You'll choose Aldo as your conjurnor, I assume?"

"Or Badru," Khaldun said. "I didn't think Aldo would be allowed since he's got Myrddin already."

"Wait a minute," said Jezebel. "How did you know he was considering Aldo? We haven't discussed that with anyone."

Enigma sat back on the sofa, exhaling deeply. "Sometimes, sorcerers can divine the future. It's not common, and it's not always reliable."

"Was Nomad able to do it?" Khaldun asked.

"No. He was young for a sorcerer. He might have acquired the ability one day, but he wasn't yet strong enough. Although Myrddin may possess the skill—as a necromancer, his power exceeds mine."

"What did you see?" Jezebel asked. "Why did you think Khaldun would choose Aldo?"

"I won't say exactly," Enigma said with a frown. "But if my vision is true, Spanbrook will need Khaldun one day."

"That's what you meant when we first arrived," Jezebel said, recalling their initial meeting. "You said you were expecting me."

"Yes," Enigma said with a smile. "I foresaw your arrival. And Spanbrook will need you, too, my lady. So we must not delay. We will rise at dawn tomorrow. You should both get your rest."

Jezebel and Khaldun headed upstairs. She stopped him at his door.

"What?" he asked.

She said nothing but gathered him into a hug. Tears welled up in her eyes as she thought of what he'd have to endure. She didn't know what she would do without him if he died in the rite.

"Careful, we don't want to get *excited*," Khaldun said.

Jezebel giggled, then sighed. "I'm scared for you."

"Me too," he confessed. "But this has to be done before we go any farther."

"I know," she whispered. "Good luck tomorrow."

Jezebel had tremendous difficulty getting to sleep. Although she drifted off eventually, horrible images invaded her dreams. She recalled her vision of Aldo's death. And she saw Khaldun dying, his body an emaciated corpse lying on a table of stone.

Jezebel woke early. She shuffled downstairs to find Enigma already up and about.

"You've got another hour to sleep," he told her.

Jezebel shook her head. She knew it would be futile. She rummaged through their provisions but felt too sick to eat. After a drink of water, she sat on the sofa waiting until it was time.

Khaldun came downstairs before sunrise. They went outside and took their positions on the carpet. Seconds later, they were flying through the darkness. They landed in the great basin. Enigma instructed Khaldun to remove his clothes.

"They'll burn to ash during the rite if you don't," he explained when Khaldun protested.

Jezebel pitied him: it was freezing. Khaldun stripped, and Enigma told him to lie on the ground. Jezebel saw goosebumps spring up all over his body.

"You should stand back, my lady," Enigma said. "Twenty feet should do it."

Jezebel moved away. Enigma did something, and shackles of stone grew out of the ground, pinning Khaldun's arms and legs. Khaldun looked down at his body, but an instant later, his head fell back. His eyes were closed, and he seemed to be unconscious.

Enigma began muttering a long string of incantations. This lasted several minutes. The sky began to grow bright. Jezebel wondered if the sun had risen beyond the eastern rim of the basin.

Suddenly Khaldun cried out; he writhed in pain, struggling against his bonds. But a few seconds later, he went still. His body glowed with golden light. Green flames engulfed him but didn't burn him. Jezebel couldn't understand this—she felt intense heat from twenty feet away.

Enigma called out powerful words of sorcery, and suddenly Jezebel found herself fading out of consciousness, overwhelmed by the power of the spell. She entered a dreamlike state, and time lost meaning. She felt as though her consciousness had become disembodied, and images floated before her, as if she were viewing them from above: Enigma as a glowing ball of fire, passing over Khaldun's body; flames engulfing the boy, then disappearing again. Hours might have passed, or even days before Jezebel fully regained her senses. Opening her eyes, she found Enigma standing over Khaldun, a silver dagger in his hands, blood dripping from the blade.

The wayfarer's body lay lifeless on the stone, a puncture wound in his chest. Jezebel screamed and ran to his side.

"He's dead," Enigma told her. "The knife pierced his heart. I have to work quickly."

Jezebel backed up a few feet, tears flowing freely down her cheeks. Enigma knelt at Khaldun's head, holding his hands to the boy's temples. A long time passed in silence.

Finally, Enigma stood up, extending his arms to both sides. He started chanting in some foreign tongue. Jezebel didn't understand what he was saying but thought she heard Aldo's name in the midst of it. This continued for several more minutes. For a time, Jezebel found herself uncertain if she was awake or asleep. Images again filled her mind that she couldn't be sure were real.

Jezebel regained consciousness. Suddenly flames erupted around Khaldun again. This time they were blue. They seemed to come from inside his body, but once again, his flesh didn't burn.

Eventually, the flames disappeared, and Enigma dropped to Khaldun's side. He pressed a finger to his neck. Looking worried, he touched his palm to Khaldun's forehead.

"What's wrong?" Jezebel demanded.

Enigma looked up at her. "I can't bring him back."

Jezebel opened her mouth to speak, but no words came out. A low moan started in her chest, and before she knew it, she was sobbing.

"NO!" she screamed.

Enigma waved his hand, and the stone shackles sank into the ground. He moved Khaldun's arms out to his sides. Standing at his feet, he held one arm in front of him as if reaching for Khaldun's head. He spoke several incantations. Nothing happened.

Enigma dropped to his knees again, pushing one hand against Khaldun's chest. The area around his hand began to glow.

Suddenly, Khaldun gasped.

CHAPTER TWENTY-FOUR
NORTHERN HILLS

e's alive!" Jezebel cried.

"Barely," Enigma said. "We should get him back to the tower. What he needs now is rest."

He called air, lifting Khaldun off the ground. Slowly he moved him to the carpet and set him down across the middle. Jezebel took a seat at the rear, Enigma in front.

Minutes later, they landed in front of the watchtower. Enigma used magic to carry Khaldun inside, upstairs to his room. He lowered him gently into bed, covering him with a blanket.

"What happened?" Jezebel asked, still crying.

Enigma stared down at the wayfarer for a moment before answering. "I don't know exactly. The rite was going smoothly. I tethered his soul to Aldo and completed the enchantments. The final step was to revive him. But his spirit would not rejoin his body."

"But you did it, right?" Jezebel asked, horror-struck. "You restored his soul?"

"Yes. But not the way prescribed by the rite. He may not wake up. Only time will tell."

Jezebel dropped to her knees beside the bed. She took Khaldun's hand in her own, sobbing uncontrollably. "Come back," she pleaded.

Enigma slipped out of the room. Jezebel stayed there for a long time, holding Khaldun's hand in silence.

"I remember the first time I saw you," she whispered. "Walking into town with Allison… I couldn't take my eyes off of you. And the day you taught me magic by that stream and gave me my wand. Who would have thought that we'd end up here? Like this. You have to come back, Khal. I can't go on alone. Please…"

Khaldun lay motionless, barely breathing. Tears slipped down Jezebel's cheeks; she whimpered quietly. She would never have made it this far without him. But now it seemed likely that she'd have to go on alone. She'd known him only a short time, and yet they'd grown so close. The thought of never seeing his smile again was too much to bear. She'd give anything to save him.

Jezebel placed his arm beside him on the bed and went downstairs. Enigma was standing at one of the windows, staring outside. He turned when she walked into the room. "Any change?"

Jezebel shook her head and took a seat on one of the sofas. "What am I going to do if he dies? I have to find Syllith and get back to Spanbrook. I don't know how to do it alone."

Enigma sat down across from her. "If you can make it as far as Highgate, I'm sure Azure will help you the rest of the way."

"But I don't even know the way to Highgate! And I'd have to cross the Forsaken Hills, and the desert…"

"Have faith," Enigma said quietly. "Khaldun is strong. He may still come out of this."

Jezebel took a deep breath. She'd hardly heard his words. "And if I do manage to get to Highgate, what will I find? Did Salerna win? I have no idea how the battle went."

"I can show you," said Enigma.

"What? How?"

"Come with me," he replied, rising from the sofa.

He led Jezebel down the stairs. After descending one level, they emerged into an empty stone chamber. In the center, a large spherical stone sat upon a pedestal. It was a cloudy white crystal of some kind.

"What is this?" asked Jezebel.

"A seeing stone of Pytha," said Enigma, running his hand across its surface. "Look."

Jezebel gazed into the crystal. At first, it was foggy. But a clearer image began to form. It was the plain of Highgate as she'd seen it from the crystal tower but horribly transformed. Thousands of dead bodies littered the land between the city and the river. Enormous pyres burned at the north and south ends of the field. Hundreds of men wearing hoods and masks carried the corpses to the fires.

Jezebel couldn't find Henry's army or the troops from the southern princedoms anywhere. Directly outside the city, she spotted what remained of Salerna's army. And to the north, she saw another camp. She didn't recognize the pennants or the soldiers' uniforms.

"Who are they?" she asked.

"Stoutwall's forces," Enigma said with a smile.

"*Stoutwall*?! But—that must have been what Salerna meant. She showed me the enemy army coming from the south, but said she had a surprise in store."

"They arrived at the height of the battle, along with Augustine's sorcerer. Salerna's forces were in trouble. Henry managed to get his entire army across the river using temporary bridges. Azure neutralized Dredmort and the wraiths, with Raphael's help. But that kept him busy, and he was unable to assist the troops. Stoutwall turned the tide."

"They survived—Azure and Raphael? And Salerna?"

"See for yourself," Enigma said, nodding toward the stone.

Jezebel peered into its depths again. She found Salerna and the mages standing atop the keep, surveying the battlefield. She breathed a sigh of relief.

"Salerna showed me the looking glass at Highgate. Does the seeing stone work the same way?"

"Not exactly," said Enigma, placing his hand on the stone again. "The looking glass can show you anything you ask to see. You can specify a location, or a person—or even events in the past or future. The seeing stone is more limited. It can only show you places. You must know a person's exact location to find him. I can't find Syllith with this, for example, unless I already know where she is. But they *can* be used for communication, unlike the looking glass."

"Could I use it to talk to Allison?" Jezebel asked excitedly.

"No, it only works with other seeing stones. The elves installed them in every watchtower. Their primary function was to keep an eye on Pytha. But this one was also used to monitor the other towers. Look here."

The image in the stone changed. Jezebel found herself looking at another watchtower, smaller than the one she occupied. It stood at the top of a peak. As she looked more closely, she realized there was a crack in the tower's foundation.

"What happened there?" she asked.

"Where?" Enigma asked, looking into the stone himself. "This is not good—I need to go."

"What is it?" Jezebel asked anxiously, sensing his alarm.

"Xythor, in all likelihood," he said, striding from the room.

"The demon who caused the earthquake?" she asked, running up the stairs behind him.

"Yes. He's the most dangerous after Nyro. If he breaks the tower, he'll puncture a hole in the spells. He's gained power as the enchantments have weakened. I don't know how much longer I'll be able to keep him at bay. I need to repair the damage immediately. I should return in a few days." He moved to the door but stopped before exiting. "Supplies are stored two levels down, behind the kitchen. You'll find bags of sugar there—mix some into a glass of water. Try to get Khaldun to drink it; he needs nourishment. And keep an eye on him."

"I will," she said.

Enigma nodded before leaving the tower. Jezebel moved to a window and watched him shoot into the sky on his carpet. After that, she ran downstairs to the kitchen. She found the sugar, a canteen of water and a mug. Once she'd prepared the mixture, she carried it upstairs.

She went into Khaldun's room and sat on the edge of the bed. He was still unconscious. She didn't know how she was supposed to get him to drink anything. Setting the mug down on the floor, she ran back down to the kitchen. She found a towel and returned to Khaldun's side.

She dipped the cloth into the mug, letting it soak up the solution. Then she dripped it into Khaldun's mouth. Although not confident this would work, she kept it up until she'd drained most of the mug.

Khaldun looked weak and emaciated—which wasn't much of a surprise considering he'd fasted for so long. But it was more than that. His hue was wrong—his skin was a paler shade of gold than usual. Jezebel didn't think he was going to make it. Imagining how she'd feel if he died, she knew she still loved him. She leaned over and kissed him on the lips.

It was true that she didn't know what she would do without him. But not purely because of the journey home. She didn't know how she'd ever fill the hole he'd leave in her heart.

Jezebel spent most of the day by his side. She went downstairs to eat and to look out the window occasionally. But Khaldun's condition didn't change.

That night she returned to the seeing stone. She looked in on Allison. The princess was sitting in bed, hugging her knees to her chest. She looked frightened. Jezebel watched for a while, trying to ascertain the source of her fear. The demon didn't seem to be present, so she couldn't fathom what was going on.

She searched the castle for Aldo, and found him in his office, alive and well. Oswald was there with him, but she could locate Myrddin nowhere.

Jezebel checked in at the farm, too. She saw her sister asleep in bed and her parents sitting by the fire. Jezebel missed them dearly, Emma especially. She'd had enough of this adventure. She wanted nothing more than to go home.

The next morning, Jezebel returned to Khaldun's side with more sugar water. He looked slightly less pale but exhibited no other change. She dripped the solution into his mouth. After that, she caressed his face, tracing his lips with her finger. She kissed him, then sat on the edge of the bed, taking his hand in hers.

"Please don't die," she said, tears falling down her face. "I need you."

Jezebel sat with him most of the day. She found a rickety wooden chair in one of the other rooms and placed it next to his bed. His breathing grew deeper as the day progressed. Jezebel found this encouraging. She held his hand, talking to him for minutes at a time. At one point, he moaned quietly, and she thought he might wake up. But he stirred no more.

Later in the evening, he took a long gasping breath. Jezebel spoke to him again—she hoped he might awaken. But nothing else happened. Minutes dragged by, and then hours, and still, he remained unconscious.

Jezebel was about to give up and go to bed when suddenly Khaldun inhaled deeply again. And then he groaned. His eyelids fluttered, and he squeezed her hand. Slowly, he opened his eyes. The irises were blood red.

"Khaldun!" Jezebel said, crying tears of joy.

"Jez," he whispered. "What happened?"

"We're not sure," she said. "Something went wrong during the rite." She told him the whole story.

He closed his eyes. For a moment, she thought he'd fallen asleep. But he whispered, "I saw you."

"What?"

"I was here in this room. I was looking down at the two of us. You were sitting next to me, holding my hand."

"Yes," said Jezebel. "I've been here almost the whole time."

Khaldun grew stronger by the minute. His voice returned, and after the first hour, he sat up. Before long, he wanted to get out of bed. Jezebel didn't think it was a good idea.

"You need to rest," she told him. "You were *dead,* and Enigma had trouble bringing you back."

But he insisted. Jezebel helped him swing his legs out of bed. With one arm over her shoulders for support, he stood up. But he was unsteady on his feet. He lurched forward and would have fallen flat on his face without Jezebel. She helped him back into bed.

"Perhaps you were right," he noted. "I think I'll rest."

"Take it slow," she said. "You're lucky to be alive at all—I don't think Enigma expected you to make it."

"I wouldn't have," he told her, "if I hadn't seen you. I thought of you journeying back to Spanbrook alone, and I knew I had to come back."

"Don't make fun of me," Jezebel said, poking him playfully in the ribs.

"No, truly," he said. "I couldn't leave you like that. That was the moment I forced myself back into my body."

Jezebel's eyes filled with tears. She leaned over to kiss him. He pulled her close, kissing her eagerly. "I love you," he whispered.

Jezebel started to reply, but at that moment, the entire tower jolted with a loud bang. Jezebel stood straight up, her eyes wide with fear. The earth shook again, and she had to brace herself to keep from falling over. After a few moments, the tremors subsided.

"Perhaps we should refrain from physical contact," Khaldun said earnestly.

"Yes, it would seem Enigma was right."

Khaldun inquired where the sorcerer was; Jezebel explained what had happened. Khaldun went to sleep shortly after that. Jezebel sat by his side late into the night. Her sense of relief drove her to tears. She couldn't believe how much stronger he looked, even in slumber.

The next morning, he tried to walk again. This time, he succeeded. With Jezebel's help, he made it down the stairs. He was famished, so they shared some of the provisions for breakfast. Khaldun ate like a horse.

His condition continued to improve throughout the day. He even tried magic. He was able to cast only a few spells before the effort drained him. But by nightfall, he could climb up the stairs on his own.

Enigma returned the following day. He was thrilled to see Khaldun on his feet.

"Tell us what happened at the other tower," Jezebel said as they sat on the sofas.

Enigma heaved a long sigh before beginning. "It was Xythor. He'd nearly broken the tower by the time I arrived. I was able to repair the damage this time, but I don't know how much longer I can keep this up."

"Won't the university send help?" asked Jezebel.

"I should be able to persuade them, but that may not be enough," said Enigma. "No matter how many sorcerers we station here, we have no way of destroying the demons. At this point, Syllith is our best hope. Until she figures out how to eliminate the old ones or restore the wards to their full power, patching holes is the best we can do.

"However, now that you've returned to the land of the living," he added with a smile, "we need to think about your training. As soon as you feel up to it, we should resume your lessons."

The very next morning, Khaldun insisted that he was ready. Jezebel doubted he was strong enough yet, but Enigma was willing to give him a chance. They flew to the great basin after breakfast.

First, Khaldun tried flying the carpet again. And this time, he mastered it. He rose fifty feet in the air before shooting around the rim of the hollow at breakneck speed. Khaldun descended low enough for Enigma to board before repeating the feat.

After that, Jezebel donned her armor, and they dueled. But it lasted only seconds. She called fire, attempting to ignite his hair. Khaldun blocked the spell. A second later, he doubled over, laughing hysterically. Enigma averted his eyes. Jezebel felt a stiff breeze between her legs; she looked down to discover that Khaldun had burned her trousers off. She was standing there semi-naked; Khaldun had rendered her armor useless. Jezebel covered herself with one hand and demanded that they return to the watchtower immediately.

"Everything feels different now," Khaldun said once Jezebel had dressed, and they sat down for lunch. "You were right—doing magic is as easy as breathing."

"Good," Enigma said, nodding his head. "We should try everything again one more time tomorrow just to be sure. But after that, you'll be ready to return to the world."

"We have a long voyage ahead of us," Jezebel said.

"Yes, you'll have to tell us how to get to Northcoast," Khaldun added. "I've been there, but I'd never crossed the desert before coming here."

"I'll do better than that," said Enigma. "You can take my carpet. That way, it should take you only a day or two."

Jezebel's jaw dropped.

"We can't," Khaldun said. "I truly appreciate the offer, but what would you do without it?"

Enigma shrugged. "I can create another. Your need is great—it would take weeks and weeks to get to Northcoast on foot."

They returned to the basin the next morning. Khaldun and Jezebel dueled, but it was pointless. Every time Enigma enchanted the armor, Khaldun removed the spell and went to work. Jezebel could do nothing against him; she was glad he didn't disrobe her this time.

Khaldun spent the rest of their time practicing with the carpet. He flew the three of them around the basin and back to the watchtower several times. They loaded their gear after the first trip just to make sure he could hold that in place in addition to passengers. But it seemed like Khaldun's control was complete.

The next morning they prepared to depart. After breakfast, Enigma walked outside with them.

"Remember, stay low until you clear the pass. The wards don't extend beyond the basin, so fly as high as you want after that. Follow the mountains until you reach the sea. Go west from there, and Northcoast will be the first major settlement you see."

"I've got it," Khaldun said, shaking his hand.

"And when you find Syllith," the sorcerer added, taking a deep breath, "send her my love."

At that moment, Jezebel had an epiphany. Syllith and Enigma were lovers. They had to be—there was an unmistakable tenderness in Enigma's voice when he uttered her name.

"We will," Jezebel promised, hugging him.

They took their seats on the carpet, Khaldun up front, the gear in the middle, and Jezebel to the rear. Once aloft, Jezebel waved to Enigma, and they took off down the pass.

Khaldun didn't go as fast as Enigma always did, but his control was reliable. As they passed the entrance to the tunnels, Jezebel spotted two dwarves standing in the cave. Khaldun cast an illusion of a giant wolf running up the pass. Looking horrified, the dwarves scrambled deeper inside. Jezebel laughed.

They turned north at the end of the pass and stayed close to the ground. Once past the basin, however, Khaldun rose hundreds of feet in the air, pressing forward ever faster. Jezebel looked back, but couldn't find the tower or the basin amidst the endless peaks.

They traveled for many hours. But at midafternoon, Khaldun set them down for lunch. They landed in a meadow, surrounded by stunted trees and shrubs. The mountains loomed over them to the east.

"We're north of the Forsaken Hills already," noted Khaldun. "We're making incredible time."

"How are you holding up?" Jezebel asked.

"I'm tired," he said. "Maintaining the spells is hard work. But I think I can go a few more hours if we rest here for a bit."

"It's amazing that you're so strong already. You were *dead* just a few days ago."

They resumed their course thirty minutes later. The day turned overcast. Jezebel found herself getting wet as they flew through the clouds. Khaldun climbed above them. The view was breathtaking. A cumulus landscape spread out beneath the carpet. The taller mountains of the northern Anthar range poked through the clouds to the east.

The day wore on. But as the sun approached the horizon, Jezebel noticed that something else shared the sky with them. She couldn't make out what it was, but some dark form seemed to swim through the clouds to the east. It was heading roughly the same direction that they were. But it seemed like their courses would converge before long.

Jezebel struggled to get a more unobstructed view. It looked like an enormous bird of some kind. Khaldun must have spotted it, too, because he headed west and dipped below the clouds. The creature followed. It was behind them now. Jezebel turned to get a better look, and her heart almost stopped.

The beast's wingspan was wider than a house. Its great ugly head resembled a horse's with scales. It had four short legs with clawed feet and a long, serpentine tail.

This was a dragon.

Jezebel could feel Khaldun increasing their speed, but it was no use. The dragon was gaining on them. Khaldun rose suddenly higher, banking hard to the left. The dragon followed, pulling up alongside them. It turned its head and shot a tongue of fire at them. Khaldun nose-dived to avoid the flames.

Jezebel realized that he'd probably be unable to block the fire while concentrating so hard on piloting the carpet. She drew her wand, clutching it as tight as possible.

The dragon approached from above, breathing fire again. Jezebel canceled the flames. The beast roared in outrage.

Khaldun swerved and darted violently, trying to shake the beast. Jezebel had a hard time blocking the fire with the carpet flying so erratically. But as the dragon swooped toward them again, she had an idea. She pointed her wand and called air. But instead of causing wind, she canceled it, creating a vacuum directly beneath the creature.

Robbed of its lift, the dragon tumbled from the sky. But as it fell, the beast belched a jet of flame directly at them. Khaldun banked hard to avoid it, but too late. The edge of the carpet caught fire.

Jezebel used magic to put out the flames, but it didn't matter. The enchantments on the carpet itself were damaged. Khaldun tried to keep them aloft, but they moved convulsively, dropping several feet at a time as the spells unraveled.

Khaldun managed to slow them down, but they were falling. Fifty feet above the ground, Jezebel felt the carpet go limp and knew the spells were gone. She called air to soften the impact but still crashed to the ground somewhat hard.

She tumbled a few yards before coming to rest. They were in a pasture. Khaldun had landed a few feet away, their gear and the singed carpet nearby. Jezebel searched frantically for the dragon. But she didn't have to look long.

A booming roar erupted from the woods to the east. Jezebel turned in time to see a tree fall as the monster stepped into the field.

"Oh no," Khaldun muttered.

Suddenly dozens of Khalduns and Jezebels appeared, running chaotically around the field. Jezebel was astounded that Khaldun could create so many illusions at once.

"Come with me!" Khaldun yelled, grabbing Jezebel by the hand. They moved south, weaving around the false images of themselves.

The dragon charged forward, breathing fire at every doppelganger it passed. Khaldun steered them into the trees. Once there, he canceled the illusions and rendered them invisible. The dragon reared, bellowing its fury.

"Now what?" Jezebel whispered. The beast quieted down, sniffing the air. Clearly, it was trying to catch their scent.

Khaldun pointed across the pasture. Jezebel followed his finger and gasped noiselessly. An enormous herd of sheep had appeared out of nowhere, bleating loudly. The dragon turned. Seeing the flock, it bounded across the pasture. The sheep bolted in terror.

Khaldun ran out to retrieve their gear. He left the tattered remains of the carpet behind. Returning to Jezebel, he led them north through the trees.

CHAPTER TWENTY-FIVE
NORTHCOAST

he trees here were small and sparse, lacking underbrush. The going was easy. They ran at first, trying to put as much distance behind them as possible. Khaldun kept them invisible and stopped periodically to erase their trail magically.

"Does that spell eliminate our scent?" Jezebel asked.

"As far as I know," he said. "I've seen it used against hounds."

"Let's hope it works on dragons, too."

They kept moving late into the night. Khaldun worried that the dragon might still find them. But hours went by, and they neither saw nor heard any signs of pursuit.

"I can't believe we're reduced to walking *again*," Jezebel complained. "Horses would be nice. A new carpet would be better. But *walking*... ugh."

"We can probably stop here for the night," he said. "I think we've lost the dragon."

"Sounds good to me," Jezebel said, plopping down on the ground.

They set up their tent and built a fire. Khaldun made their camp invisible. Jezebel was freezing. Autumn was upon them, and it was much colder here than it had been near Highgate. The mountains had been cold, too, but she hadn't had to sleep outdoors. She sat by the fire for a while, trying to warm up. But finally, fatigue overcame her. She crawled into her bedroll and fell asleep almost instantly.

She woke to find that it had snowed. Khaldun was outside already, eating breakfast. Jezebel found some food herself and sat before the fire. She ate for a few minutes before realizing that Khaldun looked troubled.

"What's wrong?" she asked.

"I'm not sure which way to go."

"I thought we were supposed to keep going north until we reached the sea?"

"True, as long as we were airborne," he replied. "We were going much faster that way—we probably covered a thousand miles yesterday."

Jezebel snorted in disbelief. "It's hard to comprehend such vast distances. Especially in so little time."

"Agreed. But now we must adjust to normal scales of travel. I'm not sure exactly where we are. And it may still be safer to keep going north. We *will* run into the ocean eventually. But… if we cut northwest, we'll get there sooner, and be closer to Northcoast when we do."

"How is that?"

"The northern end of the continent is concave."

"But going north, we can navigate by the mountains," Jezebel pointed out. "If we try to go northwest, we'll lose sight of them. And the last time we tried to cross an unfamiliar wood, we went the wrong way."

"Yes, but Stiles was different. The forest was much denser there— we couldn't simply strike out in any direction we wanted. Getting the horses through the underbrush would have been impossible. But here we'll have no such trouble."

"I guess you're right," she said, gazing out through the trees. "Tell me something… The wards protecting Pytha don't extend any farther north than Enigma's tower. Why not?"

"That watchtower sits on the spot where the Mystic Mountains branch off the Anthars. Pytha ends there—Kong occupies the northeast corner of the continent."

"Ah… Have you ever been there?"

"To Kong? No. The troupe stayed in Dorshire and Maeda the whole time I was with them. I know they journeyed through Shifar before I was born. But I don't think they ever went to Kong. Nobody *I* know has been there, at least. They speak a different language in Kong, but I don't know much else about that land."

They broke camp and set out a few minutes later. It snowed again later in the morning. Not much accumulated, but it was enough to make Jezebel's feet cold.

They walked all day, heading northwest. The weather cleared in the afternoon. As the sun began to set, they stopped for the day and made camp. Unlike the first part of their journey, they didn't have to look for a clearing. The forest was thin enough that they could pitch their tent wherever they happened to be.

It was cold again. Jezebel built a fire and sat close to it, trying to soak up the heat. Khaldun sat next to her.

"You're not cold?" she asked, her teeth chattering.

"No," he said with a shrug. He moved closer to her, rubbing his hands up and down her arms to help her warm up. After a minute, he simply held her. She was surprised at how much body heat he was emitting.

"You're so warm," she said, turning to face him.

Without warning, he kissed her. It was deep and passionate; Jezebel kissed him back despite herself. Before long, he pulled her into the tent.

They lay on top of the bedrolls. Jezebel felt considerably warmer now. Khaldun kissed her with an urgency she'd never experienced with him before. But Jezebel pulled away.

"You said you loved me back at the watchtower," she said. "Is that true?"

"Yes," he whispered, staring deep into her eyes. "It took my death and resurrection to realize it… But it's true. I am in love with you."

Jezebel sighed, rolling away from him slightly. "Why couldn't you have decided that back in Madison?"

"It's not a choice, Jez. I can't help the way I feel."

"I'm still in love with Allison," she told him. "And I'm going to go back to her. My love for her is the driving force behind this whole crazy quest. I'm determined to restore my faith to her. And making love to you now would shatter that."

"You truly have made a choice," he observed.

"Yes. It's too bad she and I aren't wayfarers," she said with a grin. "Then, I could have you both."

"That's not a bad idea, you know. The two of you could join the troupe."

Jezebel shook her head. "Allison would never agree to the idea. And besides, she's the heir to a princedom. She can't just go off gallivanting across the continent."

"Perhaps… But I can't stop thinking about this. Traveling with the wayfarers might truly provide an escape from the demon."

"But you heard Enigma," Jezebel reminded him. "The demon would find her again eventually."

"Only if she stayed in one place long enough. The troupe is always moving. And who knows. Maybe over time, Allison would grow to accept our lifestyle. Then you *could* have both of us."

"I'll admit, it's certainly tempting," Jezebel said, imagining being able to live that way. "But we can't—Allison's the heir, and *you* are bound to Aldo now."

"Good point," Khaldun conceded.

"We still have to find Syllith. If she can help us, our problem will be solved. But maybe, if all else fails…"

"It's going to be odd," Khaldun said quietly. "Living at the castle, knowing you two are together, while I can't have either of you."

They fell silent. Jezebel fell asleep in his arms before too much longer.

The next day they kept moving northwest. Snow squalls came and went, but there was no significant precipitation. They arrived at a lake the day after that, much larger than any Jezebel had ever seen. Going around it cost them a few hours.

For three more days, they kept up their steady march. They stopped for lunch early the following afternoon. Jezebel dropped her pack and dug out some dried meat. She sat down and took a deep breath.

"What's that smell?" she asked.

Khaldun sniffed. "I don't smell anything."

"It's salty, I think…"

Khaldun sniffed again. "Ah—yes, that's the sea. I first noticed it yesterday morning."

"We must be getting close then," Jezebel said excitedly.

"I think so. We may get there today. You're right—the smell is strong here. And this feels like a sea breeze."

Jezebel led the way after that. She'd never seen the sea but was eager to do so. They walked quickly. The trees grew sparser as the afternoon wore on. Khaldun pointed out seagulls soaring high above them.

An hour before sunset, Jezebel saw it. They crested a hill, and she froze in awe at the sight before her.

Water—as far as the eye could see, the ocean stretched before them. Jezebel ran the last quarter-mile. She reached the beach, dropped her pack, and kicked off her shoes. Walking across the sand, she hiked her trousers up above her knees.

Waves rolled in and receded. Jezebel walked timidly into the sea, gasping when she felt how cold the water was. She ran back to shore when a high wave moved in. The water rose to her knees before she made it back to the beach.

Khaldun caught up to her then, smiling ear to ear.

"It's quite a sight, isn't it?"

"It's beautiful," she said, gazing out across the water. Several sailboats were cruising along, and Jezebel could see a few small islands beyond them.

"We should camp on the beach tonight," Khaldun suggested. "But let's try to get farther west before we stop. I'd like to get an idea of where we are, exactly. Those boats are encouraging—there are bound to be some fishing villages nearby."

They walked along the beach for the next thirty minutes. Sure enough, they came upon a small settlement. There was a short pier extending from a rocky jetty. A fisherman was tying up his boat there.

"Excuse me," Khaldun called out as they approached. The man turned to see who was there.

"Hello there," he yelled, looking surprised and a little scared—Jezebel wondered if he'd ever seen a sorcerer before. The man was short, with sandy blond hair. He wore no shirt despite the cold. His whole body was tan.

"We're trying to get to Northcoast," Khaldun said as they walked down the pier. "Can you tell me how much farther we have to go?"

"You're already there," the man said with a laugh.

"What about the town?"

"Ah, Northcoast Town is five days' walk from here. Maybe four if you move fast."

"Terrific, thank you," Khaldun said.

"You folks need somewhere to stay?" the man asked. "The missis wouldn't mind a couple of guests, as long as you can stomach her cooking."

Khaldun turned to Jezebel.

"No—but thank you," she said. "I've been looking forward to camping on the beach."

The man nodded.

"Suit yourself. Hope you've got some warm blankets—cold wind blows off the water at night."

They thanked him again and moved on. Twenty minutes later, they made camp. Jezebel collected a pile of driftwood and started a fire. The flames burned blue.

"What's causing the color?" she asked.

"It's the salt in the wood," Khaldun told her.

They sat for a long time, gazing up at the stars and listening to the waves. The fisherman was right—a cold wind started to blow. Jezebel was freezing even though she was nearly on top of the fire. But it was worth it for the beauty she was experiencing.

They walked along the beach all of the following day. But Jezebel grew tired of it by nightfall. She felt like she was covered in sand—it was in her shoes, her mouth, her hair—even inside her clothes.

The day after that, they moved inland. Khaldun found a dirt road, which he guessed would lead directly to Northcoast Town. They followed this for three more days. The terrain grew more hilly and rocky as they progressed. The ocean was still in view, and Jezebel enjoyed taking in the sight and smell of it without the sand.

As the sun began to set on the third day, Jezebel noticed tall masts and sails poking out above a hill in the distance. She pointed this out to Khaldun.

"That must be Northcoast," he told her. "It's a thriving port town. We're probably a few hours away still. Do you want to camp here, or keep going?"

"Let's keep going," said Jezebel. "I'd love to stay at an inn tonight." Khaldun didn't argue.

It ended up taking over four hours to reach the town. Yet despite the lateness of the hour, many people were still out and about. When they walked by the docks, Jezebel saw a crew unloading a giant ship. The dockmaster was arguing with its captain. Farther along, they ran into several couples strolling the boardwalk.

A few minutes later, they found a large inn right on the water. They walked inside the front of the building. Khaldun secured a room for the night. They went upstairs and unloaded their gear.

The room was spacious. Two large windows overlooked the sea. Khaldun collapsed on the bed. But Jezebel said, "I'm starving—and I've had enough dwarf provisions to last me a lifetime. Let's go see what they've got for real food!"

Grudgingly, he joined her.

Downstairs, they found the tavern in the rear of the building. The common room was almost empty. But Jezebel insisted on sitting at a table outside on the patio, despite the cold. Only one other patron was out here—a scraggly old sea captain.

The waitress brought them menus and recommended a local ale. She served the alcohol a few minutes later and took their order. The woman flashed Khaldun a flirtatious smile and batted her eyelashes, practically ignoring Jezebel. Khaldun didn't seem to notice, she noted with satisfaction. Although she had to admit, the girl was rather cute. She had long blond hair, big blue eyes, and full breasts.

"Here's to finding Syllith," Khaldun said, raising his mug once the serving girl had walked away.

Jezebel clinked her mug to his and took a sip. "This is good," she said. "It's almost… fruity."

"You'll find that a lot in this region," Khaldun said, taking a long draft. "I once had a pumpkin lager at a tavern here that was quite tasty. I wouldn't mind trying to find the place while we're here."

The waitress returned a few minutes later with bowls of clam and mussel chowder. She dropped off the captain's main course before running back inside. After the soup, Jezebel had stuffed shrimp and lobster tails.

"That was delicious," she said once she'd finished, leaning back in her chair.

"Indeed."

"It's pleasant, being able to walk around in public with you, not having to worry about Henry's men chasing us down," Jezebel observed.

"You're telling me," Khaldun said. "I wonder what *King Henry* is up to these days."

"Pardon me," the captain said from across the patio. "I've been out at sea for many weeks—do you two have any news about that bastard from Fosland?"

Jezebel laughed. "Do we ever."

"He tried to conquer Highgate," Khaldun told him.

"You're joking," the captain said. "Is he mad?"

"He failed," Jezebel said.

"Well, 'course he did," the captain replied. "Have you *seen* Highgate?"

"We have," she said. "But Henry brought in thousands of troops from the southern princedoms. Stoutwall sent reinforcements at the height of the battle, though. From what we gather, Salerna decimated Fosland's armies."

"I'll be damned," the captain muttered. "Guess that'll keep him on his side of the Mayne."

"Let's hope," Jezebel said.

"Say, do you know where we can find a witch named Syllith?" Khaldun asked. "She's not from around here, but as far as we know, she's staying in Northcoast."

"Sorry, can't say that I do," the man replied. "I'm from Oldport myself, off on the west coast of Dorshire. I only get to Northcoast twice a year."

Khaldun and Jezebel said goodnight a few minutes later and went inside the tavern. Khaldun asked the bartender if *he* knew where to find Syllith.

"Don't know," the man said. "But I'm new here—came up from Stiles to get away from Henry. Milton'll be here tomorrow—he owns the place. He might know."

"Thank you," said Jezebel.

They returned to their room and went to bed.

"I wonder how hard it's going to be to locate Syllith," Khaldun said.

"I don't imagine she's hiding or masking her identity this far from Fosland," said Jezebel. "We'll find her."

Khaldun woke her first thing the next morning, and they went downstairs for breakfast. They ate at the bar.

"You're the innkeeper?" Khaldun asked the bartender.

"Yep," he said proudly. "Milton's the name."

"Have you heard of a witch called Syllith?" Khaldun asked.

"Syllith… Doesn't ring any bells. No mages at the castle by that name, that much I'm sure of."

"She's not from Northcoast," Jezebel said.

"There's a witch down at the market—you might try asking her," said Milton. "She's old, and not the sanest woman I've met. But she's the town gossip. Likes to keep tabs on other mages in particular."

After breakfast, Khaldun and Jezebel took a walk through Northcoast. The market occupied the heart of the city, directly in front of the castle. Lots of fishermen were selling all varieties of seafood. Many merchants offered wares essential to a seaport—fishing supplies and sails and rigging—everything necessary to operate a marine vessel.

But right in the heart of the market was a tent unlike any of the others. It was bright red, covered in odd-looking runes. The smell of incense wafted from its interior.

"That's the place," Khaldun said. "I can feel the magic from here."

They made their way through the crowd. Jezebel was amused at the way everyone hurried to stay out of Khaldun's way. She wondered how many of them had ever encountered a sorcerer before.

They walked into the tent. Jezebel's eyes took a few moments to adjust to the darkness. The place was cluttered with bins of unusual stones and crystals, vials of different colored potions, books, incense, and countless other products the novice mage might find interesting.

In the far corner, a fat old lady was sitting on a stool. Her face was craggy and wrinkled, and she was missing one eye. Long strands of wispy white hair hung from her head.

"And who might you be?" the woman inquired.

"Hello," Khaldun said pleasantly. "My name is Khaldun. This is Jezebel of Spanbrook."

"And what do you want? I don't imagine a *sorcerer* has any need for fortune-telling."

"Ah, no," he said. "We're looking for a witch."

"Found one, you have," she replied, cackling to herself.

"Yes… But have you heard of a mage named Syllith?"

"I might have if the color of your coin is pleasing to me."

Khaldun rolled his eyes but gave her a piece of silver. The witch pulled out a wand. She called a small flame at its tip, examining the coin in her hand.

"That'll do the trick," she declared. "There was a witch by the name of Syllith who came to town some time ago. Pretty little thing— pale, long dark hair. She was asking lots of questions up at the castle. I understand they gave her free rein in the library. Must've been after something important. But she's long gone."

"Gone!" Jezebel said. "Where'd she go?"

"Don't rightly know," the witch replied. "She just vanished one day. But I bet she'll be back eventually. She has a house not too far away. Cottage west of the town, on a bluff right over the ocean. The place hasn't sold or anything. You might want to check there."

"Yes, I think we will," said Khaldun. "Thank you for your time."

"It was *your* time, laddie," the witch replied with a cackle. "You paid for it, after all."

They left the tent. Jezebel found the sunlight blinding after the darkness inside.

"Let's go for a walk," Khaldun suggested. "We should be able to find some clues in Syllith's cottage."

They headed to the water and walked along the shore. A high hill rose beyond the western edge of the town. They could see a house sitting at the top. They found a path and climbed the slope.

It was a single-story structure built of stone. A wooden porch spanned the front of the cottage, facing the sea. Jezebel tried the front door. It was locked.

"Allow me," Khaldun said. Jezebel stood aside. She didn't know what he did, but the lock clicked open, and the door swung wide. Jezebel walked inside.

"I don't believe this," she said in dismay.

The house was empty.

CHAPTER TWENTY-SIX
CLUES

ezebel rushed through the cottage. A second room opened off the first. Behind this was a kitchen. There were two bedrooms as well. All were empty. She found a door that led into a cellar—there was nothing there. A trapdoor in the hallway opened to reveal a crawlspace above. Jezebel climbed the rickety ladder that dropped down and poked her head up. Nothing.

"This can't be!" she shouted in frustration. "Now what are we supposed to do?" She sat down with her back against the wall and pounded her fist against the floor.

"Hold on a minute," Khaldun said. "Something strange is going on here."

"What is it?" she asked.

Khaldun didn't reply, instead walking around the house. He held his hands out in front of him as if he were searching by touch as well as sight. He felt along every wall, from floor to ceiling.

Khaldun stopped right in front of Jezebel. He turned to her and smiled. Holding her gaze, he swept his arm around in a great circle. There was a popping sound, and suddenly everything changed. Furniture burst into existence—a chair materialized right next to Jezebel, a sofa behind Khaldun. A writing desk appeared in the corner, and pots and pans turned up on the shelves in the kitchen.

Jezebel ran around the house, shouting with glee. This place looked lived in. "I don't understand," she said. "The stuff wasn't simply hidden, or we would've run into it."

"That's correct," he confirmed. "It was pushed into the void. I was never able to do that kind of magic before—it's incredibly advanced."

"If it's so advanced, how were you able to cancel it?"

"There was nothing to cancel. I could feel that things were tucked into the void, and I just… brought them back," he said with a shrug.

"Must be nice being a sorcerer," Jezebel muttered.

They spent the next twenty minutes wandering around the house, searching every nook and cranny. Jezebel went through the desk, the shelves, the kitchen cabinets—and she examined the cellar and crawlspace again. Khaldun tore apart the bedrooms and tried to sense if anything else was being magically concealed. Still, they came up empty-handed.

"Ugh!" Jezebel exclaimed, plopping down on the couch. "Nothing!"

"Yes, and yet I wonder…" Khaldun muttered, standing in the middle of the living room. "Powerful magic has been performed here." Suddenly he gasped, backing up a step.

"What is it?" Jezebel asked.

Khaldun was staring into space, and yet his eyes seemed to follow action invisible to Jezebel.

"What do you see?" she demanded.

"Wait…"

Jezebel's impatience grew as she sat there for the next few minutes.

"Syllith *was* here," he said finally, "but she was forced to leave."

"What the hell are you talking about?"

"Watch," he said, beckoning her.

Jezebel walked across the room, stopping directly in front of him. He turned her around. She gasped.

Suddenly, it was dark outside. A woman was sitting on the sofa Jezebel had just vacated. A fire was burning in the hearth. The woman was young. Her face was pale. She had green eyes and long, black hair. Jezebel thought she was beautiful—and she recognized her from somewhere, although she couldn't place it.

"Jezebel, meet Syllith," Khaldun murmured.

"This isn't real..." said Jezebel.

"No," Khaldun agreed. "At least, it's not the present. But this *did* happen."

Syllith was curled up on the couch, reading a book, sipping a glass of wine. At that moment, there was a knock on the door. Syllith started. She rose to her feet slowly, picking up her staff and moving toward the door.

"Who's there?" she called out.

There was no answer. Syllith did something, and the top of the door became transparent. Nobody was there.

Syllith backed away to the center of the room. Suddenly the door burst open. A woman stepped inside. She had long, red hair and held a staff.

"Nineve," said Syllith.

"Good evening, you little bitch," said Nineve. "Lovely home you've got here. You covered your tracks well—it took a long time to find you."

Syllith's eyes darted toward the windows.

"Don't worry, I'm alone," Nineve told her. "This is between you and me."

"Somehow, I doubt that," said Syllith.

"You should know that you never fooled *me*," said Nineve. "The whole time you were sleeping with Dredmort, I knew you were prostituting yourself for information. He refused to listen to me, but he rues that decision now."

"I can't blame you for being jealous," said Syllith, holding out her staff. "But Dredmort keeps only *one* whore."

Nineve thrust her staff in front of her. A sheet of blue energy formed over Syllith's head. But Syllith shouted a spell, and the energy passed right through her as if she weren't there.

"Tell me how to open the portal!" Nineve demanded.

Syllith called earth. An invisible weight slammed into Nineve's stomach. She flew out the door. Syllith ran out to the porch; Jezebel and Khaldun followed.

Nineve had landed flat on her back, ten yards from the house. She got to her feet and called fire. Flames erupted around the cottage, but they didn't touch the structure.

"I pity you," Syllith shouted.

Nineve growled at her, moving forward. But suddenly, a howling sound erupted over the ocean. Nineve turned. A waterspout had formed directly offshore. It hopped onto land, climbing the bluff in seconds.

Nineve screamed, holding her staff in front of her. She tried to cancel the spell, but the waterspout overtook her. It sucked her high into the air, expelling her again seconds later. She was thrown into the sea.

The waterspout disappeared, and Syllith moved toward the ocean. Far below, Nineve swam to shore and disappeared. Syllith walked back into her house.

Jezebel followed, watching her in awe. The woman looked out the window once, then sat on her couch, set down her staff, and picked up her book as if nothing had happened.

"That was incredible!" said Jezebel. "Did you *see* that?! She called a *tornado*. I had no idea…"

Khaldun shushed her. "There's more."

Syllith read her book for a minute. She turned the page and took a sip of wine. But at that moment, there was a horrible shriek somewhere outside, answered by three more.

"Wraiths!" said Jezebel.

Syllith dropped her book. She jumped to her feet, staff in hand. After looking out the window again, she moved to the center of the room. A second later, her door burst open. Two wraiths rushed inside. Syllith called fire, but it did not affect them.

The wraiths summoned earth; Syllith blocked the spells. Something slammed into the coffee table, shattering the wine glass. She backed away toward the kitchen.

A moment later, the back door flew open. Two more wraiths jumped inside. Syllith turned and hurled spells at them. A ball of fire hit one of the monsters, igniting its robes. A jet of water exploded against the other but did nothing.

The wraiths had Syllith surrounded. She looked around once, then disappeared. Chaos erupted. Jezebel cowered, hiding her face in her hands. The wraiths cried. Fires flared, and there were crashing sounds. Jezebel heard heavy footsteps, and she looked up to see what was happening. In that instant, Syllith reappeared, diving through a window. Glass shattered, spraying everywhere, and the witch was gone. The wraiths fled out the door in pursuit.

Finally, the scene returned to normal. The glass was restored, the broken furniture repaired, and daylight returned outside.

"That explains *why* Syllith disappeared," Khaldun said.

"For sure—the wraiths caught up with her," Jezebel agreed. "But it doesn't tell us *where* she went."

"Or when," Khaldun pointed out. "She must have come back at some point."

"How do you know that?"

"The damage to the house didn't fix itself," he said.

He wandered around the house for a few minutes, examining everything one more time. Jezebel sat on the couch, her head in her hands.

"I think we're done here," Khaldun said.

They walked outside. Khaldun strolled around the house once.

"I can't sense a trail," he told her. "There's nothing else to find here."

Jezebel and Khaldun walked back to the inn. They found the common room crowded. Jezebel was starving, so they sat down for lunch.

"Now what do we do?" she asked once the waitress had left.

Khaldun took a deep breath. "I don't know. This seems to be a dead end."

"We can't give up now," Jezebel said desperately. "We're so close— where could Syllith have gone?"

"Anywhere," Khaldun replied. "It's a big continent, Jez. I don't know what else to do."

"It's like the old witch said, she's bound to come back here eventually," said Jezebel.

"So, what? Do we move into her house and wait for her to return?" Khaldun asked.

"I don't know," she replied dejectedly.

They ate their lunch in silence. Jezebel felt depressed.

"How did that magic work earlier?" she asked once she'd finished her food. "When we watched Syllith's encounter with Nineve? Did she do that somehow? Was it a message like the one Enigma left at his mansion? Or did you do that?"

"I did," he replied. "I'm not exactly sure *how* though. It's like Enigma said—I can sense magic everywhere now. I felt an echo of what happened there, and when I paid attention to it, I saw everything."

"That's pretty impressive," Jezebel said.

When they got up to leave, Milton came over to them.

"How'd you two make out with the old lady?" he asked. "Any luck finding your witch?"

They told him that they'd found her empty house, but nothing else.

"Is that so?" he asked, shaking his head. "I've been asking around here for you, too. A couple of people remember her, but no one's seen her in months."

"*Months*?" Jezebel repeated.

"You know, if I were you, I'd inquire up at the castle," Milton suggested.

"One doesn't simply walk up to a castle and knock on the door," said Jezebel. "We'd need some sort of formal invitation somehow."

"With him in tow?" Milton retorted, pointing at Khaldun. "I don't imagine many castles would turn away a sorcerer."

"He's got a point," said Khaldun. "I don't know anyone in Castle Northcoast…"

"That's probably a blessing," Jezebel muttered, recalling their ordeal in Stiles.

"But we don't need an audience with the prince or anything," Khaldun continued. "One of his mages will do."

"Burman's the one you want," said Milton. "He's a regular here—friendly fellow. He'll help you out if he knows anything."

Khaldun and Jezebel left the inn. They walked through the market again and made their way to the castle.

"This looks more like a palace," Jezebel said. There was no proper gate. The road continued right into the courtyard. Large bay windows lined the outer wall. Where the gate should have been, there was a fountain. A stone basin sat on each side of the thoroughfare, featuring intricate sculptures of naked men and women.

"Those are the mythical gods of the ancient kingdoms," Khaldun told her. "The old religion died out with the rise of the Pythan Empire. But you still see them in paintings and sculptures in some of the princedoms."

On each side, water shot from various sources—from an archer's arrow, a man's hand, and a woman's mouth, to name a few—and arced overhead into the opposite basin. Children playing in the street jumped from the edge of the pools and tried to touch the passing streams.

Within the passage, immediately before the courtyard, Khaldun found an administrative office on the left. He opened the door, and Jezebel followed him inside. An older woman was sitting behind a desk.

"I'll be right with you," she muttered absently without looking up.

Jezebel stood there impatiently for a minute, tapping her foot on the floor.

"Now, how can I… help you…" the woman stammered, her jaw dropping at the sight of Khaldun.

"We're looking for a wizard named Burman," Khaldun told her with a smile.

"Oh, yes—of course," she said, jumping to her feet. "Wait here—I'll be right back." She scampered from the room.

They didn't wait long. The woman bustled back into the room, a beefy man behind her. He wore brown robes, and a big bald spot sat on the crown of his head.

"Well, hello," he said, smiling congenially. "Lydia told me a *sorcerer* was asking for me, but I'll confess I was skeptical."

"Told you so," the woman muttered, retaking her seat.

"My name is Khaldun," he said, shaking the mage's hand. "This is Jezebel of Spanbrook."

"Spanbrook?! You've certainly come a long way. What can I do for you?"

"We wanted to talk to you about a witch named Syllith," said Khaldun.

Burman's smile vanished. "Perhaps we should talk outside," he said. "Follow me."

He led them into the courtyard. Jezebel couldn't believe her eyes. Ornate statues surrounded the square, as tall as real people. Frescos covered the arched walls, and tiles lined the walkways. Burman continued to a large fountain in the very center of the courtyard.

"What do you need with Syllith, precisely?" he asked them.

"We're having trouble with a demon," Jezebel explained, unwilling to tell him the whole story. "Syllith knows how to banish it."

"Ah, yes… Well, that would be her *specialty*, now wouldn't it?" Burman said with a frown. "Nasty business… You *do* know about her business, don't you?"

"If you mean the demons in Pytha," Khaldun said, "yes."

Burman held a finger to his lips, looking around as if to make sure nobody had heard Khaldun. "Not so loud," he whispered. "We don't want to start a panic, do we?"

"We found Syllith's house," Jezebel said, "but she's gone. Do you know where she went?"

"Not exactly," Burman replied. "I know she discovered information in our library. I let her take the book with her—I wouldn't want anyone else stumbling upon that sort of thing."

"What information?" asked Khaldun.

"She believed she'd found the location of one of Nyro's lesser mages—or his demon, I guess. I don't fully understand…"

"Where?!" asked Jezebel.

"I don't know," Burman said. "Somewhere out west, that's all she told me."

"When did she leave?" asked Khaldun.

"Weeks and weeks ago," said Burman.

"Did she say when she'd be coming back?" asked Jezebel.

"Friendly woman," said Burman. "Quite intelligent—and pleasant to look at, that's for sure. But honestly, I hope she *never* returns to Northcoast. She had *wraiths* chasing her! We don't need that sort of thing here. This is a peaceful princedom."

"It won't be for long if Syllith fails," Jezebel told him.

Burman shushed her.

Khaldun and Jezebel returned to the inn. They sat in the tavern to have a drink.

"Syllith is off chasing demons," Jezebel said. "That's not exactly news. We know nothing more now than we did when we left the watchtower."

"That's not entirely true," Khaldun replied. "Burman said she went *somewhere out west*. Around here, that means Dorshire."

"But Dorshire's enormous! Are we supposed to search the whole kingdom?" Khaldun started to reply, but simply shook his head instead. Jezebel felt defeated. "I haven't spoken to Allison since Highgate—that was nearly a month ago. I can only imagine the torment she must be enduring. We need more information—we've got to find Syllith!"

They spent the rest of the afternoon in the tavern. Milton came to check up on them. When they told him about their failure to learn anything useful, he took it upon himself to help. The common room filled up as dinner approached, and Milton asked every patron if they'd seen Syllith or heard anything about her whereabouts. Nobody had.

Khaldun and Jezebel ate dinner and retired to their room. With nothing else to do, they went to bed early. Jezebel started to drift off, but Khaldun lay awake, tossing and turning. His restlessness kept her up.

"What's wrong?" she asked.

"I don't know," he mumbled. "I think... There was something wrong with that house. I can't put my finger on it. Forget it. Go back to sleep."

"I would if you'd stay still!"

She finally dozed off. But she woke again to find Khaldun shaking her.

"What is it?" she asked groggily.

"I figured it out! We have to go back to the house!"

"Now?" she asked, rolling over. "I want to sleep. There was nothing there—we can go tomorrow."

"It is tomorrow," he said, pulling her out of bed. "It's almost dawn."

Jezebel groaned. But she rose out of bed and got dressed. She followed Khaldun down the stairs, and they set out into the night.

Twenty minutes later, they arrived at the house. Khaldun worked his spell to unlock the front door again. They walked inside. Khaldun stood in the living room, beside the writing desk. He held out his hand, and a silver glow emanated from the very air around them, illuminating their surroundings.

"You remember back at Enigma's mansion when Raphael told us that sometimes one spell could be used to conceal another?" he asked.

"Sure," she said with a yawn. "That's how Enigma hid his message. What of it?"

"Watch this," he said. He moved his hand over the desk. Suddenly, piles of books and papers appeared on the desk. Every inch of it was covered—there were even volumes stacked up underneath it.

Jezebel stared in awe. "How did you know?"

"I felt so much magic when we were here earlier that I couldn't identify all of it. But I knew there was still another spell after I showed you what happened with the wraiths. I finally realized what it was. Somehow, Syllith created one void inside of another—I didn't even know that was possible."

"We should go through all of this," Jezebel said, wide awake now. "There must be something here to tell us where she went."

"My thought exactly," Khaldun agreed.

They sifted through the materials. Jezebel started with the books. But much to her dismay, most of them were in a different language.

"That makes sense," Khaldun told her. "Anything old enough to be about Nyro and her reign would have been written in Pythan."

"I don't suppose you can translate this stuff," she said.

"I'm afraid not."

Jezebel found two volumes written in the common tongue. But they were tomes of magic that seemed unrelated to their cause.

"I've got something," Khaldun said suddenly. He was holding several sheets of paper covered in a handwritten scrawl.

Jezebel dropped the book in her hands and moved to his side. "What is this?"

"It's a list of every necromancer and demon that Nyro and the Sacred Circle controlled," he told her. "Look—these are the ones locked in Pytha. There's Nyro and Xythor. That same word appears next to the name of every demon… I'm pretty sure that's Pythan, but I don't know what it means."

"The three names at the bottom are crossed out," said Jezebel.

"Those must be the ones Syllith and Enigma destroyed. This next page shows all the mages who went uncaptured."

"That's a long list," said Jezebel.

"Yes… But look at the notes. All the ones with an asterisk were destroyed in ancient times. Those with two stars are the ones Syllith managed to find…"

"And those with three, she destroyed herself," Jezebel finished for him. "That's interesting, but it's not going to help us find her."

She returned to the books. But the very next one she picked up contained nothing but blank pages.

"Who would bother creating an empty book?" she asked, tossing it aside.

"What did you say?" Khaldun asked, dropping what he was doing.

"It's nothing—that book contained only blank paper."

"Show me," he said.

Jezebel retrieved it from the pile, opening it to show him. Khaldun took it from her. He passed his hand over the first page. A long, flowing script appeared in black ink. Jezebel gasped.

"What does it say?" she asked.

Khaldun stared at the paper for a minute. "It's Syllith's journal!"

"And?!"

"This page is old. It's about her arrival in Northcoast."

"Jump to the end!"

"I am, relax," Khaldun said with a chuckle. "The last few pages truly are blank. Wait—here we go. These are the ones we want."

He waved his hand over several pages, one at a time. Jezebel took the book from him and started reading out loud.

"I found an interesting volume in the library. Burman let me take it. Some old traveler wrote it when he retired in Northcoast. He'd spent his whole life journeying across Dorshire and Maeda. In his writing, he chronicled the most interesting places he'd seen.

"I know for a fact many of them no longer exist. Some do, but a few I'd never heard of before. One of those is somewhere in northern Dorshire. It's difficult to pinpoint its location; the volume is ancient, and many place names have changed over the years.

"But it's certainly the type of site that would attract the old ones. For all I know, there may be dozens of them there—if it still exists. It was reportedly a burial ground for some ancient civilization. The traveler hinted that human sacrifices might have been performed there at one time. He called it Rockhedge. I've decided it's worth investigating."

Jezebel froze, staring at Khaldun; he looked shocked. "She went to Spanbrook!"

CHAPTER TWENTY-SEVEN
HIGH SEAS

ezebel laughed. "This is just my luck, isn't it? We've traveled halfway around the world, and now the place I need to go is *home.*"

"It does seem fitting somehow," Khaldun said, shaking his head.

"Maybe she's destroyed the demon already," Jezebel said. "I'd love to be able to return to a quiet life on the farm."

"That does sound nice," Khaldun agreed. "But we still have to get to Spanbrook. That's no easy journey."

"It never is," Jezebel muttered. "We should hide everything again before we go. Henry's people might return—we don't want them to find this. Can you do it?"

"I hope so, but I've never tried," he replied. "Let's put it all back how we found it first."

They spent a few minutes returning the books and papers to their original locations. Jezebel was sure things were rearranged a bit, but they'd stacked it all as neatly as they found it.

Khaldun backed up a step and held out his hand. The contents of the desk vanished with a pop. He touched the desk, and it disappeared, too.

Jezebel stood in the space it had occupied, swinging her arms around. "You did it! There's nothing here."

It took Khaldun fifteen minutes to restore the entire house to the empty state in which they'd found it. Once he'd finished, they locked the door and headed back to the inn.

The sun rose as they walked. Inside the common room, the morning crew was just starting breakfast. Khaldun and Jezebel sat at a table and ordered their food.

"So tell me the bad news," said Jezebel. "How long will it take to get back to Spanbrook?"

Khaldun thought about it for a minute. "I'm not exactly sure—it depends which way we go. We'll certainly travel along the coast until we reach the River Torsa. From there, we could try to find passage upstream on a boat or barge. We would probably disembark in the north end of Cambry, take the road to the castle, and then return to Spanbrook the way we came. But I wonder… It may be faster to go by foot to the Ember."

"Then we could take a barge up the river to Spanbrook," Jezebel said.

"Yes, precisely. But either way, we're probably looking at three weeks or more."

Jezebel heaved a long sigh. "Winter's almost here. We may encounter quite a bit of snow."

"And that will slow us down," Khaldun said with a frown.

Milton showed up a few minutes later. He served them their food and took a seat at the table. "I'm sorry your quest hasn't been more successful," he said. "Seems your witch disappeared without a trace."

Jezebel told him the news.

"Spanbrook?" he said. "That's where you're from, isn't it?"

Jezebel nodded. "And we have to go back there as quickly as possible. I imagine we'll probably set out today—we've got weeks of walking ahead of us."

"You'd get there much faster by water," Milton suggested. "The Steadfast is setting out in a couple of days, heading to Rockport. Her captain's boarding here, matter of fact. He's usually down here for dinner—gruff-looking sailor type. Name's Tibold. I reckon he'd be happy to have a sorcerer on board."

"That sounds like the gentleman we met the first night we were here," Khaldun noted.

"Rockport is directly north of Spanbrook," Jezebel said excitedly. "At the mouth of the Ember!"

"That would get us there much more quickly," Khaldun said. "Thank you, Milton!"

Jezebel took a nap after breakfast; she was exhausted from her lack of sleep the night before. Khaldun was gone when she woke up. She wandered downstairs to look for him, but he wasn't in the tavern or the common room. She sat down for lunch, miffed that he hadn't bothered to tell her where he was going.

As Jezebel finished her food, Khaldun walked into the room. He was with the blond serving girl who'd flirted with him the night they arrived. She giggled and kissed him before running out the door. Khaldun strolled over and took a seat next to Jezebel.

"Did you have a pleasant nap?" he asked.

"Hmph," she replied without looking at him.

"What's wrong?" he asked.

"What's her name?"

Khaldun didn't respond for a few seconds. "You're not jealous, are you?"

"It was a simple question."

"Her name is Marianne," he said.

"Did you and *Marianne* have a nice time?"

"We did. She was extremely… ah… enthusiastic."

"Hmph."

"You have no grounds for jealousy," he told her. "You made it clear that our relationship is platonic. I did nothing to…"

"I'm not jealous. I just wish you had told me where you were going," she said. "With everything we've been through, waking up to an empty room was a little disconcerting."

"I'm sorry," he said. "I didn't want to wake you."

They spent the afternoon strolling along the beach and exploring Northcoast Town. Despite what she'd said to Khaldun, Jezebel had to admit that she did feel extremely jealous. But what did she expect? There was no reason for Khaldun to refrain from becoming intimate with whomever he wanted. He was right: she had ended that aspect of their relationship. But she couldn't deny that she was still in love with him. Seeing him with someone else made that fact impossible to escape.

They returned to the inn for dinner but didn't see Captain Tibold anywhere.

"Usually comes in late," Milton told them. "But don't worry, he'll be here. Never misses a meal, that one."

Sure enough, Tibold walked in after most of the patrons had departed. Milton introduced them, and Tibold sat with Jezebel and Khaldun.

"Found your witch, did you?" he asked.

"We did, and she's in Spanbrook," Jezebel told him. "We need to get there as quickly as possible. Milton tells us you're taking your ship to Rockport."

"I am indeed," he confirmed, eyeing Khaldun.

"How much would it cost us to catch a ride?" he asked.

"No charge for mages," the captain said. "So long as you agree to work for your passage."

"That's a bargain," said Jezebel. "But I'm afraid I know nothing about sailing a ship. I'd never seen the ocean before we arrived here."

"The crew'll take care of the sailing, my lady," he replied. "That's not the sort of work I'd ask you to do."

"What, then?" asked Khaldun.

Tibold took a swig of ale. "High seas ain't always that friendly. I'd just ask you to help us cope with any trouble we may encounter."

"Agreed," she said. "How long does it take to sail to Rockport from here?"

Khaldun looked at her with a frown but said nothing.

"Typically five or six days," Tibold said. "But with your help, we can probably make it in three."

"Terrific!" said Jezebel.

"Done deal," the captain said, shaking their hands. "We leave at dawn, day after tomorrow. You're welcome to come aboard tomorrow evening and spend the night on the ship if you'd like."

They kept the captain company while he ate, then retired to their room.

"This is so exciting," Jezebel said, lying in bed. "I'm finally going home. And we'll be there in no time. I wish I could tell Allison."

"I'm curious to see what kind of trouble he was referring to," said Khaldun.

"Probably bad weather or rough seas," Jezebel suggested. "If nothing else, we could call air and provide greater speed. He seems to expect as much—he said we'd arrive sooner with us on board."

"Yes, perhaps you're right," he said pensively.

"You don't trust him?" she asked.

"I'm withholding judgment," he replied.

"Do you think he works for Henry or something?"

"He did seem overeager to get a sorcerer on board, don't you think? He might be planning to deliver me to the enemy."

"But he saw us the night we arrived and has done nothing this entire time—Milton introduced us to *him*! And in any event, how would Henry know we're here?" Jezebel asked skeptically.

"He does have spies embedded in many places," Khaldun pointed out. "It wouldn't be so hard to keep his people on alert."

"But you're stronger than you were," said Jezebel. "You could handle them—and besides, you're bound now. Capturing you wouldn't do Henry much good."

"You're probably right," Khaldun admitted.

"He may be up to *something*," said Jezebel. "But I'm willing to trust him to some extent. And I can't tell you how happy I am that he's granted us passage—no more walking!"

Khaldun chuckled. "I wonder how Aldo will react to my assignment. It's sure to have come as a big surprise."

"He can't know already... Can he?"

"He won't know the circumstances. But he would have become aware of my bond to him the moment Enigma performed the rite."

"Then he must know your true name," said Jezebel.

"Indeed."

"Well, Myrddin seems to enjoy his service there. He lives like a king—I'm sure Aldo will accept your appointment graciously."

"It'll take some adjusting," said Khaldun. "I've never settled down anywhere. But I'm looking forward to it, especially after this journey."

Khaldun and Jezebel bade farewell to Milton after dinner the following evening. They gathered their belongings and walked down to the docks. The Steadfast was the biggest ship in the port, and the only one with four masts. The crew was loading the last of the cargo when they arrived. Most of the men were little older than Jezebel. They reminded her of the hands on her father's farm.

A slightly older man came over to them and introduced himself as the first mate. "Captain Tibold told me we'd be taking on passengers," he said, shaking their hands. The rest of the crew gathered behind him, staring at Khaldun in awe. "Don't mind them—they've never seen a sorcerer before. They'll leave ya alone, I reckon. Come on board, and I'll show ya to your quarters."

Jezebel walked up the gangplank, fearful and excited at the same time. The ship was larger than many buildings she'd seen. They walked across the deck to the rear of the vessel. The mate led them inside, to a cabin in the starboard quarter.

"These are normally my quarters, but we use them for special guests," he explained. "Not that we get many of those… But there you are. Should be comfortable for the two of you."

Jezebel dropped her pack and looked out the small porthole to the stern. All she could see was the ocean. Tibold came to find them a few minutes later. He gave them a tour of the ship. They walked around the main deck first. He showed them the bridge and the forecastle and told them where to find the head. Below deck, they toured the galley and the cargo hold.

"We set sail at dawn," he said. "You can find breakfast in the galley after that. I'd be honored if you'd join my officers and me for dinner—it's in the captain's cabin, one deck above yours."

"We'd love to," said Khaldun.

Jezebel and Khaldun strolled the main deck a little while longer before heading to bed. Jezebel drifted off to sleep to the sound of a bell ringing somewhere in the distance.

By the time she woke in the morning, they'd already left port. She ran up to the main deck with Khaldun. They were under full sail, Northcoast fading in the distance.

They took a light breakfast in the galley and spent most of the day above deck. It was sunny and cold, with a stiff easterly wind. Khaldun guessed they'd make excellent time.

Jezebel found the sea enthralling. By early afternoon, there was no land in sight, only water as far as she could see. She looked up at the crow's nest and wondered if the sailor there could still see the shore. But she had no desire to climb up there herself, especially with the ship rolling on the waves. Her plunge from Azure's carpet and the near-disaster in the mountain pass had done nothing to assuage her fear of falling.

At dinnertime, they joined the captain and his officers in his cabin. Tibold introduced them to everyone—there were only three besides the first mate, whose name was Bosley.

"My crew has been hounding me," said Tibold. "They want to know what sorts of magic you can do. Most of them have seen wizards and witches, of course. But I'd imagine that as a sorcerer, you possess a greater degree of skill than the average mage."

"I haven't been a sorcerer for long," said Khaldun. "I'm still learning."

"You've no need to be modest here," said Bosley. "Go on—show us something."

Jezebel could tell that Khaldun was uncomfortable with all the attention. "I'll do it," she said, pulling out her wand. She called a small flame in the palm of her hand.

"O-ho!" said Tibold. "I didn't realize you were a witch!"

"I'm only a novice," she said. "Do an illusion for them," she added, nudging Khaldun. He still looked reluctant.

"Illusion?" Bosley asked, sounding interested.

Khaldun nodded. He pointed at the captain. Bosley and the other officers burst out laughing: Tibold had transformed into a female version of himself. He had long, blond hair, heavy makeup, and large breasts.

"What's so funny?" he grumbled. The crew laughed even harder.

The food was served a moment later, and Khaldun returned the captain to his regular appearance.

"Is it true Spanbrook's haunted?" one of the men asked Jezebel. "I've heard the whole princedom is overrun with specters and ghosts."

"Not so," she said, unwilling to discuss Allison's situation. "The princedom as a whole is quite peaceful and ordinary."

"You ever seen the necromancer?" another asked fearfully.

"Loads of times," she said. "He's perfectly friendly." The man stared at her in disbelief.

"What about you, Khaldun," Tibold said. "You from Spanbrook, too?"

"No. I grew up a wayfarer."

"Is that so?" the captain replied. "You must have traveled pretty extensively then."

"Sure have," he said. "But only in Dorshire and northern Maeda. How about you? How far do you typically sail?"

"We stick to Dorshire and Maeda these days," he said. "We sail back and forth around the northwestern end of the continent, from the southern ports in Maeda, all around Dorshire and up to Northcoast. We used to go out to Kong, but those waters have grown dangerous in recent years."

"How so?" asked Jezebel.

"Pirates," said Bosley. "Kong's not like other places. There are no proper princedoms. Gangs fight for control of the cities—and those are huge. Much bigger than anything you see in these parts."

"Took our lives in our hands every time we docked at one of them ports," said Tibold. "The sea used to be safe, at least. But one of the gang leaders took over a couple of merchant vessels. Now he controls the shipping lanes north of Kong. To hell with them, I say."

"Should we expect to see any pirate ships on *this* voyage?" Khaldun asked slyly.

Bosley looked away from him. Tibold stared at his plate.

"That's the type of work you expect me to perform, isn't it?" Khaldun pressed. "You brought me on for protection in case any pirates show up."

"It's true," Tibold confessed. "We normally have to hug the shore on this journey. The pirates haven't grown bold enough to come close to land yet. They know the mages at every castle on the coast of Maeda would fight them. But on the open sea… You think you're up to the challenge?"

"No doubt," Khaldun said confidently. "But you could have been more forthcoming. Why didn't you tell us about this before?"

"Didn't want to scare you off," the captain said. "Figured if I told you the danger, you'd go overland. Didn't want to take that risk. We cut days off the trip going this way."

Jezebel was surprised by this revelation but knew that Khaldun wasn't. "You knew they were up to something," she said when they returned to their cabin.

"They had to be," he said. "Captains of merchant vessels rarely take on passengers under any circumstances. But to do so free of charge is unheard-of. I didn't guess pirates until they broached the topic. But I knew there had to be some sort of ulterior motive—and I didn't believe it would be something as simple as storms or rough seas."

"Very shrewd," she said appreciatively.

"Our danger will diminish as we sail farther from Kong," he told her. "If we're going to experience an attack, I'd expect it to happen tonight."

"Terrific," she replied sarcastically. "I was looking forward to a good night's sleep."

Khaldun stayed up, sitting in the corner. Jezebel tried to get some rest despite Khaldun's warning. She managed to doze off after a while but woke a few hours later to the sound of alarm bells and a pounding noise.

Khaldun opened the door. Bosley was standing there.

"Time to see what you can do," he said gravely. "We're under attack."

They followed him up to the main deck. Sailors were running around frantically, adjusting the riggings. Khaldun and Jezebel ran up to the bridge. They found Tibold at the helm.

"They're gaining on us," he said, pointing aft.

Looking to the rear, Jezebel could see the dark outline of a ship in the moonlight, some distance behind them.

"I'd appreciate a little more wind in the sails," he said pointedly to Khaldun.

"Outrun them, and they'll attack again," Khaldun said. "Let them get closer. I'll implement a more permanent solution."

"Now you're talking," Tibold said with a grin. He barked orders to his crew.

Jezebel watched as the pirate ship drew ever closer.

"That should do it," Khaldun mumbled. He held out his hand and called fire. Nothing happened. He rounded on the captain. "You didn't tell me they had a mage!"

"What are you talking about?" Jezebel demanded.

"Someone on that ship blocked my spell," Khaldun told her.

"I didn't know!" Tibold said. "Although that explains a lot—they always seem to move faster than the wind."

"This just became more interesting," Khaldun said. "Captain, keep your speed down. Will they board you?"

"If we let them, 'course they will! It's my cargo they want."

"Excellent. Allow them to come alongside."

"Have you lost your mind?!" Tibold demanded.

"Trust me," Khaldun said. He motioned Jezebel out of the wheelhouse.

"What's your plan?" she asked.

"Their wizard is strong," he said. "I can overpower him, but I don't want him to realize I'm here. I want you to cast the spells for now."

"But that's crazy—I'm not going to be any match…"

"I'm counting on it," Khaldun said. "For this to work, you must do exactly as I say."

Jezebel agreed. A few minutes later, the ship caught up with them. Khaldun told the captain to take evasive maneuvers—but only for show.

"When their archers fire, I want you to incinerate their arrows," he said to Jezebel.

She wished she knew what he was up to.

Tibold steered the Steadfast away from the pirate ship. But that was the end of the chase. The enemy mage canceled the wind in his sails. They were dead in the water.

The pirates drew closer. Sure enough, arrows flew. Jezebel called a wall of fire, burning them to ashes. Tibold's archers returned fire. Their bolts struck an invisible wall and fell into the sea. Jezebel tried to ignite the next volley from the pirate ship, but their mage canceled her spell. The sailors took cover.

Moments later, the vessel came alongside. Pirates crawled onto the Steadfast like ants. Khaldun disappeared.

Jezebel panicked as hand-to-hand fighting broke out all over the ship. One of the pirates lunged at her with a sword. She ignited him from within.

But now the pirates knew she was the mage. They focused their attack on her. She hit a few with earth and lit two others on fire. But they overwhelmed her within seconds. Jezebel screamed as they tied her up and confiscated her wand.

Where was Khaldun?

Two of the pirates dragged her to their ship while the others disarmed the rest of the crew. They pulled her below deck to a chamber in the bow of the vessel. Jezebel hadn't seen any windows in the front of the hull, but the walls here were transparent. She could see the water all around her.

In the middle of the room, an old woman sat on a high-backed chair. Her gray hair fell around her face in filthy mats. Jezebel's captors positioned her in front of the woman. One of them handed the witch Jezebel's wand.

"Who are you?" the witch asked, pointing her wand at Jezebel.

But before she could answer, the witch's wand flew from her hand and disappeared. The woman jumped to her feet, looking around frantically. Jezebel's wand clattered to the floor. The two pirates screamed for an instant before they were incinerated from the inside. Their charred corpses broke and fell to the deck.

The witch lunged at Jezebel, but a sheet of blue energy blocked her path. She stopped short, backing away from it. It surrounded her, pinning her arms and legs. She teetered but suddenly rose several inches off the floor, suspended by some unseen force.

A second later, Khaldun appeared next to Jezebel. She punched him in the chest.

"What was that for?"

"Don't ever do that to me again! I had no idea what was going on! You could have told me what you were planning!"

"You wouldn't have played your part convincingly if I had," he said apologetically.

Jezebel growled at him. She retrieved her wand, and they returned above deck, the witch floating eerily before them.

Several pirates ran toward them but stopped when they saw that a sorcerer had captured their mage. They backed away in fear, letting them pass.

Khaldun and Jezebel climbed back over to the Steadfast. They made short work of the pirates now that their witch had been neutralized. Khaldun let Jezebel do most of the work. She called fire against a few, and the others fled back to their ship.

Tibold and his men joined Khaldun and Jezebel. They brought the witch into the cargo hold. Two of the men tied her to the base of a mast. Once she was secure, Khaldun lifted his spell. The woman babbled angrily in her native tongue. Jezebel didn't understand a word.

"Keep this in your cabin," Khaldun said to Tibold, handing him her wand. "She's powerless without it."

"I'll just throw it overboard," he said. "That'll remove any possible threat."

"As you wish," said Khaldun. "I can destroy their vessel if you want. That would be one less pirate ship you'd have to worry about. But I'd suggest letting them go back to Kong and report what happened here. It may be useful to let their leaders believe you've hired a sorcerer."

"Aye, that it would," Tibold agreed. "They'll think twice before returning to these waters. But… Do you think maybe you could *damage* their ship? Keep her in good enough shape to limp home, but make sure she's not seaworthy anymore?"

Khaldun chuckled. "I can do that."

They returned to the deck. The pirate ship had already pulled away. Tibold tossed the witch's wand into the sea, and Khaldun went to work.

He broke the main mast in half, punched giant holes in the hull just above the waterline, and torched the crow's nest and forecastle.

"That should do it," Tibold said happily.

Khaldun and Jezebel headed back to their cabin. The whole crew cheered for them as they left the deck.

"We could make a career out of this if things don't work out in Spanbrook," Jezebel said sarcastically.

CHAPTER TWENTY-EIGHT
FULL CIRCLE

he remainder of their voyage proved uneventful. The crew treated Jezebel and Khaldun like royalty after their performance against the pirates. Jezebel spent the majority of her time sitting at the bow of the ship, staring out at the ocean. The world had never felt so big.

"It's astounding," she commented on the afternoon of the second day. She was gazing out at the horizon before them, Khaldun by her side.

"What's that?" he asked.

"It took us what, seventy days to go from Spanbrook to Northcoast? And now it's only three days at sea, and six or seven more by barge to make the return trip?"

Khaldun shook his head. "We've been moving back in the general direction of Spanbrook ever since we left the watchtower—that was the farthest point on our journey. Don't forget that we covered at least a thousand miles on the carpet. And we traveled more than a week on foot to reach Northcoast, every mile bringing us closer to Spanbrook."

"Ah," Jezebel said, nodding her head. "That makes more sense." She was silent for a moment. "I hope we're not too late. To save Allison, I mean."

"Have faith," Khaldun told her. "We'll be successful."

At midafternoon of their third day at sea, a sailor in the crow's nest cried out: he had spotted land. Before much longer, Jezebel caught sight of it as well. As the day wore on, she could make out other vessels sailing in and out of a distant port. She grew alarmed later in the day when a smaller boat with a single sail approached them at high speed.

"Oh, no," she muttered. "Not more pirates, I hope."

"I don't think so," Khaldun replied. "But, let's check with Tibold to be sure."

They walked back to the bridge to find the captain. He chuckled at their query.

"That's just the pilot," he said. "He'll come aboard and guide us into the harbor."

"Don't you do that?" Jezebel asked.

"Sea captains travel too widely to be familiar with the local peculiarities of every port they visit," Tibold replied. "That's where pilots come in. It's their job to navigate oceangoing vessels into the local waterways."

Jezebel watched as the pilot used a flimsy rope ladder to climb up the side of the ship. She definitely didn't want to try that.

Less than two hours later, they tied up at the dock. Jezebel and Khaldun bade farewell to Tibold.

"You think maybe you could help me bring that old hag to the local authorities?" the captain asked before they disembarked. "Don't want no trouble from her."

"Don't worry," Khaldun told him. "She's completely powerless without her wand."

"I'll take you at your word," Tibold said, shaking his hand. "And I thank you for helping out."

"It was our pleasure," said Khaldun.

Rockport was smaller than Northcoast, although the port seemed equally busy. Crews scurried about like ants, transferring cargo back and forth between ships and barges. Khaldun found a barge captain willing to transport them to Spanbrook. But they weren't departing till the morning, so Khaldun and Jezebel stayed at an inn for the night. The place was small and rundown—nothing like the lodging they'd enjoyed in Northcoast.

They set out at dawn. The going was slow on the barge, driven by men with long poles pushing against the riverbed. They traveled day and night for six straight days. The crew rotated in shifts. Khaldun and Jezebel slept under the stars on the deck every night. Jezebel found herself missing the sea. Its vastness had been so mesmerizing, filling her with an almost meditative calm. She wondered if she'd ever see the ocean again.

Not long after sunset on the sixth day, Khaldun sensed something odd.

"What is it?" Jezebel asked while he stared intensely toward the eastern shore.

"I'm not sure," he said. "There's some sort of trail out there… Someone magical has journeyed through these woods. Repeatedly. I'm sure of it."

"We're getting close to Spanbrook Town," Jezebel observed. "And Rockhedge is somewhere in that general direction. Do you think it's Syllith?"

"I do," he replied.

Khaldun went to talk to the captain. He tried to get him to pull up to shore, but the man refused.

"We run aground in the shallows, and it'll take us all day to get going again. Forget it."

Khaldun and Jezebel ended up jumping off the barge into the river. The water was chest-deep, and they had to hold their packs over their heads as they waded to land.

"This is simply terrific," Jezebel complained when they arrived onshore. "I'm soaked, and it's freezing!"

Khaldun called air. Suddenly a hot wind started blowing. Jezebel dropped her pack and held her hands out to her sides, rotating slowly to let the breeze dry her off. Khaldun did the same.

"I didn't know you could do that," she said.

"Neither did I," he replied with a shrug, gazing off into the trees. "Let's get going. The faster we find our quarry, the sooner we can help Allison."

They located a path through the forest and set out. Less than two hours later, they came to a clearing. Jezebel could see enormous stones standing in the moonlight. She could hardly believe her eyes: she was home at last.

"This is it," she whispered. "Rockhedge. But there's nobody here."

"No one alive, anyway," Khaldun replied, looking frightened. "There are spirits here—hundreds of them."

"You can see them?!"

"Faintly… It's almost like I can see their shadows, not the specters themselves. This place has an evil feel to it."

"Can you tell if Syllith is nearby?"

"I'm not sure. But her trail leads off to the northeast," he told her. "Let's see where it goes."

Although she didn't voice it, Jezebel felt relieved that they wouldn't be staying at Rockhedge. The place was spooky, and she remembered her last visit here all too vividly. They skirted the edge of the stones and started down another path back into the woods.

They followed the trail for several minutes until they came to a small clearing. Khaldun stopped.

"What is it?" asked Jezebel.

"There's something here," he said. He held out his hand, and suddenly a big tent appeared, seemingly out of nowhere. It was larger than what they'd been using on their journey, more closely resembling those the wayfarers inhabited. Jezebel followed Khaldun inside.

"This is Syllith's," he whispered. "She's been staying here for quite some time."

There was a bedroll in one corner. A carpet was rolled up next to it. Two large logs had been turned on their ends as tables. On one sat a big crystal ball in a silver stand. Upon the other were several books. Jezebel opened one of these, but suddenly someone else entered the tent.

Jezebel turned. In one moment, she saw Syllith standing in the opening, holding her staff. In the next instant, the witch cast a spell. A sheet of blue energy hovered in the air for a second before enveloping Jezebel and Khaldun, squeezing them together.

"Who the hell are you?" Syllith shouted.

Khaldun did something. The energy disappeared; Syllith backed away a step.

"I'm Jezebel from Spanbrook—and this is Khaldun. Enigma sent us to look for you…"

"Hah! Do you take me for a fool?" Syllith demanded, brandishing her staff in front of her. "Henry's tried this trick before. I'll tell you nothing."

"She's telling the truth," Khaldun insisted. "We traveled across half the continent before we found Enigma at the watchtower. We know that Nyro and the Sacred Circle are imprisoned in Pytha…"

"Of course you do! That's what Henry's after—but you have no idea how dangerous it would be to release them."

"We don't work for Henry!" Jezebel shouted. "My cousin is Princess Allison. A demon is haunting her. We went to find Enigma to find out how to destroy it. But he told us that you're the only one who can do it."

"We went to Northcoast to look for you—Enigma gave us his carpet," Khaldun added. Syllith glared at him still, seemingly unconvinced. "We went to your house and found your notes about Rockhedge—"

"You did *what*?!" Syllith looked alarmed. "Fool! If anyone finds that information…" She pushed past them, grabbing her carpet.

"Nobody will!" said Khaldun. "I put everything back how it was before we left."

Syllith stopped. "You tucked it into the void?" she asked suspiciously.

"Yes!" he told her. "Exactly like you did."

Syllith appeared to be considering the veracity of their story for a moment. But suddenly she pointed her staff at them and shouted a word of command. Nothing happened.

"Come with me." She led them out of the tent. She started a fire and sat down in front of it, laying her staff on the ground. "I'm not sure if I trust you yet. But one thing is clear: you don't work for Henry."

"How do you know?" Khaldun asked, sitting down across from her. Jezebel plopped down beside him.

"You truly are a sorcerer. I assumed you were one of Henry's mages in disguise. But I just tried to cancel your spell, and nothing happened."

Jezebel didn't understand. "What difference does that make?"

"If Henry had managed to capture a sorcerer, he'd have him working on a way to capture one of the Sacred Circle, not out here looking for me," Syllith said. "But tell me… How is Enigma?"

"He is well," Khaldun told her. "He sends his love."

"The wards are holding?"

"Yes," said Jezebel. "He found a crack in one of the other watchtowers. But he repaired it."

"Xythor," Syllith said knowingly. "They're getting stronger. It's only a matter of time before they escape—unless we can find a way to stop it." She let out a long sigh.

"What about the demon here in Spanbrook?" asked Jezebel. "We disturbed it at Rockhedge, and it's been haunting my cousin ever since. Have you found it? Is it one of the… old ones?"

Syllith nodded. "It is. Although I don't know its identity yet. When I first arrived in Spanbrook, I spoke to some of the locals. I told them about the information I'd found regarding an ancient ceremonial burial ground. They directed me to Rockhedge. I spent a couple of days examining the site. Hundreds of specters dwell there, but I could find none of the old ones.

"But the third night I was here, a group of local juveniles threw a party there. Lunacy, if you ask me. That's when the demon showed up. I felt its presence and went to investigate."

"I was there!" said Jezebel. "Allison wanted to talk to her mother—she died a year and a half ago. A friend of ours brought a spirit board—"

"You used a spirit board at Rockhedge?! That was extremely foolish. It's no wonder the demon imprinted upon one of you. And yet… I wonder how you were able to make contact when I was not. That's curious."

"I think I saw you there," said Jezebel, recalling the incident. "There was a flash of lightning, and the demon was looming over a small figure…"

"Yes, that was I," said Syllith. "I battled the monster and attempted to exterminate it. I failed. The demon escaped."

"So you *do* know how to destroy it?" Jezebel asked hopefully.

"Yes, I have learned several methods in my travels. The spells I invoked the night you awakened the monster had worked before on many lesser demons. Yet this one was unaffected. I went to Myrddin after that encounter to seek his help. He wouldn't listen. He refused to grant me an audience with Prince Aldo, throwing me out of his office instead."

"I saw you in the castle!" said Jezebel. "I *knew* I recognized you from somewhere—you were there the day after Rockhedge!"

"That's correct," Syllith acknowledged. "Tell me about your cousin's haunting. I've heard strange stories of spectral activity inside the keep—I didn't realize the princess was involved. The demon followed her back to the castle, I assume?"

"Yes," said Jezebel. "It was horrible. It appeared in Allison's bedchamber several times. And when the wayfarers performed at the castle, it possessed Nomad and… raped her. Aldo ordered Myrddin to kill him…"

"*Myrddin* killed Nomad?" Syllith said, sounding shocked. "I heard rumors that the sorcerer died inside the castle that night, but was unable to learn anything of the circumstances surrounding his death. Was Nomad wearing his ring when the demon possessed him?"

"He was," Khaldun said, holding up his hand. "I've got it now, though. Enigma said I should wear it."

"As well you should," Syllith agreed. "But this bodes ill. The demon must be more powerful than I thought if it was able to overcome that protection. That might explain why my spells have been ineffective against it."

"Myrddin said he knows a way to destroy it," said Jezebel. "But Aldo refused to allow it."

"That's not entirely surprising," Syllith replied cryptically. "And I can't say I blame him. Myrddin surely knows the same methods I do. I have to say that necromancer remains a mystery."

"How so?" asked Khaldun.

"Necromancy has been dead for centuries," said Syllith. "The secrets Dredmort unearthed in Fosland's library had been buried since the time of Nyro. And yet somehow, Myrddin discovered them too. That's where my research started, to tell you the truth. Before the wraiths appeared, I was worried that Henry might discover the rite the same way Myrddin did. So I spent two years digging up information on the necromancer.

"He entered the university a common mage with an affinity for the spirit world. He transformed during his second year, but he wasn't a particularly powerful sorcerer. After his metamorphosis, the university assigned him to Spanbrook. He entered the service of Prince Allister Barclay after he graduated, near the end of Allister's reign."

"*What*?!" said Jezebel. "Allister was my great-great-grandfather—that had to be a hundred years ago."

"One hundred and four, to be precise," Syllith confirmed.

"But Myrddin can't be that old," Jezebel protested. "He doesn't look much older than Aldo."

"Sorcerers and necromancers live much longer than the rest of us," said Syllith. "Enigma is nearly two hundred years old."

"It's true," Khaldun said to Jezebel. "Nomad told me the same thing."

"Allister died shortly after Myrddin's arrival," Syllith continued. "Albany ascended to the throne. Northern Dorshire was in a state of constant turmoil at the time. The prince in Newberry was much like Henry, a warlord attempting to conquer the rest of the kingdom. Together Albany and Myrddin opposed him. Albany built the wall around Spanbrook Town. But it wasn't enough. Newberry conquered the surrounding princedoms. They marshaled their forces and marched on Spanbrook. Myrddin wasn't strong enough to repel them.

"But on the day of the final battle, Myrddin emerged from the castle a necromancer. He decimated the opposing forces almost single-handedly. Newberry made a few more feeble attempts to take Spanbrook, but Myrddin was too powerful to overcome. By the time Allain ascended to the throne, Newberry's power had waned. The region has known peace ever since."

"Prince Allain was my grandfather," Jezebel muttered, still struggling to accept that Myrddin could be so old.

"Did you ever discover how Myrddin learned the secrets of necromancy?" asked Khaldun.

"No," said Syllith. "He left the university a sorcerer of ordinary skill. Yet he entered the battle with Newberry a necromancer. I can only guess that Spanbrook's library must harbor the same secrets Dredmort found in Fosland's. I don't know for sure. But if that's true, the information is certainly safe. No mage of Henry's will ever be able to penetrate Castle Spanbrook without Myrddin's knowledge."

"You saw the book containing the rite in Fosland," Khaldun observed. "What does it entail?"

"I didn't get a chance to examine it closely," said Syllith. "Dredmort caught me in his study, and I barely escaped. But the part I saw resembled the rite of binding for a sorcerer. And I've been able to piece together some information since leaving the watchtower.

"I found a document in Highgate that lists every mage who served Nyro—and the demons they controlled in the case of the necromancers. Next to the name of every demon was inscribed the Pythan word for 'bound.'"

"We found those papers!" Jezebel said excitedly. "We were wondering what that word meant."

"Bound?" Khaldun repeated. "Bound, how? To whom? The necromancers?"

"I believe so," said Syllith. "I came across an interesting historical text in the library at Roses. A court mage recorded it during the early years of Nyro's reign. He and a band of rebels were trying to find a way to defeat the Sacred Circle. His narrative made many references to the necromancers 'relinquishing' their power to a demon. He believed that if he could isolate Nyro from her demon, she'd be completely defenseless.

"I'm convinced that to become a necromancer, a sorcerer must bind his or her soul to a demon. That rite endows the demon with the sorcerer's full power, but binds it to the mage."

"Wait," said Jezebel. "You're saying that a necromancer has no power without his demon?"

"That's correct," said Syllith.

"But you don't know this for a fact," said Khaldun. "You're only guessing."

"That's true. But this idea is corroborated by one further piece of evidence. You understand that a demon is nothing more than the spirit of a powerful sorcerer or necromancer?" Khaldun nodded. "Nyro and the Sacred Circle are incarcerated inside of Pytha. Enigma and I confirmed that; we identified every one of them. Yet other than a handful of lesser spirits, they are the *only* demons inside the wards."

"But I thought the elves trapped the necromancers *and* their demons?" said Jezebel.

"They did."

"I don't understand," said Khaldun.

"The necromancers' souls *merged* with their demons. When they died, their spirits lived *as one* with their demons. They were no longer separate entities. Enigma and I couldn't comprehend it at the time, but now it makes perfect sense."

"But if that's true," said Khaldun, "and someone managed to bind *Nyro's* spirit, they'd be even more powerful than she was…"

"Yes," Syllith answered gravely. "Their power would combine with hers. But it would take an immensely powerful sorcerer to bind Nyro—not even Enigma could manage it. If he attempted it, Nyro would possess *him*."

"But their powers would still combine," said Khaldun. "Nyro would add Enigma's strength to her own."

"Precisely," said Syllith. "And that is the very fact that seems to escape *King Henry*. In his thirst for power, he is hell-bent upon capturing a sorcerer and binding him to a Pythan demon. He fails to understand that Nyro herself would dominate anyone who were to attempt the rite. Instead of conquering the continent himself, Henry would be slain. His mages and armies would enter the service of Nyro and help bring about a new empire."

"Myrddin battled the demon at Rockhedge the night we disturbed it," Jezebel told her. "He said it nearly broke him—does that mean it's stronger than the one he controls?"

"So it would seem," Syllith replied. "And only three or four of the demons on my list possess that kind of power."

They sat in silence for a moment, considering Syllith's words.

"This is all very interesting," Jezebel said finally, "and equally terrifying. But what about Allison? We have to save her. You said you tried to destroy the demon, but failed—what else can we do?"

"There is yet one method I have not attempted," said Syllith. "It is almost certainly the very rite that Aldo forbade Myrddin from performing. We are lucky in a way—the demon's attachment to your cousin will greatly facilitate this process. As will you, Khaldun."

"What?" he asked, startled. "How? I don't understand."

"I'm sorry, but for this to work, I'll need to speak to Lady Jezebel alone."

CHAPTER TWENTY-NINE
DILEMMA

hy?" asked Khaldun. "I risked my life to help Jezebel find you and save the princess. Surely I can be trusted…"

"It's not a matter of trust," said Syllith, rising to her feet. "The information I'm about to give Jezebel must be hidden from you for this to work. Don't be offended—I had to keep this knowledge from Enigma as well, and I assure you, I trust him completely. Take a walk, sorcerer."

Khaldun got up and moved away from the fire, looking disgruntled. Syllith motioned Jezebel inside her tent.

"You must understand something before I begin," she told her. "What you're going to attempt is exceedingly dangerous. When we die, our spirits live on, free of physical form. Yet they *remember* what it was like to be inside a body. They yearn for the pleasures of the flesh. It is this desire that drives the demon to haunt your cousin. When you used the spirit board, the monster caught her scent, so to speak, and followed her to the castle. Its desire for her will have increased since the rape. And that is what will allow us to capture and destroy it."

Syllith reached inside a pouch hanging from the side of the tent. She pulled out a slender golden spike and handed it to Jezebel.

"Allison must have intercourse with Khaldun. Doing so will lure the demon into his body—as you've probably heard, sorcerers are highly susceptible to demonic possession. Once that happens, you must drive this spike into his flesh. Powerful enchantments have been placed upon it that will trap the demon inside the metal."

Jezebel laughed. "You must be joking! The princess has to have *sex* with Khaldun to destroy the demon?! That's the most absurd thing I've ever heard."

"Magic is founded in human thought. And sexual energy is particularly potent. The metamorphosis that turns mages into sorcerers is often triggered—"

"By sex! I know—that's what Khaldun and I were doing when *he* transformed," said Jezebel. "But still—this is insane! You're talking about luring the demon into *raping* Allison again!"

"And that's exactly why Aldo would have forbidden Myrddin from performing the rite."

"No… Myrddin couldn't possibly have suggested having intercourse with Allison," said Jezebel, repulsed by the idea.

"I'm sure he wouldn't have done so himself," said Syllith. "Any male would have sufficed. Myrddin would have opened him to the spirit world before the rite. And Myrddin would have been the one to drive the spike into the boy's flesh."

Jezebel shook her head, unable to believe that Syllith was serious. "What if *I* make love to Khaldun, instead of Allison. Would that work?"

"No. The demon has imprinted on the princess, not you," Syllith told her. "*She* must be the one we use as bait. That's the only way to lure the demon into possessing the sorcerer."

"I can't agree to this. I won't put my cousin through another ordeal. The idea is utterly barbaric."

"This is how Enigma and I destroyed the spirits in Pytha," Syllith said. "It's the only way I have yet to try. But I have been unable to locate the demon in recent weeks."

"Of course—it's been inside the castle traumatizing the princess!"

"Exactly, and Aldo has issued an edict forbidding foreign mages from entering the castle. Only his own witches are allowed inside. I was puzzled by that move initially—I could only guess that it was directed against me. Myrddin must have tired of my constant demands that he help me banish the demon. But now it's clear that Aldo wished to keep anyone who might be an easy target for possession away from his daughter. Getting Khaldun inside is going to be difficult. It may be easier to bring Allison outside the castle at this point."

Jezebel laughed again. "I can get Khaldun in. But Allison's never going to agree to this."

"It's the only way," Syllith told her. "I've tried everything else. If you fail, the demon's obsession will continue to grow. It's only a matter of time before it overcomes Myrddin's protections and starts possessing the princess herself. Once that happens, it will wear her down, and she will descend into madness."

Jezebel recalled a conversation she'd had with Khaldun right before they left Spanbrook. He told her about a witch Nomad had known. A demon had haunted her and driven her to insanity. The woman ultimately took her own life.

"I'll present the idea to her," Jezebel finally agreed. "But I can't force her to do it."

"You must do everything in your power to convince her," said Syllith. "Khaldun has to know what you're planning, *but you must not tell him about the spike*! If he knows, the demon will also be aware. It may be able to cancel the magic.

"And you should wear the ring. We don't want to hide Khaldun from the demon, but it may help *you* avoid its notice during the act."

Jezebel sighed. "That's all I have to do? Drive the spike into Khaldun's flesh?"

"Yes. You must wait, of course, until the demon has possessed him. But that's the only action you need to take."

"There's no guarantee this is going to work," said Jezebel. "What if they have sex, and nothing happens?"

"That's highly unlikely, given the strength of the demon's hunger for Allison, and Khaldun's susceptibility to possession. But... I must request one more thing of you when you perform the rite."

"What?"

"The demon will be trapped inside the metal the moment the spike pierces the sorcerer's flesh. But Khaldun will be paralyzed until you remove the spike. And the demon will still be able to speak with his voice. I need you to identify the monster."

"You want me to ask it its *name*?" Jezebel asked in disbelief.

"Yes," Syllith said simply. "It's the only way to find out which of the old ones we've captured. Removing the metal from Khaldun's body will place the demon beyond the reach of any spell. Once you bring it back to me, I will destroy it."

Jezebel stared at the innocuous-looking spike in her hand, unable to believe that she was agreeing to this. She left Syllith's tent and found Khaldun a few yards away sitting against a tree.

"So are you going to let me in on your secret?" he asked sullenly.

"Most of it," Jezebel said, grasping the spike in her pocket. "But not here. Let's take a walk—I need time to think. We can go to Trey's."

They walked off through the trees. Within minutes they came to the trail Jezebel and Allison had used when they fled Rockhedge months before. They followed it to the road and headed west.

Jezebel was thankful to be home. But she dreaded the task that now lay before her. She wished she could turn around and go to the farm, leaving this whole dreadful business behind her.

It was late. They didn't meet anyone on the road. The frost covering the adjacent fields reminded Jezebel how long she'd been gone; it was summer when they left. She was surprised how quickly Spanbrook Town came into view—it had always seemed like such a long walk before her journey across the continent. And she was stunned by how *small* the town appeared. In her memory, it was much bigger. She supposed experiencing places like Arthos and Highgate had altered her perspective.

Before long, they passed within the town's wall. Trey's tavern was nearly empty when they arrived.

"Jez!" her uncle called from behind the bar. Jezebel and Khaldun walked across the room to meet him. Trey gathered her into a big hug. "I've missed you! Do your parents know you're back?"

"Not yet," she said. "We've just arrived."

"Well, have a seat—you must be starving. I'll get you something to eat."

"I have no appetite, unfortunately," Jezebel said with a frown. "But, I could use some mead."

She sat at a table with Khaldun. He eyed her expectantly, clearly eager to find out what was going on. Jezebel waited until the mead arrived. She took a long drink and spent several minutes telling him the whole story—leaving out only the part about the spike.

Khaldun's jaw dropped lower and lower as she spoke. "I can't believe… You're not serious…"

Jezebel laughed. She caught Trey's eye and held up her mug—she definitely needed more mead.

"So, you'll perform the spell once the demon enters my body?" Khaldun asked.

"That's the idea," she replied.

"And you're sure you know how to do it?"

"I'm quite certain—it's not difficult."

They sat in silence for a few minutes; Khaldun looked as distressed as Jezebel felt. Trey arrived with their drinks.

"Everything all right?" he asked.

"Oh yes, just marvelous," Jezebel replied sarcastically.

Khaldun took a swig of his mead as Trey walked away.

"Look on the bright side," said Jezebel. "You get to take yet another princess to bed. I know how attractive you find Allison."

"This is *not* what I had in mind," he replied. "You don't think I'm happy about this, do you?"

"No, of course not. I'm sorry. I just can't believe this is the only way. Although it certainly explains Aldo's refusal."

"We can't force Allison to do this," said Khaldun. "The decision must be hers."

"I agree. And I don't think she's going to do it."

"What then?"

Jezebel took a deep breath. "Then, I take her with me to find the wayfarers."

"I can't accompany you. I'm bound to Aldo now."

"I know," said Jezebel.

"When are we going to tell the princess?"

"Well, that's going to be a little difficult," said Jezebel. She explained Aldo's edict. "I'm sure they'll allow *me* inside—I am family after all. But we're going to have to smuggle you in."

"Any ideas about how we're going to manage that?"

"I know exactly how we're going to do it," she replied. "But I'm not ready to confront Allison with this yet. I'm exhausted—let's do it in the morning. We can stay here tonight."

"Sounds good to me," said Khaldun.

They took a room on the second floor. Khaldun drifted off to sleep, but Jezebel lay awake. She didn't know how she was going to break the news to the princess. She couldn't bear the thought of telling her cousin that she'd have to allow herself to be victimized again.

Jezebel gave up trying to sleep. She climbed out of bed, left the room, and wandered back downstairs. Finding the common room dark and empty, she took a seat at one of the tables.

Her uncle's tavern had been like a second home to Jezebel her entire life. When she was a little girl, she used to stay here with Trey whenever her parents would let her. But something seemed different about the place tonight. Jezebel couldn't put her finger on it.

Suddenly there was a noise behind the bar—someone was walking out of the kitchen. Jezebel jumped to her feet, wand drawn.

"Who's there?!" a voice shouted.

"Trey?" said Jezebel, her heart in her throat.

"Jez," her uncle replied, emerging from the shadows. "You about gave me a heart attack. I was just taking out the garbage—what are you still doing awake?"

Jezebel retook her seat. "I don't know. I've got a lot on my mind, I guess." She called fire, lighting the candle in the middle of the table. Trey ambled over and sat across from her.

"It'll take a little getting used to, seeing you do tricks like that," he said, indicating the candle. "Tell me about your journey. Vivien said you were headed to the university?"

Jezebel nodded. "We were seeking a great sorcerer. We had some trouble getting there—Henry's forces were in the way."

"I've heard about him," said Trey, giving her a dark look. "Folks have come through here, traveling west to get away from that bastard."

"We ended up hooking north through Arthos to get there. But the sorcerer wasn't at the university anymore. We went to Highgate right before Henry attacked there, and eventually, we found the sorcerer at a watchtower in the Anthar Mountains."

"The Anthars," Trey said, awe in his voice. "That must be a thousand miles from here…"

"More than that, I think. Anyway, the sorcerer wasn't able to help us, but he sent us to find a witch who could. We went all the way to Northcoast, only to find out that the witch has been here in Spanbrook the whole time."

"Well, did you find her?"

"We did," said Jezebel, taking a deep breath.

"And did she help you?"

Jezebel chuckled softly. "Oh, Trey, I don't know. Allison has a problem, and the witch told us how to solve it. But…"

"You don't like the solution," he guessed.

"No. And I don't think Allison will, either."

Trey stared at her for a minute, the candle flickering between them. "It's only been a few months since I saw you last, but you've changed, Jez," he said finally. "You look older. Wiser, maybe. I don't know what kind of trouble the princess found, but if it's bad enough to send you halfway around the world, she must truly need your help. Best you can do is tell her what you've learned and let her decide. You didn't make that trip for nothing, did you?"

"Of course not," Jezebel said with a sigh.

"Things'll work out," he said, rising from his seat. "They always do in the end. But you should try to get some sleep. You look exhausted!"

"I will. Thanks, Trey."

Jezebel returned to her room. Her uncle's words had soothed her somehow; she fell asleep within minutes. She and Khaldun rose at dawn.

"Before we leave, you need to look… normal," Jezebel advised him.

"Oh, yes," he said, holding his hands out in front of him. His skin changed back to its original color, no longer golden.

"Your eyes, too," she reminded him. As she looked at him, his irises turned deep brown. "That should do it… Let's go."

They went downstairs and left the inn. Jezebel led the way across the town. Vendors were setting up their shops in the market. She worried that someone would recognize Khaldun; perhaps he should have disguised himself as someone else. But then she reminded herself that he hadn't transformed until after they'd left Spanbrook. No one here would know that he was a sorcerer. But given Aldo's dislike for wayfarers, it would still be best to enter the castle covertly.

They turned north. Close to the wall, they came to a smithy. The blacksmith hadn't arrived yet. Jezebel walked around to the rear of the building. There was a metal grate in the ground.

"Help me with this," she said, squatting down. Together they lifted the grate out of the opening, moving it to the side.

"We're going in, I assume?"

"How astute," she mumbled.

Jezebel sat on the edge of the opening and jumped. Khaldun landed next to her. She had him lift her onto his shoulders so she could move the grate back into place.

"Which way?" he asked once he'd put her down. They were standing in a tunnel that faded into the darkness to the east and west.

"Follow me," said Jezebel, heading west.

Khaldun stopped her. "Wait."

"What is it?"

"I should return to my normal appearance," he told her. "If I enter the castle like this, Myrddin will detect my spell."

Jezebel nodded. Khaldun closed his eyes, and slowly his skin turned golden again.

They set out. Jezebel held her wand out in front of her and called a small flame to light their way. They hadn't reached the castle yet, so she figured this would be safe.

A few minutes later, they came to an intersecting tunnel. Jezebel turned left. Before long, they arrived at a stone wall.

"Now what?" asked Khaldun.

Jezebel pointed straight up, grinning. Above their heads was a circular opening in the ceiling, barely wide enough to admit a person.

"Help me up," she said.

Khaldun squatted down slightly, lacing his fingers together in front of him. Jezebel held onto his shoulders and placed one foot in his hands. He hoisted her up. Jezebel grabbed the edges of the aperture and scrambled inside. The space was small, no more than a crawlway. She reached down and gave Khaldun a hand climbing up.

They climbed through a hole in the stone wall. Beyond was an opening in the floor. Jezebel dropped through it, Khaldun right behind her. He looked around in amazement.

"I know where we are!" he hissed.

They were standing in an alcove recessed into the corner of a cavernous chamber. A channel ran through the middle, filled with water. Arches spanned the water, steps protruding from their stone faces. There were crews unloading cargo from barges.

"We're inside the castle—this is where the Ember runs through the building. You brought me here the night… Well, right before the incident with Nomad. This was one of the secret passageways you told me about."

"Yes, although I never imagined I'd be using it to break *into* the castle," she said. "I wish you could make us invisible—we need to get to that far passage, preferably without being seen. Hopefully, if we act like we belong here, they won't bother us. Come on."

Jezebel and Khaldun started across the chamber. Before they'd gone twenty feet, someone shouted at them.

"Hey! What are you doing down here?" It was one of the prince's guards. He'd been hidden by a pile of crates.

"Go!" Jezebel yelled, breaking into a run. But as they drew up to the far wall, six more men came charging down the stairs. Jezebel stopped short. She pointed her wand and called earth, knocking them back. Khaldun grabbed her by the arm, and they dashed toward the water.

Jezebel led the way across one of the arches. She moved slowly, pressing herself against the stone, afraid of falling into the river. Safely on the other side, they pelted across the chamber to the nearest exit. Jezebel turned in time to see a dozen guards giving chase.

"Now can you make us invisible?" she pleaded as they ran up the stairs.

"Might as well," Khaldun muttered, casting the spell.

They emerged into the courtyard; it was crawling with guards. Badrick, the prince's master-at-arms, was standing in the center, shouting orders to his men.

"The whole castle's been alerted to our presence," said Khaldun. "There must be guards outside the princess's chambers."

"We'll deal with that when we get there," said Jezebel. "Let's go."

They crept along the wall to the armory. Jezebel was about to walk inside when three more guards dashed through the door. She backpedaled after nearly running into them. But she was successful—the guards didn't touch her.

Inside, she led Khaldun to the far end of the room. She ran through a door into the keep. But as they rounded a corner, Jezebel ran into someone. She backed away a few steps and realized it was Myrddin.

"It's good to see you again, my lady," he said. He looked much older than he had before. His face was drawn and haggard. There were dark circles under his eyes. "But I'm afraid we'll have to take your friend into custody."

Jezebel pointed her wand and called earth. Nothing happened. She turned and ran, pushing Khaldun in front of her. "Move!"

They charged back through the armory. But as they entered the courtyard, everything went black. Jezebel could see nothing but Khaldun.

"Cancel the magic!" she yelled.

"I'm trying!" he shouted back. "Myrddin's too strong."

Suddenly a sheet of golden energy wrapped around Khaldun. The blackness dissipated, and Jezebel saw Myrddin approaching them with a dozen guards.

"I'm sorry, my lady. The prince has prohibited mages from entering the castle. *You* may see the princess, but I'll have to confiscate your wand."

Jezebel knew she had no choice. She handed it over.

"Was your quest successful?" the necromancer asked.

"No," she lied. "But how do you know I was on a… quest?"

"Her Highness confided in me," he said, turning to face Khaldun. He snapped his fingers, and the sorcerer rose several inches off the ground. Myrddin strode away, Khaldun floating along behind him. Jezebel followed, along with the guards.

"What are you going to do with him?" she asked, recalling the incident with Nomad.

"It's up to the prince to decide," said Myrddin.

"He's done nothing wrong. We were only going to see the princess."

"I must do as my prince commands," Myrddin told her, a note of apology in his voice. "But I don't think there's any immediate danger. His Highness plans to let your friend cool his heels for a few days."

"He already knows we're here?"

"He's been expecting him," said Myrddin, "ever since he became aware of the boy's true name. I informed him the moment you entered the castle."

"But how did you know? We used no magic…"

"And that would have worked perfectly against a sorcerer."

"But why imprison him—he's bound to Aldo!"

"Bound or not, it would be unwise to allow a sorcerer to wander about the castle in the present circumstances."

Myrddin led them to the southwest tower, Jezebel begging him the whole way to let Khaldun go free. At the top of the stairs, they came to a chamber enclosed with iron bars. Myrddin moved the sorcerer inside, closing the cell behind him. As the door clanged shut, the perimeter of the enclosure began to glow with golden energy. The spell encasing Khaldun disappeared, and he stood on his own.

"His Highness asked me to prepare this cell after the unfortunate episode with Nomad," said Myrddin. "The enchantments protecting the chamber seal it against magic." He locked eyes with Jezebel. "The spells can only be removed by unlocking the door."

Jezebel stared at him in disbelief. Had he just told her how to free Khaldun?

Myrddin and his entourage started down the stairs. Jezebel looked pleadingly at Khaldun. He merely shrugged. She dashed down the steps after the necromancer.

"Please, let him go! We'll leave the castle—I promise he won't come back." As she said these words, she was already plotting a way to sneak Allison out, too.

"My hands are tied," said Myrddin. He stopped at the bottom of the stairs and turned to face her. "I will confess that I've grown weary of this constant struggle—I desperately wish Aldo would allow me to banish the demon. And I was hoping you'd find a way, even though I'd have no choice but to stop you. *If* I caught you." He strode away, leaving Jezebel gaping in his wake.

CHAPTER THIRTY
ALLISON

ezebel ran up to her cousin's bedchamber. She opened one of the doors slowly, peering inside. Allison was sitting in the bay window. She turned to see who was there.

Jezebel was stunned: Allison looked terrible. Her hair was a mess. It appeared that she hadn't slept in days; the circles under her eyes were darker than Myrddin's. But when she laid eyes on Jezebel, she smiled radiantly, and her natural beauty shone through.

Jezebel moved into the room, closing the door behind her. Allison ran to her, uttering a soft cry. She hugged Jezebel tightly. Tears of joy slid down Jezebel's cheeks.

"Three months," Allison murmured. "You've been gone for *three months.*"

They held each other for a full minute until Allison pulled away slightly. Jezebel looked deep into her eyes and kissed her passionately.

"I've missed you so badly," Allison said. "There was a commotion, and the guards whisked me away to Myrddin's tower. I returned only a minute ago. Were you the cause of the fuss?"

"I was—I sneaked into the castle with Khaldun, but Myrddin sensed us."

"Yes, they've forbidden mages from entering—sorcerers in particular. Did you find Enigma?"

Jezebel let out a long sigh. "We did. But this is a *long* story." They sat in the bay window, and Jezebel recounted her tale. She told her about their journey from Highgate to the watchtower, the demons locked inside Pytha, Khaldun's bond to Aldo, Syllith's house in Northcoast, and tracking the witch to Rockhedge.

"She's been in Spanbrook this whole time?! That's incredible… But she does know how to banish the demon… Right?"

"Yes, and she told me how to do it," said Jezebel. "You're not going to like this."

"What? Tell me!"

Jezebel didn't know how to break the news gently. So she cut to the chase. "You have to make love to Khaldun. That will lure the demon. It will enter his body, and I…" She touched the spike in her pocket. "I will perform a spell to trap it and bring it to Syllith to be destroyed."

Allison fell silent, giving her a blank stare.

"Did you hear me?" Jezebel asked.

"I… Yes, I heard… But…" she stammered. "My father didn't want the demon to rape me again… That's why he refused to allow it. Did Myrddin plan to… himself?"

"Unlikely," said Jezebel. "Syllith thinks he would have used someone else and opened them to the spirit world. Myrddin would have performed the necessary spell.

"I told Syllith you'd never agree to this. Our only other choice is to leave. The demon will find you eventually, no matter where we go, unless we stay on the move. So I thought we could join the wayfarers…"

"Join the wayfarers?! What are you talking about? *We have the solution*!"

Jezebel was shocked. "You mean… You want to go through with it?"

"No question."

"But… I thought…"

"You thought because I'm not interested in men, I wouldn't want—"

"Allison, we're talking about rape!"

"Not this time we're not," she countered. "I'm entering into this willingly. I understand exactly what's going to happen, and I *want* to go through with it. You don't know what it's been like here! The monster has tormented me almost incessantly. I have to sleep with guards in the room now, and that only works some of the time. The demon nearly killed one of them last night. Myrddin visits almost daily and does whatever he does... But that only works for a few hours. The demon *always returns*! It watches me when I bathe, and it follows me to the dining room and the stables... I want this to end! I'll do anything!"

Allison covered her face with her hands and sobbed. Jezebel moved across the window and pulled her into a hug.

"Why does it have to be Khaldun?" Allison asked once she'd calmed down. "You said Myrddin would have used someone else, so why couldn't we?"

"Myrddin knows how to open someone's channels to the spirit world," Jezebel said. "We don't—but Khaldun's are already open. As long as he removes his ring, the demon will have no trouble possessing him."

"Yes, but that will still be true if I make love to *you* instead of him. He only needs to be nearby—our lovemaking would still attract the demon, right?"

"Well... yes, I suppose it would..."

"Then let's do it that way! The demon will still possess Khaldun, and then you can perform the spell!"

Jezebel thought about it for a moment. "I think you're right—this should work. Syllith doesn't know we're lovers, so doing it this way wouldn't have occurred to her."

"How soon can we do it?" Allison asked.

"Well, that's going to be a little bit of a problem," said Jezebel. "Myrddin's locked Khaldun in the tower—on your father's orders. He's sealed the cell against magic. But the strangest thing happened before I came to see you..."

"What?" asked Allison.

"I might have been imagining things, but it almost seemed like Myrddin *wants* us to do this. He essentially told me how to free Khaldun."

"He did? How?"

"He said that unlocking the cell removes the magic."

"That's easy then," said Allison. "I know where the keys are!"

"You can't be serious…"

"Come with me!"

Allison jumped from the window seat and dashed across the room. Jezebel followed her to the other end of the hallway. There was a small room there that served as a guard station. An older man was sitting behind a desk.

"Harold, I need the keys to the southwest tower," said Allison.

"Not a chance," the guard replied, shaking his head. "I'm under strict orders from the prince himself. *Nobody* gets those keys."

"I am your princess! I demand that you give them to me!"

"I'm sorry, Your Highness," he said, jumping to his feet and saluting her. "I cannot comply."

Allison growled in frustration and stormed from the room.

"I'm sorry," Jezebel muttered to Harold before going after her.

They returned to Allison's chambers. The princess flopped down in her bed.

"Now what?" Jezebel asked, unsurprised by what had happened.

"We wait until Preston goes on duty," she said with a grin.

"Who's Preston?"

"You remember—he's the young one who's smitten with me. He requested regular night duty after that first time I saw the demon," Allison explained.

"Ah yes," Jezebel said, recalling the boy in question. "I'm sure he's just hoping to get another glimpse of your breasts."

Allison giggled. "No doubt. But we can use that to our advantage."

Jezebel lay down next to her. "Poor Preston."

"Forget Preston," Allison said, moving right next to Jezebel. "Poor *me*. You were gone far too long."

They kissed. But then Jezebel pulled away.

"What's wrong?" asked the princess.

"We don't want to disturb the demon—yet. And besides… We need to talk…"

Jezebel didn't know where to begin. Allison stared at her, waiting for her to say something.

"What is it?" she asked.

"I was… When we were in Madison… I suppose it's not important *where* we were…" she stammered. "I made an awful mistake."

Allison looked concerned. "What happened?"

"I… Khaldun and I made love."

Her words seemed to hang in the air between them as if Allison hadn't heard them yet. Jezebel felt awful as her cousin's face finally registered comprehension of what she'd said.

"I'm so sorry," Jezebel pleaded.

"Was that the only time?"

"Yes," Jezebel said. "I was drunk and…"

Jezebel held her breath for a moment. Allison got out of bed and moved to the window. Jezebel sat up. Allison shook her head and stared out the window. Jezebel hated adding to her pain like this, but she had to tell her the truth.

"We never did it again after that. I was sorely tempted, I'll confess, but I resisted…"

"Good for you," Allison said.

"I resisted it because I love you!" Jezebel cried. "I saw us together in the looking glass, and *that* is the future I want!"

"Perhaps you should have thought about that a little sooner. And what about Khaldun? Do you love *him* too?"

Jezebel sobbed. "Yes."

Allison tutted impatiently, returning her gaze out the window. Jezebel sat there for a few minutes, staring at her cousin, crying freely. Allison didn't move. Jezebel rose from the bed and started to walk out of the room.

"Why did you come back?" Allison asked.

Jezebel stopped in her tracks, turning to face her cousin. "*What?*"

"If you love him, why did you return? The two of you could have run away together and escaped this insanity."

Jezebel stared at her in disbelief. "Do you understand nothing? We walked halfway across the continent and back—*for you*! I can't count the number of times I nearly lost my life, all to find Enigma and save you from this hell! How can you possibly ask me that?"

Allison didn't reply. Jezebel strode from the room. She didn't know where she was going, but she knew she had to get away from Allison. How could things have gone so horribly wrong?

Jezebel went out to the courtyard and sat on the same bench from which she'd watched Allison's lesson with Badrick so long ago. Sobbing uncontrollably, she thought of how things had been before her journey. She wanted that life back. But she couldn't blame Allison for being so angry. She knew she'd violated her trust.

Jezebel sat there for a long time, staring at the ground. She didn't know where else to go. If she walked to the farm, she'd just have to turn around and come back again. She assumed Allison would still go through with the rite.

Suddenly Jezebel looked up. Badrick was walking across the courtyard, toward the stables. Jezebel joined him.

"Welcome back, my lady," he said gruffly, retrieving his saddle from a hook on the wall. "I'm sorry about your friend. But this business with your cousin seems to be pushing our prince toward madness. I petitioned for the sorcerer's release, but His Highness will not listen to reason."

"Thank you for trying," she replied softly.

He asked her about her travels. Jezebel recounted her story while he saddled his horse. She was careful not to say anything that might lead him to guess her plan, but Badrick seemed most interested in her encounters with Henry and his armies.

A few minutes later, he bade her farewell and rode away. Jezebel followed him out of the stable. She stopped short before she'd taken three steps.

Allison was approaching from across the courtyard. Her hair was wet from a bath, and she was wearing a simple dress. She looked as beautiful as Jezebel had ever seen her.

Allison stopped a few feet away from her. They gazed at each other for several moments, saying nothing. Jezebel didn't know what to think. Was she here to banish her from the castle? Or to offer her forgiveness? She couldn't tell from the expression on her face. Jezebel wanted so desperately to be with her, for everything to be how it used to be.

"I'm sorry," Allison said quietly.

Jezebel closed her eyes, relief filling her very soul. "So am I," she whispered.

"But I forgive you. I still want to be with you if... if that's what you want, too."

Jezebel cried tears of joy. "Yes! Of course, it is!"

Allison hugged her tight, seemingly unconcerned that anyone would see them. Jezebel cried on her shoulder. They held each other until she calmed down, then walked hand-in-hand back inside the keep. The two of them took their supper in the private dining room. Jezebel was struck by how normal this felt. There was no sign here that a demon was haunting her cousin.

After dinner, they returned to Allison's chambers and waited for Preston's shift to start. Allison led Jezebel down the hall once it was time. Sure enough, Preston was sitting behind the desk. Jezebel couldn't get over how young he seemed—she had to remind herself that she wasn't much older.

"Your Highness!" Preston said, jumping to his feet. He saluted her awkwardly, unable to keep his eyes off of her.

Allison moved into the tiny room. "Relax," she said, standing very close to him. "I was wondering if I could just *borrow* the keys to the southwest tower."

"Oh... Well, you see... I can't..."

"I know my father has forbidden it," she said, rolling her eyes as if that were only a minor inconvenience. "But, I'd be forever grateful if you'd overlook that little issue."

"I'm sorry, Your Highness. I cannot," he said, seeming to rally himself.

"Please," Allison cooed, leaning her face in closer to his.

"I… No…"

Allison kissed him. Preston tried feebly to push her away but gave up after only a second or two. Allison kept kissing him and reached between his legs with one hand. Jezebel cleared her throat. Allison pulled away. Preston had turned bright red.

"Did I mention how *thankful* I would be?" Allison asked. Jezebel could tell she was fighting very hard to stifle a giggle. But Preston gave in.

"You have to promise me that you won't tell your father about this," he said.

"I give you my word," Allison told him solemnly. "And I'll promote you when I ascend to the throne."

Preston opened a drawer in the desk and pulled out a ring of keys. He handed them to Allison. "The big one unlocks the chamber at the top of the tower. I assume that's why you want these."

Allison smiled at him once more, and they left the room. They ran to Khaldun's cell. Allison held the keys tight, trying to stop them from jingling.

Khaldun was sitting on the floor. The energy around the enclosure was glowing brighter than ever. He sprang to his feet when he saw them. Allison unlocked the door, and the spell vanished immediately.

"Let's get out of here before someone catches us," Jezebel said nervously.

"I'd make myself invisible, but Myrddin would sense it," said Khaldun.

"Don't do that!" Jezebel replied. "I think he wants us to succeed, but he did say he'd have to stop us if he caught us. I'm already worried enough that he'll realize we've removed you from the cell."

They stopped at the guard station. Allison gave the keys back to Preston, and they returned to her chambers.

"There's been a little change of plans," Jezebel told Khaldun as she shut the doors. "*I'll* be the one making love to the princess—sorry to disappoint you."

"Then how do we lure the demon into possessing me?" he asked.

"You'll need to be nearby," said Allison. "Our actions will still attract the demon. And if you're here, it's sure to possess you."

"You still get to watch," Jezebel told him with a sly grin.

"Ah… so…" Khaldun said uncomfortably. "When are we…"

"Right now," said Allison.

"Are you sure?" asked Jezebel. "There's been no sign of the demon today. Perhaps we should wait until…"

"Until what?" Allison demanded, jumping into bed. "It'll show up. It *always* does. Let's get this over with." She started unbuttoning her dress.

"I'll just… wait over here," Khaldun said, moving toward the bathroom.

"Not too far," warned Jezebel.

"Wait," said Khaldun. He took off his ring and handed it to Jezebel.

"Oh, right," she said, taking it from him and putting it on her finger. It was much too big for her; she put it on her thumb.

"And what about your wand?" Khaldun asked in alarm. "Did you get it back?"

"Oh—yes," Jezebel lied. "I got it back."

Allison had removed her clothes. Jezebel climbed into the bed and kissed her passionately. She reached into her pocket and pulled out the spike, keeping it at the ready, and made love to the princess.

After a minute, Jezebel gazed over at Khaldun—he was spellbound, but no change had come over him. The demon had not made an appearance.

Moments later, Allison moaned with pleasure. But an instant later, something went wrong. The princess squealed in pain; Jezebel pulled away. Nothing could have prepared her for what she saw next.

Allison was writhing in agony. She started foaming at the mouth and went into convulsions. Within seconds, her skin began to turn golden.

"I don't believe it," Jezebel said with a gasp. "She's transforming!"

Allison moaned low in her throat. But suddenly there was another noise—a snarl.

Jezebel looked up just before Khaldun's fist connected with her skull. She tumbled out of bed, dropping the spike. Jezebel tried to get to her feet, but her equilibrium was off, and she saw stars.

She forced herself to focus. Khaldun was removing his clothing, growling the whole time. Jezebel looked around frantically for the spike. She couldn't see it anywhere.

"I've been watching the two of you your entire lives," Khaldun said. His voice was off—it sounded feral. And his eyes were glowing. "And now I'll finally have you both."

He lunged at her. Jezebel tried to dodge, but he grabbed her, spinning her around. He ripped her shirt clean off her body. Jezebel pulled free and ran toward the doors.

But Khaldun tackled her from behind. He threw her to the floor and sat on top of her. With one hand, he squeezed her breast; it felt like he was ripping it off. Jezebel screamed. Khaldun punched her again.

Jezebel's vision started to go black. She could feel him trying to rip her trousers off. Suddenly she heard the doors opening and turned to see who was there.

It was Preston. He was standing in the doorway, frozen with terror.

"Help!" Jezebel cried, willing herself to stay conscious.

A snarl ripped from Khaldun's throat. He threw out his hand, and something invisible crashed into Preston, propelling him into the wall across the corridor. The doors slammed shut.

Jezebel screamed again. But suddenly, Khaldun leaned back, howling in rage. Allison was on her feet; she'd thrown her arm around Khaldun's neck, trying to pull him off her cousin. Jezebel wriggled free, scuttling away from him. She realized Allison was still naked—her entire body had turned golden. The princess looked horrified as she wrestled Khaldun to the floor.

Jezebel scrambled across the room, searching desperately for the spike. She heard Allison scream—turning, she saw that Khaldun had thrown her on her back and was trying to mount her. Allison struggled to push him away.

The spike was nowhere to be seen. Jezebel dropped to her knees and scanned under the bed. Nothing. She looked under the nightstand. It was too dark—she couldn't see a thing. She clutched it with both hands and toppled it over. And there it was: the golden spike was lying on the stone floor.

Jezebel grabbed it and raced across the room. Khaldun was on top of Allison—he had her arms pinned with one hand, trying to pry her legs apart with the other. Jezebel wasted no time. She lunged forward and embedded the spike in Khaldun's shoulder.

Khaldun fell to his side, howling in pain. But his voice was normal now.

"What did you do?!" he demanded, trying in vain to pull the spike out of his flesh.

"Khaldun?" asked Jezebel.

"Yes—the demon left my body right before you stabbed me. What were you trying to accomplish? You can't harm a specter that way!"

"No, of course," Jezebel said anxiously. "Let me do that." She yanked the spike out of Khaldun's shoulder and pocketed it before he could see what she had.

"Where is it?" asked Allison, scrambling to her feet and frantically searching around the room. "Where did the demon go?" She made no attempt to cover her nakedness, so fearful was she.

"I don't know," said Jezebel, edging toward the doors. "But I fear we've missed our chance. Perhaps I should go get Myrddin—this has gotten out of hand."

"No!" said Khaldun. "He'll incarcerate me again, and we'll never be able to end this!"

"What do you suggest we do?" demanded Allison. "We failed. I'll leave the castle and join the wayfarers. There's no other choice now!"

Suddenly there was a growling sound. It seemed to come from the walls. The three of them looked around anxiously.

"Where did that come from?" asked Jezebel.

"There," said Allison, pointing across the room. "Inside that wall!"

"No," countered Khaldun. "It was over here, by the bed."

"Enough of this. I'm going for Myrddin," said Jezebel.

She opened the door and spotted Preston lying unconscious on the floor. But something ripped the door out of her hand, slamming it shut again. Jezebel backed away with a little scream.

There was another growling noise, louder this time. Jezebel huddled together with Allison and Khaldun in the middle of the room. A shadow grew out of the floor, right in front of the doors. It loomed over them, filling Jezebel with cold and dread. Suddenly it reached out with one arm and lifted her into the air.

Jezebel screamed. But the shadow muffled the noise like a thick fog. She felt its icy touch caressing her body. Faintly, as if from a great distance, she heard Khaldun's voice uttering some sort of spell. And suddenly, the shadow crackled with energy. She felt its tingle along her skin. But the demon reached out and threw Khaldun across the room. He crashed into the wall and fell to the floor.

The shadow disappeared again, dropping Jezebel. She landed on her stomach on the cold stone but jumped immediately to her feet. Allison was next to her. Jezebel pressed against her, scanning the room to see where the demon would show up next.

Allison grabbed her hand, lacing her fingers into Jezebel's. Jezebel squeezed her tight. But with her other hand, Allison reached out and fondled her breasts. Jezebel stared at her cousin in sheer terror. Allison's eyes were glowing red. The demon had possessed her.

"NO!" Jezebel screamed, trying to free her hand and get away. But Allison grabbed her and tossed her onto the bed. Jezebel attempted to scurry away, but the princess jumped onto the bed, mounting her.

"I'll taste you this way, you little slut," said Allison, her voice a snarl.

She lowered her head to Jezebel's, plunging her tongue inside her mouth. Jezebel tried to turn away, but Allison kissed her hungrily. The princess bit Jezebel's bottom lip, piercing the skin. Jezebel tasted blood. She screamed, trying to push Allison off of her.

Suddenly the princess sat up and gasped.

"Allison?" asked Jezebel.

Allison stared down at her, fear and confusion in her face. "What happened?"

"The demon possessed you!" said Jezebel. "Don't you remember?"

But at that moment, a shadow appeared behind the princess, moving closer. It was Khaldun. With a snarl, he ripped Allison away from Jezebel, throwing her to the floor. Allison scampered away, but Khaldun grabbed her, turning her onto her stomach and trying to mount her from behind.

Jezebel sat up and pulled the spike out of her pocket, grasping it tightly in one hand. "NO!" she yelled. "Leave her alone! Take me instead!"

Khaldun turned, staring at her with his glowing eyes. He roared like an animal, rose to his feet and dove into the bed. Grabbing Jezebel by the throat, he pinned her to the bed, climbing on top of her. As he kissed her on the mouth, Jezebel caressed his back with one hand. With her other hand, she plunged the spike into his shoulder.

Khaldun straightened up and froze, releasing his grip on her. Allison ran over and tried to pull him off of her cousin, but knocked him off the bed in the process. He landed on his side on the floor. Jezebel jumped off the bed. Allison stared down at Khaldun, shaking uncontrollably.

Jezebel dropped to her knees beside him. "Identify yourself," she commanded.

"I am Tamalan of Highgate," Khaldun said, his voice wrong.

Allison stared incredulously at Jezebel. "Who?"

Jezebel shrugged.

Khaldun groaned. "And Myrddin of Spanbrook."

CHAPTER THIRTY-ONE
LONG SHADOW

ezebel couldn't believe her ears. She must have heard wrong.

"Tamalan and... *Myrddin*?"

"Tamalan of Highgate and Myrddin of Spanbrook."

Jezebel reached across Khaldun's body and yanked the spike free. It was hot. Khaldun stirred, rolled onto his back, and groaned. "What happened?" he asked weakly.

Jezebel told him everything. Allison went to the bed and wrapped herself in a sheet.

"Myrddin," Khaldun whispered, shocked.

Jezebel put her shirt back on, tattered though it was.

"I don't understand," said Allison. "What does that mean? How can it be two demons—and what's Myrddin got to do with it?"

"To become a necromancer, a sorcerer has to bind his soul to a demon, relinquishing his power to it," Khaldun explained.

"And a demon is just the spirit of a dead sorcerer or necromancer," Jezebel added.

"When a sorcerer undergoes the rite, his soul merges with the demon. They become one single entity," Khaldun concluded.

"Myrddin's demon has been haunting you," Jezebel told her. "He's the one that raped you."

"But that can't be," said Allison, shaking her head. "Myrddin wouldn't do that to me... This is impossible!"

Jezebel stared at her cousin, not knowing what to say. This was difficult for her to believe, too. She felt that there must be some other explanation—Myrddin had always treated the princess like family.

And at that moment, another realization hit Jezebel. It was already clear that Allison had undergone the metamorphosis into a sorcerer. But Jezebel thought back to the vision she'd seen of their wedding day, recalling the way Allison had seemed to glow. And she finally understood. Allison's skin had reflected the sunlight as only a sorcerer's could. But it shouldn't have been possible for Allison to become a sorcerer…

Suddenly the doors burst open. Aldo charged into the room with six of his guards. "What the hell is going on here?" he demanded, shaking with a cold fury.

Khaldun rose unsteadily to his feet, still naked. The scene reminded Jezebel forcefully of the last time a sorcerer had entered this chamber. She locked eyes with Allison as a terrible thought occurred to her: Aldo knew Khaldun's true name.

"SOMEONE ANSWER ME!" Aldo roared.

"We captured the demon," Jezebel said, showing him the spike. "It won't be able to haunt Allison ever again. Syllith is going to destroy it."

"Explain to me why this man and my daughter are standing here without any clothes on!" he shouted.

Allison stared at Khaldun. And at that moment, the full danger of the situation seemed to dawn on her, too.

"Father, you have to understand—what we did was necessary to trap the demon! Khaldun did nothing wrong! You mustn't…"

"How did he escape his cell?" Aldo yelled. "He raped you, didn't he?!"

"*Khaldun* didn't do anything!" Jezebel told him.

"Jez—no!" shouted Allison.

Jezebel didn't want to inflict Aldo's wrath upon Myrddin, either, but she wasn't about to let Khaldun take the fall. "It was Myrddin's demon," she told him. "That's who attacked your daughter, Your Highness —*not* Khaldun!"

"Myrddin… What is this nonsense? What are you talking about?"

"A sorcerer has to bind his soul to a demon to become a necromancer," Khaldun told him.

"I know that! Guards—where is my necromancer right now?"

"Probably in his tower," one of them replied.

Aldo left the room. "Come with me—*all of you!*" he called back.

The guards ran after him. Khaldun and Allison rushed to put their clothes back on before the three of them followed. They hurried down the stairs, caught up with Aldo in the courtyard, and hurried up the stairs to Myrddin's chamber.

The necromancer was sitting at his desk, his head in his hands. A woman was standing across from him. Jezebel didn't know if it was Gemma or Camilla—she could never tell the two witches apart. But she turned around, and Jezebel realized it was Syllith.

"What the hell are *you* doing here?" Aldo demanded. "I thought I made it clear that you are unwelcome."

"He summoned me," she said, indicating Myrddin. "Something about the security of the princedom. I flew here immediately; I arrived only a moment ago."

The necromancer looked up. He appeared diminished somehow. His face was more drawn than ever. And Jezebel realized with a shock that his irises had turned blood red.

"Is it true?" Aldo asked him, disgust on his face. "It's been *your* demon haunting my daughter?"

Syllith gasped; Myrddin nodded slowly. He didn't seem to be in his right mind.

"It's true. I never wanted to become a necromancer. But I was left with little choice. When Newberry attacked during Albany's reign, I wasn't strong enough to defeat their mages. They commanded so many…

"I'd discovered Tamalan of Highgate at Rockhedge. He was one of Nyro's sorcerers—he'd been powerful in his day. I bound his spirit. And with that power, I defeated Newberry and protected Albany.

"I thought I could control the demon. And for decades, I was successful. But it grew stronger over time—Leda was the one who initially forced me to realize it."

"*Leda*?!" Aldo bellowed. "What does my wife have to do with this?"

"I am so sorry… Her Highness and I had an affair…"

Aldo snapped. He flew across the room, shouting unintelligibly. Syllith and two of the guards had to stop him from diving across the desk at Myrddin.

"Father!" Allison yelled. "Master yourself!"

The prince backed off, yanking his arms away from the guards.

"It started after Allison was born," Myrddin continued, gazing at her fondly as if he hadn't noticed Aldo's eruption. "I regularly slipped a potion into Her Highness's drink to prevent pregnancy."

"That's why my mother never had any more children!" said Allison. Aldo wailed with despair.

"But one day, tragedy struck. My demon possessed me as I made love to Leda. Using me, it raped her, committing unspeakable acts. Naturally, the princess was terrified. When it was over, she told me what had happened. Leda knew I was losing control. She insisted that I tell Aldo.

"But I could never admit to my prince what I'd done. And I believed I could regain control of the specter. I broke off the affair and modified Leda's memory. I made her forget the incident."

"You fool!" Syllith scolded him. "The university banned those spells for a reason!"

"I know," Myrddin said, bowing his head. "And they were right. The charm I used made Leda sick in mind and body. It wasn't long before she lost the ability to recognize her own family."

"You did that?!" Aldo said in a hoarse whisper. "You killed my Leda?"

Myrddin nodded sadly. "I never meant to harm her—I loved her. And for years after that, I kept the demon in check.

"But Leda was right. The monster was too powerful. When I watched Allison and Jezebel venture out to the Devil's Wood, I lost control again. The demon sensed Allison's energy when she used the spirit board, and it went berserk. It had tasted the pleasures of the flesh when I was with Leda. And now it yearned to do so again. It took me hours to rein in the beast.

"Matters only grew worse. It wasn't long before the demon acquired the ability to act without my knowledge. When the wayfarers came to perform, it knew a sorcerer had entered the castle. Nomad's ring prevented it from locating him. But it saw him with my eyes and possessed him. I didn't become aware of the rape until it left Nomad's body.

"And at that moment, I knew I had to destroy the demon. I explained the rite to Aldo and begged him to allow me to perform it. But he refused."

"Wait a minute," said Syllith. "If you'd done it, you would have lost your powers."

"A small price to pay to protect the princess," said Myrddin. "It was a step I was prepared to take."

"But how would you have explained your loss to His Highness?" asked Syllith. "Would you have admitted the truth?"

"I could have attributed it to being overpowered by the demon," he replied. "His Highness never would have known what really happened.

"I did my best to keep the monster away from the princess. But it found ways around my protections. I began to despair until I learned of Jezebel's quest. I hoped against hope that she would find a way.

"When they returned today, I had no choice—I had to inform the prince. He'd ordered me to report to him directly if any mage attempted to enter the castle. But I dropped hints to Jezebel. It would seem she correctly interpreted the clues I provided her. She freed the sorcerer without my knowledge and prevented him from using magic for a time. But then I sensed him casting a spell inside Her Highness's chambers, and I alerted my prince.

"I lost track of the demon today. But I became aware of its presence inside the sorcerer when Jezebel drove the spike into his flesh. I knew that they'd succeeded, and I was happy."

Everyone stood in silence for a minute. Aldo stared at Myrddin in utter disbelief. But suddenly, he cried out, "Myrddin Longshadow—I name thee!"

"Father—NO!" Allison screamed.

It was too late. Myrddin fell to the floor, howling in pain. Fire consumed him from the inside out. In seconds the necromancer was gone.

"Everyone out," Aldo said quietly. "I want to talk to my daughter and my niece alone." He sat at Myrddin's desk as the others filed out of the chamber. When they were gone, he motioned the girls to the chairs.

They sat down. Jezebel shot Allison a questioning look. Allison shrugged. The three of them sat in silence. Suddenly Aldo broke down and sobbed.

"Father…"

He held up his hand to stop her, trying to regain his composure. "I am so sorry," he said, tears streaming down his cheeks. "It is my duty to protect this princedom, yet I failed to save my wife and daughter from that necromancer. You two were forced to move on without Leda in your lives. It is clear that I am not fit to rule."

"Father, don't say that," Allison pleaded. "That's not true…"

He continued as if she hadn't spoken. "I was too busy managing the vassals, negotiating *trade agreements*…" He sobbed, unable to go on for a moment. "I never told Leda how much I loved her. Maybe if I'd told her…" He looked directly at Allison. "I have always loved you, my daughter. You are my whole world, and I am so proud of you. And you, my niece—you have always been like a second child to me. I am so grateful for the way you've taken care of Allison. I don't know what we would have done without you."

Allison moved around the desk and hugged her father, crying on his shoulder. Jezebel felt uncomfortable—she knew she didn't belong here.

But a second later, Aldo asked to be alone. Jezebel and Allison left him in the chamber. They descended the stairs, but as they arrived at the bottom of the tower, someone outside screamed. Jezebel ran into the courtyard to find out what was happening.

And that's when she saw it. Aldo was lying on the stone, flat on his back. Blood was pooling by his head. A few passersby had run over to him. Allison screamed and staggered to his side. She dropped to her knees, taking his hand in hers.

Jezebel realized this was the exact vision she'd seen in the looking glass. And at that moment, she discovered that she knew Khaldun's true name.

CHAPTER THIRTY-TWO
PRINCESS

ews of Aldo's death spread throughout the castle. A black flag was flown over the keep to notify the citizens of Spanbrook that their prince had passed away. Oswald told Allison, Jezebel, and Syllith that there would be a conference with the prince's advisers the following morning.

Jezebel and Allison retired to the princess's chambers once the commotion had settled down. They changed into their nightgowns and lay in bed. Allison cried for a long time. Jezebel held her. She shared her grief, though she knew it wasn't as intense. Both of her parents still lived. Now Allison had none.

"I don't understand it," the princess said softly.

"Which part?" Jezebel asked.

"How can I be a sorcerer? I've never done magic."

Jezebel could provide no answer. She didn't understand it herself. Only someone who had inherited magic from *both* parents could become a sorcerer. She knew Allison had magical blood on her mother's side. Robert had told Jezebel there was no magic in his family, yet Allure had sounded certain that Jezebel had inherited magic from both of her parents. Allison's transformation seemed to prove her correct about Robert's side of the family.

Allison fell asleep in Jezebel's arms. It felt good to be home, Jezebel thought, despite everything that had happened.

They woke early the next morning. Once they had dressed, they headed directly for the great hall. Oswald, Badrick, Camilla and

Gemma, Syllith, and Khaldun were already there. Jezebel feared she knew precisely what was coming. And she desperately wished it didn't have to happen so soon. Her cousin deserved more time to grieve, at the very least.

Allison and Jezebel took the two chairs the others had left for them, Allison at the head of the table and Jezebel to her right. Jezebel found her wand sitting on the table in front of her.

Oswald rose to his feet. "Good morning, everyone, and thank you for coming. The purpose of this meeting is to invoke the rite of succession and name the new ruler of Spanbrook. This is mostly a formality, as circumstances have already dictated a clear course of action.

"Princess Allison was Prince Aldo's sole heir. However, as she is no longer eligible to rule, the throne must pass to—"

"*Excuse me?*" said Allison. "What do you mean, 'no longer eligible'?"

"Sorcerers and necromancers are forbidden from sitting upon any throne," Syllith told her.

Allison was stunned. "But… This is madness! I am Aldo's only offspring—our line has ruled Spanbrook for centuries. You don't have the power to remove me…"

"I'm afraid that's not correct," said Oswald. "As steward, it is my sole responsibility to oversee the rite of succession. Typically, the naming of an heir is simply a legal matter. However, because Myrddin served Spanbrook, Gemma formalized Aldo's line using the ancient rites to ensure the necromancer's bond passed to his heirs. And in this case, Jezebel must ascend to the throne, with her sister Emma as heir apparent."

Jezebel had known this was coming ever since becoming aware of Khaldun's true name. But Allison was shocked. She looked back and forth between Oswald and Jezebel, her eyes wide.

"Jezebel Barclay, do you accept the position of ruling princess of Spanbrook?" Oswald asked.

"I do," she said quietly, staring down at the table.

"And do the court mages swear fealty to Princess Jezebel?"

"I do," Gemma and Camilla said in turn.

"As do I," said Khaldun.

"Very well. Your Highness, at this point rule of the princedom officially passes to you. The coronation will memorialize your ascension to the throne in front of the people of Spanbrook."

"Thank you," Jezebel murmured.

"We will meet in the coming days so that I might familiarize you with the duties of your office. In the meantime, I will continue to attend to the business of the princedom on your behalf, with your permission, of course."

"Yes, please," she replied.

"And Your Highness, we should discuss plans for establishing a standing army as soon as your schedule allows," said Badrick. "With Myrddin's passing, the landscape has changed dramatically."

"Indeed," Syllith murmured.

Jezebel nodded.

"Your Highness, I offer my services to you as well," said Syllith, "for the short term, at least. Your court sorcerer will need training."

"Enigma taught me how to conjure properly," said Khaldun. "To stop thinking like a wizard, I mean."

"You can replicate any magic you perceive, but you lack experience," said Syllith. "You still have much to learn, and I can teach it to you. In the fullness of your power, your presence will keep Spanbrook strong—which is essential to maintain stability in this region.

"Also, I'm still curious how Myrddin learned the rite of necromancy—I should like to conduct some research in your library, if you approve, Your Highness."

"Yes, definitely," she said, feeling somewhat overwhelmed at being thrust into this position of power so suddenly. It was strange to hear the honorifics and know they were referring to her.

"Very well," said Syllith. "I will begin my duties as soon as I return from the university—we must transport your cousin there as soon as possible."

"*What*?!" Allison demanded, standing in alarm. "What are you talking about?"

"You're an unbound sorcerer," Syllith told her. "Henry will attempt to acquire you if he learns of your transformation. We cannot allow that to happen. I will bring you to the university to be bound, and there you will begin your studies."

"I don't want to go to the university—why can't I stay here?" Allison demanded, panic in her voice. "Jezebel, don't let them take me away!"

"Can you bind her to me?" Jezebel asked. "I know two sorcerers are not customarily allowed to serve the same ruler, but Enigma made an exception for Khaldun."

"I cannot speak to Enigma's decision," said Syllith. "But the university strictly forbids the binding of more than one sorcerer to the same conjurnor."

"But you've defied the university before," Jezebel pointed out.

"I did so only because I feared that Nyro and the Sacred Circle still existed—and that Henry would attempt to control them. And if he obtains a sorcerer, that's exactly what he'll do."

Jezebel realized that Enigma must have foreseen Myrddin's death. He'd said that Spanbrook would need Khaldun—that was the only explanation for his willingness to violate the interdiction.

"Not only that," said Oswald, "but no member of a ruling family who undergoes the metamorphosis is ever allowed to serve her native princedom."

"That's correct," Syllith agreed. "Allison will probably be bound to someone at the university. But she may enter the service of one of the other princedoms."

Allison stared at the two of them in dismay. "Are you saying that I'm never coming back to Spanbrook? How can you do this? I grew up in this castle—this is my *home*! You can't take me away from here forever—Jezebel, tell them they can't do this!"

Jezebel already knew everything they'd said was right, but she hadn't thought it through. The reality of the situation hit her hard. She might never see Allison again.

"I'm sorry," she said, a tear rolling down her cheek.

"NO!" Allison wailed. "HE didn't train at the university," she shouted, pointing at Khaldun, "and he's allowed to stay here. Why can't I?"

"The situation is completely different," said Syllith. "He's bound to the princess. Whatever Enigma's rationale, the deed is done. And in any event, I've never performed the rite of binding. We must get you to the university right away."

Allison was crying freely now. "Can't I at least stay until Jezebel's coronation? And my father's funeral?"

"No," said Oswald. "It will take several days to prepare Aldo's service. And the coronation won't take place for weeks. Your presence here severely jeopardizes our security."

"I agree," said Syllith. "Henry may well have spies in Spanbrook. We should depart after sunset."

"*What*?! You mean tonight?"

"Yes," said Syllith. "Flying with the cover of darkness, it'll only take a matter of hours to get you to safety."

Allison stared at her in disbelief.

"That should conclude our business this morning," said Oswald. "Unless anyone has any objections… Very well."

Allison ran from the hall, crying hysterically. Badrick huddled with the two witches, and Syllith went to talk with Khaldun. But Oswald pulled Jezebel aside.

"Your Highness, it is now imperative that you select a husband and produce an heir," he said.

"Now is not the time—"

"I beg to differ," he said. "Your cousin's stubborn delay caused the end of Aldo's direct line. If you should make the same mistake, the princedom will fall into the hands of a lesser lord. We must not allow that."

Jezebel knew he was right. But she didn't want to think about it right now. "Can you send a messenger to my parents?" she asked. "I haven't seen them since my return. They'll need to be informed of… Well, everything."

"Right away, Your Highness."

She parted his company and waited for Syllith to finish her discussion with Khaldun.

"I need to speak with Syllith for a moment," she said to Khaldun. "Alone."

He nodded and left the hall.

"Your Highness?" asked Syllith.

"First of all, I need to give you this," she said, handing her the golden spike. It was still hot.

"Yes, of course," Syllith replied, taking it from her. "I will take care of this at once."

"Also… There's something I'd like to do for Allison before she leaves," said Jezebel. She explained the idea she'd had.

Syllith smiled. "I think I can help you with that. I'll need to fetch something from my camp, but I'll return soon."

After that, Jezebel went to find her cousin. Allison was in her chambers, lying in bed, utterly disconsolate. Jezebel tried to talk to her, but she made no response.

Twenty minutes later, there was a knock on the door. It was Syllith. Jezebel moved into the corridor, closing the door behind her. Syllith handed her a heavy velvet pouch. Jezebel looked inside.

"How does this work?" she asked. "Is it like a normal one?"

"For the most part. You both need to touch it directly, but the interaction is much more lifelike."

"Thank you," said Jezebel.

"Good luck," Syllith replied. "And please have Allison in the courtyard immediately after sunset."

Jezebel nodded and went inside. She sat before the hearth and placed the contents of the pouch on the floor in front of her.

"What's that?" Allison asked, sitting up in bed.

"Come and have a look," Jezebel suggested.

Allison slid out of bed and moved across the room. A smile lit her face. "Is this safe to use now?" she asked, sitting next to Jezebel.

"I don't see why not," said Jezebel. "The demon's gone, so contacting your mother shouldn't present any danger."

The board in front of them was black and unadorned.

"There's no planchette," Allison observed.

Jezebel placed the fingers of one hand upon the wood. "We both have to touch it," she said. Allison reached out with one hand. "We want to speak with Leda of Spanbrook. Are you with us?"

For a moment, nothing happened. Jezebel felt stupid, even though she knew this should work. But suddenly, the air in front of them began to shimmer. The image of a woman formed above the board, as large as life. She was tall and slender, with long, golden hair. Her face resembled Allison's, but with softer features. Jezebel had forgotten how beautiful she'd been before she fell ill.

Allison gasped. "Mom?"

"Hello, Allison," the woman said with a smile.

"I miss you," Allison said, tears welling up in her eyes. "I miss you so much."

"I will always be inside your heart," said Leda. "And I have to say that I often wondered if you might become a mage."

"What? Why?" asked Allison.

"You have sorcerer blood in your veins," she replied. "Both of you."

"How?" asked Jezebel, shocked by this revelation.

Leda sighed and smiled. "Myrddin was your great-grandfather."

"*What*?!" they both said.

Leda chuckled. "After the defeat of Newberry, Prince Albany was seldom home. He was on the road for months at a time, rebuilding the princedom. The princess was lonely. She gave Albany a son but never told him that Myrddin was Allain's father. Robert and Aldo never knew their grandfather was a necromancer. And Myrddin was much more careful in the future. He invented a potion to magically block conception."

Stunned silence greeted this pronouncement. But now Jezebel understood: Allison was able to transform because she *had* inherited magic from both of her parents.

"How dare he," Allison whispered. "I misjudged his character…"

"Don't think of him too harshly," Leda said. "He saved the princedom. And the life of a court mage can often be a lonely one. Myrddin was only human."

"Mom," said Allison, taking a deep breath. "Did you love Father?"

"Yes," Leda answered, smiling. "Always."

"But then… Why the affair?"

Leda sighed. "Aldo and I started to drift apart after you were born. He was busy with the princedom, and I was focused on raising you. I couldn't bear to leave my child with a nursemaid the way most nobles do.

"And Myrddin was a constant presence, always by my side during your father's absences. I suppose it was fated."

"But you married for love," said Allison.

"Oh yes," Leda agreed. "Aldo swept me off my feet."

"I…" A tear slipped down Allison's cheek. "Why couldn't he understand that *I* wanted the same thing? He tried to force me into marriage… All he cared about was preserving his line!"

Leda smiled at her. "Do you remember when you first learned to ride a horse?"

"Of course I do—how is that relevant?"

"You were too small to reach the saddle on your own. Your father had to lift you. But one day, you figured out how to climb the stall to get onto your horse. Aldo forbade you from ever doing that again. He was afraid you'd fall."

"I remember… But that's how I *always* used to do it. He never forbade me—"

"He did, but you wouldn't listen. And many times, you did fall—but you always got up and tried again. It pained your father greatly to watch you struggle, but you refused his help. He came to accept that you had to be allowed to do things your way.

"Aldo was a stubborn man. And I know he pressured you to continue his line. But he loved you dearly, and ultimately he would have accepted whatever choice you made."

With her final words, Leda nodded toward Jezebel. Allison cried. "I love you, Mom."

Leda smiled. "I have to go now, Allison. I won't be able to come back like this anymore. But remember, I will always be with you."

"Goodbye," Allison whispered. "I'll never forget you." Leda faded away.

Allison sat there for several minutes, crying quietly. Jezebel thought about what Leda had told them. Myrddin's blood explained her magic, as well. And it accounted for the fondness he'd always shown both girls.

Jezebel thought back on her relationship with the princess. She recalled their very first encounter and the sense of danger and excitement she'd felt. And she remembered the night they first tried to contact Leda, when Allison had revealed her true feelings for Jezebel. At that time, Jezebel had been so caught up worrying about which man she would marry, she'd never considered the possibility of spending her life with Allison. The idea had surprised her. She reflected on the irony: now, the princess was the only one she wanted.

Allison rose to her feet and walked back to her bed. Jezebel replaced the board in its pouch before lying by her side.

"I wish I didn't have to leave," Allison said quietly. "Now, your vision will never come true."

"You never know," said Jezebel. "I realized yesterday that you were a sorcerer in that vision. Perhaps the rest of it will happen, too."

"Would you have married me if I stayed?"

"Without hesitation," Jezebel said with a big smile.

They lay together in silence for a while. Jezebel reflected how truly happy she felt with her. She wished this could last forever. The thought of Allison undergoing the rite of binding terrified her. Enigma had almost lost Khaldun; what if they couldn't bring Allison back? The thought was too much to bear.

But… did Allison know that the rite would involve her death and resurrection? Jezebel doubted it, but she didn't have the heart to break it to her after all the other horrible revelations. Allison might never forgive her for *not* warning her, but Jezebel felt it would be cruel to do so under the present circumstances.

"Everything is happening so quickly," Allison said. "For my entire life, I assumed that one day I would inherit the princedom. Father groomed me for it—the lessons with my tutors and my training with Badrick were meant to prepare me to rule. I'd never imagined any other future. But now I'm leaving completely."

"The university isn't so bad," Jezebel consoled her. "I met some of the governors, and I read some of the texts… To be honest, I'm a little jealous."

"Truly?"

"Yes—I started to think that maybe *I* could go there. I would have returned to Spanbrook when I was done, of course…"

Allison sighed. "I wouldn't mind this so much if I could return. It wouldn't matter to me which of us became the ruling princess, so long as we could marry."

"You know, I didn't think of that…"

"What?"

"This will take some getting used to…"

"*What?*"

"I'm the ruling princess now," said Jezebel. "That means I'm the one in charge. So if I want to go off and visit you at the university for a while, nobody can stop me."

"You have a princedom to run now; you can't just disappear…"

"Why not? Your father spent a month touring the countryside, and everything was fine. And Oswald is running things for me until I learn how—he could do it again."

"But Father had Myrddin," Allison reminded her.

"True. But I've got Khaldun. I'll have to wait until he trains up a bit. But I *will* come to visit as soon as I can."

Allison embraced her. Despite what she'd said, Jezebel knew this might be the last time she'd ever see Allison. They made love more passionately than ever—as if they were trying to squeeze a lifetime together into the span of a few hours.

But much too soon, her bliss came to an end. Allison got dressed and got to work packing her things. For a moment, Jezebel thought she saw a golden glow in the corner of the room—reminding her of the encounters she'd had out in the woods at the university so long ago. When she looked again, it was gone, but suddenly she heard a sound like tinkling bells.

"I'll be watching you, *Princess*," a voice said in her head. "May the experience always prove so… provocative." Although the voice was not audible, Jezebel thought it sounded distinctly female.

"Who are you? Allure? And why would you have any interest in *me*?" she asked quietly, pushing aside her exasperation that the woman had watched her making love to Allison.

"I know what you saw in the looking glass," the voice said. It did not sound like Allure—this voice was deeper. "I've seen it too. We'll meet again, you and I."

Somehow, Jezebel sensed that the presence had departed.

"What did you say?" Allison asked.

"Nothing," she replied. "I was talking to myself."

Jezebel escorted Allison outside to the courtyard after sunset. Syllith was waiting for her there, the carpet spread taut on the ground. Allison regarded it apprehensively.

"Do you think you could make one stop before you leave?" Jezebel asked.

"I don't think that would be wise…"

"Just to bring me to my parents' farm," Jezebel said. "It isn't far— and it's on the way."

Syllith sighed. "I guess I could do that. Let's go."

The witch placed Allison's bag in the center of the carpet. She positioned the girls near the edges before sitting at the front. Staff in hand, Syllith spoke words of command. Allison screamed as the carpet rose high in the air and shot into the eastern sky.

They reached the farm in no time. Syllith set them down in front of the barn. Allison got to her feet and hugged Jezebel tight.

"I love you," Jezebel whispered. "Forever."

Allison only whimpered in reply.

Syllith had her sit in the middle of the rear edge, and they took off again. Jezebel watched for several seconds until the carpet disappeared into the night.

She walked to the house and found her father on the porch. Robert was sitting in his rocker, smoking his pipe. He nodded to her as Jezebel took the opposite chair. They sat for a while, gazing at the stars. Jezebel was grateful for the silence.

She tried to wrap her mind around everything that had happened, with Myrddin and Henry—and the demons trying to escape Pytha. And she missed Allison. The irony of her removal from Spanbrook was too cruel to fathom. It was difficult to believe that *she* was the princess now. Things certainly hadn't turned out the way she'd expected. She'd been right when she left the farm: life would never be the same.

"I reckon there's a storm coming," Robert said eventually. Jezebel looked up—there wasn't a cloud in the sky. "I don't mean the weather. I can see it in your face."

Jezebel heaved a sigh. "You always know what I'm thinking."

"You want to talk about it?"

Jezebel shook her head. "Not now. For tonight, I just want to be your little girl again."

Robert drew on his pipe. "You'll always be that," he said.

To be continued…